HOSTILE
TAKEOVER

JOEY W. HILL

ELLORA'S CAVE
ROMANTICA®
www.EllorasCave.com

An Ellora's Cave Publication

www.ellorascave.com

Hostile Takeover

ISBN 9781419965920
ALL RIGHTS RESERVED.
Hostile Takeover Copyright © 2012 Joey W. Hill
Edited by Briana St. James.
Cover art by Syneca.

Electronic book publication January 2012
Trade paperback publication 2012

HOSTILE TAKEOVER

๛

Acknowledgements

ॐ

Bringing together a story that completes a full circle of books involving five extraordinary men and the exceptional women they love required a lot of fact checking and review of the past works for consistency. My fingers are crossed that we caught everything, but of course that's likely wishful thinking. Still, it was not for lack of helpful resources. I want to give heartfelt thanks to the following:

To the JWH connection fan forum, particularly the participants of the Ben and Marcie thread, whose insights into the characters, their recollection of details about Ben and Marcie from previous works, and their overall enthusiasm, helped drive this book forward.

To Janine, for the legalities of rummaging through trash containers.

To Karen, for the wonderful timeline you put together — it was a godsend!

To Michele and Mandy, for medical advice regarding the aftercare of an especially stressed submissive.

To Mindy, for your delightful command of anatomy terminology.

To Minuet, for your observations about the positive effect a good Master has on a woman's confidence and self-worth. These observations helped connect some key dots about Marcie's motivations and personality.

To Ritu, for helping me locate the right setting for Jeremy.

To Sandy, one of my dedicated "Ben" fans. Despite your insanely busy schedule, you took the first look and assured me that *most* of the readers wouldn't run screaming from the more controversial areas. Thank you also for the great photos and information you provided to guide my research on New Orleans.

To Sarah Frantz, whose academic exploration of popular romance led her to write an essay about one my works for the upcoming *New Approaches to Popular Romance Fiction: Critical Essays* (spring/summer 2012). Your insights actually furthered my understanding of my own characters, such that I was able to direct Ben and Marcie's areas of conflict much better.

To the folks of the SouthEast LeatherFest, thank you for exponentially increasing my practical knowledge of the D/s world, and for making a new attendee feel so at home at your wonderful con.

I'm sure I missed someone, but as always, I thank everyone who contributed in ways large and small to the creation of this work. As always, any remaining missteps or errors are entirely my own.

Finally, a loving thanks to my mother, who wanted to go on the Voodoo/Cemetery tour of New Orleans. It's not something I would have done on my own, and as a result, I discovered a very special place for Ben to go to clear his head, as well as many other details that enhanced the book. Thanks for going with me on this trip, Mom. You were the best travel companion ever. I'll miss not having you with me for future trips, but I'll try to carry your spirit of adventure in my pursuit of future stories.

The best advice I can give you is to start every day with chocolate cake. That way, no matter what else happens, the day started with something perfect.

Ben, letter to Marcie during her freshman year

Chapter One

❧

"Goddamn it, I don't have time to nursemaid a damn baby." Ben snapped his phone closed. "I'm meeting with Senecorp at ten this fucking morning, and that contract was supposed to be ready."

Peter gave him a sidelong glance as he made his coffee. Out of habit, he poured Ben's, leaving it caffeine-coma black as he added sugar and cream to his own Colombian blend. "Janet hears you barking like that, she'll wash your mouth out with soap."

"I'll shove Irish Spring dry up the ass of whatever moron in Personnel decided to send me an intern while Alice is on vacation. Christ. I would have come in this weekend if I'd known, but Alice said she had it handled. Fuck."

"Alice doesn't usually make mistakes. Whoever the intern is, she's probably top of her class."

"Great. She knows her way around a stack of books. Doesn't mean a fucking thing in the real world."

"Mr. O'Callahan?"

Turning, Ben saw Janet, their CEO's imperious admin, standing in the doorway of the office kitchen.

"Since I and everyone else can hear you," she said coolly, "your finished contract is on your desk. The baby intern scaled the walls of her crib and spent most of the weekend getting up to speed on the negotiations with Senecorp so you'd have it first thing this morning. You'll find her sucking her thumb at Alice's desk. I've given her a handful of Cheerios to keep her happy. I trust you'll handle any diaper changing personally."

Peter shot him a droll *I-told-you-so* look. Ben narrowed his gaze, but when he turned that irritated expression on Janet, she didn't blink. She and Alice had worked for Kensington & Associates long enough to know they were utterly indispensable. Alice had been Matt's admin before she took paralegal training, after which she became Ben's assistant, but both women routinely handled the diverse personalities of the five men who comprised K&A's executive management.

That included Ben's formidable Irish temper, which he knew had been rising to the top more often of late, enough that he'd had to suffer jokes about male menopause at the ripe old age of thirty-two. And send apology bouquets to both admins more than once.

"Thank you, Janet," he said. "I appreciate your excellent hearing."

"Hmm." She gave him a reproving look and then vanished, her heels soundless on the carpeted hallway.

"The contract will probably be fucked up five ways to Sunday," he muttered. "Only thing worse than an intern who doesn't know anything is one who thinks she does."

"Maybe she'll have a great rack and a nice ass."

"I can get that from a Playboy centerfold. Doesn't help me when Matt is tearing me a new one for sloppy prep work."

"You're way tougher on yourself than Matt could ever be." Peter gave him a thoughtful look. "You're pretty grumpy these days. I know you're getting plenty, so maybe you're fucking the wrong type of women."

"There is no such thing, Dr. Phil. Bite me."

"Pass. Haven't had my shots. I know where you've been."

Ben snorted. "Places you can only dream about now, ball-and-chain."

10

Taking his coffee, he headed for his corner office. He balanced the cup with his briefcase as his phone buzzed with several incoming messages. He had forty-five minutes to review and fix that contract, and then he had a meeting with Johnson in Matt's office that would take up the hour before his ten o'clock. If the intern hadn't totally screwed it up, he could have her run the contract over to Senecorp so they could digest it before he arrived.

The desk where Alice was normally stationed, a few paces from the door of his office, was vacant. The baby intern had escaped from her high chair or the Cheerios hadn't been sufficiently entertaining. Setting aside his briefcase, he took a seat at his desk, his eye on the contract sitting neatly in the middle of it.

When he had a free weekend, he spent it immersed in sweet female ass and Irish whiskey, his reward for work weeks often eighty-plus hours long. He worked hard, played hard, with exacting demands in both areas of his life. Which was why Alice's voicemail this morning had set him off.

The revisions for the Senecorp contract will be done by the intern Personnel has hired. Don't worry. She's good. And don't curse when you get this message.

"I'll fucking curse if I want to," he muttered. Just not around Alice. Or Janet. Cognizant of her superhero hearing, he'd have toned it down in the kitchen, except he hadn't realized she'd arrived as early as he had this morning.

As he scanned the contract, his brow eased. Well, hell. The revisions were damn near perfect. Some of the points had even been tweaked for smoother language, keeping his original meaning intact. Not a typo to be found, not even a random crayon mark or a smudge from fingers stained with Juicy Juice. His lips quirked. Putting the document down, he rubbed a hand over his face.

Hell, what *was* the matter with him these days? He didn't used to get so worked up about shit like this. Yeah, he was an ogre on details, but in the past he'd had a scathing sense of

11

humor about it. From Peter's sidelong glances, he knew he and the others had ongoing theories about him, especially Jon, Mr. Touchy-Feely-Let's-All-Hug. He gave them credit for sticking to the guy code, though, giving him room to steer the boat the way he needed to steer it for right now.

Still, he had to push down resentment at Peter's teasing. It was easy to be smug about the hollow state of a single guy's sex life when you were married to the submissive of your wildest dreams, the way Peter was. Though Dana was blind, she had the courage and unbridled sensuality of a woman with all her senses intact. Ben knew it firsthand, because on one memorable night, Peter had enlisted his help to make one of her fantasies come true, to be taken by two men at once.

All five members of Kensington & Associates executive management were hardcore sexual Dominants, and four of them had found their perfect submissive match. Soul mates, if you believed in that bullshit, and it was hard not to, looking at how they got along with one another. Ben remembered the aftermath of that night with Dana. He'd gone into the bathroom to clean up, and when he came out, he'd seen her curled inside the curve of Peter's muscular body. His arms were wrapped around her like she was the beginning and end of everything, his lips cruising over her temple and cheek, his deep voice rumbling soft in her ear. Ben felt like an intruder. He'd slipped out without another word. He didn't really do cuddling, anyhow.

So here he was, four years later, still single. That didn't bug him. If he wanted a more serious relationship, he could seek it. Yeah, maybe in his few off hours he'd started opting for whiskey and strolling through the Quarter, rather than seeking female companionship. No big deal. His tastes were the most extreme, so club submissives had been good enough for him for the past year or two. Dating was too much effort, always the wrong ingredients, a meal he had to eat to be polite, but couldn't wait to finish and step away from the table.

Things had changed, and much as he knew that was the way of the fucked-up world, it didn't always sit so well. It stirred up shit he didn't want stirred, and maybe that was what kept griping his bowels. Hell, maybe it was time to take a vacation, go somewhere tropical where he could seduce pretty women and get his boxers out of their permanent bunch. Except all he seemed to see when he imagined that vacation was a stretch of empty beach, nobody on it but him.

Christ, was he *lonely*? He didn't need down time. He needed more up time, juvenile sexual pun intended. He'd drive down to Baton Rouge, do an extra session at Club Surreal this week. In the past couple years, Surreal had opened a sister club here in New Orleans, appropriately called Club Progeny, but he preferred to go to Baton Rouge when he didn't want to run into one of the other guys. He'd find one of his regulars, or a new submissive looking for a club-only experience. Take her on one of his extreme roller-coaster rides, not letting her off until she was too shaky to walk.

When he was breaking down her shields, opening her up to everything he demanded, getting the maximum level of response, far beyond what she imagined was possible, time stopped for him. It was all about that moment. It was the same feeling he'd had when he was doing trial lawyer work, earlier in his career. When he felt the steel jaws closing around his opponent, knowing he was the guy with his foot on that spring lever, it was almost as good as sex. Negotiations with Matt's acquisitions gave him the same sensation, particularly when it was a hostile takeover.

Jon had recently observed that Ben was Genghis Khan in a previous life, happy with nothing but conquering. Asshole. Their mechanical genius didn't do barbed digs, though. If Jon said something like that, he was sending a message. Ben chose to ignore it.

The light tap of heels moving from the carpet to the wood floor around the admin desk alerted him to the arrival of his intern. He bit back a sigh. He really wasn't in the mood to be charming and welcoming, but he'd make the effort. He wasn't in the habit of snarling at women even on his worst days, particularly young ones right out of school and wet behind their ears.

Then he glanced out his doorway, and discovered another way time could stop, one he hadn't experienced in a while. His gaze got stuck in full lock.

She'd turned to the file cabinets, so he'd missed her face. Instead, he saw a classic Audrey Hepburn slim hourglass shape, complete with tailored skirt that nipped off above her knee. When she sat down, a hint of thigh would tease male senses. She was wearing those provocative nylons with the old-fashioned lines up the back, and they were perfectly straight. Following the contour of calf, the sweet valley behind the knee, they ran up the back of her thigh and disappeared beneath the snug hold of the skirt. Her pale yellow blouse was translucent silk that showed the impression of her bra in the same color, making him wonder if there were panties in that same butter color beneath the skirt.

Her dark blonde hair would fall a little farther than her shoulder blades, but right now it was clipped shorter by a wide bronze barrette, a Celtic knot design with a tiny shamrock done in emerald rhinestones. As she put the files away, he saw well-kept nails, a French manicure with white tips that drew attention to capable, feminine grace. There was something familiar about the way she moved.

He didn't know what scent she was wearing because he wasn't that close, but he wanted to be. His gaze slid back down to that tempting ass, shaped nice and round by the tailored skirt. If she'd bend down to the lower file drawers, he could let his mind go some pretty interesting places. Not that he'd be anything but professional with her, of course. Baby intern and all that.

She turned then, and his attention coursed up the flare of hips, registering generous breasts, probably a C-cup, cradled in a lacy, low-cut bra, thank the lingerie gods. The two-button opening of the blouse collar was modest, but would still give him a glimpse of bare curve at the right angle. She was perfectly put together, office executive with appealing woman, class and style all the way. Jesus, *this* was an intern? Then he reached her face and was poleaxed.

Holy Christ, it was *Marcie*.

Snapping his chair back to an upright position, he managed to send his pen spinning off his desk when he set down his coffee. He damn near splashed the document she'd prepared for him.

When Lucas, K&A's CFO, had married Cassandra, she'd been the guardian of five younger siblings. Marcie was the next oldest girl, about to turn seventeen when Ben first met her. She'd already been pretty, but pretty teenager had obviously given way to breathtaking young woman.

For the past four years, she'd been away at college. During her freshman and sophomore years, he'd seen her briefly at holidays, because the five K&A men were a family. They'd congregate at Matt's family estate in Texas, or Jon's second home in Baton Rouge for family get-togethers. But for the last two years, Marcie hadn't been home, though Lucas and Cass had flown out to see her once or twice. She'd been doing work co-ops in Europe, then New York City. If not for the occasional postcard, he'd have had no contact at all.

During the first two years of college, she'd sent him lots of letters. Not just emails. Handwritten letters on scented girly stationery, with clippings from her studies or the college paper to interest or amuse him. At the beginning, when she told him she was going to write him, he'd told her he wasn't going to become her pen pal. She'd fixated on him in high school, a crush he'd always carefully managed with platonic affection. While she seemed to accept that, she sought his advice on a variety of things, often inappropriate. The guys had teased him about his wary navigation of those treacherous waters, but he'd opened the letters, read each one, and even answered a few.

Yeah. He'd become her regular damn pen pal.

She *was* family, damn it. She was like having an annoying little sister, one he'd taken under his wing. All the kids had needed some one-on-one in the male role-model department, given that Cassandra's father had bailed years before and Jeremy, the oldest son, had been a drug addict living on the street. When it was obvious Marcie was gravitating toward Ben, Lucas had trusted him to give her that big brotherly protection and guidance while he and the others focused on the rest of the family.

Honestly, she got under his skin. Her worries and fears, her successes and missteps. Used to being "second Mom" when Cass was working her ass off to take care of all five of them, she was a serious kid, too locked down, one who'd had too many responsibilities thrown on her too early. He knew enough about that to feel a kinship with her right off.

When her letters and phone calls slowed to a trickle in her junior year, he'd received the infrequent postcards, sometimes a passed-on hello when she talked to Cass on the phone. It was all normal for a girl growing into a woman, of course. She shouldn't be spending all her time writing to a guy almost a decade older.

He admitted he missed those letters, the things she talked about with him, no matter how wildly unsuitable some of those past topics might have been. They'd been friends — in the ultra-cautious way that an older man and jailbait could be. He almost snorted at the thought. She wasn't jailbait now, but God above, he knew trouble when he saw it.

"Baby intern?" She'd come to his door, was studying him. Jesus, her voice. How had she developed that sultry little purr to tag her syllables? She was…how old was she? Twenty-three. Barely. "You're still such an asshole. I'm surprised Janet doesn't smack you down a couple times a day."

"She leaves that to Alice. And Alice is out of town." Ben kept his gaze fastened on her. "When'd you get home?"

"Couple weeks ago. Hi." Marcie's voice softened. There was a touch of shyness to her smile, something he remembered from her teens, but it was also openly glad to see him. "Did you miss me?"

"Hi yourself." He realized his voice had become husky, and he cleared it. "Who are you again?"

She crinkled her nose, stuck her tongue out at him. When she'd done that as a teenager, he definitely hadn't reacted the way he did now. He watched that tongue go back between her full lips, touching them briefly, an involuntary gesture. Leaning in the doorway, she crossed her arms beneath her ripe breasts, hooking a delicate ankle around the other heel. "Cass told me you needed someone to fill in while Alice was island hopping, so I had her set it up with Matt as a surprise. I've heard working for you is like working for Satan, and I figure that'll look good on a resume. Especially if you give me a glowing reference letter."

For some of the thoughts he was having, he was going to get up close and personal with Satan. He needed to stand up, go give her a friendly hug, stop acting like something else was happening in this room, in the way they couldn't seem to stop looking at one another. She was a kid. Like a little sister.

She was also apparently tired of waiting on him. Straightening, she moved across the carpet. The heels she wore were pencil thin, four inches and made her legs look ready to wrap around a man's hips. She still had those solemn, steady brown eyes. Her features had traces of the girl he remembered, but they'd become more refined. Her makeup was applied with a light touch, because with those doe eyes and thick lashes, the cushion of her bottom lip frosted with a light gloss, she didn't need much. A few wisps of hair strayed over her brow and around her temples, increasing the focus on her face while emphasizing the delicacy of it.

He realized then why her movements had seemed familiar. They were like Cass'. Lucas' wife was a top negotiator who could hit a guy broadside with understated female wiles

17

and nerves of steel. She'd move in for the kill so smoothly a man died with a smile on his lips. Her younger sister had obviously inherited some of that, but this was also Marcie, a separate and unique entity with mysteries of her own.

She had a gymnast's grace. In high school, she hadn't had the time to join teams or clubs, but she'd pursued gymnastics on her own, used the school equipment to stay flexible and lean, and he knew she continued that in college. She'd excelled at everything she attempted, studying business principles practically from the time she was in middle school. Majoring in business and minoring in pre-law, she was as brilliant and driven as her sister, who'd been a child prodigy of Pickard Consulting, a negotiation and corporate investigations firm.

The slim choker she wore caught his attention. The pendant was a crystal disk with a tiny trio of blue flowers pressed under the glass. Forget-me-nots. Something about that niggled at his mind, but the fact there was a lock above the pendant, a small keyhole decorated with scrollwork, was even more distracting. It could be an affectation of course, not a true lock.

She was coming around the desk, giving him a warm look. Since he hadn't moved, he saw a flash of uncertainty behind it, something hard to pin down, as if she wasn't sure a hug would be welcome. *Get up, asshole. Say hello, be nice. What the hell's the matter with you?*

Why wasn't he getting up? When he'd been younger and more street raw, Matt's father and then Matt himself had hammered courtesy into him as a mandate, not just as a way to hustle marks. Like Matt's unbreakable rule about not cursing around women, that and the rest of it had become part of who Ben was somewhere along the way, the instinctive breeding of a Southern male rising above the circumstances of his birth.

But he was also a Dom with extreme preferences, whose radar was on full alert. Something was keeping him right where he was, studying her with firm, unsmiling lips and a calculated gaze he intended her to see.

It was a weighted moment, that indefinable quality teetering on a scale between them. When her gaze shifted to the floor between his knees, her lashes lowering, it hit him in the solar plexus. But then her smile became a wry twitch of her lips. Putting her hand on his shoulder, she gracefully squatted and picked up the pen by his polished shoe. Her fingers slid down over his biceps, an exploratory touch. When she placed her palm on the desk to lever herself back up, she caught the edge of his notepad, knocking it off as well.

"Oops." With a glance at him beneath those long lashes, she knelt fully to reach farther under the desk. As she did, she reached over his polished shoe, stretching out to retrieve the pad. He got an eyeful of Marcie on her hands and knees before him, her ass turned up, her back that shallow valley that made him imagine caressing the sweet, naked line of it. Her skirt was pulled drum tight over those toned cheeks, the cleft nicely teased. His palm would make a firm smacking sound on it if he gave her a swat for dropping his papers.

What would it be like to cover her with his body, hold her there on her elbows as he ripped the fragile silk open, her breasts filling his hands so he could squeeze? She'd gasp, rub her ass against his cock, wanting, begging...

Christ. Okay, if he invoked that name one more time, he was going to have to go to mass or confession, something he hadn't done well...ever. To be a lapsed Catholic, you had to be a practicing one first, right?

She'd knocked that pad off deliberately, was doing this deliberately. He wrapped his mind around that as she straightened, turned in the span of his knees to put the note pad on his desk next to the pen. She took her time, straightening things, making sure they were exactly the way they'd been before she'd disrupted them. Kneeling there, her back to him, she had her hair in range of his fingertips. He could unclip that barrette, bury his fingers in those thick strands, pull her head back to set his teeth to her throat. She smelled the way a candy shop did, so many flavors to sample and explore.

Now she shifted back toward him, her hands settling on his thighs as if to push herself back to her feet. He was surprised the heat coming off him didn't burn her fair skin, even through his slacks. Her gaze traveled along his thighs, lingering over his groin, where it was starting to be very obvious he was responding to her. He stifled a growl. She was putting off every signal in the world, challenging him to take over. When she moistened her lips at the size of his reaction, her eyes widening slightly, he almost gave himself away by putting a death grip on the chair arms. Those sultry lashes lifted, her brown eyes meeting his.

"Something else I can do for you, Mr. O'Callahan?"

He saw it in her eyes. She wanted to go down on him, wanted to feel his hand fisted in her hair, driving her according to his will. Since she wanted it that bad, he wouldn't give it to her right away. He'd make her get up, turn around so he could grasp her hips, work her against him in a lap dance then and there, make her show him how much her pretty ass hungered for his cock. And then he'd blister it good, so that he'd wring a few tears out of her before he fucked her right here on his desk.

Holy fuck. She was teasing him the way a sub did, trying to goad a Dom into action. He had to be mistaken, but the set of her chin said she could get more determined about it, until she'd be outright bratting, blatantly topping. What the hell was going on here?

He didn't know, but while one part of him was reeling, the part of him that was sure of this ground, as sure as breathing, steadied and locked like a collar clamping around a pale white throat. He knew this terrain, even if being on it with Marcie was unexpected.

"What are you doing?" As she rose, he met her eyes squarely.

"Just helping." She wasn't up to that direct stare. But that only made it worse, because what she did wasn't calculated. She responded the way a natural submissive did when a Dom finally got his shit together and took the reins. She looked down. Back at his desk, straightening the contract unnecessarily, shifting his coffee farther out of the way. Then she stepped back, and she was smiling again, though it was a little forced. As she put that distance between them, she shrugged, tossed back her hair.

He'd seen that look before, usually when she'd been figuring her way through the difficulties that had been their home life until Lucas and Cass had gotten together and moved things in a better direction, with the K&A men becoming their extended family to help out.

"Hey, why don't you let me take you to dinner tonight?" She held that smile, probably trying to pretend that whatever she'd been trying to pull hadn't taken an unexpected turn for her as well. Her cheeks had a light flush. "You can bring me up to speed on the things you need me to do, and I can tell you all about my co-ops in the Big Apple and Europe. Don't say no, because I've never paid you back for that trouble you bailed me out of in college. It can be an adult thank-you for helping me out when I was a kid."

"You're still a kid."

That smile disappeared. He was getting an overwhelming compulsion to lick at that frosted color, see if it tasted sweet. As her brown eyes became more thoughtful, she leaned in, reaching out to touch his face. He caught her wrist, holding her there.

"Don't."

She blinked at him. Her fingers closed, touching his knuckles in a light caress. "I'm not a kid anymore, Ben. Will you let me take you to dinner?"

"To catch up."

"Among other things."

"No," he decided. She reacted with a brief flash of hurt, which quickly disappeared behind an unfathomable expression. He needed to make this right, put it on the proper footing. She was still Marcie. He needed to talk to her about this kind of behavior. If she used it on the wrong guy...well, it wouldn't be good for a lawyer to have a murder rap hanging over his head.

"I'll take *you* to dinner. Old family friends don't pick up the tab." He managed a charming smile he hoped didn't look like a big bad wolf salivating. "Pretty girls especially don't have to pay."

"Not with money." She slipped his hold with a devilish grin and a little sass to her walk as she headed back to the door, contract in hand. It was as if that hurt look had never existed, but he knew better. Whatever Marcie had been trying to do, she wasn't the duplicitous kind when it came to emotions. "I better get back to work," she added, throwing him a look, the blonde hair spilling over her shoulder. "My boss might paddle my ass if I don't get this contract over to Senecorp this morning. At least a girl can dream he might. Oh and Matt said he wanted to meet with you about fifteen minutes before Johnson arrives. I've pulled the file and the notes you'll need."

"Marcie—" He was going to give her a piece of his mind and then some, but of course Peter buzzed him. By the time he'd glanced toward the phone and debated whether to answer, she'd grabbed up some other folders on the desk and was gone, moving with breezy energy on those thin heels.

He couldn't remember the last time he'd been so outmaneuvered, taken by surprise, flat out punched in the gut. By a freaking kid, a twenty-three-year-old baby. He had about a hundred things to wrap his mind around from that little interchange, but there was one thing his aching hard-on was telling him, loud and clear.

That's no baby, buddy. She's a freaking natural submissive, hungering for a Master.

What the hell had happened to Marcie? Did she know she'd just thrown down a gauntlet to an experienced Dom, daring him to pick it up?

He was afraid she sure as hell did.

I'm really glad to be here, very grateful, but sometimes — don't tell Cass and Lucas — I feel so isolated. A lot of these kids came straight from high school, from lives where they didn't have a lot of responsibility. They talk about being on the basketball team, in clubs, with loads of friends they miss, because they hung out together so much. I miss my siblings. It's crazy. I miss taking care of them, feeling like they're counting on me to look after them, even though I remember days when I had to step outside the kitchen and scream, pull at my hair, because it became too much. Sometimes I think I should have gone to a community college with single moms, or adult students, where the intention is to learn, not to party or be on my own for the first time. I don't really know what this kind of freedom is supposed to feel like, Ben. If it's supposed to feel good or bad. Or how to even handle it.

Letter from Marcie to Ben, freshman year

Chapter Two

❧

Marcie bolted for the fire stairwell, avoiding the elevator. Once she was three floors down, she stopped in the echoing stillness of concrete and metal. Leaning against the rail, she put her hand on her stomach, calming the butterflies. She'd done it. She'd fired the first shot, and she was pretty sure she'd scored a direct hit. Oh God, she was *so* over her head.

That was the only toe-to-toe volley she'd get, she knew it. She had to come at him from a more unexpected angle next time, keep him off balance. Once Ben O'Callahan rallied, he'd either rebuff her like an impenetrable fortress or... Her cheeks heated at that loaded *or*.

Don't tease the wild animal. Isn't that what they posted at the zoos? Kneeling between his thighs, she'd seen up close what she was poking with a stick, had felt the heat coming off him. She'd heard the rumors about his size, but if that was a partial erection, there were monsters in Japan who would run screaming.

It gave her a half chuckle, which helped calm her down some. Age wasn't a factor in negotiation, unless you used it to your advantage. Cass had told her that. It was all about confidence, will, commitment, being prepared. More prepared than anyone else, one step ahead.

Only that was the irony. She didn't want to be one step ahead. Her goal was to be a step behind. Following a Master, following his lead, serving his desires, no matter how extreme they were. Following Ben.

So while she was experiencing a somewhat hysterical form of exultation at what she'd just accomplished, making him see her as a submissive, even if only for a second, she also had a wrong sort of coil in her belly. She was approaching the problem from the only direction that would work right now, but it didn't mesh with who she really was or wanted to be. This was a means to an end, that was all.

She couldn't deny the forces at work seemed to know what they were doing. Right before she'd stepped into his office, she hadn't been sure what the hell she was going to do, but when she saw him, something else had taken over, guiding her into that crazy maneuver with the pen and pad.

A girl's gotta do what a girl's gotta do, as the song said. Before she could serve him, she had to push him past any reservations about wanting her. The whole "kid" thing. Touching the pendant at her throat, her fingers glided over the words engraved on the flat back. She knew what she knew. She wouldn't start doubting herself now, no matter how scared she was of opening a tiger's cage and stepping back to see what would happen. She could handle herself. She would. The stakes were too important.

* * * * *

25

Ben sat back in his chair, the contract forgotten, his coffee cooling. *That trouble in college...* Well, he'd been kind of obligated to help, hadn't he? Since he was the reason she'd needed bail.

Under her serious nature, he'd glimpsed something struggling to get out. A fresh wildness, the reckless innocence of youth she'd never been able to indulge. He remembered one of her freshman letters, talking about how out of sync she felt with the other students. He told himself he remembered it nearly word for word because he had a damn near photographic memory. Not because he'd read it a little too often, feeling an uncomfortable connection to what he'd experienced in college.

He'd called her, because her loneliness had been too much for him to address through the written word. He didn't remember half of what he'd said, but he'd stayed on the phone for an hour and a half with her, until he had her giggling uncontrollably and calling him names. He'd told her to loosen up, stop worrying about everything. Do something unexpected, stretch her wings and relax her inhibitions. Get in trouble occasionally, for Chrissakes. Not real trouble, okay, but you know. "Stay out overnight, get a little tipsy on Budweiser, kiss a boy you don't know very well who has a cute butt."

"*Ben!*"

He'd laughed at her embarrassed outrage, but then he'd sobered, fingers tightening on the phone. If he was there, he would have hugged her. It bugged him to know she was hurting. "Learn how to have fun, Ella-Marcella." Marcella was her full name, and he'd made up the pet name for her because it annoyed her. "I know you'll ace the studies. You're too responsible to do otherwise. But Jesus, cut loose and be a kid. See how it feels. You may like it so much you'll decide never to grow up."

"Like you?"

"Cute. I have a life, so I'm getting off the phone now."

"You just have a date with some woman with big boobs and no brains."

"If they have the big boobs, the brain's not really necessary."

"Sexist pig."

"Smartass." But before he hung up, he added, "Go. Have. Fun. Don't worry. If you end up in jail, I'll bail you out. And don't do the Budweiser thing around boys. Only girls."

So maybe he felt a little responsible about the actual need for bail. One night, late, she and six other kids decided to jump in the beat-up Toyota she'd bought with her own money. All packed in with snacks and pillows, they'd driven overnight to Mammoth Cave in Kentucky. They were near their destination, close to dawn, when her passengers decided to moon a passing motorist just for the hell of it. Unfortunately, it was an unmarked police car, and one of her passengers was carrying a bag of weed, something Marcie hadn't known until it dropped out of the kid's pocket when he stumbled out of the car.

Ben got the call in a morning meeting, Alice breaking in with the pointed look that said *You need to take this.* He'd talked to a tearful, apologetic Marcie, but what he most remembered was her pulling it together, enough that he heard her audible swallow on the phone, the sudden attack of dignity as she stated, as solemnly as a defense attorney nailing the key point, "You said if I got into trouble, you'd bail me out. Right?"

Telling Matt he had something personal to handle, he took the private jet to Kentucky. He worked it out, getting them released without anything going on their records. Fortunately, the sheriff was a decent sort who could tell Marcie was a straight-arrow kid and no one had any other priors. Marcie didn't make Ben cover for her for long; she told him she would tell Lucas and Cass about it, and she did, a couple weeks later. Her main concern was making it go away before Cass had to worry about it, because her older sister had spent so much of her life protecting them. Marcie couldn't bear to give her another moment of worry on her behalf.

On the drive back to the school, where he took the wheel of her Toyota, and the other kids followed in a chauffeured van, she'd freaked out to the nth degree, resolving never again to leave the campus grounds until graduation. He'd been able to convince her she shouldn't stop being adventurous and going after things she wanted just because she got set back on her heels now and then. Life was about the experience, not just the nose to the grindstone.

Why did he have a feeling he was about to pay dearly for that advice?

* * * * *

"What happened to that guy?" Ben poured Marcie a second glass of her preferred after-dinner white zinfandel as she finished chuckling over the recap of her Kentucky mishap. He'd chosen one of his favorite casual cafés, with a table outdoors so she could enjoy the New Orleans' nightlife.

"Allan milked the whole anti-establishment pothead image as a freshman, but he was too smart to stick with it for long. He was a chemistry genius, so he's working for one of the major pharmaceutical companies now. He'll probably discover the cure for cancer. Thank God he cut those gross dreadlocks. He was actually a decent-looking guy without them, a real Michael Bolton makeover."

"Do you want dessert?"

"Have you ever known me *not* to want dessert? I'd have started with it, but I'm convincing you I'm a grown-up. Then I'll be the oldest one at the table, right?"

"Yeah, yeah, keep it up, wiseass." He passed her the dessert menu so she could consider her choices for later. As he watched her eyes flicker over the selection, her teeth worried her bottom lip in an altogether distracting manner.

He'd kept their conversation to her school years, the work education co-ops in Europe and New York, because it helped him remember who she was, who she was supposed to be to him. A little smile played around her lips now and then, a knowing look as if she was wise to the ploy, but he found himself absorbed by her experiences with corporate offices in Paris, Milan and Stuttgart, the differences in legal practices, as well as the sights she'd indulged. She'd always been detail oriented, and she recalled everything with ease, answering his questions and frankly impressing the hell out of him.

"You were smart, integrating the co-ops into your studies. I knew you were impatient about it putting your graduation a year later than your classmates."

"Yeah, and you all didn't have to go to one of those mind-numbing graduation ceremonies. They mailed me my diploma. But I admit, when you said it would give my resume that extra polish, it did." She gave him an eye roll and a smirk. "I've already been invited back to two of the European firms and the New York one wanted to hire me then and there."

He licked his finger, touched her with the sizzling noise of hot stuff, and she laughed. "Yeah, yeah, go ahead and be smug. It gave me valuable work experience as a corporate investigator, which is the field I intend to pursue. Steve Pickard's already given me a couple projects to do while I'm home. I can't wait."

"Just so they don't interfere with the vital tasks of collating, copying and organizing paper clips for me."

"I'm going to tell Alice and Janet you mocked what they do. They'll load your stapler with C-4 and wait for the boom."

"They don't need any help creatively planning my demise."

"I'll bet." She grinned at him, then gave him a mock scowl. "You didn't warn me what the absolute best experience in Europe would be."

"All-night orgies with rugby teams?"

"No, but that was a close second. Oh my God, the food. If you ate everything you wanted you'd exceed the weight limit for the plane trip back. I thought of you so often, because you're such an amazing cook. You really need to go to Italy sometime and do one of their week intensives on Italian cooking. You'd love it. Do you still bring something for the monthly family dinner at our house?"

"Still."

She sighed, sat back. "Whatever you brought was always our favorite. Well, not Nate's, but that was because he had a serious hot dog and macaroni fetish going then, but those orgasmic desserts, or the bread... I don't think I've ever tasted bread as good as what you bake, not even in Paris. If you ever decide not to be a lawyer, I think you should open a bakery." Her gaze went back to the menu, then up. "Will you choose for me, like you did dinner? I trust your instincts."

She'd implied it was his culinary expertise, but if he was the suspicious sort, and of course he was, she'd maneuvered him into taking control of the meal, deciding what she would and wouldn't eat. The way a full-time Master might.

The candlelight on the table flickered, catching her eyes, the gleam of her freshened lipstick. Glinted off that pendant. Reaching out, he touched the disk. His fingers were large, couldn't help whispering over her throat, just a brief touch, but he saw her register it, her fingers tightening on the stem of her wineglass. His own skin tingled with heat. "That's a pretty piece."

"You gave it to me. The forget-me-nots?" At his puzzled expression, she prodded his memory further. "My senior prom, the night my date stood me up?"

"Oh yeah. I remember. What happened to *that* clueless loser?"

"I have no idea, but I've often hoped it involved several flights of stairs and a year in traction. I was mortified that Cass

30

told you about it. The other guys were okay, but it embarrassed me that you knew."

He decided not to touch the why of that, because it was too uncomfortably obvious. Marcie was continuing anyway, relieving him of the need to do so. "I was crying on the back-porch swing. You came out with a corsage of fresh forget-me-nots and roses, and a handkerchief. You told me any guy worth my time would always come to me with flowers and a handkerchief. One to make me smile, and the other to dry my tears, because a smart guy knows women need to cry as much as they need to laugh. It was good advice on judging which guys were worth my time."

She touched the disk. "So I pressed three of the forget-me-nots, and a friend who likes making jewelry designed the collar and pendant."

He paused in lifting his whiskey. Before he could respond to that startling statement, the waiter was there, asking for their order. "We need a few more minutes," he said brusquely. When the waiter nodded, retreated, Ben leaned forward. "Marcie—"

"You sat on the swing with me, kept me distracted." She was lost in the memory, tracing the edge of the wineglass. "Everyone else decorated the front yard with lights, turned on music. Any of the neighbors who wanted to relive their prom day were invited. There was food, dancing. It became a party. You and I danced. Do you remember?"

They were near Frenchmen Street, which meant there was always music in the air. He'd chosen a restaurant across the street from a hole-in-the-wall club renowned for local-band favorites. As a result they'd enjoyed the music while eating, but it hadn't been so loud they couldn't talk. Now she tilted her head, drawing his attention to the bluesy jazz piece playing. Giving him an infectious smile, she rose from the chair, tugged on his hand. "Let's dance now. Just one song. I can't believe I'm back in New Orleans. I've missed it so much here."

He closed his fingers on hers, holding her in place. "Marcie."

She leaned against his grip, trusting him not to let go as she swayed back and forth. "Are you worried about what people will think, us dancing on the sidewalk? Have *you* forgotten how to cut loose and have fun, Ben?"

He sighed, tossed down the napkin. Their outdoor seating was cordoned off with a painted iron fence hung with bright beads and fresh potted flowers. He delighted her by putting his hip on it, swinging over, and in the same motion, curled a strong arm around her waist and brought her over as well. He rolled her into an easy Cajun two-step, twirling her out and under his smoothly moving hands, taking her around his body.

She laughed out loud as he caught her hips, kept her in place as he stayed behind her, doing the footwork in tandem and out to the side, then bringing her back for the turns and the two-step basic again. It didn't take much to get people in New Orleans to dance, so several couples joined them almost immediately.

Marcie reveled in the feel of his hands on her. She knew the steps, but not as well as he did, so she followed his lead. He more than met the challenge, directing her without hurry or hesitation, comfortable in that role as he always seemed to be. To the outside viewer, he was just a capable dancer, but anyone who had the craving in her blood as she did would see it, feel it.

She knew he'd picked up on her ploy, having him order the meal for them both, but he had no idea what it did to her, watching him assume command of a situation where her only preference was to trust his direction. And now, how he took control of her movements so easily…she was content to stay in this moment forever.

This man was meant to control and lead a woman in ways that would overwhelm her with pleasure, open the deepest wells of her heart, the places she was afraid to surrender. She'd put the white flag in his hands, happy to have him tie it around her wrists, binding him to her.

They did two songs, going from the Cajun two-step into the faster jig, improvising some freestyle steps that had them both laughing. It brought her heart in her throat. Ben hadn't laughed during dinner, not once. Cass had mentioned he'd gotten more serious these past couple years. Marcie had seen it when she first stepped into his office, in his green eyes, the tighter set of his mouth. He'd always been the jokester of the group. But even then she'd known what they saw now, that sometimes it was more habit than true levity. Whatever demons plagued him, she hoped she was helping to push them away. She wanted to do it forever.

On those turns and brushes, she took full advantage, making sure his grasp fell lower on her hips than he intended. She worked herself in closer to his body, pressing full against it before she stepped back for the next turn. He was solid and strong, so sure on his feet, his large hands bringing heat and pleasure even in a casual touch. She was glad for the nature of dance itself, the way it let worries be set aside for a little while, allowing what both dancers wanted to come to the surface.

The band took a break, the club switching to a DJ. Recognizing the Jennifer Paige song *Crush*, she bit back a snort. Perfect timing.

It didn't matter. Ben was a smart guy. Her feelings at sixteen wouldn't have evolved and persevered this many years unless they were something else. The song actually illustrated the point, the lyrics suggesting the singer knew it was far more than a crush, that she was just trying to fool herself. Ben was probably doing the same, maybe even trying to convince himself *he* was the one suffering a crush now. She would love knowing that, that she was starting to be an inseparable part of his thoughts, the way he'd been of hers for so long.

Those two years of travel and staying away from home had been hell. But Cass always said you couldn't enter into a challenging negotiation without believing a hundred percent in what you wanted. Marcie had needed to prove it to herself before she could prove it to Ben. And she had, in spades. Nearly seven years, and she'd never wanted anyone else to touch her. Every time a boy had, something inside her turned off, and she could only imagine Ben. She'd made herself do those dates, though. While she tried to avoid the emotional entanglements that might hurt the male in question, she needed a certain level of experience to achieve her goal. Those dates had been a testing ground for this, a game with very real stakes.

"Do you remember our slow dance, at my home prom?" He was still wearing his suit jacket, additional armor against her, she was sure. Rather than putting her hands on his shoulders, she slid her hands inside his coat, along the firm, heated skin over his ribs, separated from her touch only by his thin dress shirt. He stilled, but she stepped closer. He gripped her upper arms, but she kept coming, until her palms were against his back, fingers stroking his shoulder blades, the male muscle beneath the shirt. Ben was over six feet, so it was easy to lay her cheek on his chest, just under his jaw.

He still had his hands on her arms, but as she sighed, let her body melt into his, he muttered an oath against her hair. She closed her eyes, triumph sweeping through her as he slid his arms around her. One at her waist, his palm against her hip, the other staying at her face, cradling it where it lay against him. He slid his thumb along her throat, touching that collar, his fingers playing in her hair. They swayed together to Jennifer's song, Ben's sure footwork keeping them moving in a slow glide.

"I put my hands under your coat, just like this. The other guys were grinning at you, knowing you were trying to figure out a way to push me away a little bit without hurting my feelings. You knew I was too old for you to dance with me like a little girl, too young for us to dance that close. Isn't that odd, how that change happens?"

When she lifted her head, Ben still had his hand on the side of her face, his gaze intent upon her. His grip on her tightened, and she knew from his expression he was done letting her dodge and retreat. His mouth had that firm set, his eyes pinning her in place. But she still had a couple key seconds, and she wasn't going to lose them.

"You'd started to get hard when you pushed me away. You covered it in your usual smooth way, but I remember it." Had dreamed about it.

Particularly when she brought herself to climax in her dorm room at night. She'd lean back from her laptop, think of Ben. She'd imagine him coming up behind her, his fingers sliding around her throat, tipping her head back against his abdomen. He'd whisper to her, tell her to spread her legs. He'd command her to put her fingers down her panties, and then watch her get so aroused she was begging him. Begging for permission to come.

She'd had submissive cravings for a long time, but it wasn't until she'd read between the lines, picked up on what she'd overheard and seen between Lucas and Cass and the others, that she'd understood what she was. Why her sexual desires were different from the vanilla sex fantasies of a high school or college girl. Her dreams had to do with her being on her knees, being spanked, restrained. Tortured and tested. By him.

She wanted to say all of that, wanted to be that brave, but something about his look now, the tightening of his fingers on her face, kept her silent.

"You're asking for trouble, little girl." The hard tone was different. It wasn't the Ben he'd always been with her, and though she knew he was trying to warn her off, it speared need and hope through her vitals. This was the predator she wanted. Hell, she'd bathe in raw meat if that was what she had to do. It gave her the courage to answer him.

"I surely hope so. I don't think I could be any plainer about it."

"Marcie, cut it out now, or your internship is over. Got it?"

"I don't care about the internship. We're close to Club Progeny. Just a cab ride away. Why don't you take me there, do everything you want to do to me, that I can feel you wanting? I've been to clubs, I've—"

"Stop." The word was a knife, cutting her off. Taking her arm, Ben led her back to her chair, this time going through an opening in the iron fence that required them to wind past the other closely placed tables. He motioned to the waiter as he held her chair, pressed her back down into it, his fingers gripping her nape in a way that made her shiver.

"A chocolate torte to go, and the check."

"Yes sir."

He sat back down. Before, with the bistro table being so small, and the other tables so close, his knee had ranged alongside her crossed legs, his other foot placed beside hers. Now he set the chair back toward the rail, putting a more circumspect distance between them. She was losing ground fast, but she'd made enough progress this battle wasn't a complete loss. Picking up her wine, she took a bracing swallow, regarded him. She'd been on the debate team in college, she knew how to hold her own. That is, if she imagined him as anyone other than Ben, who was looking as if he could eat her in three sharp bites.

"You're in over your head, and you need to quit this."

"If you think that, take me to the club and show me what it's really like. I think what you're really worried about is that I won't scare. How would you punish me? Spank me? Tie me up. Fuck—"

In a snap of motion, his hand closed over hers, forcing the wineglass back to the table. He caught her chin, leaning forward so she was staring into brilliant green eyes.

"Where is the key to this?"

Since her senses were reeling from his proximity, it took a moment to realize he was asking about the collar.

She could go with the coy, smart-ass answer, like "Where do you want it to be?" or "Why don't you search me to find it?", but while she knew what she was, it was more fantasy than experience. She'd never had it tested under the searing regard of a fully unleashed Master. This wasn't a practicing Dom with protocols and reasonable discussions of limits. Ben was an actual, in-his-blood Master, who demanded only one response from a submissive. The unembellished truth, delivered promptly.

"It's... The key's attached to my navel jewelry."

His gaze still locked on hers, he dropped a hand to pull the blouse free of her skirt. When he found the tiny key, his attention dropped to examine the connection. She bit her lip at the pressure on the catch bead, a jeweled flower that provided the fastener to hold the key there. His touch passed over her navel, and she couldn't help it, a small noise came from her throat, her thighs tightening at the moisture that came from her sex. His eyes flickered up to her face. "Part your legs," he said in that same hard tone.

She obeyed, but as she did, everything quivered. Her nipples were stabbing against her bra, and her palms were damp.

He unhooked the key, smoothed her blouse back down over the area. "Lift your chin."

As she did, he fitted the key to the lock. The collar loosened, came away in his hands. He laid it on the table between them. Her neck felt too bare, too light without it. Once she'd made her decision about Ben, she'd put it on, resolved not to take it off, and she'd been wearing it over a year. His gaze lingered on her neck, then lifted to hers. "Look down at the table, and don't look up unless I give you permission."

She was going to hyperventilate. Everything was tightening up inside. Her skin was cold and hot at once, and that trembling continued. It was as if she had the flu. Was he having the waiter box up the dessert to take her to the club? Was he going to agree to her desires? Was she ready for that?

"A slave doesn't collar herself," he said, his voice low. Uncompromising. "If you've ever set foot in a club, that won't happen again. That's not your world. You defy me on this, I won't hesitate to take it to Cass and Lucas."

He was chastising her like a child, but his orders, his touch, had been that of a Master taking sexual control. Another emotion swept through her now.

Anger.

She lifted her gaze, locked with his. Before she could respond, the waiter came back, carrying a to-go box. Ben rose, lifting his hand for one of the slow-cruising cabs patrolling for evening patrons. The waiter handed her the dessert box when Ben brusquely gestured for him to do so, then the man wisely retreated. They were too crowded in the dining area for her to try digging in her heels, so she set her chin, allowed herself to be guided back to her feet and out of that area to the waiting cab.

However, once there, she stopped and faced him, extricating her elbow from his grasp. He'd pocketed the choker, and she wouldn't wrest it from him, no matter how much it meant to her. If he was right, and she knew he was, it was his to put back on her. She wondered if he'd read the inscription on the back of the pendant. If he did, would it have the same meaning for him it had for her?

Giving her a hard look, Ben spoke to the cab driver, telling him Cass' address and handing him enough to cover fare and tip. He opened the door for her. "Get in. You're going home."

She set her chin. "I'm twenty-three. I'm no longer a child, Ben. Cass and Lucas don't have any say in my decisions about this." She drew a breath. "If you're not willing to be my Master, you don't either."

The anger was strong enough she was tempted to tell the driver to take her to Progeny instead, right in front of him. But she wasn't going to go without him, and she couldn't bluff a man like Ben. She had to be willing to do everything she said she was going to do.

She got into the car with quiet dignity, though she was vibrating with emotion. As he closed it, he stepped back without saying anything more. He'd reverted to that unsmiling expression, his eyes so calculating, seeing so much. She wondered if he was going to end her internship, try to block her from seeing him again. But that was what could happen tomorrow.

While she hadn't been completely prepared for the emotional impact of his rejection, she had anticipated something like it happening. There were always snags in a negotiation, setbacks. The key was a backup plan, and she had one. When she'd come up with it, she'd wondered if she'd have the bravery to pull it off. Now, galvanized not only by his stubbornness and anger, but those moments she'd seen and felt something entirely different from him, she had the courage to use a battering ram if necessary.

As the cab moved away, leaving him behind, it gave her the space to take some deep breaths, marshal her thoughts. It was time to stop reminding him of the child she'd been and hit him full force with the woman she *was*.

* * * * *

Ben brought the choker back out. It was still warm from her skin. Staring at the forget-me-nots pressed under the glass, he knew he needed to go to Progeny himself. He'd find a submissive, fuck her brains out, work her over hard. He'd pay a staff member to do the aftercare so he could walk away. Finish out the night at his favorite bar filled with questionable characters and the odor of stale beer. He might get a drink, or two or three. The Irishman's crutch. He knew the dangers. Which was why he'd probably go straight to the bar.

Progeny wasn't where he wanted to be. Doing a scene with a submissive required precision, control, artistry. A mutual exchange of pleasure. What he needed was a down and dirty whore, one who'd blow him off, let him fuck her in the ass with enthusiasm, and then leave him with a knowing half-smile and a pocketful of his money.

In the past when this mood took him, he'd go find one of the guys, hang out at a sports bar or one of the classy burlesque clubs, eye naked females, and it would be okay after a while. When Peter had been single, they'd often trawl the streets together until dawn. It was why they'd called the ex-National Guard captain Nightcrawler. Ben had even given him an original signed cover of the famous comic book character for his birthday. It was framed on the wall of Peter's office.

But things were different now. Savannah was seven months pregnant. Matt wasn't going out in the evenings right now, because her pregnancy hadn't been an easy one and she was on bedrest until the baby came. Lucas and Cass still had three of her siblings at home, Cherry, Talia and Nate. He could call Peter and Dana, or Jon and Rachel, but it felt wrong. It all felt wrong.

He'd told her she was asking for trouble, and she'd parried with that half-smile, the taunt in her gaze. But she hadn't been making light of the threat it was, and that made it worse. If she would act like a clueless kid, reckless and naïve, he could brush it off easier. But the knowledge was in her eyes.

She wasn't experienced; if she'd been to a club, he'd bet money she'd only watched, not participated or given herself to a Master. Something ugly tightened in his chest at the thought of her being anywhere near a Dom in that setting. He pushed past that. No, she wasn't experienced, but she understood. She knew what she was, what he was. She was daring him to let it loose, wanting to see if she could handle what he'd dish out.

He thought about calling Lucas, sounding him out on it, then played out how that conversation would go. "Hey, just wondering. Did you know your wife's little sister is a submissive, and oh, by the way, have you been taking her to clubs to have her ass smacked by random Doms?"

Oh yeah. That would go over well. Luc would say, "Stay right there, Ben. I'll be by directly with a baseball bat to beat your fucking brains into the sidewalk."

He returned to the table, paid the check. He had some work he could handle at the office, but he wasn't in the mood to go back and do that either. Jesus, she'd be there tomorrow. Alice was gone for two weeks. It was too much to hope he'd taken care of the problem tonight, spooked her. He'd read the stubborn jut of that chin when she got in the cab. She'd been one breath short of telling the driver to ignore his directions and take her to Progeny. If she'd done it, he would have yanked her out of the cab and blistered her ass right there up against it until she was moaning...

Holy fuck. He'd walked down the street several blocks, and now he decided to sit down on a bench. Seedier elements who kept an eye out for the solitary pedestrian traffic gave him considering looks and he met their gazes square on. *Yeah, you want to be fucked up, you give it your best shot.*

There were some working girls, and he motioned to one of them. When she approached, he shook his head before she could start her spiel. Instead, he nodded to the cigarettes in her purse. "A fifty for one of those and a light, darling."

"For a fifty, I'll give you two, sugar." When he handed over the cash, she proffered the two cigarettes. He cupped his hands over hers to protect the flame as she used her lighter. She had wicked long nails, scarlet with some flashy stuff on it. Nodding, he sat back, and she trawled back to her friends, recognizing a man who wanted to be alone. Good whore. On another night, he might have taken a second look. Yeah right. He hadn't tapped that risky kind of pussy since he was a dumb-ass teenager.

Drawing deep, he closed his eyes and laid his head back against the wall of the old brick building behind the bench.

Marcie lost her virginity at nineteen. Christ on a cupcake, she'd called him to talk about it. He'd given up lecturing her on what was appropriate to discuss with him. The last time he'd tried, she'd teased him, told him he was her best girlfriend, earning a snort. Then she'd become more serious.

You listen. You always give me the right kind of advice, and you know when not to give me any at all. You're my friend, Ben.

She didn't know him or what he was. He and that whore had way more in common. It was showing in the smoking, in the proliferation of f-words in his vocabulary lately. His increasing apathy about all of it.

Marcie had sex at nineteen. By the time he was nineteen, he hadn't been a virgin for years. Those experiences weren't innocent gropings in the back of a Mustang. They were the type of memories best left buried like the rotting corpses they were.

He didn't want to dwell in those dark spaces, so he thought back to that phone call. In truth, he'd been surprised she'd waited that late, given that most teens these days lost their virginity in high school. She'd stumbled around a bit, but she'd wanted to talk about it. The guy had been an okay sort who'd done a decent job, not completely screwed up. She didn't say so baldly, but he could tell she hadn't had an orgasm, not unusual for a girl's first time, but she'd felt those stirrings that suggested it could go that way sometime down the road. He'd confirmed her experience was normal. Without endorsing her going out on a Debbie-Does-Dallas pilgrimage to find the ultimate orgasm, he'd told her it would get better.

He'd cautioned her to be careful, told her what to watch out for. She'd gotten a little teary. After he made sure the tears were just typical female catharsis over an important turning point, and not because Bill What's-His-Name needed to have his dick twisted off, he'd reassured her they were normal too.

Not too long after that, the letters and calls stopped coming so regularly. Cass had said she didn't have a steady boyfriend, so Bill hadn't lasted. However, dinner tonight clearly suggested she'd figured a lot of things out, and not just about sex.

Was the brat smart enough to realize the importance of that break in contact with him, setting a clear demarcation line between the relationship that had existed between man and teenager then, and man and woman now? Plotting it out so she could show up in his life as a sexy, grown-up young woman, homing in on him like a sleek barracuda? That kind of calculation was a bit scary, but she'd always been precocious.

She had self-confidence, determination, and the Dom in him who recognized it, recognized what she was, hungered for it. He wanted to hurt her, give her pain, and she acted like she'd welcome it. She was off limits, but a big portion of him — entendre intended — was just not giving a rat's ass. The combination of innocence and sexual drive made her damn near irresistible.

So if that was all there was to it, why wasn't he going to a club to blow off steam? Or calling up his preferred reputable escort service to take care of his more functional and dangerous cravings?

Because she was in his head. Hell, her scent was still on his clothes, where she'd rubbed up against him during the dancing. He'd smiled at her during the Cajun two-step, and kept smiling. It was hard not to appreciate her, especially when she was utterly serious and yet had that dancing light in her eyes.

It had reminded him of something he couldn't deny. While he may have helped the teenage Marcie let loose and laugh again, her dry wit and self-deprecation, unexpected for her years, coupled with the occasional dose of teenage omniscience on every subject, had kept him grinning and impressed back then. Plus, as the others had found their "one" and gotten married, affecting him in ways he hadn't expected, she'd seemed to understand when it was getting to him. She'd loosened up things inside him about that.

That was the problem, wasn't it? His relationships with women were about the physical, and the pure psychology of D/s. Marcie had an emotional connection to him he couldn't deny, something no other woman—other than the K&A wives who had more clear boundaries—had with him.

He imagined her eating that dessert at home, alone, the chocolate melting in her mouth. The tines of the fork imprinting on her lips, her moist tongue coming out to catch a bit of sweet. He could see her brown eyes, thinking over the evening, analyzing, planning her next attack. Hell, Marcie had started studying for her SATs when she was eleven. Superhuman focus and drive was a family trait. Except in her older brother Jeremy, unless you counted a superhuman determination to self-destruct.

He drew on the cigarette again, a shadow passing through his mind at the thought. It had been awhile since he'd asked Lucas how that was going. For the past few years, Cass went to Thailand monthly to visit Jeremy. She took one of the kids with her each time. Sometimes Lucas went. Through him, Ben knew Marcie had made the trip a few times as well. But the last report Lucas had given the group said Jeremy's time was running out.

Of course, if Jon hadn't found that clinic trying an alternative treatment, and mixed it up with some Eastern hocus pocus by having Jeremy stay in a Buddhist temple near the clinic, the kid would have been dead over six years ago. With full-blown AIDS, he'd been living every day on borrowed time, a fucking miracle. Of course, all of them were living on borrowed time, weren't they?

Lately it felt like he wasn't doing shit with his.

Jesus, he wasn't even fit company for himself. He was beating himself up for sending her off in that cab. He thought of the way she'd sneaked in those little brushes of her body, her wandering hands during their dance. He'd had her turned against him once, her backside soft against his groin. It would have been so easy to cup her breasts, hold her tighter against him, bury his nose in her hair.

He was going to go home, stand naked under a cold shower, wrap his fingers around his dick and jack off until his legs buckled. He already knew he'd be imagining her on her knees, working him in her mouth, that blonde hair slick on her skull. He'd probably have to spurt three or four times tonight. When he was finally drained, he'd lie in bed, stare at the blinking light of a mute television, make his way through a bottle of whiskey, and try not to think about the fact he was starting to backslide into a person he'd vowed he'd never be again. But the monsters were always waiting, weren't they?

Some shit was best not stirred up, and she was like a great big wooden spoon, ready to attack that cauldron with a double-fisted grip. She'd get scalded, and he couldn't allow that.

Marcie: I can't believe you couriered French bread and capellini to me in a warmer. It was so fresh, it was as if I was sitting in the kitchen at home watching you pull it out of the oven. The only thing more perfect would have been if you brought it yourself, though maybe that wouldn't be a good idea, since half the girls on the floor are now in love with you.

Ben: Hmm… Not really interested in the "in love" part, but a floor of co-eds in lust with me? I'll be right there. That Mercedes you're always mocking can do well over a hundred on interstate. Prepare the Jell-O tub and wet T-shirts.

Marcie: Pig. Yes, your car is fast, but you have to stop for gas every hour. Of course, it was pretty thrilling, taking it from 0 to 60 in four seconds. But I'll deny it if you tell any of my green friends.

Ben: That's green with envy, brat, not eco-conscious. And you better not tell Cassandra I let you do that. She'll want to do it too. I only let you do it because you nagged incessantly.

Phone call between Ben and Marcie, freshman year

Chapter Three

❧

"You know, all the greats — Lou Gehrig, Babe Ruth — they could pick up any old bat and hit it out of the park. You only need a caveman's club if you can't hit the side of a barn without one."

"Just keep telling yourself that, Luc. Whatever you need to feel good about that inferior equipment of yours."

Jon snorted, coming into Ben's office. "Glad to see you two are getting some real work done this morning."

Ben braced his foot against the side of his desk as he drank his morning coffee. He eyed Lucas, who had his ass planted on the arm of his couch. "You know Lucas can't resist talking about my dick. It fascinates him."

Lucas raised an unimpressed brow. "You brought up the distasteful subject of your dick. I was just asking how your new intern is doing."

"I hope he's doing *her*." This from Peter, coming into the door with a box of donuts. "I saw her winging her way down the hall yesterday. Only got a profile shot when she turned to say something to Janet, but what a gorgeous pair of — "

"It's Marcie," Ben snapped, bringing his feet down to the floor with a resounding thud. "Jesus, Peter."

Peter shot a glance at Lucas. "Oh *shit*. Sorry about that, bro."

Lucas smiled wryly. "She's grown into a beautiful woman, like her sister. And just as strong-willed, God help the man who falls for her. But her assertiveness will stand her well. She wants to be a corporate investigator."

Assertive, hell. There was an understatement. Ben snorted into his coffee.

"She did exceptionally well at the intern level in Europe," Lucas continued. "She's had a few lucrative entry-level offers from firms in Milan and Stuttgart. Cass hopes she won't go that far away from home though."

"At least that puts one family member closer to Jeremy," Peter offered.

Ben remembered his thoughts of last night. "What's the latest on that, Luc?"

"Not so good." Lucas' expression became more somber. "We talked about bringing him home, letting it end here, like a few years back when we thought it was going to happen then, but he seems truly at peace at the monastery. It's a good place. Cass wants to be with him, though, so she's talking with Pickard about a leave of absence in the next couple weeks. She'll go spend his final days with him there, and I'll fly back and forth as needed. I intended to talk to Matt about it today."

Shit, Ben hadn't realized Jeremy's time was that close. Because he'd been tuning out a lot of the domestic discussion crap of late, he wasn't staying connected to each of their lives on the things that mattered. Maybe he wasn't the balloon who'd been cut loose, but the one who'd untied himself from the rail.

The men were quiet for a few minutes. "I'm so sorry, Lucas," Jon said. Their philosophical boy-genius leaned forward in the guest chair, his blue eyes sad. "I knew it was a long shot, but I hoped that treatment would help turn the tide."

"It did." Lucas shook his head. "We thought he was going to die years ago, Jon. You gave him every moment since then. Nearly seven years not to be a junkie on the street, seven years for his life to be something better. It meant the world to Cass, to the whole family. You gave him back to them."

Ben cleared his throat, rose. Coming around his desk, he put his hand on Lucas' shoulder. "Whatever you need, you've got it, from all of us. If Cass needs you with her full time, we'll cover here, no problem."

Lucas studied Ben with shrewd gray eyes. "You know same goes, right? Whatever you're fighting, Ben, we're here. You don't have to marinate your liver and walk the streets looking for a fight. You dumb Cajun-Irish brawler."

"Don't forget his sporadic New England accent from that fancy education. Or the midwest drawl to put our more country clients at ease." Peter grinned, defusing the sudden tension in Ben's chest. This was about Jeremy, not him, damn it. "You know you can call me and Dana any night," Peter added. "We'll go out or, if it's a guys-only thing, she'll cut me loose without a second thought. Especially if it's you."

"Yeah, she's got a thing for me. Good for you to be a man and accept it."

"In your dreams, horse-dick."

"Now see, that's just rude. And reveals your raging insecurity. I'm *fine*, guys." Ben glanced at Lucas. "I'm just working too hard. I've actually been thinking about taking some time off." Though that would now wait until whatever happened with Jeremy happened. He'd want to be close for that, to support Lucas and Cass. And Marcie.

She'd had a hard relationship with her brother. Before he'd become an addict, she'd idolized him. Then, when she was thirteen, one of his friends had tried to rape her while Jeremy was stoned in the other room. That was the end of him living under the same roof with Cass and the other kids. The past few years had mended things, but it reminded him now why he needed to keep their relationship where it had always been. Yeah, they'd stepped way the hell over that line yesterday, but he'd taken that step back. End of story. Time would take care of the rest. Marcie couldn't afford having another male let her down.

"Mmm. A vacation may be a good idea." Lucas rose then. "Once we get the Senecorp issue off the table, you'd be clear."

"Lucas is just trying to cut Marcie's internship short." Peter chuckled. "We all know what a corrupting influence Ben is."

"Can you blame me?" Lucas said dryly. He gave Ben a shove. "Up until the last couple years, she pretty much hung onto everything you said and did, so hell, I figured you'd already corrupted her."

Great. Just what he wanted to hear. He managed an amused expression, no small feat when he'd swallowed nails.

"Time to get to work." Lucas turned toward the door. "Did Janet say if Matt was coming in today?"

"Yeah." Jon had been studying Ben's expression, but now he thankfully turned his attention to Lucas. "He'll be in around lunchtime. Savannah wasn't feeling too great this morning, so he wanted to stay with her awhile. Even though she nearly took his head for telling her he was coming in late."

"She's tired of being in bed, and she hates to feel like the whole world is waiting on her, particularly Matt. No worse patient in the world than a submissive female," Peter noted.

"Except Dana," Ben snorted. "She has no problem with foot massages and being handfed bonbons."

See? He'd jumped in with that one. Proof that he was fucking fine, right?

Peter took the bait with a chuckle. "Just don't tell her she can't drive the Batmobile or scale tall buildings with a nail file. She likes to be pampered, but on her own terms. She doesn't like being helpless."

"Why don't we all go hang with Savannah and Matt tonight?" Jon suggested. "We haven't gotten together in a few weeks. Ben, can you make it?"

"I'll see. Maybe."

Lucas met Jon's gaze, what Ben privately called the secret decoder ring glance, because Lucas tried to cover it with a shrug. Ben knew what it meant, regardless. *He'll spend another night alone drinking.* Jesus. Sometimes working with four guys known for their incredible intuition as businessmen and Doms was a pain in the ass. At least they weren't women. If they were, they'd want to talk about feelings, and he'd have to throw himself off the top of the building.

He decided to ignore the look. He still had enough whiskey in his system to keep him mellow, and that's where he wanted to stay.

"Sir?"

Glancing toward the doorway, Ben saw Randall Caldwell, the K&A security chief. "Morning, Randy. What brings you?"

The man shrugged casually. "Just need a minute of your time, Mr. O'Callahan, once you get done with your morning bullshit session."

Peter gave the man a punch as he went by. "There's important corporate strategy going on in here, rent-a-cop."

Randall effectively blocked the blow, giving him a grin. "Yeah, yeah. A bunch of suits who don't know what hard work is."

There was some more banter back and forth, but Ben was focused on the steadiness of Randall's pale green eyes. He was teasing to lighten the atmosphere, to distract focus. The others picked up the hint, though none were fooled. Lucas gave Ben that same look again, the look that was supposed to convey solidarity. Ben wasn't sure where to go with that, given he'd been imagining the girl Lucas had shepherded to adulthood going down on him like a high-powered vacuum. *Christ.*

After they filed out, all traces of humor left Ben. "What's up, Randall?"

The security head pulled a disk out of his coat, laid it on Ben's desk. "That's the only copy, sir. If you don't want it returned, that's fine. I'll need to mark it on my monthly report to Mr. Kensington, but it'll go no further than that. If this is something you want us to investigate further or file charges, we will. But I wanted you to see it first. No damage appears to have been done to your vehicle."

That brought Ben's attention up sharply. "Someone was fucking around with my car?" He hadn't retrieved the Mercedes from the parking deck last night, but when he checked on it this morning, it had looked fine. "When did this happen? How the hell —"

"Time stamp's on the disk, sir. Best to look at it first. I've taken disciplinary action on the security detail assigned that shift, but... Well, I'll be in my office to discuss questions, *after* you look at it." Randall had moved to the door. Without further explanation, he stepped out and pulled it shut after him, so Ben wouldn't be disturbed unexpectedly.

Ben stared after him. *What the hell?*

Putting the disk into his laptop, he called up the footage. To better see the details of the black-and-white security tape, he put it on his wall screen.

The time stamp was 12:50 a.m. The security patrol went through each level of the parking deck once an hour, though they rotated that time by a varied amount each night so no one could anticipate their schedule. Apparently, whatever had happened had occurred right after the detail went through, because he watched the guard walk past, checking between the cars and in the shadows near the stairwell as always.

So the perpetrator had anticipated their schedule, known to do his worst when he had at least an hour to pull it off. There was a guard in reception to watch the cameras pan through the buildings and decks, but he didn't pay close attention unless one of the guards called in a camera check. The footage was merely for history, flagged if a problem cropped up. Ben wondered what had caught Randall's interest if there'd been no damage to the car.

He parked on the top covered level, the back corner. It was a secluded area, but one camera was focused directly on that section. He sat down, his attention sharpening. And then everything else disappeared.

She was walking toward his car. In five-inch heels that had a plethora of straps over her ankle and a little tassel teasing the back. She was crossing one leg over the other, putting a serious sway to her hips. As he watched, she unbelted the thin coat she was wearing, let it slide down slow, until it fell below her bare shoulder blades. Her hair was slicked back and in a tight knot on her head, the black and white of the camera making it look darker. But he already knew that hair was blonde and thick. With a faint scent of perfumed coconut.

The garment dropped to her waist, the sleeves holding her elbows to her sides. She stopped in front of the grill of the car as if studying it, her back to the camera. Then the coat fell to the ground. Milk-cream skin, slim arms and legs, a gentle flare of hips. An Audrey Hepburn figure in truth. Completely naked.

"Fucking Jesus." He snapped up straight in his chair as if he could throw a coat over her, ask her if she'd lost her mind, even realizing he was looking at something that had happened hours ago.

She moved another several steps toward the car, keeping his gaze glued to the swing of her ass. She didn't play it up, just put everything that was female and perfect into the movement, the slight quiver of the buttock as her heel made contact with the deck concrete, the shift of hip as she moved forward. When she put her knee on the nose of the car, Ben stifled a groan as she braced her hand on the hood and then looked over her shoulder at him, right at the camera.

She was wearing a mask. A Mardi Gras mask with deep purple and teal green feathers, the gold thread edging drawing attention to her lips and sweet line of chin. The feathers brushed her temples. A tiny waterfall of rhinestones emphasized the eyes.

Holy fuck. He'd seen this mask before. Her movements at the file cabinets had been familiar for reasons other than inheriting her sister's grace. Marcie hadn't been lying. She *had* gone to a club. She'd been at Surreal ten days ago.

He usually played private, but lately the privacy mocked the intimacy he really wasn't getting with his subs, so he'd decided to go for a public playroom scene. He'd gone over the top, chosen three women. Clara, Sharon and Myra. All staff regulars up for hire, and his preference that night because they thrived on rough edge play.

He'd put them in a triangle of stocks, the kind that bound neck and wrists, and then he'd locked their feet to the floor in the anchored boots that increased the sense of vulnerability. He'd gone to work on them with a flogger, then wielded a paddle with expert precision and force until they were crying, the marks showing on their asses, but they were also soaked as honey hives. Drawing out that honey with clever fingers that had them on the cusp of orgasm, he'd mixed that natural lubricant with a stimulant that would heat up their rectums, make them even more sensitive to his penetration.

He'd been ruthless that night, wringing two or three orgasms out of each woman before he'd plunged his cock into them. Three different condoms, three different orgasms. When he was done, his chest was heaving and his vision was a little gray, so when he sat down on a nearby bench to watch their aftercare, handled by the staff, he was almost spent. But not too spent to notice her.

He'd been peripherally aware of her during the session, which was unusual in itself, because once in a scene, it usually absorbed him completely. In this case, as the scene became more intense, he noticed her more. She kept circling, so he saw her first on his left, then right, at a distance, then closer. She'd eventually found a stationary spot, near the wall across the floor of the public play area, blending with the shadows.

She'd been wearing a simple black cocktail dress, no rubber club bracelet that gave a clear indication of her status. No jewelry except the silver collar and pendant he'd never seen close up, not until last night. She'd worn a killer pair of strap heels then as now, and the dress's neckline framed her swelling cleavage in an eye-catching way. Because the dress was snug, he'd had a few tempting glimpses of her ass.

Throughout his scene, she'd stayed riveted on what he was doing. She was a sub; he'd felt it from her like a beacon call, and just the kind of sub he took pleasure in breaking down, breaking open. She'd be a virgin to having her ass fucked, he was sure of it.

By the end, it was almost as if he was performing for her. When he was balls deep inside Myra, listening to her grunt deliciously at the power of his strokes, he saw the mystery woman's lips part, her tongue touch her lips, a delicate movement of need and yearning. Her fingers had gripped the rail so that he suspected her knuckles were white, and her body was pressed against it. If she'd been closer at that point, he would have told her to lift her skirt, put her fingers on her wet pussy and masturbate for him, show him how wet she was, how she wanted his cock inside of her when he was done here.

After he got his breath back, she was gone. The staff remembered her, said she was a guest, but of course he didn't pry beyond that, respecting the privacy rules that didn't reveal names. He'd thought of her more than once since then. If he saw her again, he'd burn down her shields, win her sweet cries and tears of surrender.

Now he was looking at her again. *Marcie.* She put her other knee up on the car hood and, with a smooth ripple of thighs and buttocks, she was on the Roadster on all fours, her ass facing the camera.

A black velvet bag was in her hand, and she laid it near the windshield. As he watched, she went down to one elbow and put her cheek to the car's hood. Holding her balance on her knees and that one cheek, she reached back, cupped both hands over her ass. Curving her fingers into the seam between, she parted her buttocks to show him that delicate puckered entrance. As she flexed, he caught the glisten, realized she'd already oiled herself up.

Dipping her fingers into her pussy, she worked them in and out, showing him she was also well-aroused, then she moved her fingers from there into her rectum. The muscles contracted and released, then contracted again, taking her.

He had his hand on his cock, he couldn't help it. It was straining against his slacks, threatening to split seams. Damn it. He hit the remote on his desk, locking the door, and then opened his trousers. When he put a chokehold on it, it convulsed under his hand.

Removing her fingers from her ass, she reached for that velvet bag. She withdrew an eight-inch dildo from it, an impressively thick size, though still not as large as him. She put it in her mouth, taking all eight of those inches to the hilt, her throat working then relaxing. She worked it in and out, lips stretched over it.

Yes, baby. That's it. Take my cock. Take all of it. He had to watch this to the end. Then he'd think about the ramifications.

When she had it slick from her saliva, she reached behind her again, parting her cheeks.

Who had seen this footage? Whose eyes did he have to put out? His fist clenched on himself, but not to rub. Something even deeper came to the forefront as she worked it in. She bit her lip, concentrating, trying to relax. She hadn't done it too often then, and he sensed some tension in her. If he were there, he'd teach her how to relax. Best way to ass fuck a woman fairly new to it was to get them so excited, their pussy so near climax, they were contracting on air, then slide right into their rear entry like butter. They convulsed on a cock like a fist that would never let go, those sphincter muscles strong and sure.

Four inches, five...she had it past the muscles, but it was thick, and he was sure it was burning. But then she had it in to the hilt. As she turned her body, she tried to hold on to her sinuous way of moving. She didn't realize it made his blood heat to volcanic lava, seeing that sensual impairment, the awkwardness caused by such a penetration.

She made it over to her back, pressing the dildo deep inside of her against the car hood. Slowly, she spread her legs. He drew in a breath as she lifted her upper body, used that gymnastic flexibility to reach down, unbuckle the straps of the shoes. What he'd thought were two sets of buckles, part of the shoe's design, was an extra set of tie straps on her ankles. She buckled one ankle to the grill. Spreading the other leg out as far as it could go, she fastened it as well. Then she eased herself to her back once again, only now her legs were spread so wide he could see her weeping pussy, the flex of her buttocks as they flattened against the hood, holding that phallus inside of her.

She placed the other hand above her head, curling her fingers around the hood edge at the windshield. She didn't restrain her wrist, but the way she held it there suggested binding. Then she slid her other hand down her belly. He saw the navel jewelry, that glittering flower, now without a key on it, because he'd taken it, removed it and her collar.

Her breasts were as fucking tempting as any Ben had ever seen. He thought Peter, dedicated tit man who he was, would agree. She was pierced there too, tiny little rings, tempting teeth. The nipples were stiff and large, her back arched as if offering them, begging. He followed the track from that irresistible view down the slope of her abdomen, over the navel piercing, down to where her hand was. Jesus, she had a clit hood piercing as well, a jeweled ring lying against her clean-shaven pussy, glistening with her juices.

She could be bound by those four rings. A collar around her neck, chains leading to her nipples, navel, clit. Chains that could be tightened and tugged to fold her over, increase the discomfort, helplessness, focusing her on her Master's desires, heightening his pleasure and her own...

She tugged on that clit piercing and moaned, arching up farther, thrusting out those beautiful tits in a way that would compel any straight man who saw this to jack off. Ben understood Randall's comment about disciplinary action now. There was no way the guard monitoring the cameras had missed her doing this. But he wouldn't put it past Marcie to have done her research, to know which on-duty guard would be most likely to hold off calling it in right away, unable to resist indulging in a little late-night adult cable entertainment.

Or more likely—given that K&A security were smart and well-trained—the man in question had realized within the first thirty seconds this was an intentional message for Ben. As such, he'd made the judgment call, decided to simply monitor her, making sure she intended no vandalism, and then reported it to Randall after the fact, earning the disciplinary action as a matter of form only.

Either way, she'd taken a calculated risk, one that had panned out.

She rocked against her touch, her lips pressing hard together. Fingers dipping in, coming out, smearing more fluid against her cunt. She was saying something, urging herself on, and when Ben recognized the words on her lips, his cock convulsed hard in his hand, demanding to spurt his response.

Please, Master...let me come. Let me serve you. Master... Master... Then, Ben...please. Master.

He traced her face, her body. Pre-cum trickled down his shaft, dampening his fingers, making him tighten his grip once more. He couldn't. This was...he was going to shake her until her teeth rattled. Security or not, she was all by herself in a parking deck in the middle of the night. If some vagrant had stumbled on her, or anyone...

She slowed then, so near climax her body had to be sheened with perspiration. Now she stretched out both her arms, a clear message of submission. She breathed deep, drawing herself back from that edge. She wasn't going to come, because he hadn't been there, hadn't given her permission.

That realization hit him hard in the chest as she at last let go of the hood. She probably had red indentations in her palms. When she pushed herself up, he saw her hair had come down, a twisted, dark tail against her neck.

She opened the tie on one ankle, moved more stiffly to do the other. Turning onto her hands and knees once more, she reversed the provocative process, sliding out the dildo until the head released with that sudden pop that made her convulse, press her thighs together. He could see the tracks of her arousal on her thighs. That tight rosebud entry point flexed as it released the phallus, such that he felt that impact all the way to his testicles.

Tucking it all in the velvet bag, she took out a handkerchief and wiped what appeared to be some drops of her arousal off the hood, then tucked that away as well. Turning to face the camera fully, she dropped to her knees and bowed her head. Then she picked up the coat, slipped it on her shoulders. Tossing her hair back, combing through it with her fingers, she managed to walk away with that same sauntering confidence she'd shown in his office earlier in the day when she'd been teasing him. When she reached the stairwell door, she even threw the same sassy look over her shoulder.

Speak of the devil. His gaze lifted as he heard the tap of heels outside of his door. A moment later, his intercom buzzed.

"I'm here, Mr. O'Callahan." That sultry purr. "So is your nine o'clock. Are you ready for Mr. Alexander?"

That effectively brought him up short. Clamping down on a variety of responses, he tucked himself back in, ejected the security footage to lock it in his middle desk drawer and tore open a sanitized towelette to clean his hands. He was proud to find his voice was even, controlled when he responded. "Yes, Marcie. Send him in."

Fortunately, Don Alexander was a no-nonsense sort who preferred to get straight to business. He wouldn't question why Ben didn't rise from his desk for a morning handshake. If Don knew where his hand had been, he'd probably thank Ben for the lack of courtesy.

The legal muscle for one of their latest in-process acquisitions took a sprawling seat in Ben's guest chair and unlatched his briefcase, already firing off the info he was here to get. Ben knew what he needed, had it ready, so his gaze slid to the view outside his door while Don did his required diatribe.

Marcie's desk was at a diagonal angle to his door. She was wearing another one of those straight, tailored skirts, only this one was a little higher and had several short, coquettish slits in the front that layered like flower petals. When she adjusted her seat, he caught a glimpse of the lace top of her thigh-high stockings. As if she was unaware of his perusal— *yeah right*—she ran her finger beneath the skirt edge, flipping up one of those layers to check the hold of the—*holy God*—garter holding the stocking in place. Her hair was twisted up in a soft, loose style, and today she wore a lightweight sleeveless turtleneck in a pale blue color. The long stretch of fabric from throat to hips drew a man's gaze right to her generous breasts. He could discern the puckered state of her nipples. A faint impression only, something that could be explained away by the well-air-conditioned office, instead of inappropriate attire, but he'd put money on the fact her bra was so thin it allowed that subtle effect, while keeping those heavy breasts up nice and high.

His hard-on wasn't abating in the least. She was wearing the heels she'd worn on his car, the little tease. Two sets of buckles, so she'd included the restraints, which yanked his mind right to the image of bending her over her desk, spreading her legs out wide and binding her ankles to the desk legs. He'd fuck her, then make her do her work in that bent-over position while he enjoyed the view from his desk.

Janet might have a few words to say about that. So would Matt. As for Lucas...hell.

He pulled his attention away from Marcie, though he could smell her unique fragrance. She'd probably shaken Don's hand, leaving a lingering scent on his palm. He gave Don some answers, asked a few questions of his own, which sent the man riffling through papers again. It left Ben free to shift his gaze back to the only thing that mattered to him at the moment.

Weren't you supposed to stay on the other side of that line, you prick?

Marcie was studying her laptop, but as if she felt his regard, she lifted those lashes. He caught the familiar moistening of her bottom lip, that involuntary tell of vulnerability, of possible uncertainty, as if she was weighing a decision. But then the decision was made. Like a flipped switch, her expression became hot, focused, challenging. With a surreptitious glance toward Don, she slipped her hand back down to her thigh, fingers following the silken surface of the stocking. Pushing under one of the front overlapping slits in the skirt, she traced the nylon up, up, into the dark shadows of the skirt fabric. Her fingers moved over, down, her knees parting. Biting her lip, she lifted her chin in reaction as she obviously found her pussy, stroked.

To someone coming down the hall, it would appear she was still working on her computer, but beneath the desk, where he could see, she was getting more stimulated, her movements a little more jerky. Which meant she'd been hot and worked up when she put her hand down there. Given that she'd come into work with a battle plan to drive him insane, he wasn't surprised. Her pussy was probably so slick and ready for his cock he could just cross the room, shove her against the wall and slam into her like a torpedo chamber ready to fire.

She kept her hot gaze on him, with those occasional maddening little flicks toward Don. If he looked left, he'd get the same view Ben was getting. Then Ben would have to kill him.

Something broke inside him. No, not broke. That was entirely the wrong word. He found his footing, something kicking in that was much stronger than concerns about Lucas and Cass, about inappropriate or appropriate behavior on his part. It was the feeling he had right before he entered one of Matt's volatile acquisition meetings. Foot in the stirrup, ass on the warhorse, lance in hand, no entendre intended. Decision made.

The whiskey and damn indecision from last night disappeared. He knew how to handle this situation. Misbehaving subs, those who stepped out of line, were his particular area of expertise. His craving.

"Is that all you needed, Don? All right then, I'll have my intern fax over…"

He dealt with Don with courtesy, showed him out the door, using iron discipline to keep his cock from straining at the end of its chain. Marcie had of course returned both hands to her keyboard, her skirt smoothed back over her thighs. She rose, smiling. Nodding to Don, she reached out to grip his hand when the man offered his. She was going to touch him with the hand she'd had on her pussy, leave that scent on his fingers. From the calculated look in her gaze, Ben knew she intended it.

He stepped between them, though it wasn't a wide space. While Don looked a little startled by the abrupt intervention, Ben ironed it out with some further BS about the documents he needed. As Don responded, Marcie's fingers brushed Ben's back, the line of his spine, tugging playfully on his dress shirt, since his coat was hanging up behind his door. Her touch felt good, too good. Ben stepped away, taking Don down the hall and back to reception.

After he turned him over to Janet, doing a few more minutes of necessary bullshit chitchat, he pivoted on his foot and headed back down the hall. Since he was striding back to his office like a wolf running down a kill, he made himself stop before he hit the corner that would take him into view of his office area. Holding himself there, he took a breath. Thought it through.

That pause didn't change anything. He knew what was needed, and wouldn't turn back from it. Wherever the hell this took them, she'd pushed it too far. Time to give her a taste of what she thought she wanted.

* * * * *

After executing her Plan B, Marcie had been too wired to sleep, her body needy, hungry, but she didn't give it the orgasm it was screaming for. She wanted to stay like this, wild, reckless, so she'd have the courage to make some really terrible decisions in judgment in the morning. Like masturbating right there where Don Alexander might have seen. But the look in Ben's eyes, the flame in those green eyes, had been worth the risk. She'd broken his chain of self-control, she knew it. He'd obviously seen the security footage, because there was an edge to that look, a promise of retribution.

As she heard his footsteps, she had a moment to be thrilled and terrified at once. She'd pushed him past anything she could control. It gave her a primal urge to bolt, but fortunately he was turning the corner, already too close. Just the smell of his aftershave, the remembrance of the heat of his skin beneath his shirt when she'd stroked him just now, without Don's knowledge, was enough to weaken her knees.

She was still standing by her desk, but he didn't pause. Locking his hand around her wrist, he strode past her, yanking her into step with him. With a little hop and skip, she was with him. He might drag her by her hair if she stumbled.

He took her to the private restroom at this end of the hall, one that had shower facilities, everything for a man who often worked long hours at the office. He pulled her in there, slammed the door behind them, twisted the locks shut.

"Ben—" That was all she got out, because in the next blink, he'd shoved her against the wall and slammed his mouth down on hers.

Oh. *Oh.* She whimpered in the back of her throat at the strength of his aroused, powerful body against her. His hands were in her hair, yanking out pins so it spilled onto her shoulders. He gripped the strands hard, fusing her mouth to his. His tongue demanded entry, and it made every part of her tight, the way he lashed it against hers, pressing it down, learning her mouth more intimately than she thought was possible.

His hands stayed on her face, though her body writhed uncontrolled against him, her tight nipples pressed to his chest. She tried to push herself against his hard groin, but he thrust his thigh between her legs so his knee thudded against the wall, flexing muscle pressing against her mound.

"You fucking slut," he muttered against her lips. "Hot little cunt."

How he could make such awful words sound like an endearment, a caress, she didn't know, but he did. She was shameless enough to nod, to confirm it. She was a slut, her pussy wet, all for him. Only for him. This was that moment she'd dreamed about, overwhelming, crazy, impossible to control, and she didn't want any control. She wanted to be chained to him. Collared and belonging to him in every dark, dangerous way that horrified the civilized world.

If it were hundreds of years ago, and he were a pasha, she'd want to be his slave girl, subject to the sting of his lash. If he was a pirate, she'd be the nobleman's daughter he kidnapped and corrupted, night after night, turning her into a wanton, willing to do anything. Fight at his side, press her lips to his polished boot. Curl next to his feet to be there for anything he needed.

She savored every millimeter of his palm against her face, her throat, his fingers buried in her hair. Her lips stayed parted, open as he plundered, took for himself. Her pulse thundered in her throat, roared in her ears. Her clit throbbed against his leg. When the thigh muscle shifted with his stance, she gasped into his mouth. But she stayed still, his to do with as he desired.

He broke the kiss, pulled her to face the mirror over the sink. "Hands on the counter," he growled, gaze pinning her in that reflective glass. "Get rid of the shoes. Keep standing straight. Press your cunt against it."

She obeyed, kicking off the shoes, knowing that her teeth were chattering with nerves. There was something raw and volatile in this room, something she'd glimpsed that night at Surreal when he hadn't known she was there. This was the kind of Master he was. Hard, ruthless, edgy. Dangerous, the kind of Dom who took the challenge of finding out what his sub was and needed down to her soul, without allowing her to say a word. He was a lawyer—he had no trust of words, though he certainly knew their power.

It didn't matter. She wanted him any way she could get him. She could do this.

Her nipples were so stiff, it was as if she was wearing no bra at all. He slid his hand along the right stocking, traced the garter as she made a tiny mewl. The loss of her heels made her feel even more vulnerable. Dipping his fingers under the hem of the skirt, he pushed it up so it folded around his wrist as he found her panties, the soaked crotch. She moaned.

"Wet as you can be. You were going to touch Don with this hand." He lifted it with his other, his fingers tight on her wrist, emphasizing how much stronger he was.

She wouldn't show fear, even though she was shaking like a cornered mouse. "Yes."

Pushing the crotch of her panties aside, he sank two fingers into her, without hesitation, knowing her body intimately. She cried out, but managed to stay still as he ordered while his thumb settled on her clit, began to rub. He brought her hand to his mouth, sucked on her fingers, took the taste of her pussy into himself. It was a good thing he was pressed up against her, because her knees would have buckled.

"You didn't come last night," he muttered, "all spread out on my car. Why not?"

"Because...you didn't give me permission."

"You'll come now."

It was lightning, whatever he did, the skillful rhythm, pinches at just the right moments, the way his gaze met hers in the mirror, the feel of his body against hers, taking her over. She had a compulsion to resist, an automatic survival instinct before the vortex about to sweep her away, but it was useless. The climax she'd held out of reach last night, stoked to trip off at the slightest provocation, swept up through her, flushing her skin.

He caught her throat, holding her face so she was staring at herself in the mirror, staring at him. Her mouth stretched wide, her eyes teared, and strangled shrieks tore from her throat. He kept working her with the other hand, had her up so high on her toes he put uncomfortable pressure on her jaw, keeping her straining, quivering, gasping.

As she cried out, he turned his face into her throat and bit, sucking on her skin fiercely, marking her tender flesh just below the top edge of the soft turtleneck collar. A glazed glimpse at the mirror showed him biting into her like a vampire, her breasts thrust out, nipples jutting, body jerking uncontrollably in his powerful hold, his hand working between her legs. With her skirt pushed up and gathered around his forearm, his large fingers were visible through the sheer cloth of her panties as he thrust and scissored, pinched her clit.

Because of that hold, the balance of pain and discomfort with the pleasure, it was the most unusual and intense orgasm she'd ever experienced. Like a whitewater rapid ride, bumpy and thrilling, scary, a cyclone of unpredictable sensations as she cried out and shuddered, made pleading noises. The waves of feeling kept hitting her from all sides, spinning her mind, making her body buck. Just when she thought she was coming down, he'd move his fingers or alter the pressure on her throat and she was bleating with helpless noises once more.

At last her body itself gave out, convulsing like a fever victim, leaving her mind blank, facial features numb, making it difficult to speak. She was panting, seeking air. At a certain point she'd unconsciously let go of the counter, had grabbed hold of his forearm across her body. Now she saw she'd dug her nails into his flesh, drawn blood. He'd have at least three crescent marks there. She was still holding him that tightly, but she couldn't make herself let go.

"Does Lucas know what you are?"

Her gaze fluttered up to meet his in the mirror. He had his jaw pressed to the side of her head, his lips cruising along the hair at her temple. It wasn't tenderness, not exactly. He looked like he was learning her scent like a predator, so he could hunt her again.

"I don't know. I don't know what he and Cass talk about." Enough belligerence slipped into her voice that she earned a deeper push of those fingers. Plus a third one, despite the constricted nature of her post-climactic tissues. She bit her lip.

"Does Cass know?"

"Yes." She swallowed against his hold, met that formidable stare. "She and I talked...when I figured it out. She also had me talk to Dana. In case I felt reservations about discussing certain things with her. I asked her not to tell Peter. So I don't think any of the other..."

"Guys" didn't fit, not at this moment. Five hardcore Masters, bonded like a wolfpack. A more respectful honorific was needed, but her brain was too foggy to figure it out.

"Christ" Though he still held her on her toes, he slid his fingers out of her. Her hands convulsed against his arm, the one she'd marked. If he rolled down the sleeve, he'd get blood on it. When he eased her back to her feet, she was already reaching for the basket of thick paper hand towels. Her fingers shaking, she tried to run one under the water.

"Got to wipe that blood off," she said, hearing her voice break. "Make sure you don't mess up your shirt."

Marcie: I know you've had sex with a million women. How many women have you had that mattered?

Ben: I'm not having this conversation with you.

Marcie: Why?

Ben: Because it's entirely inappropriate, and none of your business.

Marcie: I'm just curious what it is you really want.

Ben: Men aren't that complex, Marcie.

Marcie: Maybe most men aren't. But I think you are. Otherwise you'd just answer the question.

Phone call between Ben and Marcie

Chapter Four

ಐ

He pressed against her back, closing his hands on her wrists. "Stop." He spoke against her hair. Pulling the towel from her hands, he set it aside. "Come here."

Since she was already right against him, she wasn't sure what he meant, but it didn't matter. Turning her in his arms, he picked her up, smooth and easy. In the small sitting area adjacent to the bathroom was a settee, probably to give him a place to sit down and put on his shoes if he was dressing in here. Now he set her down on the firm cushions. "Stay there."

Returning to the sink, he blotted the blood off his arm, quick and functional. Then he wet another paper towel and brought it and a couple dry ones with him. Nonplussed, she watched him drop to one knee beside her, bringing them to eye level. Cupping her chin, he dabbed at her mascara, dried tears she hadn't realized she'd shed when he took her over so completely. She didn't understand why that would make her cry, but it felt right, like it should.

Reaching out, she touched the pocket of his shirt, her fingers hooking briefly in it, caressing the man beneath. "No handkerchief," she managed.

"It was in my coat," he said. "We'll make do with this."

He sat back on his heels then, out of her reach. Bending his head, he gripped her ankle, began to massage the strained arches, her toes, through the silk of her stockings. "Oh." She suppressed a moan of sheer joy at the sensation. The little ripple between her legs at the intimate touch surprised her, her body responding as if that hollow of her foot was an erogenous zone.

"Unzip your skirt," he ordered, his head still bent over his task. It took a little fumbling, since coordination wasn't happening right now, but she managed to reach behind her and do that. Rising, he lifted her back onto her bare feet, and then worked the skirt off her hips himself. The strength and yet precision of his hands captured her, the way he was able to remove the skirt with firm pressure, no jerking or awkwardness. On one hand, it was a reminder of how many women he'd undressed. On the other, it was undeniably sexy, the competent way he did it, no haste.

"How you breathe in this is beyond me."

"Lycra and cotton blend. It's a wonderful thing." She hiccupped on the chuckle, felt a little silly and more than a bit nervous, flushing as he flicked a glance at her. The skirt dropped to the ground around her bare feet. She wanted to cross her arms over herself, rub arms that now had goose bumps. Instead, her hands had landed on his shoulders as he'd bent to free the skirt, and they were still there. Until he straightened, and then they slipped to his forearms, her fingers curling into the folds of his sleeves. He took her wrists, lifted her hands away from him, but gave them a squeeze.

"At your sides, Marcie. You don't have permission to touch me."

It was odd, how it kicked in. That post-climactic lassitude, the numbness of her brain, didn't make her numb to instinctive obedience to her Master's order. Though he said it in a relatively mild tone, she immediately put her arms at her sides. Keeping them there became a little more difficult when he hooked her panties, drew them down her legs, his fingers following the same track over her thighs. She twitched, made a small noise. He stopped, glanced at her, and she stilled again.

Giving an approving nod, he continued, taking them down to her feet. "Step out of them."

When she did, he set them aside. Now she was wearing only the snug sleeveless turtleneck and her garter belt and stockings, framing her bare sex. In the mirror over the sink she saw the silver glint of the clit jewelry against her pale skin. It was a barbell with a slender chain dipping from each of the ends, a faint tease to her clit and labia when she moved, though of course she hadn't needed the additional stimulus today.

Ben sat back on his heels, studying her. She dared a glance down at him, the strong face, those brilliant green eyes, the dark hair falling over his forehead. He had such a strong face, a solid jaw, the slope of his cheek bones beautifully sculpted. He was everything a man should look like. Even the casual power of his pose, resting on one heel, arm on his thigh, the other reaching out now. She bit her lip as he touched that tiny chain, his thumb and forefinger pinching it, giving it a tug. She closed her eyes at the sensation. God, she'd just climaxed, and yet her body was so attuned to him, so hungry.

She had damp tracks on her inner thighs, her labia wet from her climax. Given his focus there now, she expected he was going to wipe away the come from her thighs with the other paper towel. Instead, he put his hands on her hips, shifted forward and put his mouth there instead.

She sucked in a gasp. He hadn't told her to widen her stance. In fact, his hands tightened, holding her still as he licked his way up to her pussy. Then he was on it, suckling away her juices, teasing her labia and clit as he cleaned her in a deliberately functional way, indulging a Master's desire to taste his toy while she stood still and suffering, aching for him. She kept her lips pressed together tight but couldn't help the pleas in her throat, the involuntary twitches from the stimulus to over-sensitized skin.

At last, he sat back. Only then did he use the paper towel, rubbing her dry, letting her feel the stroke of his fingers through it. Lightheaded, she swayed, and he put his hand back on her hip, steadying her.

"Don't lock your knees."

She'd forgotten, but he'd noticed. He noticed everything. Now he eased her down to a sitting position on the couch, perching her on the end of it so her pussy was exposed to the cool air. "Spread your legs, Marcie. Put your hands behind you, straighten your back, then I want you to meet my gaze."

He rose, moved back to the sink while she obeyed. Lifting her gaze was more difficult than expected. He hadn't even taken off his clothes, while she was half naked, the bottom half, which was a far more vulnerable feeling than topless. He was leaning against the sink, watching her. His cock was a thick root against the restraint of his slacks, making her wet her lips. She'd of course seen men get aroused, but not to such obvious thickness, and not with the complete lack of self-consciousness he had about it. He'd given her a climax, but taken nothing for himself. She wanted to service him the way a slave should, sucking his cock until he had his own release.

When he'd taken her collar, he'd said *A slave doesn't collar herself.* He even understood that about her. Yes, she was a submissive, but in her mind she preferred the far more stark and aggressive term of slave. Myriad definitions in the D/s world for each status didn't matter to her. It was what he meant when he said it, and the way it made her feel. His.

71

"My brain might be in my cock, Marcie, but my eyes aren't."

She brought her gaze up to his, reluctantly. His lips twisted, seeing it. If things were different, if he truly accepted her as his, she knew he would have dished out some punishment for the infraction, minor as it was. Ben was the kind of Master who didn't let anything slide. She hungered for that, loved the idea of that kind of structure, safety. She craved the sharp edge of his discipline enough to challenge that side of him, again and again. But right now, she had enough to do controlling her own body. Her knees wouldn't stop quivering, no matter how much she tried to make them do so. She wasn't sure they'd ever support her weight again.

"How did you know about me? About us?" he asked.

To pull it together and answer him, she imagined she was in a meeting, being asked for a report. It wasn't easy in this setting, but she let familiar practice guide her. "Once Lucas and Cass got together, I picked up on things, but I always knew, in a way."

He was still waiting. She hadn't answered the question fully, so she backtracked a few steps. It was truly odd to do this naked, and right after a climax besides. Like a surreal Penthouse letter. She quelled a strange hiccup of laughter at the thought.

"My passion's always been investigation, research." *And you*, but she didn't add that. "I'm freelancing a couple cases for Pickard Consulting now." She moistened her dry lips again. "You remember, I was studying K&A, how you all do things, when I was in middle school. As I went along, I also read the social blogs, picked up hints. Things others would miss. Then at home...as I said, I noticed things. Really subtle, because Lucas and Cass were pretty discreet, given all the kids. But because of what I am...I picked up on it."

It was like hearing a song she knew, over and over. One day she'd put together all the clues, found the name of it.

She saw an ominous flicker in his eyes, but she straightened, made her voice as firm as she could manage. "I could see it, in the way you interact with each other at family barbecues, Christmas, whatever. When I was eighteen, I found Cass' membership card to Surreal. By that point, it confirmed what I already knew."

She stopped, not sure what else to say. But it didn't matter. He was closing up on her. Picking up her skirt, her panties, he dropped them on the couch. "Get dressed. We'll talk more in my office."

He was headed for the door, going to leave her here. The spell where he'd been caring for her, all of his focus on her, was breaking. He'd draw back, rationalize. If he took this away from her, if it stopped, she'd die. He'd opened the door, and he couldn't close it now. She couldn't let him.

"I've known what I am for a long time, Ben." She blurted it out. He paused, his hand on the latch, but he didn't turn. "I mean, you don't call it that when you're young, but when you fantasize about superheroes tying you up, and your favorite game is Ken torturing Barbie in a dungeon, you start to realize... You want to know the first really great erotic dream I had, the one that made me feel like, *yes, that's what I am?*"

He didn't say yes, but he didn't tell her to stop either. Not that she gave him much of a chance, the words tumbling out. "I suspected Lucas was Cass' Master, that you were all Doms. I wasn't completely sure, because I was still exploring it in myself."

Her rational mind might not have been certain, but the part of her that controlled her dreams had known. "I fantasized I was blindfolded, led into a bedroom by Jon. I recognized his hands, even though I never saw him. I heard noises, soft cries. Then I could see things, even though the me in the dream was blindfolded. Cass was tied, all spread out on the bed, her knees bent over the edge of the mattress, calves bound to the bed rails. I'd been pushed down on my knees on the floor, right between her spread ankles. Peter turned me so my back was against the foot of the bed, and my arms were tied to Cass' calves. My thighs and…ass hurt, as if they'd been whipped. It felt good, sore that way. Then Lucas was there. He ordered me to open my mouth, fed his cock into it."

Ben turned, his eyes narrowing. Though she pushed onward, she focused on the wall next to his head, not sure she could meet his gaze for this. "I was pushed back against the mattress as he leaned over me, his cock going deeper down my throat. He made me service him as he went down on my sister, made her scream out her climax. He came just as she did. I was burning up with the desire to come, but I knew I wasn't allowed. Not until you said so."

There was a stillness in the small room now, a heated intensity that was building. She dared the flame at last, meeting the green fire of his eyes.

"You were there. When Lucas moved, joined Cass on the bed, you picked me up, told me I was a good girl, that I'd taken care of Lucas just the way you'd ordered me to do it. Then, in that very same room, while Lucas was fucking Cass, you bent me over a chair, spread my legs and began to fuck me. You were so hard, so big, I was afraid I couldn't take you all, but I wanted to. I wanted to do anything to please you. When you pushed against me, you pinched the places that you'd whipped, made them hurt more. It only made me hotter."

His jaw flexed, but she wasn't done.

"It freaked me out," she admitted. "But you dream what you dream. And it wasn't an incest thing, because Cass and I…we were just…we were both there to serve Masters. A bond no less strong than blood. It was all about serving a Master. Serving you, and them. I know how it works, Ben. The women…Dana, Cass, Rachel, Savannah. You play together, you share together, but each woman belongs to only one of you, her soul all his. I'm that person for you, Ben. I know it. I've wanted you since the moment I met you, and it's only gotten stronger. Everything I am tells me I can handle whatever kind of Master you are."

Boy, she'd overplayed that hand, big time, but she'd crested the hill and rushed down it, unable to stop the coaster that was her mouth. His expression had shuttered, of course. Guys never liked hearing shit like this, but she didn't care. "Take me to a club," she said. "Let me prove it to you."

"That's a weird dream for a kid to have," he said in a flat tone.

"All teenagers have sex dreams. I'm not ashamed of them. Then or now. Lucas is my sister's husband, not my father. Any red-blooded woman who had to sleep in a room near the two of them, hearing the things he could do to a woman, no matter how much Cass tried to muffle it, would get turned-on by him."

His brow rose, but his mouth also tightened, as if he didn't particularly care to hear her appraisal of his CFO. Of course, the idea of him being jealous was probably wishful thinking on her part. Since it was obvious he'd let go of the leash he'd picked up for far too short a time, she wriggled into her panties and the skirt. Retrieved her heels. That put her within a couple steps of him. Stepping into the shoes, she ran her fingers through her hair, tossed it back.

"I was top of my class, won a full scholarship to college, and I'm damn good at what I do. And I'm only going to get better at it. I'll pay my taxes, pull my weight, and I've never avoided my responsibilities. So..." Glad she was back in her heels, reclaiming the sexual advantage they gave her, she took a step toward him, cocked a hip, drawing his attention to the angle of the body he'd just sampled. "I can be as deviant and twisted as I want, as long as I'm not hurting anyone. The only one craving pain is me. From you."

He stepped away from the door, right up to her, her breasts brushing his chest. His mouth was thin and tight. Everything in her screamed she should give way before that Master's stare, that alpha demand for submission, but she couldn't, no matter how everything in her wanted to do it, no matter her stomach was jumping hurdles like mountains.

"Don't." As he caught her chin, his fingers pressed against that mark he'd left on her throat, the impression of his teeth, the suction of his heated mouth. "Don't try to act more experienced than you are. I know you're scared to death and putting on a brave face."

"So?" She swallowed against his touch. "I want you, Ben. I know you want me." She dared herself, closing her hand over the front of his slacks.

He caught her wrist immediately, but she'd tightened her grip, feeling the shape and weight of him. Holy God. He really was...enormous. Her gaze flicked back up to his face. She saw a coldness there that would have sent an icy shiver through her if not for that overwhelming heat in her hand.

"Let go of me."

"Let your slave give you release. Let me suck on you, bring you to climax."

"For Chrissakes, Marcie. I'm a decade older than you." He pushed her away.

"Nine years. Not so much difference."

"It makes all the difference in the world."

"Jon says you have the emotional maturity of a thirteen-year-old, so I'm technically older."

"Jon is a New Age geek...*ass*," Ben retorted.

They both paused. Marcie blinked. Her lips curved, tremulously. Ben swore, but his own mouth twisted wryly. "Fuck, this is a mess."

Not from where she was standing, but she stayed quiet, recognizing the turning point where the negotiator had to stand back and let the client argue with himself, reach the appropriate conclusion. At least she hoped that was what he was doing.

"No more of this shit at the office," he told her sternly. "I mean it, Marcie. You won't be doing your internship here if you keep pushing it."

She bristled at being scolded like a child, given that she could tell he was still impressively aroused, but she suppressed the dangerous urge to point it out. Instead, she gave him a short nod. "Okay." She kept the fingers of her other hand crossed, behind her back.

He studied her, sighed. "I'll think about it."

"Think about what?"

He gave her a narrow look. "I'll think about taking you to a club. Not as your Master. As your mentor. Make sure you know what you're doing, show you around, keep you safe. That's not a definite yes. I may wake up tomorrow and change my mind. You'll just have to live with that."

She didn't nod, didn't give anything away, agree or disagree. Her fingers were a damp knot. Faster than she could anticipate, he reached behind her, yanked her wrist to the front.

"Finger crossing? Really?"

She shrugged, knowing she was flushed to the roots of her hair. "It's a universally accepted escape clause for untenable verbal agreements."

Ben stared at her a heart-pounding moment. Then a devastating grin crossed his face. Her pussy dampened again, telling her she'd have to seek a panty liner in the women's room of the main bathroom or she'd soak through her panties and skirt, right onto the cushion of her office chair. Particularly since she'd be thinking for the rest of the day about what had been done here, what tinder had been lit.

"That mouth of yours is going to be your undoing, little girl." He stepped back. "I want you back at your desk. I have work to get done, and so do you. You don't get to shirk it because of this. Since HR made you my personal slave for the next thirteen days, I plan to take full advantage."

He stepped out, shutting the door firmly behind him. She wondered if he had any idea of the images that one potent word had conjured in her mind.

"I sure hope so," she whispered.

* * * * *

She had the reckless bravado and stalwart courage of her sister, despite her lack of experience. He could cut through that shit pretty quick— break her down and leave her in tears. Which was when Lucas would kill him, rightly so. Even if she seemed to be begging for such rough treatment.

Marcella Ann Moira. Marcella meant young warrior, and damn if that didn't fit. She reminded him of Eowyn in *The Two Towers*, disguised as a man on the battle line, shaking in her armor but still screaming out *"Death"* with all the veterans. She wasn't backing down on this. Goddamn it.

Okay. He shifted in his chair, considered the view of downtown New Orleans, an assortment of rooftops and brick buildings, an old cathedral tower rising in the distance. She was a submissive. He wasn't going to argue an indisputable fact. And fuck him, one aspiring to be full hardcore, though he didn't much care for that word when it came to Marcie. Everything about her was soft, sweet, tempting. Too tempting. A sweet, tempting masochist who wanted pain as part of her pleasure. *You pinched the places that you'd whipped, made them hurt more. It only made me hotter...* Christ.

She was right, no matter how unsettling hearing the truth had been. With her being a natural sub, and having that curious mind, it wasn't a surprise she'd figured out they were all Doms. She'd had a crush on him young, so the current fixation was normal, particularly with her exploring the way of it. It might make sense to take her to a club, show her the ropes—figuratively, not literally—give her some tips, guide her. Maybe even facilitate a pairing with a young Dom he trusted to help guide her. Then he'd leave it there, let her continue her life's journey.

Shit, and maybe he'd go live in a swamp like Yoda, Great Jedi Master, content with what he'd taught his student. *Go forth, young Grasshopper.* What a load of bullshit. He rubbed a hand over his face. His cock was still settling, but the slightest provocation would have it at the ready again. He could jerk off in the bathroom, but he didn't trust himself with her this close. Hell, he didn't trust her. She wanted to suck him off. He'd given her a wrenching orgasm, and within seconds her eyes had been back on his cock, because she hadn't done what a sub needed to do to feel complete. She hadn't serviced her Master.

It was his own fault. When he'd yanked her into the bathroom, he'd let the Master take over, responding to her exactly as he would a sub displaying that kind of behavior. Trouble was, she'd more than held her own. He wanted to berate himself for an error in judgment, but the problem was, it didn't feel that way.

It didn't matter. Bottom line, he couldn't do this. She might get exactly what she was asking for. There was a reason he chose experienced, hardcore subs, ones well-trained in extreme submission. He liked cracking those hard nuts, finding the inner core they thought was impregnable, and taking it to an even deeper level. He was after a woman's soul. That was the challenge when he did a scene. But after that mission was accomplished, he let go of the soul, as easy and gentle as he'd been hard and ruthless when pulling it out of its fortress. He had no desire to keep it for his own.

You're a conqueror. You conquer and move on, never finding true contentment. Jon's words of course.

He needed to be the adult here. A thirteen-year-old's maturity or not—he was so getting even with Jon for that one—he was going to rein himself back.

* * * * *

The problem was Marcie had no appreciation for his restraint.

Mini-cake donuts covered with white powdered sugar, fresh from the local bakery, were one of his favorite indulgences. Apparently Alice had told Marcie that, because the next morning she arrived with a box. He detected the aroma the moment she set it down on her desk, along with a coffee for him. Glancing up from his laptop, he saw she'd worn a longer skirt today, but it held her tight from waist to just below the knee, with a little flare to the skirt at the bottom when she walked.

He'd seen Cass wear a similar style, and it made Lucas just as batshit as Ben felt now. It triggered something in an alpha male, seeing a woman wearing something sexy that also hampered her movement, making her easier prey to catch. It also gave her a hell of a walk, lots of shifting curves and provocative movement.

She wore a scoop-necked shell blouse in a pale tan color. No necklace, but simple silver earrings. Was she keeping her neck bare on purpose, cognizant he still held her collar? He wouldn't put it past her.

"Good morning." She paused at the door, giving him a smile. She was holding his coffee and two of the donuts on a napkin. When he met her gaze, acknowledging her, she lowered her lashes, sending a shot straight to his groin. As she crossed his carpet, her heel hooked one of the fibers, putting a brief hitch in her step. She stopped, lifted it free carefully to make sure she wasn't taking any fibers with her, then she was on the move again.

When she rounded his desk to set the coffee and donuts next to his elbow, he saw some of the sugar had gotten on her breast during that jerk in her step. It was right above the scoop neckline. When she bent to put the donuts and coffee down, the blouse shifted, giving him a brief glimpse down the front, to the barely there bra that seemed to be a lot of lace and sheer tan mesh.

It wasn't one of her calculated tricks, not this morning. She seemed oblivious to the sugar, was already talking about the day's work. He'd left her a shitload to get done yesterday, not holding back in the least. Part of it was him wanting to do right by her, give her the most out of her internship, because she did take the job seriously and the opportunities and experience it could provide her. His other hope was that the work would keep her out of trouble. Off car hoods.

Right now, giving him a status on the work she'd finished, she was obeying him to the letter. A hundred percent professional, going a hundred miles a minute. While that white powder was teasing him like crack to an addict, stark and tempting against the curve of flesh.

He had a full plate today. He'd be out of the office at a meeting with Matt and Lucas for most of it. No time to play. But there was always time for the important things.

Touching the remote on his desk, he heard the door swing close and lock, but he kept his eyes on her. She stopped in mid-sentence, brown eyes widening as he turned his chair toward her, set his hands to her waist and brought her between his knees. She was still holding the hot coffee.

"Put it down on the desk," he ordered. She complied, her simple obedience a sweet drug. Pulling the blouse free from her waistband, he slid his hands beneath it, along that soft skin. She kept her hands lifted, clear, so there was no impediment to what he wanted.

When he reached the bra cups, he curved his palms over them, squeezed to make her breasts swell up over the neckline. Leaning in, he inhaled that powdered donut and coffee smell. Then he licked away the sugar. She strangled on a breath as he took his time with it, tracing a pattern on her quivering skin. He was tempted to dip down into the bra cup, find her nipple with the curl of his tongue, but he reined himself back. She was swaying on her heels when he sat back, savoring the taste of sugar on his tongue. "Fix your blouse, Marcie."

He was satisfied to see her a little dazed and fumbling. "Sounds like you have a full day ahead," he commented casually. "Everything you're doing is fine. Have those three documents on my desk by day end for review."

"Yes sir." A flick of those lashes showed him a quick glimpse of her bemused eyes before she lowered them. When she backed out of the space, she'd recovered enough to add even more of a fuck-me-now sway to that mouthwatering backside, though he noticed she was a little wobbly on her heels. The combination made him hard as a rock. Might be good he was spending most of the day offsite, or he'd be in excruciating pain by lunchtime.

"That skirt's so tight there can't be any panties under it."

She glanced over her shoulder, her brow lifting. The sparkle was back in her gaze. "It would ruin the line of the skirt over my absolutely perfect ass, don't you think?"

"Behave," he reminded her. "Or else you'll get that ass smacked, and it won't be pleasant."

Her lips curved, completely unrepentant. He had the urge to grin at her like a feral wolf. Jesus, he was losing his mind. He was *mentoring* her. That was what this was. He'd told her as much yesterday. Or rather, he'd told her he'd think about it. He'd also told her to cut this shit out in the office. It wasn't like him to send mixed signals, and with an already difficult, headstrong sub, that was a recipe for trouble. Of course, with the heat boiling in his balls, he was working his way up to craving some serious trouble.

"Mr. Kensington, Mr. Adler." Composed now, at least on the surface, she smiled as Matt and Lucas came into Ben's area, ready to head offsite with him.

Yeah, just as soon as I get rid of this raging hard-on.

Lucas gave her a snort, a lifted brow. "Mr. Adler?"

"We're in a professional office environment." Marcie gave him a cheeky grin. "I have to behave. Ben says so."

"Well, there's a first for everything." Lucas looked toward Ben. "It must be a trick. I've never known you to be a good influence on anyone. Especially an impressionable young girl."

Was he really that bad? He bit back a scowl at the second reference to his dark reputation in less than a day. Jesus, you'd think he raided convents.

"Woman," Marcie said, an edge to her voice. When Lucas glanced back at her, she held onto that polite mask, but her next words were a direct, kick-in-the-balls contrast. "C-cup, vibrator in my nightstand drawer, and I can drink you under the table in tequila shots."

Okay, so maybe that one *was* his fault. He'd revved her up not only with the sugar thing, but with what had happened yesterday. Though the look on Lucas' face was worth money, another instinct took precedence now.

"Marcella."

The sharp edge of command was in his voice, cutting across anything Lucas had been about to say. Marcie's gaze snapped to his desk, a startled look on her face.

"That was disrespectful. I'm disappointed in you. Apologize."

She flushed, but he'd been looking for a particular reaction, testing those waters further. He got it. He saw the chagrin, that pained response a slave had when she disappointed her Master. Her hands slipped off the desk, folded in her lap, and she bowed her head. "I'm sorry, Lucas."

"Mr. Adler," Ben corrected her. "That's what he is here."

Even as he said it, he imagined her dream again. Her lips wrapped around Lucas' dick as he ate his wife's pussy. Marcie on her knees, servicing him at Ben's command. Ben's slave entirely, to do with as he wished.

Mentoring. He was mentoring.

"Mr. Adler." Marcie's voice was a near whisper, but he didn't have to correct her this time. She cleared her throat, repeated it, more loudly.

"What's going on here?" Lucas' gray eyes narrowed.

"Discipline," Matt said mildly. He exchanged a look with Lucas that said whatever this was, they weren't talking it out here. The Kensington CEO moved his shrewd dark gaze to Ben. "Are you ready? We've got about fifteen minutes to get there. And Marcie?"

She looked up then, her expression still wary.

"You're right. You probably *can* drink Lucas under the table in tequila shots. He's always been a lightweight."

She dimpled, though she stole a glance at Ben. He'd picked up his laptop case, was acting as he always acted now, and he saw her register it, her shoulders ease, though there was still a cautious set to them. He'd taken her off balance with that one, but she'd responded to him on instinct, responded to him as her Master, over and above the other two Doms present. He didn't know if that made things better or worse. Probably worse, because now he also had to deal with those two Doms. Particularly one of them, who looked as if he was deciding whether they needed to head for their meeting or make a brief stop in an alley to leave Ben's bleeding and broken body there.

"I need a few minutes to give my assistant direction for the day," he said casually, meeting Lucas' level stare. "Why don't I meet you in the car?"

Matt nodded. "Five minutes."

Ben made a gesture of assent as Lucas gave him a *Get the hell downstairs so we can talk this out* look, then followed.

Once they were gone, Ben came out to her area, braced his knuckles on her desk. Marcie's cheeks were still stained that attractive red. He wondered if her ass would be the same color after he went after it. Leaning down, he watched her press her lips together as he got close to her mouth, stopped short to meet her gaze close up. "That vibrator better stay in the nightstand unless I tell you that you can use it. I want you hot, wet and suffering."

"Are you going to take me to a club?" He saw that little flash of defiance, the high set of her chin. He had just the thing for that. A five-inch-width collar that locked into place under the jaw, making her hold it at that defiant angle until her neck ached and she remembered better manners. Alternatively, Peter had shown him an intriguing rope bondage design — the "haughty pose" — where the slave could be tied in a way that forced her to hold her head up until she was begging to bow it down in a deferential manner. Choices, choices.

Jesus, he needed to stop thinking about this stuff, or he'd have a lot more to explain to Lucas as he hobbled to the car with his briefcase and massive erection.

"Taking you to a club is my decision. I'll let you know when I make it."

"Remember what I said," she returned, giving him a glare. "If you're not willing to be my Master, you don't get to say what I put in my pus — "

"Whether I take you to a club has a lot to do with whether I think you can follow direction, obey a Master as you should, or if you're just a spoiled brat who thinks you can keep running things. No Master wants a slave like that. I won't be your Master, but I will be your mentor. *If* you show me you can behave. Those are my terms. No revisions, no loopholes, no games. If you can't handle that, collect your stuff, take your fuck-me-now slut attitude, and get out of this office."

She didn't flush this time. The color drained out of her face, her cheeks paling. He'd startled her, hurt her. He'd intended it. His gut told him that was the way to go, except he wasn't sure if his intent was to drive her away, crush her spirit or test her mettle. He wouldn't question himself in front of her though. He held her gaze, waiting to see the outcome, even while that gut twisted, telling him he was a complete and total bastard.

No newsflash there.

She wasn't at all sure of this Ben, this cruel side. But one thing she did know. He'd spoken to her like a Master in front of Lucas and Matt. No, she hadn't had much experience, but every time he exercised this side of himself, it resonated somewhere in her, in shadowed corners that were waiting for the right touch, the right motivation, to rouse that natural response in her.

Earlier, she'd known to counter his will with defiance. However, this was a true chastisement. She'd pushed things too far, showing her ass in front of Lucas and Matt and now him.

"I'm sorry, Master." She lowered her gaze to the desk, feeling the strange need to push back tears. "I'm sorry I disappointed you."

"Call me sir. I'm not your Master." But there was a pause there, making her wonder if that was what he really wanted to say. "Go into my office, to my desk. Pull your skirt up over that bare ass, spread your legs. Bend over, your nose and hands an inch above the wood. Do it quick. I only have five minutes and I don't want to be late to this meeting."

He was brusque, glancing at his watch. She moved on jerky legs, but she hurried into the office, did as he said. It took some effort to get her skirt up to her waist, but it sort of underscored his point about its tightness, didn't it? Bending down, nose to desk. Holding it that way required some precision, a little stress on the muscles. The air from the air conditioning vent in the ceiling put gooseflesh on the small of her back, her buttocks. She had *brought* panties. She just hadn't worn them. They were tucked in the top desk drawer.

The door closed, the locks clicked into place. The tendons of her calves quivered, making her heels wobble. Because of the shoes' height and her position, her ass was tilted up, exposing everything between her legs. As she imagined what he was seeing, the spiral of anxiety and arousal in her lower belly grew tighter.

"Close your eyes and open your mouth."

She did. What felt like a rubber ball was wedged past her teeth. He cupped her skull to hold her steady, allowing him to push it in that space, because it was so large it pressed down on her tongue, held it fast, held her mouth open. He hadn't used a cloth behind it, so saliva immediately began to pool around the ball. She would be drooling on his desk, nothing to stop the embarrassment of that, unless she disobeyed him and tried to wipe it away.

When her fingers flexed, uncertain, his hands covered them, curled them into closed fists, hovering just above the desk surface. Her stomach muscles were tight, holding herself in the position, and it wouldn't take long for them to start to ache. Ben would have made a hell of a teacher in an old-fashioned one-room school. She'd misbehave every day for his punishment.

"You don't make any contact with my desk. Keep your nose and hands where they are. As I do each stroke, you count it off with your fingers. It'll be ten."

She was breathing hard against that ball. Her fists trembled in their suspended position. A trickle of response slid down her thigh.

"Little slut," he muttered. She reveled in hearing that hoarseness in his voice. That impressive cock was baseball-bat hard, she was sure of it. If only he'd let her go down on her knees, suck him off. She could make him come in five minutes. It would make her impossibly hot, knowing he was at his meeting with Matt and Lucas, her lipstick marking his cock. She'd savor the taste of him in her mouth for hours, the abrasion at the corners she was sure his thick size would cause.

He'd removed something from the walk-in closet, and she caught it in the corner of her eyes. It was a short, slim cane, no more than ten inches long, perhaps made of carbon. Not so intimidating, but she revised that opinion as the first strike landed. *Fuck.* Like most canes, it hit fast and was gone, but the pain zinged through all her nerves.

She bit down on the ball in shock and pain. There was no titillation in this, no soft flogger that hit with a nice slap and teasing sting. She'd played with one of those in her dorm room, one she'd made out of nylon rope, imagining him using it on her.

"Count it, Marcie."

She managed to get the first finger out. She was pretty sure she was losing her mind, because she chose her middle finger. Damn it, he wasn't going to break her, or scare her off, or...

He chuckled, a dangerous threat. "You just doubled it, sweetie, and I don't have time to slow it down. You better keep up with the count, or I'll triple it. I plan to leave pretty welts on that rebellious ass of yours."

She didn't think. She tried to push up off the desk. His hand clamped down on the back of her neck, and he pushed her cheek down to the desk surface, locking her down, like a schoolmaster holding down a naughty, struggling student in truth. She snarled against the ball, but it was too big for her to spit it out. Then she had no room to think, because he lived up to his word.

Two, three, four...in rapid succession, striping over her ass in different places, setting her skin on fire. She started shuddering on number five, her fingers fluttering out on the one hand, palm pressed hard to the desk because she couldn't balance herself with that powerful hand on her nape. He allowed it. She was crying out against the ball gag with each stroke, no way to bite it back. Her toes curled in her shoes.

"Lift up against my hand. Don't you tuck down like a beaten dog."

She arched her back, thrust her buttocks up defiantly, screamed as another blow landed. Six...seven, eight, nine... Teeth sunk into that rubber, saliva marking her chin, ass high in the air, legs spread. Every muscle clenched like iron against the pain, she nevertheless got her palms back up where he'd told her to put them, even as he held her face down. She'd show him she could do it. Oh God, there were ten more to go.

She howled at the eleventh stroke, a direct slap against her labia. Her legs gave out, the pain overcoming her, but he caught her by the waist, her abused buttocks abraded by the summer wool of his slacks. But it also pushed his erection between them, against her throbbing pussy, making her whimper. She tried to rub, she couldn't help herself.

"Uh-uh, none of that. You'll get your cream on my clothes. Be still or you'll get the other nine now."

She stilled, because hell, she didn't think she could do nine more, now or later. He guided her palms down to the desk surface, did a quick stroke and tug over her mussed hair. "Stay in the position you're in. Keep your eyes closed."

She heard him move around his desk, unlock a drawer, come back. Then she swallowed against the gag as a smooth and thick plug was pushed into her pussy, worked in and out a few times, then removed to be inserted into her ass instead.

"Figured you'd have enough honey to lube that up." She made a wordless plea as another plug was inserted back into her cunt, with a piece on the outside that closed over her clit. She felt straps dangling against the backs of her legs, then they were run up between them, and around her waist, cinched tight so all of a sudden she felt those plugs held deeper, more securely.

"A little chastity device to keep you from playing with what's not yours, hmm?" Ben pulled her skirt down, a functional tug, gave her ass a firm smack. "Keep your eyes closed until you hear me leave. That to-do list better be finished before I get back today, or I'll add another ten to the nine you owe me."

His footsteps, moving away. The door opening, then closing, the sound of him voice dialing Johnson's office, telling them they were on their way, his voice steady, authoritative. It was as if he weren't the least affected, though she knew he was. He was just that damn much in control. Marcie waited until she couldn't hear his voice any longer, then she cracked open her eyes. He'd left the handkerchief he carried in his coat neatly folded up near her hand to wipe her mouth...and the tears.

The considerate gesture against the ruthless nature of what he'd just done took her breath, almost made her knees buckle. She'd imagined so many things...but she hadn't imagined this. He sent her spinning from one direction to another so effortlessly. She'd known she was in over her head, but this was like being at the bottom of the Laurentian Abyss.

As crazy wild as all this was, she was sure of one thing. She wanted more. He claimed to be acting as her mentor, but that wasn't the way she was viewing it. This was a job audition, and she was going to prove exactly what she'd said she would. That she was the slave he needed, that she could handle everything he dished out.

Though that had certainly been more than she'd ever experienced before. When she moved, she winced at the light movement of fabric over her ass. Removing the gag, she moved to the full length mirror in his closet, where he kept spare changes of clothes. Holding her skirt at her waist, she twisted around to look at her abused flesh.

Holy God. It was not only red, but she could see the individual marks of the cane, short lines, welts. It should horrify her. Instead, it made her pussy clench against that thick plug he'd put there, her anus contract on the other one. That night at Surreal, he'd left marks like this on the three women. Ben was a sadist who enjoyed exploring the top limits of pain. He wanted the women who served him to earn the pleasure he gave them. It was all tied up together. She thought she would endure almost anything for that. Her body was vibrating with stress, shock...and raging desire.

He'd put a chastity device on her, so she'd keep herself only for him, preventing not only the touch of other men, but her own touch. Her body was his, not hers.

She fixed her hair, her face, did some deep breathing. Nothing seemed to steady her hands. The plugs were short, so she could move in them, but that clit piece was sheer torture, rubbing against her as she walked. It wouldn't move enough to make her come, but she'd remain hyperaware of the desire to fuck, to be fucked, to have an orgasm that would shake the foundations of the building with her screaming.

He'd left something else at her desk. A small pillow. Like the handkerchief, the gesture made her smile, squeezed her heart. But when she lowered herself to it gingerly, she came back up just as fast. That was when she saw the note he'd left on her desk.

"Sit on this to reinforce the lesson. Else you'll be thinking too much of misbehaving. No perching on the edge. Square in the middle. If you need to go to the ladies' room, you may remove what's necessary, but then the plugs go right back in."

Passing her hand over the pillow, she felt the tiny pricks through the fabric, like a vampire glove. Not long enough to penetrate skin, but enough to make it feel as if she were being stuck with pins.

Holding white-knuckled to the edge of the desk, she lowered herself onto it. When the barbs dug into her tender ass, she suppressed a groan. She could do this. She could. Though she really wished he'd given her a different punishment, like writing *I will not sass Master* a million times.

A desperate smile crossed her face. No, that wasn't Ben's style. He wasn't treating her like a child. That was what was important. He was making a point. If she couldn't handle this, she needed to give up now.

She took steadying breaths, picking up the file she was going to review, the first thing on his to-do list for her. Every minute movement of her body shifted her against that pillow, renewed the agony. One small mercy — the plug for her pussy and the covering for her clit protected those more tender tissues. Though her outer labia were pricked, the clit and inner petals were protected.

Despite the fact she had no idea how she was going to endure this for the hours he was gone, she was all too aware of the fact she was soaking wet. All she wanted to do was hump herself against the clit piece until she came, screaming through the pain and pleasure.

Yeah, she was twisted. Twisted for him, willing to endure anything for him, just for the right to call him Master to his face. She used his handkerchief to wipe away the tears that kept falling from her eyes, the result of stress and shock. Her mascara was wasted today.

"I'm yours, Master," she whispered, looking toward his office. "You won't break me."

At least not that way. Not until the breaking had to do with him accepting her as his slave, now and forever, and breaking her down so that she could surrender to him utterly.

She was well aware that wasn't the most difficult problem she faced though. Could she make him believe she truly loved him? Even more challenging, could she get him to realize that he loved her? Because he did. She was sure of it.

I know it's silly, but I love hand writing letters. How many emails do you think they'll find in the future, versus packets of love letters people have kept in their treasure boxes, tied up with ribbon? A dried, pressed flower in between them, the fading scent of perfume where a woman offered a man her scent? Plus, I think better when I write it out, and I like the way cursive looks. I could be one of those monks who did the calligraphy and hand printed each book.

Marcie, letter to Ben, sophomore year

(in cursive, on elegant, scented stationery)

Not silly. Little things matter far more than big ones. We remember them longer. We can't control the big things, brat. If you think about what's happened in the past, it will be the small moments that come to the forefront, not the big transitions. The big things were just history. The small moments are yours. The books those monks printed are still preserved centuries after they were gone. Little things matter.

Ben's reply

(in block print, on preschool writing practice paper, oversized and lined)

Chapter Five
❧

"You going to explain what the hell that was?"

Lucas asked the question as soon as Ben got in the limo. Matt had already lifted the privacy screen between them and Tobias, their driver.

Ben wished he'd figured out some credible way to meet them there. He needed some space, big time. But his ability to keep every hair in place during a shit storm was one of the reasons Matt paid his exorbitant salary. So he sat square across from the K&A CFO, met his cool stare with one of his own. "You know exactly what that was."

Marcie might claim not to know what Cass had told Lucas, but Ben knew. Cass wouldn't keep secrets from her Master, no more than Dana would. Though Lucas had reacted with aggression to what had happened upstairs, surprise at Marcie's behavior hadn't been part of it. So he knew Marcie was a submissive. He probably *didn't* know whom she'd decided, come hell or high water, her Master was going to be.

Jesus, she was a headstrong brat. He couldn't believe that middle-finger maneuver—he'd barely been able to strangle back the laugh. But what sobered him, inflamed him, was knowing she was sitting her sore ass on that barbed pillow, obeying his every order. Every order except not to think of him as her Master. It made his gut twist in an unusual way, a way he didn't like.

"Yeah," Lucas said, after a considering pause. That was Lucas. Like Jon, always thinking it through before shooting off his mouth, even when his emotions were involved. "But seeing you do it in the office, and with my wife's little sister? That's fucked up."

"How so? She's pretty much a blood-deep sub. She responds to it, in the office or out. It was instinct."

"What are you doing, Ben?" Matt was sprawled out in the opposite corner, looking as usual like a very well-dressed hawk, the sharp eyes missing nothing, the lazy power of the body suggesting he could strike for the kill in less than a heartbeat. But that was in business negotiations. This was a look Ben knew. Matt was the only one who could make him squirm, even if Ben would rather key his own car than show it.

His jaw set. "She's asked me to be her mentor. Show her how it works. She's ready to find a Dom, enter the scene. She hasn't really done that yet, right?" He arched a brow toward Lucas, got a reluctant lip curl that admitted it. When it loosened something in his gut, he chose to ignore the inexplicable reaction. "I was one of her first real crushes, so it makes sense she's hooked on me for that role."

Okay, that was a misdirect, but he was the one member of the pack most likely to get away with some minor dissembling. He was damn good at concealing his hand when he needed to do so. From Matt's sharp glance, he could tell he didn't quite pull it off, but Lucas seemed to be mulling it over.

Her pussy had been soaking wet when he slid that chastity device in place, cinching it up good to keep her from playing with herself. He knew she'd do it up just as tight after any trips to the restroom. She'd follow his direction to the letter, until that pretty ass of hers was a raw mess and she was crying in her chair from the pain, all while hard at work on those files. Which was why he'd left a folded and sealed note with Janet to give to Marcie thirty minutes after their departure. It would tell her to replace the barbed cushion with the bed pillow from his private closet, where he kept linens for all-nighters.

Those happened more often these days, even when he didn't really have to work late. He'd dick around over this or that email, but then end up sitting on the couch, sipping his whiskey. He'd watch the lights of the New Orleans' business district slowly wink out until all that were left were the lights of apartment hallways, the dwellings over the businesses. Lights shining on nothing, because people had gone to bed, leaving the small hours of the mornings to people like him.

He turned his mind back to how badly her ass would be hurting from that punishment. He imagined laying her out on his couch tonight, putting cloth strips of cool balm on those luscious cheeks. He'd spread her hair over her bare shoulders, stroke through it, caressing the silken skin beneath while she lay completely still, on his orders. Her hair was lustrous thick and curled some, so it curved over her shoulders and lay just the right way to catch a man's eye, make him think about the way it would feel on his skin. Particularly when he was moving her on a direct line down his chest and stomach to take care of his cock with her pretty mouth, the wet heat of her eager tongue.

Her aftercare would be as tender as the punishment had been ruthless. It was always a balance, one that broke down a certain type of woman's shields, cracked open her emotions, kept her spinning and in touch with her raw feelings, no dissembling, nothing but pure, honest reaction.

Lucas shifted, drawing him out of his thoughts and irritating him further. His mind was wandering around like a damn cow grazing in a pasture. Matt cocked a brow in his direction, that gaze still way too sharp, but when he spoke, he wasn't addressing Ben. "You okay with this, Luc?"

Lucas glanced out the window, a muscle flexing in his jaw. His index finger was tapping a slow, pensive beat on the car door. Not a great sign, but not Def Con 1 either. "We've been together a long time, Ben. I know things about you. I know you push hard. Your way of handling a sub…it's what they want, you prove that over and over, and so there's no reason I should doubt your judgment, but Marcie…hell."

Since Ben had stepped into the car, he'd had his shields up, ready to ward off any frontal assault. Just like that, seeing Lucas' worry, the focus changed. They'd been part of one another's lives too long. Beyond that, when Lucas had claimed Cass as his own, she and all her siblings had come under their protection and care. He wouldn't deflect, not when it came to that side of things.

"You feel responsible for her." Ben inclined his head. "And you're the best at reading people of all of us. But you're not objective about this one. I can be, to a certain extent."

"He shouldn't be," Matt said quietly. "Neither should you. We all know how important family is, particularly the ones we create for ourselves."

Matt had tapped on that door of his psyche on purpose he was sure, a reminder of the darkness behind it. "What I'm saying," Ben responded evenly, with effort, "is she's at the beginning of it, but that doesn't mean the signs aren't there. She's a 24/7, Luc. Rachel's got a gentle form of that, the way she defers to Jon even in front of others, but Marcie craves the hardcore brand of it."

He knew what that would look like. When she came home from work, she'd follow a Master's protocol from the time she walked through the door. He'd have the heat programmed to bump up a couple notches a half hour before she arrived home. Once there, she would shed her clothes, all of them, hang them up. She'd slide on a thong fitted with a small clit stimulator. It would be set on a low vibration to keep her distracted as she moved to do the things she was required to do for her Master. Set the table, light the candles. Put out his dinner.

Well, the dinner he'd have her heat up, because he preferred to do the cooking. Marcie appreciated good food, but she could burn break-apart Nestle Tollhouse cookies.

Right before dinner, she'd remove the thong, lie down on the table. At his Garden District townhome, he had a dining room table of glossy cherry wood, with carved legs that looked like a griffin's feathered and taloned feet, a heavy antique piece that had been created during the Baroque period. She'd brace her feet on the arms of his chair, her spread thighs framing his plate. When he sat down to eat, he'd have the pleasure of seeing that pussy wet and glistening, needy. The candlelight would glint on the clit piercing, and her arousal would give her that sexy little quiver, her nipples high and tight...

He'd place one candle in either hand, making her hold them stretched out to either side of her body as he lit them. He'd get the tallow kind with wax drippings, so she'd feel the tiny burn as each drop hit her wrists, her knuckles. When he finished his dinner, he'd eat her pussy until she came. Then turn her over, give her a good paddling that would have her squealing and begging before he slid into that tight little puckered hole, feeling her submission to him, to anything he wanted to do to her. Utter, total surrender of self, belonging to him forever.

After that, they'd watch TV. She'd curl up next to him naked, tolerate the business reports and his acerbic comments about the idiots in Washington. But then she'd steal the remote and put it on some romantic chick flick she wanted to watch. Maybe she'd be wearing one of his shirts, left open to give her Master access, but allowed because it kept her warm and drowsy. They'd share popcorn and he'd watch her fall asleep against him, her head against his heart. He'd carry her to his bed, and when he was restless in the middle of the night, he'd find her curled around him, arm across his chest, body snugged up so close…

He was the night owl; she was the morning person. So he'd wake to find her perched like an adorable sex kitten near him, holding his coffee out of reach, teasing him with the aroma. He'd wrestle her for it, carefully, so she didn't get burned, then when he got it away from her, putting it on the side table, he'd snatch her to him by the waist. She'd straddle him, run her fingers through his hair, smiling, then her mouth would soften and he'd turn her beneath him…

Someone to wake up with, someone he wanted to see next to him in the morning.

"Ben?"

He snapped out of it to find Lucas and Matt looking at him like he'd just sprouted a second nose. Thank God he had the briefcase on his lap. As it was, the weight of the damn thing was making his cock hurt like a son of a bitch. He was lucky it wasn't knocking against it like a door. But that wasn't what freaking rocked his foundation. He was fantasizing about…nesting with a woman. *Holy Christ.*

"Yeah." He cleared his throat. "Sorry. Thinking about the meeting."

Lucas raised a brow. "Yeah right. Subs don't usually get under your skin. She messing you up?"

"Well, the whole family relationship thing threw me for a loop." Ben forced a casual shrug. *Jesus, let me out of this car. I can't breathe.* "I've got my feet under me. But it would have helped if you'd let us know you suspected this about her way the hell earlier."

"I expect I didn't for the same reason you didn't tell me where you were on it. It wasn't something I felt comfortable tossing out there. I assumed when she started to actively pursue it, it would be with someone her own age, her own group."

Ouch. That hurt more than expected, but it was nothing more than what he'd told her himself. He kept his expression blank.

Lucas rubbed a hand over his face, shook his head. "There were always clues to it, even before we realized it straight out, but of course talking about it when she was underage was a quagmire I wasn't about to touch. She was sixteen when I came into her life, so she never saw me as a father figure, more as a friend, her sister's husband. Cass was in charge of keeping an eye on it, helping to direct and manage it in subtle ways. But I figured it out from the way she watched me and Cassandra. Sometimes the way she acted toward me."

Ben lasered in on those words. "What do you mean?"

He sensed Matt's interested shift, decided he wouldn't look toward him to see if his curiosity was about what Lucas was saying, or that Ben had just tried to cover a surge of annoyingly possessive heat.

"Not like she was looking for me to be her Master, but acknowledging me as one, respecting what it means." Lucas tossed his leather portfolio onto the seat, stretched his arm out on the back of it. "One night I came out of our bedroom, after I'd worked Cass over pretty good. We'd done laundry earlier and all the washcloths were in the laundry room. I needed one to soak with warm water and put on some of the more tender parts."

His lips curved, a Master's absorption the other two men well recognized. "Marcie was home from college, up late studying in the kitchen. She asked what I needed. When I told her, though of course I didn't tell her why I needed it, she immediately got up, found a cloth. Soaked it, heated it in the microwave, placed it in a basin then handed it to me with this little nod of her head. She knew exactly why I needed it, and she'd provided it exactly like I'd get a staff slave assist at the club."

Fuck. Ben could see her doing it.

"That's just one example. When Marcie was in New York, Cass suggested I let Marcus Stanton and Thomas take her to a few clubs, just to observe. Marcie didn't tell us about her experiences, but I know she took advantage of the contact. Damn, Ben, you can't tell me you never noticed. All of us pick up on this shit, and you spent more time with her than anyone."

"My focus was elsewhere. I was busy managing the teenage crush thing." But Lucas was right; the clues had been there when she was in her teens. It had probably crossed Ben's mind once or twice, given the fact he was a Dom, but it would have been an interesting factoid only: "hey, this girl has the tendencies of a natural submissive". It hadn't involved him or his role in her life. Until now. He sure as hell hadn't been prepared to be part of her journey of sexual discovery. Like Lucas, his job had been to prove a male's presence in her life could be a positive thing.

"How deep does it go?" Surprisingly, Matt directed that question not to Lucas, but to Ben. When Ben raised a questioning brow, Matt gave him his no-bullshit look. "That call-down upstairs says you're in a better position than either of us to make the assessment."

No way was he looking toward Lucas when he answered that one. He also hoped Matt wasn't going to pry any deeper than that in front of him. But he wouldn't lie. "She's a full-blown masochist. Craves the pain. The right Master could go after her with a fucking baseball bat and she'd still come at his command. She needs strong guidance, training to help her protect herself from that extreme. She's a lethal combination — as headstrong and adventurous as Dana, but deeper in the psychology of it than even Rachel."

When Lucas swore softly, Ben tightened his fingers on the briefcase, even though he tried not to show his tension. Matt shifted his attention to his CFO. "Lucas?"

The man shook his head. "I'd like to say it surprises me, but it doesn't. It fits what I know of her personality. The submission is natural, but the degree of it has been affected by her experiences. Her father's love was unpredictable, weak. She latched onto her older brother, and then he betrayed her as well. It makes sense that she'd need that strong hand, something rock-solid, to open herself up fully."

Matt gestured at Lucas. "Don't sell short the experiences you and Cass have provided her. For at least two years she lived in a household where a healthy Dom/sub dynamic was operating. Your stability, your influence on Cassandra's sense of self-worth, her confidence as a woman, have been obvious. Those things would have also encouraged Marcie, given her confidence to pursue her own submissive inclinations to a deeper level."

"Cass already accomplished a whole hell of a lot without me."

"No argument there." Matt waved a hand. "My point is, I am a better man, more assured of my direction, knowing Savannah is at my side. If I'm the husband and Master I should be, I serve the same purpose for her. I've no doubt you do that for Cassandra, because she is a much more relaxed and happy person than she was when we met her."

Yeah, this was making him feel heaps better. Ben could be a rock-solid Master, but in the stability and happiness department? Jesus. He cleared his throat, considering a different direction. "Have you picked up on her desire to be...part of the group?"

While hearing that Marcie was a hardcore sub hadn't surprised him, Lucas now turned a startled gaze to him. "We only share a woman, all of us, if—"

"Not going that way," Ben said quickly, dispelling that issue before Lucas could react in horror to it, as he was sure he would. "But we have a different situation here. She may not belong to one of us, but she already has a foot inside the circle, because of the family relationship. She's been fantasizing about it. If you're cool with the mentoring, I can keep tabs on it, redirect it if you want. Make sure it doesn't become a bigger issue. But I wanted to warn you it's there."

They rode in unresolved silence for several blocks. True to form, it was Matt who broke it.

"The key to this is you, Ben. You have the lead. You'll be able to tell us where it needs to go, what needs to happen. We can talk it out once you have a better feel for the situation. Remember, we're here if you get in over your head." His dark eyes met Ben's, again stirring that past shit that Ben really didn't want dredged up, but of course Matt didn't let anyone get away with much.

God, he needed air.

* * * * *

When they pulled up to their destination, Ben was the first out of the car. He muttered something about needing to see someone in Legal first and that he'd meet them upstairs, then disappeared through the front doors.

Lucas looked toward Matt. "He has the lead on this?"

"Because he's right. You're too close, and in the wrong position to help her embrace her submissive nature. You have to trust him."

"I do. With my life. Not so much with Marcie's." Lucas sighed. "You know his M.O."

Matt straightened his cuffs. "Ben is one of the most disciplined Masters I've ever seen. He never loses control, because he puts all his energy and focus into holding the reins, into getting the sub to give him everything. He's brutal, going to the edge of edge play. But he always gives a woman the experience of her life."

"And in return, he takes nothing but the challenge of having broken her down. He doesn't let her in. Doesn't let any of them in." Lucas grimaced. "The problem is, she's already inside him, because she's family. I know what he carries around, and so do you. I'm not sure that's a place I want her to be."

"Marcie has been starry-eyed in love with Ben since she first laid eyes on him," Matt pointed out. "We all saw it. As improbable as it is that it might have survived the transition from childhood to adulthood, from what I saw this morning, that girlhood crush has become a woman's passion. It's possible we're witnessing the very rare instance when a teenage crush was never a crush at all."

Matt's handheld buzzed with an incoming message. When Matt glanced at it, his lips quirked. Leaning forward, Lucas saw the screen. *Not texting you. Bully.* He raised a brow, his lips curving.

"Savannah?"

"Yes. I told her to text me every so often while she was awake. The last one was 'Bite Me'. She's getting more conciliatory. The first one was 'Fascist Asshole'." Matt shook his head. "I have the housekeeper texting Janet as well, to let me know if she does too much."

"She's going to stab you in your sleep."

"If Savannah ever decides to take me out, she'll do it toe-to-toe while I'm fully conscious." Matt gazed at the handheld screen fondly, thumb passing over it as if he was caressing the woman sending the barbed missives. "She's a mountain lion."

"Like Cass. And like Marcie, truth be known."

"I know. I also know this is hard, Luc." Matt met his gaze anew. "She wants in, and she's determined to get there. It makes sense she chose the man she's always trusted the most. But yes, Ben has some very dark places in him. For most of his life, he's kept them buried, but the events of the past few years are opening them up. We've all tried various ways of offering our help, but he's not there yet. I'm not sure what will be the trigger, but if she forces her way into those rooms, eventually he's going to lose a grip on the reins. It's possible she'll get hurt."

Lucas' hand tightened on the console between them. "If Marcie went to him for mentoring, that's a front. She wants more than that. The mentoring is just all she's been able to get him to agree to do...so far."

Matt nodded. "Ben's loyalty to you, to us, is unquestioned. If you want to put an end to it right here, right now, you need only tell him. He'd do it, in a heartbeat. But if you're not going to make that call, you need to let it play out. Sometimes you have to step out of the way and see what Fate decides."

"Jesus. You've been talking to Jon."

Matt's lips curved. "No, but he's rubbed off on me, as we've all rubbed off on each other over the years. It's time for a change in Ben's life. He feels it, as do we all. Unfortunately, what we're suggesting makes Marcie a guinea pig. Normally, I'd trust my gut, take the risk, but this part *is* your call, Lucas. Yours and Cassandra's."

"Cass will get worked up about it, initially, but in the end she'll say Marcie's of legal age. That if what she wants is Ben, she has a right to take her shot. To get hurt like any other adult. But she'll worry, same as I will. Marcie is so fucking young." He sighed. "I don't know how I'll react if he breaks her heart, even if he's dealing with his own knee-jerk fight-or-flight instinct. Fair warning."

"We'll protect her if she needs protecting. We've always put the well-being of our women first. It's in Ben as strong as any of us, for all that he hasn't found a singular focus for it. Maybe he has now."

"Whoa, wait a minute." Lucas caught Matt's arm. "Did you just suggest what I think you suggested?"

Matt gave him his trademark piercing expression. "Have you ever known him to act this unsettled about any woman? Or ask the question he asked about her being part of the group?"

"He said it was just a heads-up, because of her fantasies. Not his."

"Maybe not consciously."

"Fuck." Lucas sat back. "Seriously? You think this could be going in that direction? I just wrapped my mind around him mentoring her."

"I wouldn't swear to it, but I do know when it comes to women, Ben isn't easily rattled."

"Damn it, Matt." Lucas sighed, ran his hand over his face. "If it's true, she will stumble on those dark places. And you know the problem isn't her inability to handle that."

"Correct. The problem is how Ben will handle it. If it's any comfort, I suspect Marcie already knows a great deal about Ben. She may not be able to withstand the storm, but she knows it's coming. She's inviting it, because she trusts somewhere in that maelstrom, she'll find Ben, and Ben will find himself."

"Okay, you have been talking to Jon too much."

Matt grinned then. "Care to place a bet? Freaked out because he's always known Marcie as jailbait, versus freaked out because maybe she's something more than that?"

"You know I have no choice but to take that bet, as a point of pride and personal comfort."

"I like to take advantage of charitable opportunities. The local animal shelter needs new fencing. Savannah's already financed it, but she wants me to match it. And adopt the ugliest dog I think I've ever seen. I believe it's the mating between a moose and a sheep. Five thousand."

"Bastard," Lucas muttered. "Fine. Five thousand. But no more talk about rubbing off on each other. Gives me some pretty disturbing images."

"Agreed," Matt said.

* * * * *

The meeting could have been about painting circles on a monkey's ass for all that Ben really cared about it. Because of that, he sharpened his focus a hundredfold and secured everything Matt wanted from the strategy session, and then some.

Such obvious proof he was on top of things was validating. It put him in a much better frame of mind. Mentor. He was Marcie's mentor. Lucas had given his blessing, and that helped. Hell, he'd always liked the brat, and now that she was a hot young woman, it could be enjoyable. He'd help her find the right path in the D/s world, know he'd had a part in bringing her into the full glory of that.

He'd have to tread easy, be careful, but every interaction with a difficult sub was a chess game. Marcie really wasn't difficult as much as she was green and headstrong. But she sure had a lot of guts. He liked that. She was also absolutely determined to prove she'd go above and beyond for him.

When he had that thought, they were doing the usual shake-hands-while-thinking-*what-a-dick* ritual, part and parcel of their interactions with this particular negotiations team. Ben stopped in mid-motion. While he jumpstarted his brain enough to finish out the hand shake with Fred Marlton, Ben turned to Matt. "I've got to go," he said. "I'll see you tomorrow."

They'd intended to catch an early dinner, but Matt nodded, reading his set face. "All right. Take the limo. We'll walk down to Acme's to eat."

Normally his gut would gripe at missing out on their po'boy sandwich, but his stomach had another issue right now.

The right Master could go after her with a fucking baseball bat and she'd still come at his command. She needs strong guidance, training to help her protect herself from that extreme... Goddamn. Had he really made such a newbie Dom mistake?

Taking the stairs, he hit the lobby with a swift, ground-eating stride. Matt had already anticipated him, because the limo was pulling up front. He wished it was Max who was at the wheel instead of Tobias, because Max could get through New Orleans' business traffic like shit through a goose. However, by unanimous agreement of the K&A team, Max was Dana's daytime driver for her job as assistant pastor at one of New Orleans' many old churches. His duties had even expanded to assisting her with some of the church's programs, like helping with the soup kitchen and doing maintenance on the building.

It was all right. K&A wasn't that far. If they hadn't been running late this morning, they probably would have walked the fourteen blocks.

As Ben got into his vehicle, he checked his PDA, which he'd kept turned off during the meeting. He bit back an oath.

One text from Janet, over two hours ago. *There's a problem with your intern. You need to get back here.*

He texted back *On my way,* and grimaced as he received an immediate reply.

About time.

When he arrived at the building, he took the private, coded elevator that went straight to their floor. As he emerged, he saw Janet sitting at her desk, waiting on him, purse at her elbow. Five-fifteen. The meeting had taken all day, fuck it. As she shouldered her bag, she gave him a steady look. "I gave her the note precisely thirty minutes after you left, just as you instructed. We had a busy day here, so I wasn't aware of the problem until I took her some files at three p.m. That's when I sent the text. She made me promise not to call and interrupt your meeting, but I was on the verge of breaking that promise when you texted me."

He needed to address the hard note in her voice, but of course the most important thing, even in Janet's opinion, would be to skip the apologies and fix the problem. He'd screwed up.

His office area was sequestered from the others because he often met with clients and adversaries who didn't need to be privy to snippets of information overheard in other sections of the office. As he turned the corner, moved down the hall toward his space, he heard her. To most, it wouldn't be detectable, but when he was in a session with a sub, he was attuned to the slightest indrawn breath, the rise of gooseflesh over fair skin, the tensing of muscles, warning him when she was reaching her limit. This was far beyond that. He quickened his step.

Tiny sobs, small expulsions of air bitten back. As he reached his reception area, something twisted in his chest. Something different from anything he'd ever felt.

Marcie was still sitting on that barbed pillow. Her body was quivering as she tried to finish up some memo on her computer. Two out of the three documents he'd left her to prepare were laid out on the side table. They'd be perfect, because she would have re-checked them a couple extra times, taking into account her distracted condition.

Instead of following his direction, she'd stayed on that pillow all day. Each time she rose to go to the printer, the file cabinet, as she would have had to do numerous times, she'd had to sit back down on it, let the hundreds of barbs stab into those welts anew.

Her hands were shaking as she typed. She'd apparently long ago stopped trying to stifle her tears, because there were dried tracks on her cheeks beneath the newer ones, tears caused by stress and pain. While her hands were moving, the rest of her body was rigid, trying to minimize any motion that could impact those barbs. She'd still feel their bite with every key typed on the laptop.

"Marcie."

She stopped abruptly but didn't look at him. Her fingers curled over the keyboard.

"Get up."

She couldn't. He knew she couldn't. But she tried, placing her hands on either side of the computer. Her elbows quivered so hard the desk vibrated. Since there was a small store of office supplies on the desk, the printer pulled closer, at some point she'd stopped getting up. Now the lack of circulation, the prolonged stiff posture, was defeating her efforts to rise. Stubborn, beautiful, pain in his ass.

Going to her, he turned the chair on its swivel toward him. Clasping her upper arms, he eased her to her feet. When she tried to swallow a pained noise, he cupped her face, turning it up to him. He was tempted to take her head off with a bellow that would scare monks in their temples in the furthest corner of Asia, but he kept his voice even, steady. "I left you an order. To remove that pillow when Janet gave you the note."

"I know. But I had to prove—"

"Stop." He cut her off with the steel injected in his voice. "A Master told you to do something, and what did you do? You disobeyed. You can call it interpreting, overcompensating, whatever the hell you want, but it's pure disobedience."

She was pale, and he could read her thoughts in the trembling of her body. She thought he might punish her further, and she wasn't sure how she was going to bear any more pain. But she would. Just to prove to him she could. *Christ.*

"Marcie." He pushed her head to his chest, curving his hand over the side of her face to hold her there, shelter her.

"We'll deal with that later. Right now, just be easy. Easy, darlin'."

A little sigh went out of her, a hiccup. "I love it when you sound Cajun."

Her hands were folded in between them, so he tightened his grip, cocooning her. He wanted her to stop shaking, but that was going to take some doing. "Where'd you put your things? Purse, girly stuff?"

She straightened, holding on to him to steady herself, but determined to show him she could do it. When what little color she had drained out of her face, he anticipated the faint. She hadn't had lunch, hadn't hydrated herself at all, because her skin was too cool and dry, despite the fact she looked as if she'd perspired quite a bit. She really needed to work on that bad habit of locking her knees.

"Okay, here we go." He'd lifted her, carried her to the reception couch. The mere pressure of the seat cushion on her ass was enough to keep her from full unconsciousness. She swayed inside his grip, her brown eyes seeking his face.

"I messed up, didn't I?"

"Yeah, you did. But not as bad as I did. Stay here just a second." He made sure he was back fast, bringing her a bottle of water from his office fridge, and a pack of peanut butter crackers. "Okay, drink some of this. Slow, just sip it. There you go. Ease back on the couch if you can."

It was difficult, her body too stiff, her ass too sore. She was starting to shiver. He was functional, brisk, sliding his hands under the skirt, along her thighs, locating the straps to the two phalluses he'd left inside her. Coiling an arm around her waist, he lifted her enough to work all of it free, then set it aside. She made a small sound as his fingers brushed her pussy, her upper thighs, the rim of her ass, a different kind of shudder going through her.

Her cheeks colored over it, but he wasn't surprised. Given what he knew of her already, the pain and stress wouldn't have completely overwhelmed the arousal caused by being under a Master's command, his direction. Being as much of a Dom as she was a sub, he of course couldn't stop his dumbass cock from hardening.

Shrugging out of his coat, he put it around her shoulders. Then he lifted her in his arms and took her spot on the couch. When he put her in his lap, he kept her abused ass in the open area between his splayed thighs, bracing her lower back and upper thighs against that vee so she made only nominal contact with the firm cushion—and his groin. Then he brought the water back to her mouth.

Cupping her hands over his, she met his eyes before her lashes lowered, suggesting that she'd felt his arousal against her hip, but she focused on drinking. For the next fifteen minutes, he didn't let her speak, just worked on calming her down, getting crackers and fluid into her. At length, she let out a little sigh, rested her head against his chest. Her fingers were curled loosely in his open collar, because he'd pulled off his tie in the limo. Her French manicure was making teasing little scratches against his flesh as she continued to shake.

"Why did you say that? That you'd messed up?" she whispered.

"Figures you'd latch on to that." He was relieved to feel her lips curve in a slight smile against him, but he tipped up her face, held her chin, made her see the serious reproof in his gaze.

"A hardcore submissive like you, an inexperienced one, tends to go to extremes. You have to be trained to understand a Master's nature, to respond to it. You don't know the difference between anticipatory service to a Master and destructive overcompensation. Part of being a Master is knowing how far to push a sub, uncovering what they really need. It's never about causing them true, lasting physical harm. You were too green for me to leave you unsupervised like that. I knew better.

"Now, that said, there's your side of things." He gave her delicate jaw a firm squeeze. "A sub's devotion is shown through obedience, not pushing past the edges of good sense. You have a responsibility to care for yourself. How can you serve a Master if he's forever having to tend to your injuries?"

He was angry. Marcie knew his logic was sound, and more than that, she could tell he was angrier with himself than with her. It shamed her, that she'd caused that, but it also revealed a side of him she'd never seen before. It mattered to him, deeply, that she'd hurt herself. She wanted to tell him she understood what he was telling her, that she wouldn't make the same error twice, but there was something reckless in her when it came to him. She wanted to give him everything. She wanted him to know her soul was his, every part of her. The more it had hurt, the more determined she'd become, until the agony and the yearning were the same thing.

He tightened his arms around her, letting out a sigh as if he could read her thoughts. "It was stupid of me to leave you alone. You're too deep in your head on it. It's irresistible, but it also means a Master really has to be on his toes with you, to make sure you don't go overboard."

No other Master would ever have to worry about that, because she didn't feel that way about any other one. She wisely held that thought to herself. For now.

He told her they were leaving, but not where they were going. He didn't let her take her laptop with her, making it clear she wasn't going to be permitted to do any work tonight. Thank goodness she'd finished most of his task list, though it bugged her she hadn't completed it all, as he'd demanded.

He had her step out of her shoes and picked them up, looping them over his wrist as they walked to the elevator. He kept his arm around her, holding her steady. They didn't take his car, the small sports car whose bucket seat she was sure would have been agony to her. Instead, they took a limo from the limo pool. Fortunately, the driver stayed in the car, Ben holding the door for her. When she got in, she saw the privacy screen was raised.

As she tried to determine how not to sit on her ass, Ben curled his fingers around her upper arm and guided her down onto her stomach on the comfortably long seat. Fortunately, he sat next to her, so she could put her cheek on his thigh and slide one hand under his knee. He smelled good. Heated male, aftershave, soap, dry cleaning for his suit.

He stroked her back, playing with her bra strap through the thin turtleneck. That intimate touch made her hold her breath. It also stirred things up inside her, crazy as that was in her current condition. But doing what he'd ordered her to do, having that vibrator inside her, had kept arousal a big part of the equation. She could imagine going to her knees in this limo, wrapping her hands around him, putting her mouth on his cock.

Her fingers inched up his leg, doing a circle on his inner thigh. She'd give so much to serve him that way, feel him climax, know she'd given him pleasure. *It's irresistible, but it also means a Master really has to be on his toes with you...* She wanted to work harder on the irresistible part.

"Hey." A soft reproof as he laid his hand over hers. "Be still."

"I don't want to. I want to touch you." This time she was merely telling him what was in her head, not sassing him. When she stopped, he stroked her hair, a reward for her obedience. She let that be enough, though her body was running hot and cold. It was like being in shock, floating and yet so wired, everything out of control. She couldn't get her mind around it, but it was okay. He was her Master. He was in control.

At length, she realized they were outside the city. When they turned off a quiet rural road into a private driveway, she realized where they were. Jon's house. It was a lot like his second home in Baton Rouge. His driveway was a quarter mile long, winding through a hushed pine forest skirted with thick foliage, so it was never unusual to see wildlife crossing a car's path. Deer, possum, raccoons, armadillo. The occasional alligator or long, slithering snake.

While she loved visiting Jon's, being here now alarmed her. Not as much as if Ben had brought her back to Cass', but still. She wasn't sure of his intent. Easing gingerly to her hip, she propped her elbow on his leg to peer through the windows. His face had a set expression, the solid planes shadowed by the night closing in outside and the dim light thrown by the limo's interior. "Why are we here?"

"Didn't I tell you to use sir? And do you have permission to ask me a question?"

"I don't know. I can't tell when you're being...Ben and when you're being a Master." But that question had its own answer, and she knew it. In her mind, he was always a Master. *She* treated him as Ben when she was trying to direct things, control them. His sidelong glance told her he already knew that, but it was the first time she'd figured it out. So she wasn't surprised that he didn't answer, only waited on her. It was more difficult than she expected. She'd engineered so much of everything that had happened until now. She was afraid if she stopped fighting for what she wanted, let go of the reins, he wouldn't pick them up. He'd just walk away and she'd lose ground.

"May I ask...why are we at Jon's, sir?"

His lips pressed together. When he shifted, that heat in her lower belly kindled further. Whether or not he wanted it to happen, her subservience had pleased him. She could tell. "Rachel has nurse training in addition to her physical therapy certification. I want her to check you over, make sure you're all right."

"I'm fine. I—" She bit her lip as he shifted that steady stare to her. She nodded, laid her cheek back down on his leg.

"Yes sir." But her fingers curled into balls, uncertain.

The porch light was turned on as they pulled up. Ben had probably told the limo driver to call ahead. She was hoping he'd let her walk, because she'd feel utterly foolish if he carried her. He did let her walk up the stairs, though he carried her to the deck steps since he wouldn't let her put her shoes back on.

As she ascended, he was right behind her, hand on the small of her back, fingers grazing the upper rise of her ass until she reached the door. Fortunately, it was Rachel who met them there, her expression warm and welcoming. Though Jon was the most deceptively gentle of the K&A men, she wasn't sure she could handle the intense scrutiny of two Doms right now.

"Marcie, it's so good to see you again. Come on in, dearest."

Why the affection made tears spring to her eyes, she didn't know, but Marcie pushed them back, with effort. Rachel's eyes held so much understanding, a kinship, as if she understood that Marcie was pure chaos right now, emotionally, physically. She and Jon were both into the spiritual chakra stuff. If Rachel read auras, Marcie expected hers probably looked like an LSD-induced kaleidoscope.

Ben withdrew his hand, a loss she felt everywhere, not just at the small of her back. When her gaze turned to him, he nodded. "You do as Rachel tells you," he said. Then he was moving across the spacious living area to Jon. Rachel's husband and Master was sitting at the kitchen island with the parts of what looked like an old phonograph machine laid out before him, complete with large conical-shaped speaker. A half-eaten dinner was on a plate at his elbow, next to a glass of wine. As Ben was approaching, he was already opening him a beer.

Jon didn't speak to Marcie, just glanced at her with that familiar measuring look. She wouldn't be acknowledged yet. Jon had turned her over to his submissive's care and would determine her well-being from Ben. Her Master.

Or at least the one she wanted to call Master, so much she knew it was going to eventually slip from her lips. When she was feeling less vulnerable, she'd do it deliberately. Master, Master. Master. She wasn't going to let him —

God, she was doing it again. But she couldn't help it, damn it. She was unwilling to back down or give up, no matter if she had to sit on that pillow for the rest of her life. Except she hoped it wouldn't come to that, because if she had to sit on it right now she might cry like a kindergartener.

"Marcie." Rachel brought her back with a warm squeeze on her arm. "Come on. You're caught in the zone. We need to get you grounded a bit better. Let's check you out, all right?"

Rachel guided her up the open staircase, to the second level that held bedroom, home office, and a room with a massage table. In that room, there were clusters of lit candles that threw flickering light onto a tall stained-glass window with the design of a lotus blossom vine. A light installed behind it allowed the vibrant greens and browns to glow, even at night. Somewhere behind the array of delicate Japanese maples in the room, a flute piece was coming through a speaker system.

Okay, she'd definitely been expected. It embarrassed her, but Rachel was being her usual gentle but firm self, not allowing any of that nonsense.

"Let's get your clothes off. No, honey, let me help. Your fingers are so cold and shaking."

"I told Ben, I'm fine. I just — "

"You're fine, but you need some help to stay that way." She removed the sleeveless snug turtleneck. Marcie tried to help, to prove she didn't need to be undressed like a child, but Rachel was right, because she fumbled over the zipper of the skirt. Rachel made a soft sound, brushed her hands away. As she stepped closer to reach around her to do that, her breasts pressed against Marcie's.

She was wearing one of Jon's soft worn T-shirts, jeans pulled on beneath it, suggesting the shirt had been a nightshirt until they received Ben's call. It seemed a little early for wearing night clothes, but then she remembered Rachel was a 24/7. It was entirely possible that Jon preferred her naked in the house when it was just the two of them. The temperature in the house was more than comfortable for it.

The shirt smelled like a pleasing combination of Jon and his wife, and Rachel wore no bra under it. As a result, when Marcie felt the give of her generous breasts against her own, her nipples got hard again. Though her mind was logy, her body was still in an alert state, prepped for physical intimacy. Turning her face into Rachel's thick blonde hair, she smelled her fragrant shampoo, the heat of her skin. She wanted to press her lips to the woman's neck, taste her. Insanely enough, she did.

Rachel let out a sensual chuckle, pressed her hand to the side of Marcie's face, allowing it a moment before she unhooked her bra, stepped back to slide it off Marcie's arms, then turned her toward the massage table. "You are spinning, love. Let's check your vitals first. Sit here on the table."

She was vaguely aware of Rachel taking her pulse, checking her heart, making her breathe deep and then shallow as she did so. The woman wrapped a blood-pressure cuff on her, pumping it tight with calm efficiency. Marcie didn't realize she'd zoned out until Rachel's voice called her out of the fog. "Good. Vital signs are fine. I'm going to have you lie down now, check some other things, but I want you to start sipping on this." She drew Marcie's attention to a bottle with a flexible straw by the massage table. "It'll taste a little odd, but it's just a hydration mix. Salt, sugar, water and a little mint and some other things I put in to soothe the stomach and nerves."

When she assumed that state, Rachel's capable hands adjusted her legs so they were slightly spread. Marcie was completely naked now. The air touched her skin, made her shiver, though she knew it was warm in the room. "We'll get a blanket on you in just a second. Oh love. You really pushed yourself over the limit, didn't you? Let's put an antiseptic salve on that broken and irritated skin right now, because we don't want infection. Keep drinking now, small sips."

When Jon's wife rolled her over, she'd put a blissfully damp towel over a soft pad right under her backside so it wasn't as uncomfortable as Marcie had anticipated. She smelled something fragrant and chemical at once, suggesting the damp pad was soaked with the salve.

"That will help for now. An additional healing balm will be added later. One of my own mixes. It has beeswax, aloe, some different extracts. Mixed with a bit of talcum." Marcie heard the smile in the woman's voice. "Smells wonderful and makes you feel like a pampered baby."

Marcie floated. The smell of the antiseptic, the way Rachel had her laid out on the table, made her remember getting her nipples and her clit hood pierced. The pain had been excruciating, but throughout it, she'd imagined Ben there as if he'd ordered it, decorating the body that was his. That night, she'd gone home and looked in the mirror at the silver clit ring. Eventually, she'd bought two emerald beads for it, the color of Ben's eyes. She'd worn them today, beads that teased her clit and labia when she moved. She wondered if Ben had noticed when he was caning her over his desk.

The night she'd purchased those beads, she'd fantasized about Ben tugging on the ring, attaching a tether to it. Her pussy had been so wet, making the ring and beads glisten even more.

Remembering, past and present coming together, her body reacted with a shocking contraction of arousal as she heard Ben's voice. She cracked her eyelids to see him at the door. Rachel had covered her with a warm blanket, now that she was on her back, but his gaze still covered every exposed inch of skin with careful precision. "I called Cass, let her know she's here for the night. How is she?"

"She's going to be fine. Dehydration was the main worry, but she's working on fluids now. The antiseptic will prevent infection, if she tends the area according to my instructions. In a little while she'll feel much steadier. Then she's all yours."

She wished. Oh how she wished for that. On her side of things, it was already the truth.

*　*　*　*　*

She must have dozed off for a while, or floated around in that weird trance state, because when she focused again, she thought quite a bit of time had passed. She did feel steadier, but when she shifted, she winced. Sheesh, her muscles were sore. She probably needed to take a hot shower at some point.

Of course, with lucidity came a bunch of nervous feelings that compounded tenfold when she saw Ben sitting where she last remembered Rachel being. The woman had watched over her as she dozed, reading at one point, then peeling some carrots, a rhythmic, comforting clink-clink of noise from the peeler. Probably preparation for some meal she'd be cooking for Jon later. Though Jon could cook and sometimes did, Marcie had noticed at the group get-togethers it was always Rachel who brought Jon his plate or a refill on his drink, unless he specifically told her to stay seated so he or another could tend to it. Another of those many little clues she'd put together.

Rachel was an anticipatory sub, one who anticipated what her Master or his guests would need and took great pleasure in meeting those needs before they even voiced them. Some Masters allowed that; others required that a sub follow their direction exactly. She had a feeling Ben was a mix, depending on the situation, but she was a hundred percent certain what he truly wanted was a 24/7 relationship, no matter that he'd never committed to a woman in all the time she'd known him.

He hadn't pursued a woman outside a club setting in the past couple years, but that only confirmed her opinion. All the intel she'd gathered said that Ben O'Callahan didn't settle for anything less than exactly what he wanted. 24/7 subs—and the Doms who not only wanted them, but knew how to manage that type of relationship — were rare. Even those who said they wanted it often really didn't, because the reality of 24/7 was a whole different thing. But like Ben, she didn't want anything less. Further, she didn't want it from any Dom in the world except Ben. He could call it youthful idealism or fantasy all he wanted. She knew differently.

She met his gaze, couldn't tell what was going on there, but she didn't have to figure out how to ask. When he saw she was awake, he rose. As he drew back the blanket, exposing her body to him without any preamble, the air now felt warm.

"On the floor, on this mat here. Obeisance pose." His voice was firm, but like the air, no longer cold. She hoped her hair looked okay. Her makeup had been ruined, but Rachel had cleaned her face with a warm cloth, so hopefully it wasn't too bad. Personal appearance aside, he'd just given her a direct command. She found her limbs a little logy, but he gripped her elbow, helping her off the cot and into a kneeling position.

Knees folded, body leaning forward, elbows to the padded yoga mat, forehead down. Ass lifted off the heels, pushed into the air against the elbows so she was balanced. He made an approving noise at her understanding of the pose. She wished she could tell him she'd masturbated in this pose, imagining that it was his hand that had pushed a vibrator into her ass and pussy, commanding her to hold the pose until she came, shuddering and screaming into the pillow she put on her dorm room floor so her neighbors didn't hear.

He took a seat on a short stool next to her, one knee crooked, the other leg stretched out comfortably alongside of her body. He was still wearing his slacks and dress shirt, but he'd rolled up the shirtsleeves. Before she went all the way down, her gaze had slid down his throat, over the light mat of dark hair revealed by the open collar. He had a cart next to him with cotton balls, gauze and an open jar of something that smelled wonderful. Rachel's balm.

Marcie had assumed she'd be doing the care, but in thinking about it now, Rachel had never said that. Instead, Ben was handling it personally. Tears pressed against the back of her eyes once more. She wasn't a crier, never had been, but for some reason, a whole backlog of the pesky things seemed to keep swelling up like a creek after a rainstorm. Shutting her eyes, she swallowed against the lump in her throat.

He had powerful hands, hands that were probably half again the size of hers. As he stroked her hair off her neck, spreading it forward on the floor around her shoulders, she made a questioning noise in her throat. He stilled. "What is it, Marcie?"

"Can I...would you put your hand under mine...sir?" Master was there, on the tip of her tongue, but she wanted this, wouldn't provoke him right now.

Blissfully, he complied. Hers was flat on the mat, and he knelt beside her to slide his palm down, beneath hers. She curved her fingers over his knuckles, aligning them so she saw she'd been mostly right. Not half a size larger, but still much larger than her own. When cupping her breast, a hand like that would almost cover it, though not quite. Thank God she and Cass had inherited their mother's generous bosom. Ben might be an ass man, but he had a healthy appreciation for breasts too. In those few days they'd shared office space, she'd seen him perusing hers more than once. Those demi-bras allowed a lot of attractive movement.

"Thank you, sir."

He removed his hand without comment, but he gave her hair another stroke. Then he started tending to her. The balm stung a bit, telling her there was still antiseptic in the mix. However, she wasn't sorry about that at all, because it had the benefit of him leaning forward, blowing gently on her buttocks where he applied it, soothing that burn and sending an erotic ripple through her, thinking of his mouth so close. Then came a light stroke of his fingers as he massaged it into her skin. It was uncomfortable, but bearable, as long as his touch was part of it.

Fluids had helped restore her, made her feel less thick-tongued and dizzy, and the shifting waves of arousal came back fast under his touch. The obeisance pose underscored complete submission to a Master's desires, the genitals and anus open to whatever he wanted to do, the forehead to the ground making surrender clear.

She couldn't help twitching, the slight lifts of her backside begging for more of that touch, for more, period. She was getting wet, she could feel it, and while she knew he'd call her a slut, it was how she reacted to him. She couldn't bear it if he thought she was this way with everyone. But there was nothing she could say to prove otherwise. She had to show him, and in this moment, being still and letting him register the arousal was all she could do.

She thought she heard a muttered oath. But then his touch slid down the seam of her buttocks, and his thumb probed the lips of her pussy, coming away wet. She whimpered.

Candlelight, heat, silence. She wondered if Rachel and Jon had gone to bed, because she heard no noise at all beyond Ben's breath and her own. Though she had no idea how long she'd been out of it, it had to be late.

Now both hands were cradling her buttocks, his thumbs parting them. His breath was there, a heated balm even better than the salve on the abraded parts. Then she nearly swallowed her leaping heart.

He put his mouth to the tight, puckered opening.

It should get better. It's always a little harder for girls, at first. Find a guy who will take the time to make it good for you. Don't settle for just lying there while he gets off in five minutes. The right guy will want you to feel pleasure as well, and even if he doesn't know how to go about it, he'll want to learn. Don't be afraid to tell him and show him. He's supposed to take care of you. Otherwise he deserves to have his dick tied in a knot."

Ben, answer to Marcie when she told him about her first time

Chapter Six

❧

Holy Mother of God, fuck, please, oooohhhh. Though she'd surely fantasized about this, there were some things electronics couldn't duplicate. A heated, firm tongue licking around that rim, teasing the ultra-sensitive center, which contracted under the pressure, welcoming him in. But he taunted her with it, kept his tongue on the outside, tickling and stroking that ring of nerves. His fingers tightened just enough on her abused buttocks, making her flinch and convulse at once. Yes. More pain, more pleasure. She could take it all from him.

She tried her best to stay still, to be a good girl, but it really wasn't her nature. She wanted to wiggle against his face, rub and squirm. She wanted that tongue. Those powerful fingers dug in, a warning, hard enough that a true lance of pain went through those broken areas.

"Keep still, or I'll stop." He spoke against her flesh. That combined threat and command stilled her more effectively than any physical pain.

But oh God, it was intense. She bit into the mat, her fingernails digging into the foam as that agile tongue made small circles among the tiny creases of her anus, touched that center point again and again. He put pressure there several times, making her think he was going to penetrate, but then he'd withdraw. Her whimpers became pleading cries. Her pussy was convulsing, warning her the very friction of the air could make her orgasm, his very proximity enough to push her over the edge.

"You won't come." Reading her body so well, he spoke sternly.

She nodded frantically, agreeing, though she had no idea how she could stop herself. He made her helpless. She knew he exulted in it, that this was his drug, making her every action and reaction a mindless, instinctive response to him.

His tongue pushed slowly inside that opening, going deep, moving, swirling, teasing, and she came apart. She didn't come, but it was more intense than any climax she'd given herself. She screamed into the mat, her nails puncturing the foam and taking chunks out of it. Her thighs trembled, her toes curling hard as she struggled to stay still. His fingers bit into those welts, and the mixed sensations were so overwhelming she thought she might black out. She fought to stay in this moment forever.

He withdrew, then penetrated again, fucking her ass with his tongue. When it became too much, he would tease and play on the outside, then thrust back in again. Every time it was more overwhelming than the last. She knew there were other people in the house, but she couldn't stop making those wailing, crazed shrieks.

When he pulled back at last, sat on his heels, she was holding on to that cliff edge with every tense, quivering muscle. Those strong hands curled around her upper arms, lifted her onto her knees, turned her toward him. "Look at me, Marcie."

His eyes were green fire, the flickering candles making love to the planes of his strong face. "Arms boxed at the small of your back, ass on your heels."

She complied immediately. He took a seat on the stool, caging her between his thighs and the massage table. Taking her shoulders, he slid her closer with an effortless move that kept her in the same position. "Close your eyes."

Oh the hell with that. She wanted to see, wanted to see him. But he wasn't going to do anything else unless she obeyed. She shut them, swallowing back the petulant protest that came to her lips.

"Behave, little slut." When she was in her teens, he'd called her brat, and now she heard a similar note of affection, though it had a new element to it, one that made hope bloom in her heart.

She heard him opening the slacks, adjusting himself, imagined his cock stretching out hard and thick so close to her face. She smelled him, heated skin, aroused male. She wondered if pre-cum was glistening on the slit. He wasn't covering himself, because she didn't detect the latex smell, hadn't heard the crinkle of a foil package. Once she was old enough for Cass to answer her more brazen questions about Ben, she'd told Marcie how adamant he was about wearing protection with his club subs, and even then it was always ass fucking or blowjobs with them—if he allowed them to touch him at all.

The fact he was going bareback now said that he was sure he was clean and wanted to feel her lips on his skin. It didn't matter how irritated Ben might get with her, or the volatile quicksand she was walking to get him to be her Master; she knew he would never risk harming her for the pleasure of the moment.

Though that wasn't wishful thinking, her hope that she was the first to touch her mouth to his cock without that thin barrier probably was. But she'd let herself have that fantasy. Especially since he was about to grant one of her deepest wishes.

Her lips parted, tongue darting out as the broad head touched them. He withdrew before she could taste. "Keep them closed," he ordered in that firm, no-arguments-tolerated voice. She did, making small needy noises in her throat as he came close again, pressed velvet flesh against her sealed mouth. He painted that pre-cum along her lips, making her want to lick them so badly it was almost an involuntary reflex.

"All right now. Part them, but you wait for me to push forward. No reaching, no movement of your mouth except for how my cock stretches it. All movement comes from me, understand?"

"Yes, Master." She did it deliberately or instinctively, she didn't care. Would he let her get away with it? As he continued to hold himself from her, her heart twinged in disappointment. She relented. "Yes sir."

He punished her by making her wait another full minute. When that rigid cock finally pressed against her lips, demanding entry, she let out a mental sigh of joy and relief. An emotion that turned to alarm and incredulity. Holy God. She knew, of course she knew, because she'd heard about it in bits and pieces and touched him through his clothes, but as her mouth opened to take him, it kept being pushed open farther, the hinge of her jaw stretching, straining harder.

Her dentist had always said she had a small mouth, such that her jaw hurt from opening wide enough for him to do his annual cleanings. But that was good, because she knew Ben would like a tight, wet mouth, one that would clamp around him like a snug pussy. She had a moment of panic, though, thinking she wouldn't be able to take his full girth. He kept pushing forward, slow, deliberate. It was a little scary to have something that large pushing toward the back of her throat, the steel and meat of him against her teeth.

How long was he? Was he mostly diameter, or did he have the length as well? She'd practiced this with a large dildo, first using benzocaine, and then learning to do it without it, relaxing those throat muscles. Now that it was truly happening, she had to force her crazy emotional and physical reactions to settle, focus enough to do what she'd prepared herself to do. She wasn't going to fail in this. A man with a cock this size needed a woman who could service him well.

There were other things she could do, teasing the ridge around the head, sucking on the tip and, if he'd let her use her hands, please God, she could let them help the work of her mouth. However, she understood this moment wasn't about technique.

He was taking his time, which made her chest constrict with a more emotional reaction. While he was ruthless, he really wasn't cruel. He'd brought her here for aftercare, and now that he was making a Master's demands on her, he was being patient. He was hard and hot, like steel pulled right from the fire. She'd had a taste of him and now she wanted his climax, wanted to swallow him down. His fingers were tight in her hair, conveying his reaction and holding her steady as well.

She got him past her gag reflex, and counted it down in her mind, a meditative thing Jon had taught her long ago. At the time, it had been to deal with family and school stress, but she'd discovered the exercise not only kept her body relaxed but those all-important throat muscles as well.

There. He'd stopped. She wasn't all the way to the base, but she had a sense she was close. She breathed fast through her nose, trying to slow it down. Easy, easy. Her body was trembling, her pussy leaking arousal on her calves. Her nipples were so tight they ached, the barbells adding to that sensation. She vibrated in guttural sound as he noticed, one hand cupping her right breast, thumb passing over the nipple and tweaking the piercing.

"That's my good girl. Hold steady, there."

As he began to withdraw, he gave her a gift. "Start sucking me. Show me what else that smart-ass tongue of yours can do."

She drew in her cheeks, ecstatic at the sensation when his shaft returned, a deep, slow thrust. She used her tongue and a little bit of her teeth. Teasing the sensitive, throbbing vein under the shaft, flicking against it like plucking a taut violin string, she won an approving grunt, a flex of his fingers.

He kept it a torturous glide back and forward. As he went out, she nipped and sucked the corona, the broad head, and when he came back in she stroked that vein beneath anew. As she started to make unintelligible noises of pleasure in the back of her throat, he began to pick up speed. It increased the strain on her jaw, but it was all about pleasuring him, serving him. Her every nerve, every brain cell was attuned to it. For him, she could go into subspace with the least provocation. During this, during pain...even listening to the sound of his voice urging her on was enough.

"There you go. Suck me harder. Fuck..."

Her fingers, clasping her forearms in that box position at the middle of her back, clenched at the hoarse note. She knew he had awesome control. He'd fucked those three subs to completion before he came for the first time. But she wanted to believe the past couple days had been the continuous teasing foreplay for him it had been for her. She wanted him to lose control, use her hard, leave her jaw aching so badly she'd have trouble speaking the next few days. She wanted to be marked by him in every way.

She was so deep in that zone she was confused when he pulled out. She reached for him with her mouth, making a noise of protest. In answer, he turned her roughly, pushed her back down into obeisance pose, her arms still boxed so she had to depend on him to guide her face to the mat without harm. He pressed her forehead to it, his hand on the back of her neck. She quivered, her stomach flip-flopping as a plastic tip pushed against her anus. At the squirt of heated lubricant going in, her fingers flexed. *Oh God, yes.*

He tossed it aside so she heard the little plastic tube roll out beside her. Then his cock head was at her entrance. "Breath deep and push out against me, Marcie."

No one had ever been inside her there. She'd saved it for him, though she'd practiced with various-sized toys to be sure she could handle him. She wasn't so sure of that now, because the largest toy she'd used had been about two-thirds of his actual girth, and it had been a difficult entry. But she was so wildly aroused she thought she could take him if he was big as a tree trunk.

She wouldn't tell him he was her first anal sex. That would change things, give it a significance that could make him withdraw, physically and emotionally. She couldn't handle that. So she obeyed, breathing deep, pushing out and hoping she could do it.

She didn't need to worry. He would care for her, help her, even while demanding she comply, submit, yield to his intent to fuck her. But she still made a female noise of distress as he entered. The lube helped him slide into the opening, but there was so much of him to take. He braced himself over her then, one hand guiding his cock, his dress shirt pressed into her bare back. Reaching beneath her, he closed his other hand over her breast. She was right, it pressed into his palm just right, his fingers spreading over the curve. When he pinched her nipple around the barbell, her hips jerked up against him, taking him an inch deeper. She moaned, undulating in reaction as he stayed still but kept teasing her breast, squeezing and playing with the nipple. God, she was so sensitive around her piercings, and as she got more violent, so did he, pinching harder, tugging.

She didn't recognize the sounds coming from her throat in rapid succession, because every touch brought something new from within her. Her hips were pumping, pushing, working against him. She realized he wasn't moving at all. She was. Taking him deep, deeper. Burning, raging fire, but she could handle it, no matter that her eyes were watering. She could handle him. She belonged to him.

She was panting in distress, pressing her forehead hard into that mat. "Please…" She was begging, she didn't know for what, but he did. His hand left her breast, slid up the slope of her belly. Her clit was already contracting when he hooked his finger in the ring, played with the beads, then tugged on it to pull back the hood. Brushing the calloused tip of his finger over that ultrasensitive bundle of nerve endings, he set off a rocket of sensation.

She screamed like a wild panther in the dead of night, being mounted in the dark by a rough and uncompromising male. He slid home, down to the hilt, his testicles pressed against her pussy, and she made another harsh cry, pleasure and distress at once.

"Hold me there, baby," he murmured against her ear. "Just hold me. You can do it. Relax. Just rock with me."

He was moving against her hips, but not to pull in or out. He held them fast together, moving their bodies in one smooth roll of motion, a soothing lift and fall like waves in the ocean. It created incremental adjustments of his cock in her ass, which felt wildly good in a concentrated, compressed way. Her pussy was so wet the fluid was sliding down her inner thighs. His testicles were against her labia, so she knew her arousal would mark his ball sac as well. He was still playing with that ring, teasing the beads, brushing his thumb more gently around her clit, keeping those waves of feeling rushing up into her lower belly, the precursor to a violent, overwhelming climax.

Oh God, oh God, oh God. He felt better than anything had ever felt. She wished he was as naked as she was, that she could feel every inch of bare flesh, but Ben kept control, she knew that. Kept his distance. Only this didn't feel like distance. It felt like intimacy at a level she'd never expected. He was at the threshold of her soul, and she was terrified, realizing that as they progressed forward, if he did as she wanted, he'd be deep in that soul, leaving her no secrets, every part of her stripped bare for him. That was what he demanded. After he won it, he walked away.

She was his slave, but more than that, she'd always been his. She had to believe that, believe she would be different, no matter how many times women deluded themselves into thinking they would be the one to get into the heart of an emotionally closed, scarred man. Because Ben was exactly that. She'd realized it to a depth she suspected few others did, except maybe Matt. Or Jon, because Jon always knew things like that, whether you told him or not.

She had to get into Ben's soul. She didn't know how except like this, through utter surrender, something he'd won from countless women a hundred times before. Those women hadn't given him their heart when they were teenagers though. She had, and she'd never gotten it back. He still had it, whether he knew it or not. That made her different.

"You're going to come for me now."

"Please...you...first. Master." She was insane, because there was no way she could hold out a millisecond more.

He pinched her clit, tugged on that ring, began to rub her the wrong way with knowledgeable fingers, holding her climax out of reach. His voice, a growl against her ear, shivered over her nerve endings. "Address me correctly, or nothing is going to happen."

"I...did." She gritted her teeth. "*Master.*"

He could pull out, leave her there. He had enough will to do it. But she squeezed down on him with all she had, eliciting an expulsion of breath against her ear, another of those muttered oaths that gave her such ferocious satisfaction.

Wrapping his fingers in her hair, he jerked her head back. It was an implicit command to open her eyes, such that she was meeting his gaze full on. His eyes blazed like hellfire, his mouth set in an implacable line. "Three seconds, and I pull out, Marcie. I'll slap ice on that hot cunt of yours until you're writhing and begging from the agony of it, and you won't come."

"I want you more...than I want that."

A muscle flexed in his jaw. Something violent passed through him, something that almost lifted the hair on her neck, instinctive self-preservation. But when he spoke in that savage rumble, his tone was even. "Prove you can obey me. If you can't do that, I give you nothing."

He meant it, she could see he did. Once again she had to concede a battle for the hope of winning the war. Closing her eyes again so he wouldn't see the tears of frustration, she relented. "Please, sir. You come first. Let me serve you."

Just like that, he released her hair, put his hand back on her nape so she was forced to look at the floor. When he started thrusting again, she began to come within three strokes.

She couldn't resist him, the internal muscles in her pussy and ass clenching down so hard, the one on empty space, the other on the massive size of him. It was indescribable, how it felt to have him there. The toys she used, they'd been rigid, unyielding, no matter how lifelike. He was living, pulsing, heated flesh, and it galvanized her reaction to a level she'd never experienced before. A long, never-ending wail tore out of her throat. She couldn't bite it back, even if she'd wanted to do so, her vocal cords pushed to the max, the same way he was pushing all of her body. She convulsed against him, completely lost.

Still massaging her clit, he slid two of his fingers into her pussy. It shot her over another edge. He thrust into her ass, then slid almost all the way out. Back in, each pass ripping another sound from her throat, another wave of her climax. She clamped down on him, working for her Master, wanting to give him pleasure. She was forming words among the screams, single words that meant so much to her. "Master...fuck...yours...God..."

Then words weren't possible. With an expulsion of harsh breath, a primal grunt, he began to release. His hips were slamming against her abused ass, driving her forehead harder into the mat, his other hand now clamped around her boxed forearms to keep from putting additional duress on her neck, an amazing awareness of her even when he was obviously letting go, pushing them both to their limits. She reveled in his groan of pleasure, the way his fingers convulsed on her, the heat that she knew had to be his seed. The flood of his semen was enough to make her cry out anew, and he muttered a savage, gasping oath, responding to her.

He kept going for quite awhile, long past his completion, as if he was savoring the clench of her muscles over his still-hard cock, prolonging and underscoring her surrender to him. For her, time slowed to a dreamy haze. Her climax spiraled down to intense aftershocks, but her body kept jerking from his thrusts. He didn't pull out until long after all those aftershocks had faded to a low tide of pleasurable ripples through her stomach. When he did finally withdraw, a soft noise of discomfort broke from her lips, that tight ring of muscles contracting, burning. Suddenly she was aware of just how sore she was. Inside *and* out. It almost made her smile, but she was too exhausted.

He didn't lie down with her, but he did lift her back onto the massage table, laying her on her stomach. One palm settled on her buttock, holding her in place. She heard Rachel's quiet voice at the door a moment later, and his touch slipped away. He was leaving her aftercare to Jon's wife. She'd called him Master again, and he was punishing her for that.

"You promised," she whispered.

"What?" Ben squatted near her head, his hand gentle on her hair, thumb stroking her temple. His other hand rested on the edge of the table and she let hers creep up, cover two of his fingers. His glance went to the touch, then back to her face. Leaning forward, he pressed his lips to the corner of her eye, and she realized he was kissing away the track of a tear. She trembled beneath his mouth, but when he drew back, those eyes still so close, she swallowed, spoke.

"The club. You said you'd take me."

"I said I'd think about it," he corrected, giving her that sexy stern schoolmaster look.

"How much longer are you going to think about it?"

His gaze narrowed, but her stomach eased, seeing a flicker of humor. She lifted her hand, traced the serious mouth. Too serious. Too stern. "You don't smile as much as you used to."

She knew she was floating, but that was the way it was after something like that. At least she'd read it was this way, overheard discussions about it. Savannah, Rachel, Dana and Cass, having their monthly tea parties on the back deck, underneath her bedroom window. It had been easy enough to crack the window that tiny amount needed and sit below the sill to listen. It became an irresistible regular habit, particularly when she finally heard the words that told her what her feelings were. Submissive cravings. They had access to a whole candy shop outside her reach, but at least she'd been able to press her nose to the glass, learn what was waiting for her there. She'd dreamed of the day she could join them.

"I have a lot more annoyances than I used to have." He tugged on a lock of her hair.

"No, that's not it. Your heart…it's all closed up. But it's okay. I'm here. When are you taking me to the club?"

His glance shifted, as if her comments had elicited some type of reaction from Rachel, but then he was back to studying her face. His thumb traced over that tear track. "We'll talk about it later. Rachel is going to take care of you now. You rest. That's an order. You're not going to work tomorrow."

"Hmm." She had another contract to finish. She didn't want him to have to cover her work. Plus, there was something else she owed him. But he was too good at reading her.

"You want me to mentor you, from this moment on, you obey my orders. Got it? No work tomorrow. Say it."

She bit her lip in frustration, but he had that look on his face, and she knew she couldn't refuse it. "No work tomorrow, sir."

He made a point of looking toward her hands, making sure nothing was crossed, and it almost made her smile. Of course, he didn't look toward her toes.

Disentangling his fingers, he gave hers a quick squeeze before nodding to Rachel. "Take care of her."

Ben cleaned up in the bathroom. He wanted to go back in to see her, but he didn't, just glanced in to confirm Rachel was still working over her. She had an herbal wash that would soothe the tissues he'd stretched so cruelly, make that afterburn hurt way less. He'd liked cosseting her, taking care of the welts on her ass, hearing her sexy little whimpers. He wouldn't mind being the one to put her in the tub, rinse out that tight passage, make her comfortable again.

But he wouldn't. It was too personal, too intimate. He had to question his sanity, though, cutting out before Rachel gave her a full-body massage. Under different circumstances, he could probably talk Jon into ordering his wife to strip so they could have the pleasure of both women naked during the massage. With warming oil involved on lots of silken skin. Marcie's skin.

Jesus, he had to get out of here.

As he walked into the main room, Jon looked up. He was stretched out on the couch, a cup of tea in hand, reading a massive book about the wisdom of ancient civilizations or some bullshit like that. He looked entirely too calm. Ben shook his head, lifting a hand before he could speak. "Thanks. I'll be back for her tomorrow. I owe Rachel a yoga mat."

"Ben—"

"Not now." He stopped at the door, looked back at the man. "Thanks for your help, yours and Rachel's. I just don't want to talk it out right now, all right?"

Jon nodded. "I'll call if she needs anything we can't provide."

"Okay."

He slid out the door, relieved to breathe the open air. Though the limo was waiting, he would have preferred his own car, so he could open it up on the quiet rural roads around Jon's house, feel the blast of wind and cathartic roar that came with pushing it, feeling the lift over the few hills as if the car was about to take off like a plane.

He told the driver to drop him off in the French Quarter. This time of night, Bourbon Street was revving up, but he bypassed the traffic and noise, getting out at Royal Street to head for the place where the night sky was close and there was full dark.

The St. Louis cemetery, the oldest one. His childhood haunting ground.

Fortunately it seemed pretty quiet tonight. A homeless person or two were probably settled into the shadows, which was fine. He slipped along the maze of vaults, the various sizes that housed whole families. As a kid, he'd come through here plenty times. Hiding from other predators, the cops, or just to be by himself. Out of habit, he traced one of the many trios of sideways crosses etched on Marie LaVeau's tomb. Didn't really know why he did it; just always had. Sometimes he left a few pennies there, because the shrewd voodoo queen liked copper. Never hurt to network and make friends where you could.

When he reached the Italian Society vault, he glanced around, verifying he was alone and unobserved. Taking off his shoes, he held the laces in his teeth, then used handholds on the sealed drawers to climb to the top, take a seat amid the tufts of grass that grew untended there. Putting his back against the cross that crowned the area, he looked out over the acres of the dead and gone.

He wished he had a bottle of whiskey or a six-pack of Guinness, but then again he didn't. He knew he shouldn't drink in this kind of mood, but lately it hadn't stopped him. Closing his eyes, he rested his head against the cross. Mistake. Marcie was beneath him again, all that pale cream skin, her hair brushing her shoulders. She was biting her lips, tears in her eyes as she concentrated on taking him inside of her, managing the pain, her cheeks flushed with arousal. Her pussy had been soaked, sucking eagerly on his fingers. When she took his dick in her mouth, she took him like an experienced hooker. How the hell had she learned to do that? When? With who?

He recalled again the letters about her losing her virginity. She'd liked the boy, but with her penchant for strategic planning, it was kind of a "to-do" — getting it out of the way. At the time it had bugged him, though he couldn't put his finger on why. It was the way most *guys* were about it, after all. Get it done, the sooner the better. But maybe that was why it bugged him. Marcie wasn't a guy.

She'd asked why she hadn't climaxed, and whether it would get better. Recalling the advice he'd given her, he winced. That poor guy. With the practical streak Marcie had, she probably used him as a guinea pig, exploring every possible thing and asking a million questions about male anatomy until the kid was clawing and screaming, trying to get out of her room. Was that where she'd learned about the throat thing? She knew how to take a larger-than-usual cock, in both her ass and mouth. She'd known how to work with him.

It pissed him off. He told himself it had nothing to do with her experience or lack thereof. He was pissed because he wasn't supposed to have fucked her at all. When he'd made her call him "sir", she thought she'd lost. She didn't realize he'd been scrambling to regain the upper ground, which was a fucking joke since he'd already lost it. In Jon's house, no less. Jesus.

Rising, he crossed his arms and stared down into the cemetery like one of the stern angel statues. One clothed in a custom-tailored charcoal suit. He wanted her back at his place tonight, in his bed, so he could turn to her during the night and do whatever he wanted to do to her, make her sob with pleasure, wear her out. Give her the rest of those cane licks to make her behave.

His idea of a leisurely Sunday at home would be to tie her over a spanking bench, totally naked and legs spread. He'd keep her there through most of the day, her pretty mouth sucking his cock before he fucked her with it. He'd make her beg for food, water, trips to the bathroom. He'd blindfold her and paddle her ass at unpredictable intervals, keeping her on edge. One evening at the club, he'd done that to a seasoned sub for five hours, until she was so deeply mired in subspace she was speaking in tongues, begging to be fucked, for pain, for anything he wanted. The memory sent a shimmer of heat through his blood, especially with Marcie overlaying that picture.

Fine line between fucking sadist and a Dom, asshole.

There was no doubt he was a sadist. He needed to give pain to release something inside of him, and a sub craving it, willing to take higher and higher levels of duress just to please him and because she herself got off on it, she was a drug.

How did Marcie know that about him? How did she know so damn much? He thought of her body stretched out on the car hood, her glistening pussy lips. He'd like to taste what was there. Yeah, he might like assfucking, but he liked diversity, would take full advantage of the other pleasures a woman's body could offer. Those piercings made him hot as hell. He liked that she didn't have tattoos, all that creamy skin unmarred. He could mark it with his teeth, the suction of his mouth, the touch of a whip or paddle. He grinned like a feral animal, thinking of the play paddles he'd seen with words cut out of the wood so they'd imprint on the flesh. Slut. That would be hers, for sure. She wore the name like a badge of honor.

He sobered. It was a puzzle, how innocent she truly was, how inexperienced as a submissive, all of it bravado, and yet she sassed and defied him, begging for the worst punishment he could inflict. As if she'd known him as her Master for far longer than this one day.

Because she trusts you, asshole. It was like Matt had said. She followed her natural cravings because the environment told her she was safe, that she could make that leap and someone would catch her. Either that or she was just that damn brave. *Fuck.*

She'd followed him to Surreal. How long before that had she been studying him? What he wanted, what he liked. Jesus. She wanted to be an investigator, was top of her class...

He shook his head, climbed down off the top of the vault. Hearing a poignant ballad being wailed out on a sax, he followed a familiar track to its source. Sticking to the shadows, he watched Marvin Troxler stand before the grave simply marked "Bernie, Musician" and play his latest composition. Best fingers on a sax Ben had ever heard locally, but Marvin only shared with Bernie. If anyone appeared while he was playing, he stopped, walked away. His communication skills weren't the greatest, but there was a pain burning in his eyes Ben recognized too well.

Ben had first heard him a year or so ago. Figuring out his habits, he'd tailed him home, figured out that he was a low-paid dock worker. He'd arranged an accidental meet one day at the docks, and offered the man a different job. He worked in one of Kensington's warehouses now, earned better pay and had a decent apartment, but as far as Ben knew, he never sought gigs or any public outlet for his music. Ben never asked him about it, never revealed that he knew about Marvin's midnight serenades. There were wounds that were private. That no one should touch.

Turning away, he slipped back through the vaults. Stopping at one that had fallen to ruin, he readjusted the broken head plate to make sure it stayed upright. To show someone remembered. Swallowing, he moved away. Couldn't get into that shit. He had a damn good life. Friends who cared about him. The only reason one of them hadn't tracked him tonight was because he'd deliberately had the limo drop him at Bourbon. If they checked, they'd think he'd gone to Progeny or one of his favorite watering holes.

They all had families who needed them. They didn't need to be chasing after him. He knew the fact he was alone bugged them, but that was his choice. Marcie might think she knew what he needed and that she could handle it, but he'd decided long ago that was too much to ask of any woman.

Yet he remembered the way her fingers had covered his, the way her beautiful brown eyes had studied his face, seeing things she shouldn't be old or wise enough to see or understand. *"Your heart is closed. But it's okay, I'm here."*

"Shit," he muttered. He was way too aware she was here. That was the problem. He'd agreed to mentor her, and he needed to live up to that, but he was also way too aware that he wanted more than that. He wanted to take her over, Master her, show her the ropes literally and figuratively.

He wasn't going to go back for her in the morning. He'd send the limo, have her taken home, and that was the end of it.

* * * * *

Marcie slept restlessly, even though Rachel had done a good job. She was only sore in the right ways when she rose, but her nerves felt all raw and exposed. He'd been inside her, around her, surrounding her. It made her twitch or shudder at odd moments as she was getting cleaned up and dressed. Rachel had hung up the clothes Ben had taken off her, a vision she couldn't forget. Her nipples became erect at the least brush of contact.

He must have found her panties in the drawer and brought them along last night, because they were part of what Rachel had included with the clothes. Along with a silk blouse of Rachel's, a pretty pale pink that went well with the skirt and was thick enough the tan bra with its mesh top, though faintly visible, didn't look out of place beneath it

Ben had told Marcie she wasn't going to work, in front of Rachel, but Rachel had provided her a new blouse. If Marcie decided to go into work, she wouldn't be wearing the same top she'd worn yesterday. Did Rachel understand her that well? Probably.

Marcie's lips twisted. Should she do it, go on in to the office, even though he'd forbidden her to do it? He had hard limits, but she hadn't quite figured out the shape of that line. He'd committed himself to mentoring, so that was progress. However, if she broke the rules too stringently, would he use that as an out? The mentoring was the only true foothold she had right now.

Sighing, she left the guest bedroom and headed to the main floor. Jon was still here, sitting at the kitchen island, working his way through scrambled eggs, tomatoes and toast. He had one foot propped on the opposite chair, elbow resting on the counter as he held a piece of toast in that hand and an engineering drawing in the other. Though he was wearing slacks, his dress shirt had been shrugged on but not yet buttoned, the tie draped over the back of the chair where his foot was propped.

As a woman, she was obligated to pause, appreciate that view. Every one of the K&A men was an utterly edible male and Jon was no exception, with his jewel-blue eyes, dark hair to his shoulders and his lean grace. His current pose demonstrated the casual flexibility that came from advanced yoga, something he and Rachel did together. The smooth pecs and ridged abdomen, the shape of his tight ass in the slacks, made her an absolute fan of the ancient practice to sculpt the male form.

Rachel was dressed for her work as a physical therapist, in attractive black slacks and a shirt that clung to her curves in a sexy but professional way. As Marcie came down the stairs, Jon glanced up. It was unsettling, how he assessed her physical and emotional state in a series of steady blinks.

But Jon was a Dom, and this was the world she wanted to inhabit. So she kept her chin up, her walk steady. When she met his gaze, she lowered her eyes, nodded, acknowledging what he was before she lifted them again.

He was a Master, but not her Master.

"Toast and eggs, love," Rachel said, sliding another plate next to Jon's. "The jelly is fresh, from the berries in our garden. I need to get to an early PT appointment, but Jon said he'll stay here with you until Ben arrives."

"Ben's coming here?"

"When he left last night, he said he'd be back for you in the morning." Jon caught Rachel's hand when she was picking up his orange juice glass to top it off. He held her there as he dipped his knife in the jelly, put a bit of it on her wrist. Bringing it to his mouth, he licked it off, considered the taste thoughtfully. Rachel held still, and Marcie saw the pulse leap in her throat, her gaze riveted on her Master.

"Hmm. It's good on toast, but better on you. Leave some of that out so it can get room temperature. I'll want to see what else I can spread it on tonight."

Rachel gave him a smile, then glanced at Marcie. "Do you want some juice, love?"

Wow. Just like that. She'd wanted to be at the adults' table, and suddenly they were doing things in front of her they never would have done before. Of course, she had nearly shattered their glassware with her screaming last night. Regardless, the change was both exhilarating and a bit unnerving.

"Yes. I can get it."

"No, you sit." Rachel gestured to the stool next to the one Jon was using as a prop for his foot. "Relax a little bit, since you have the day off."

"I guess so." Marcie pressed her lips together, glanced at Jon. "I'm sure Ben will go to the office first before he comes here. It's silly for you to be late. Just take me to the office. I can

142

meet him there, and if he's not quite ready to leave, I can finish up a few details I left yesterday."

It wasn't like she was disobeying him. She was just making it easier for him to find her. Or less easy to change his mind about coming for her personally.

Jon gave her a level glance. "You sure you want to do that, Marcie?"

Busted. She didn't flinch though. "I won't let him avoid me, Jon. Last night, he told you he'd pick me up today. But he's going to just send a car, and the driver of that car will be instructed to drop me at Cass'. Then I'll go back into work tomorrow, and he'll be on a flight halfway across the world, dealing with some unexpected legal problem. By the time he returns, my two-week internship will be over."

Rachel made a noise that sounded suspiciously like a dry chuckle, an *I-told-you-so.* Jon gave her a fond and amused glance, but when he looked back at Marcie, he'd sobered.

"It's his decision. You need to accept that."

"It's his decision if he's making it for the right reasons," she said. "Not because he thinks I can't handle what he wants."

"*Can* you handle what he wants? Stop." Jon's tone sharpened enough to startle her, make her hold her tongue. "Don't simply react. Think it through."

Marcie glanced at Rachel. She was standing at the sink, watching the two of them, but her calm look bolstered Marcie.

"I don't know," she said at last. "Each of you found the one woman who was…everything for you. You knew it pretty much from the first moment. You and Rachel, Peter and Dana, Lucas and Cass, Matt and Savannah. That's the way you guys work. Ben might think he's different, but in my heart, I know he isn't."

Jon considered her. "You believe you're that one for Ben?"

"Yes. I feel it." She braced herself for that look people adopted when a younger person said something incredibly naïve. But Jon merely looked toward Rachel.

"Head on to your appointment. I'll decide what to do after I talk to Marcie awhile."

Rachel nodded. When she came around the counter, she put her arms around Marcie and hugged her. "We'll talk later," she murmured.

In high school, Marcie had called Rachel's embraces "Earth Mother hugs" because they brought comfort and warmth, this amazing desire to stay inside of her armspan forever. It was amusingly similar to the tranquility that Jon emanated the moment he stepped into a room.

However, Rachel's lips touching her temple was a different kind of caress. Marcie was still worked up enough from last night to respond to it. When the woman turned her head, Marcie couldn't resist brushing her lips across hers, stroking her fingertips over the strands of Rachel's beautiful blonde hair. She was careful not to muss it, but she wanted to dig her fingers deep into that luxurious softness.

She imagined the two of them intertwined and naked, engaged in a full girl-on-girl kiss, driving Ben and Jon crazy hot. She knew Rachel was sometimes self-conscious about her age, almost fifty, but all she saw when she looked at the woman was a loving female submissive with a smoking body and a warmth anyone would crave to share.

"That would be great," she said, meeting Rachel's amused eyes.

Jon raised a brow, but stood when Rachel came to him. Apparently, he could pick a woman's thoughts right out of her brain just like Ben, because everything Marcie had stolen in her fantasy, he now took as his undeniable right. He kissed his wife deep, strong, tangling his fingers into her hair. He didn't care that he mussed it. In fact, he unclipped the barrette, pocketed it, and then let that hand wander around her hip to rest on her buttock. Her kiss was no brush of lips either. When he lifted his head, his blue eyes full of his wife, Rachel was clinging to his forearms for support. Marcie didn't blame her. She was sitting, but *her* knees were just as weak. "Be careful," he said. "I'll talk to you at lunch. I love you."

Rachel nodded, left them with another smile at Marcie, her lips moist and somewhat swollen from the demand of that kiss. While it had aroused her, Marcie found it had done something less pleasant to her emotionally. The desire for physical demand and intimacy together was overwhelming, and came with a quiet sense of despair. She'd started the ball rolling, and though she had no idea if it would get to its destination, if it did, that would bring a whole set of problems, problems that might prevent her from ever being on Jon and Rachel's kind of stage.

Jon sat back down, pushed her plate closer to her. "Eat and keep talking," he said. "Tell me what's bugging you."

There was a different tone to his voice now, reminding her Jon was a good listener. It probably seemed odd that she'd gravitated toward Ben as her confidante as a teen, but once she'd understood why, it hadn't been much of a surprise to her. Still, Jon provided perspective, a calm she needed desperately right now. She was going on gut feeling, recklessly daring the fates to strike her down, and Jon had prompted her to rein it back a notch, think about it. Which was exactly why she preferred the steamroller approach. She had to have superhero confidence to do this. Pausing for reflection invited doubts, and a whole wealth of them crowded forward into this moment.

"I went to watch him…at Surreal. He didn't know I was there, watching."

"Does he know now?"

"Probably." She remembered how he'd kept looking toward her that night, noting the mask she'd later used on his car.

"I expect he wasn't entirely pleased to know he was being stalked."

"It wasn't stalking." She wrinkled her nose at him, reassured when he gave her a smile. "He was with three women, Jon. I don't like seeing him with others, but in some weird way, I guess that made me feel better about it, because it's so...impersonal. I don't know if I can keep up with him though. The stamina he showed, how much each of them took..." Last night, when he pulled out of her, he was still hard. She'd seen it when he'd adjusted his clothing. "If I can't be all he needs in that department, no matter how much I want him, I don't know how I'll feel if he wants me to be one of many, versus just...the one."

She was smart enough to know last night was his relatively gentle side, yet it had pushed her to her limits, physically and emotionally. Of course, it was the first time she'd actually experienced something like that. She could learn, get better, get stronger. "Is that what he wants, Jon?"

"Hmm." Jon slathered more jelly on another piece of toast, handed it to her. "The word *want* is a tricky thing. It's far more subjective and unstable than *need*. Nature aligns us, Marcie. We may differ in our physical capabilities, but nothing overrides what our hearts really desire. Think about extreme adrenaline junkies, the things they do that can get them killed. What are your thoughts about that?"

"They're running. Trying to outrun death or fear, or something else. They push their limits so they don't have to stop, be still and face that."

"Exactly." He chewed on his own toast, studied her.

"Okay, you're going all Yoda on me. Giving me the 'Luke, you dumbass — figure it out' look."

He grinned, appreciating her, but then he sobered. "Ben is a very demanding Master. However, if you're right, if you are what his heart truly desires, you won't have to worry about keeping up with him, or being one of many women. When each of us found the woman we knew was the one for us forever, that was it. She could have been an invalid, and she'd have been plenty for us physically. You've said you believe Ben is no different from the rest of us in that regard, so that's your answer."

She frowned, looking down at her plate. "Finding that one person," he added, touching her hand to bring her gaze back to him, "it's a shift of paradigm that changes everything. What we always thought we wanted, what we know, what we don't. But when it clicks into place, that's also when everything makes sense, often for the very first time in our lives."

"You're scary," she decided. Picking up the toast, she took a bite. "This is fabulous."

"Just think how it will taste on Rachel's skin." Those blue eyes gave a wicked flash that made her toes curl.

"Another important point." He pointed at her with his piece of bread. "You have to be who you are, Marcie. If you believe deeply you belong together, then you must do it on your own terms, as who you are, because you can't pretend to be someone else. Not for a lifetime. Don't sell yourself short. He'd know anyway. There's a reason he's a very good lawyer. He can scent a lie like a bloodhound."

He rose. "I'm going to finish getting dressed. You can stay here or I can take you into the office. The choice is yours. But remember this. You're pushing a Master pretty hard. For everything he's done so far, I can tell you that Ben has showed a great deal of restraint, given what he's capable of doing."

There went that shiver again, part fear, part...longing. She wasn't brave enough to share with Jon some of the things she'd imagined Ben doing to her. She would stand in a stock like those women, her neck and wrists bound, body bent over in servitude. Ben could put her on display in the center of his living room and she'd stay that way all day while he went about his routine, enjoying his Sunday coffee, reading his paper, working out, whatever.

He'd gag her of course, so she'd be unable to do anything but await his pleasure. Whether it was fucking her in that helpless position, smacking her ass, clamping and weighting her nipples, whatever. He could punish her endlessly for her defiance, because she knew he wanted to be pushed. He wanted someone who wasn't afraid of his form of Mastery. At least not in the wrong kind of way.

As much as she craved that, she also hungered for the other side of that mountain. Him removing the restraints, bathing her, brushing her hair, holding her against his body at night. Laughing with her, dancing with her. Sharing everything with her. He was the two sides of that coin, and she just wanted to spin with him, taking either side, whenever, however she could get them.

"Marcie? One more thing." Jon stepped closer, tipped up her chin with two fingers. He held her in place with a firm, unexpected touch, pulling her out of her reverie. "Hugging my wife, affection, is one thing. But you want to touch her other ways, you need my permission. She's mine. You understand?"

Wow. His unyielding tone was in direct contrast to the mild conversational attitude from before. It was potent, seeing the Master inside him up close and personal.

"Yes sir."

He nodded, stepped back. When he retrieved his plate, took it to the sink, other things rose inside her, demanding to be said. "I know I'm out of control, irrational about some of this. I've planned this for a while, Jon, and now that the reality has kicked in, I'm following this feeling inside me. The more he tries to push me away, the more it tells me to push back. I know a lot of what I'm doing is wrong, but I can't seem to calm myself down, make myself take it slower, especially now that I've opened the door."

She'd raised a forkful of eggs, but the more she talked, the more her fingers shook, such that she put it back down, uneaten. That raw feeling was back.

Jon's brow creased in concern. Coming back around the counter, he slid his stool closer. Picking up her fork, he nodded. "Open up."

She gave a nervous laugh. "I can—"

"No arguments. Open up."

She nodded, opened her mouth. As she chewed the first mouthful, he scooped up another, patiently waiting on her. "Breathe, and eat. No talking."

She obeyed, because his calm command steadied her nerves. It was odd to have Jon feeding her, his thigh pressed alongside hers on the outside of the stool. As she ate, the knot in her stomach loosened. She realized suddenly, with mortification, that tears were trickling down her face. Putting aside the fork, Jon patted at them with the napkin, and then slid his arms around her. Before she realized it, he was lifting her, taking her to the couch to sit her down in his lap.

"Cry now," he murmured. "Just cry."

As if a dam broke loose, she did. Nerves and stress, pleasure and pain, all the memories of the previous night, good and bad, were rolled up into her sobs. She buried her face in Jon's bare chest, held onto his dress shirt and wept. She wasn't a crier. She really wasn't. It astounded her, even as she couldn't stop it.

Jon stroked her hair, her back, the line of her hip. He wasn't infringing on what was Ben's, but they all understood this. Ben should be sitting where he was sitting. When a Dom broke a submissive wide open for her very first time, it made her impossibly vulnerable. For a short period, she would be overcome by vacillating emotions, her body hot and cold, aroused and calm, completely unpredictable. The wilder and stronger the sub, the wider that pendulum could swing.

Her Master was the touchstone for keeping a handle on that, helping her find the center, calm down again. Since her Master wasn't here, Jon would take care of it, at least in this moment. But he thought Ben was going to regret not doing it himself, because Marcie was as wild and strong as they came, fueled by the idealism of youth and the determination of an old soul, a lethal combination.

Faced with the choice of leaving her alone here, waiting for Ben to never show, or taking her to the office and letting her throw the gauntlet down, Jon decided he was taking her to the office. He hoped he wouldn't regret it.

I'm going to fail sociology. The professor blames everything from cockroach infestation to pimples on corporate greed. I've explained to him that corporations are run by people, which means they're as diverse and generous as whoever is managing them. I also pointed out that since individuals are the largest source of donations in the country, if they don't have jobs, which corporations provide, they can't donate. He said I was a corporate drone. He was probably sitting on his ass in his office when you guys were trucking in supplies to Gulfport, MS, after Katrina. Do you still make that industrial spray foam at the Costa Rican plant? I want to fill up his Prius like a cream horn.

Letter from Marcie, sophomore year

I'll ship you a case of it. Remember to wear gloves and don't leave fingerprints. And burn this letter. Morons like that don't realize a good teacher teaches you how to think for yourself. Their job isn't to impose their own agenda.

Ben's reply

Chapter Seven

❦

When Marcie walked past Janet's desk, she could tell from her expression that the admin was surprised to see her. So he'd told Janet she wasn't coming in.

"I don't know how long I'll be here," she said. "I'm just checking on a few things."

Janet gave her a handful of pink message slips. "He's on a conference call right now in Matt's office. They'll probably be in there for an hour or so."

Good. Maybe her stomach would move down from her throat and back into its proper area by then. All she'd been able to handle were those eggs. Jon had packed up the leftover toast, tucking it into a sandwich bag with a small jar of the jam. He'd suggested she eat some of that later. A nurturing Dom. He and Rachel were perfect for one another.

Marcie pulled out the document she'd been unable to finish yesterday and got to work. Her concentration was for shit, though, so she stopped to return some of the messages. She answered the calls on her feet because her ass still hurt enough to make sitting uncomfortable. But other symptoms concerned her more. Remembering the concern in Jon's eyes as he held her, she wondered at it herself, how shaky she felt today. Her nerves were on high alert, her body vibrating like a hummingbird. She did carry a personal massager in her purse. Maybe she should take the edge off?

That vibrator stays in the nightstand drawer until I say otherwise. She shivered deliciously at the memory, the look on his face as he issued the order. He kept switching between taking over all her decisions, and wanting to cut her loose. It gave her hope and drove her crazy at once.

Her intercom buzzed. Janet. "Yes?" Marcie asked.

"Mr. O'Callahan says to use the pillow on the top shelf of his closet."

"Did you tell him I was here?"

"No, I did not."

"Jon told him?"

"Mr. Forte isn't in the meeting." Janet's tone suggested she would very quickly tire of twenty questions. Truth, the woman was kind of scary, so Marcie thanked her and clicked off. How had he known? Was he pissed? Had she messed things up?

"Stop it, Marcie," she muttered. "Get a grip."

Going into his office, she found the pillow on the top shelf. When she brought it down, she couldn't help herself. She pressed it to her face, inhaling his scent. She imagined him using it, the long, powerful body stretched out on the office couch. He'd kick off his shoes, probably shrug out of his shirt, and then flop down, one arm casually hooked over his head, studying the ceiling as he ran through the details of whatever had kept him late enough to decide to sleep here.

Now she visualized herself curled against his body, her head propped into the valley created by that raised arm. Her fingers would play with the light mat of hair across his chest as she gazed up into that strong face. Those beautiful green eyes would shift to her, studying her from such a relaxed position. She imagined waking up together. They could pull all-nighters together, because of course she'd love to work as part of his staff, his investigator.

She wrapped her arms around the pillow, hugging it to her. Folding herself down on the couch, she rested on her hip so she didn't aggravate her abused buttocks. Just a quick second to lie here, where he had been. He didn't sleep long hours, she was sure. There was such incredible energy to him.

She remembered the way he'd played with the younger kids on the evenings or weekends when they all got together. He was tireless, wrestling with Nate, racing the girls on their bikes, hauling the younger ones around on his shoulders in the pool. Some of her most intense early masturbating fantasies had to do with the way his broad chest and shoulders looked with beads of water rolling down them. The way the sun played across the dark silken hair that arrowed down to his waist.

He wore those modest oversized shorts that most guys did for a swimsuit, but she preferred to imagine him in far more fitted swim trunks. Ones that would cling to his ass and groin like a second skin when he hefted himself easily out of the pool on strong arms, one of her siblings clinging to his back.

If he was lying behind her now, she'd feel the hard planes of his body, that impressive groin pressed up against her ass. He'd cup her breast, play with the piercing jewelry as he dozed and she got more aroused, until she was squirming against him, rubbing against his cock, waking him up on several levels. Of course he'd probably grumble at her for disturbing his rest, threaten to punish her. Push her down under the blanket so she had to service his morning erection. Maybe he'd let her use her hands, to cup his muscular ass, stroke the taut lines of his thighs.

Her lids were drooping. She really had slept poorly last night. She needed to get up, finish that work. Hold it all together, even though she was afraid everything was falling apart. She was just so tired... If she had a nap, she'd be better off. She wasn't going to give up, even if she had to go through a hundred days like the last two. Which would technically be two hundred days...

* * * * *

"It's going to be a pain in the ass."

"Yeah, yeah, bitch, bitch. Stop being such a little girl about it. Think how much better production will be after the turnover."

"We'll lose about a million during the outage."

"You could pull a million out of your ass right now. This will triple our investment in two years."

Slowly, she surfaced. Where was... Oh holy hell, she'd fallen asleep on the couch, apparently some time ago, because Ben was back in his office. With at least Peter and Matt, the two who'd been arguing with him. Was Lucas in here? She froze, wondering if she should just keep her eyes shut and hope they hadn't noticed her. Yeah, that was likely. From the direction of Peter's voice, he was in the chair that faced the couch.

She'd fallen asleep like a sleepy, trusting child, her nose nestled in his pillow, arms wrapped around it like she'd wrap them around him, never wanting to let him go. God, she was like a Taylor Swift song, probably *not* the picture of mature woman at the moment. If they were looking at her, they'd know she was awake, because she was turning the color of a tomato.

The hell with it. She opened her eyes. Peter was actually standing, leaning on the wall behind the chair, all that restless energy too out front to be contained for long in a chair. Though he'd retired from the National Guard to be here for Dana, he still looked like he should be carrying an assault rifle, ready to lead a unit into a firefight. He was built like a muscular tank, and to the delight of every woman who met him, he was the one K&A man who usually wore khakis or dress jeans and form-fitting heavy weight tees that emphasized that physique. Since he oversaw a lot of the plant operations, the casual look was more appropriate for him.

Matt was as intimidating and riveting as ever in his dark suit, polished shoes. He was in what Marcie privately called his raptor pose. Though he appeared relaxed, ankle on the opposite knee, hands loose on the chair arms, there was something about the position of his head, the focus of the dark eyes, that suggested he was about to swoop down five hundred feet and pluck a hapless field mouse out of a dense meadow.

Ben had his chair pushed back with one foot against the edge of the desk. He was tapping a pen against the arm. None of them were looking toward her, but they all realized she was here. They hadn't woken her. It was as if her being in Ben's office made her part of his other belongings. She wondered how Lucas would feel about that. Had he already been here? Seen her?

"I have something else to handle now," Ben said, tilting his head in her direction. "Are we done?"

"Yeah. Hey, don't forget next Friday's benefit." Peter pushed off the wall. "Black tie. Stale finger foods, open checkbook. The girls are really looking forward to it."

Today was Thursday. Were they anticipating him being gone for the next seven days, such that Peter was mentioning it now? She held her tongue, though cold dread filled her stomach. Had she known him well enough to anticipate his escape out of town?

Then Peter gave him a grin. "It will take you that long to get some unlucky woman to agree to be your date."

"I'll ask your wife," Ben said dryly. "You know she'll choose me."

"Yeah. Keep it up, I'll wrap your oversized appendage around your throat and choke you with it."

"Don't you wish yours was long enough to do that?"

"Gentlemen," Matt warned in a mild voice. She knew he was a stickler about talking crude around women, at least in normal conversation. The others followed the same code, though she'd always noticed Ben strayed outside the lines more than the rest.

Through Cass, she knew he'd lived on the streets as a kid. Maybe that was why he slipped in the manners department more often, though she'd never seen Ben treat the K&A women with anything but the greatest respect. That street experience probably contributed to his versatility as a lawyer, but he'd have made a good investigator as well, because he could easily adopt different personas. He'd delighted her siblings with his command of accents. Cajun, Irish, Midwestern, New England. What she found interesting was how the accents would show up unconsciously when his moods changed, as if the situation called forth that particular personality.

When Matt rose and he and Peter headed toward the door, neither of them looked toward her, even though she pushed up on one elbow. Same situation as at Jon's. She was Ben's, a submissive waiting on a Master's attention, and therefore not to be acknowledged by the other Doms in the room unless it was part of the plan. Given her immediate reaction to that thought, a nap hadn't helped settle her as much as she expected.

"Remember what we talked about."

Jon *was* in the room, standing by the door. He was addressing Ben, holding his gaze. Ben inclined his head, his mouth tight. "I'll handle it the way I see fit."

"Just be sure you handle it."

Okay, she'd never heard Jon with that edge. Ben registered the challenge, eyes turning into shards of glass. "I said I would. Back off."

Jon nodded, his blue eyes just as cool. Then he turned, pulling the door closed after him.

She wasn't sure what to say. She was pretty sure that had to do with her, but she didn't know what corner of the sheet to grasp to straighten it out. Surely Jon wouldn't have told Ben what they talked about? Yes, of course he would. From her tea-party eavesdropping, she knew it caused Cass, Dana, Savannah and Rachel various levels of frustration. The well-being of their women came first, over and above issues of privacy, and all of the guys were hugely overprotective.

The Knights of the Board Room was what they'd been dubbed by a columnist, years ago, and though the guys would roll their eyes if anyone brought it up, it fit. It was as much about their old-fashioned code of chivalry as it was about their behavior in business and charitable circles.

Ben turned his chair then. She couldn't read his countenance, but he rose, came to the couch, dropped to his heels next to it. His gaze covered her face, the open neck of the pink blouse, following the lines of her body down to the tailored skirt. As his gaze came back to hers, she was warmer all over, and more flustered.

"I told you not to come here today. Why did you?"

"Because you told me I had twenty strikes coming, and you only gave me eleven. So I still owe you nine."

His lips tugged, a sexy half-smile, but as he studied her, the smile thinned. "That was what you meant by unfinished work."

She nodded. "That, and that last document I didn't complete."

Ben sighed. He put his hand on her hip, and before she could anticipate him, he'd slid those capable fingers to her right buttock, cupping it firmly. When she flinched, his eyes darkened. "I'm a sadist, Marcie," he said softly. "But not that kind." His touch eased and he stroked her curves, giving her body another glance. "You have no idea what you look like, sleeping on my couch, your neckline showing that lace edge of your bra, your killer legs curved up. All this beautiful hair." His other hand threaded through it, cupping her face. "Come on, get up. I'm taking you out for a beignet."

"Café du Monde?" Her expression brightened. She loved the view of Jackson Square, the artists, the musicians and impromptu performances.

"Maybe another day. I want a good beignet, one where the dough is still handmade each day, not squirted out of a mass-production tube and served in a corral with a dirty floor and wall-to-wall tourists."

"Ouch. I love it there."

"Well, you're young and stupid."

"Better than old and grumpy."

He gave her a pinch that made her yelp. "On your feet and leave your purse. I'm paying."

She rolled her eyes. "You never let anyone treat you."

"We split the check all the time. Just not with women."

"Sexist pig."

"Oink, oink."

He took her to Café Beignet, which was a few blocks off Jackson Square, but she had to admit it was more intimate and relaxed, and the beignets melted in the mouth. They enjoyed them first, though he made her order a lunch she was sure she wouldn't finish. Everyone seemed determined to make her eat.

As she finished off the last of the beignet, she was aware of his silent regard. She was licking the sugar off her fingers, because no one could resist doing that with a good beignet. She wished he'd let her clean his fingers with her mouth. She'd take them in deep, a clear reminder of what he'd let her do for him last night. The hinge of her jaw was sore and all she wanted was to do it for him again.

Reaching across the table, he caught her wrist. Bringing her fingers to *his* mouth, he sucked the remaining sugar off, sending electricity crackling all the way from her wrist pulse to her toes, awakening every major erogenous center in between.

When he was done, she had that queer little shake happening again. She couldn't stop it. "Ben..."

"Ssshh." He reached out, slid his knuckles over her temple. "Easy. Just breathe."

"I-I don't know why I k-keep doing that."

"I do. Last night was your first time, wasn't it?"

When she would have looked away, his grip tightened. "Marcie, any question I ask, you'll answer, and you won't lie to me. Not now, not ever. You understand?"

She managed a nod, though her teeth started to chatter. "Damn it..."

"Focus on me, what I want. Answer."

"Yes." She met his eyes, gripped their steadying influence, so her voice could stop quivering as much. "I've been to clubs, like I said. I just watched. I did a lot of Internet surfing." Plus enough fantasizing to launch an adult Disney World.

"Did you go to the clubs alone?"

"I took one of my friends with me the first time. She isn't into the scene, but I thought she was okay with me being that way, and would go with me to make it safer. She didn't like how...mesmerized I was by it. It kind of freaked her out. After that, she pulled away from me, and I became more careful about who saw that side of me."

"You went alone after that?"

"Only a few times. They were safe places, classy clubs. Then when I was in New York, Lucas' friend, Marcus Stanton, took me fairly often. He went as a chaperone," she added. "He's a great Master, but he's utterly devoted to Thomas. I got to watch them have a session, hand him things. I'm not stupid, Ben."

His jaw eased a fraction. "No, but you're reckless as hell."

"That's the pot calling the kettle black. What do you call that death trap you drive?"

"A high-performance driving machine, an engineering piece of art."

"An expensive metal phallus." She snorted. He was still holding her wrist, playing with her fingers, and it was extremely distracting. She hoped he never stopped. "So are you going to take me to a club?"

"Nag, nag, nag." He sighed, sat back.

"As my mentor," she persisted. "You can show me how the deeper stuff works. We're already...I mean, I could go as your sub-in-training. You could help me."

Ben regarded her with those sharp green eyes. "Marcie, do you think you can con me?"

"No."

Just that steady look, an unspoken correction, and butterflies swarmed. "No, sir."

He inclined his head. "I'm willing to give you a short mentoring period. If you're using it to get something more from me, you're setting yourself up for heartbreak. I've no intention of taking things beyond that."

"Why not?" She met that stare dead on now. "Am I not good enough for you?"

"I'm not looking for that. Not with you."

In her lap, her hands curled into fists. "Ben, do you think you can con *me*?"

He leaned forward. Something dark moved in his expression, something more than a little bit scary, but there were things that scared her far worse than pissing Ben off.

"Do I have to rip your fucking heart from your chest to prove my point, Marcie? Do I have to break you?"

"You can't. You won't. Give it your best shot." He could probably hear the rabbit thumping of her heart, but she'd have a full-scale cardiac arrest before she'd back down. "It's all bullshit," she said quietly. "Everyone's looking for *that*. You'd walk through Hell for me, for Cassandra, for every member of your family. But I'm not the one afraid of surrendering myself fully. You are."

That darkness became something full blown, something ugly, lonely and violent. Then it was gone, the smooth lawyer back in place. It was a startling transformation, one that made her more uncomfortable than she wanted to admit.

He sat back now, picked up his beer. "We'll see about that," he said casually. "Because if you want me to mentor you, full surrender is what I'm going to demand. As well as full honesty. How did you know how to do what you did last night? You weren't new to it." Something deadly entered his gaze again, only this time it had an erotic edge to it. "Who taught you to take a dick that size down your throat, in your ass?"

Thank God they were in a quiet corner. He'd spoken in a low voice, but some words just had a way of carrying. She kept her gaze fastened on his, sure she'd be mortified into speechlessness if any heads turned.

"There was no who, not exactly. I went to chat rooms, asked questions. Talked to Thomas because…" She stopped. She was pretty forward, but she wasn't sure she could finish that statement.

"Because when you were in the club you noticed Marcus is pretty good sized."

161

"Yes." She pressed her lips into a line. "I also talked to Dana."

"Excuse me?"

"Well, Dana...she's seen you. I mean, not seen you, since she's blind, but her tactile senses..."

Despite Ben's black cloud expression, she suddenly had to fight against a laugh, remembering some of Dana's more colorful descriptions. "Before that, I eavesdropped a lot. All of them—Dana, Rachel, Cass and Savannah—have been meeting for third Sunday tea at Cassandra's house since they came into your lives."

Her cheeks colored. "So I practiced. Mostly on inanimate objects."

Maybe it was best if he didn't ask further questions. If CSI had seen the back of her dorm closet they would have profiled her as a full-blown stalker. That was where she hid all her notes, pictures, articles and other data on him—particularly those letters. She'd run copies of them so she could make notes, underline certain parts. Yeah, that would seem a little stalker-crazy.

Except she knew her prey. If she wanted him, she had to come prepared. He was the first investigation she'd ever undertaken, and the longest she'd pursued. She knew how wrong it was, a submissive stalking a Master, but she hadn't known how else to go about it.

If she could crack Ben O'Callahan, get him to claim her for his own, everything else would be a cinch. She could uncover secrets that would bring down governments. Or build new ones.

He could look at her like she was a stalker—which was sort of what he was doing now—but she knew she wasn't. The letters gave her confidence, the full picture. At a key point, she'd known she had his heart, no matter that he was trying to convince her that its weight in her hands was an illusion.

"You'll stay at my Garden District place tonight," he said, startling her. "I'm taking the day off tomorrow. We'll spend the day preparing you, then we'll go to Progeny in the evening. And that's it."

Her mind raced over the possibilities. She couldn't believe he'd agreed to the club, let alone an overnight at his house. "You want me to stay with you?"

"Don't read too much into it," he said bluntly. "I've decided you can't be trusted on your own until this is resolved."

That pricked her ire a little, but she pushed it down. "I think I can probably handle one night at your place," she said lightly.

In point of fact, she could cartwheel from Royal Street all the way to his house. Or, more appropriately, walk on her knees…if he required that.

* * * * *

They returned to work and finished out the day, though Ben made her use that pillow while she completed the paperwork for him. While she was on her best behavior, infallibly professional, her blood was simmering below the surface every time she stole a look at him. Working at his desk, moving around the office talking on his hands-free, interacting with the others as they came in and out for different things. She would be spending the night at Ben's. The idea of it, of what might happen, made her flushed and high strung, though she did her best to cover it.

When the day was over, instead of taking his car, they took the trolley. Marcie had never appreciated how narrow the wooden two-seat bench was. Ben necessarily stretched a long arm across the back, pressing her against his side, his thigh against her leg as they clattered along the track from downtown. Though she'd grown up in Baton Rouge, she was well acquainted with New Orleans. Still, it had been awhile since she was here.

She enjoyed recalling the landmarks as they went along, the crush of people wandering Canal Street, that view streamlining into St. Charles' never-ending offering of restaurants. Each had a unique flair, like bohemian middle-aged women, old enough to be comfortable and confident in their skin, yet young enough to exude color and style. As they passed through the religious school district, she saw a few students still on the grounds in their uniforms of crisp white shirts and navy pants or skirts.

Ben had them get off at Audubon Park to join the joggers and cyclists along the walkways there. In the quiet nooks where statues and gazebos sat by the water, they occasionally glimpsed homeless people camped, absorbing the tranquility the way they were. Ben guided her hand into the crook of his elbow, and they strolled that way. She imagined them doing it a hundred years ago, her in petticoats and a stylish hat, him in a suit that wouldn't differ too much from what he wore now, at least in cut and style. The man did know how to dress.

"Your work today impressed me," Ben said. "The Kelly-Bergerson brief was pretty much perfect. I've had rookie lawyers serving under me who don't have your command of the terminology."

She warmed to the praise. "I'm good at business languages. My roommate at college was pre-med. To help her memorize, I'd string together her medical terms in a dirty way. Want to hear?"

Ben quirked a brow at her. "Is your mind always in the gutter?"

"No more than yours. Besides, it was for a good cause, to help her become a better doctor." Marcie nodded to a shirtless jogger who passed them. "His rectus abdominis is well defined, but his external obliques still need work. Though his rectus femoris just invites the tongue."

His gaze glinted. "Careful, there."

Marcie freed her hands to clasp them together, sighing with dramatic effect. "His phalanges gripped her pes anserinus to pry them apart. Pushing his rectus femoris into her gluetus maximus, her pubic symphysis was pinned against the bed. He forced his pollicis into her suboccipitals, pressing her frontal bone into the mattress."

"I don't think romance fiction has anything to worry about from you."

She sniffed. "I might open up a whole new field. Doctors reading romance."

"I think they'd prefer the layman terms. Otherwise, it would be a busman's holiday."

When they left the park, they strolled along the broken sidewalks that led them into the residential areas. Tilting her head back, she studied the thick waterfall of colorful beads hanging from the oaks, competing with the Spanish moss. "I love that they let these stay in the trees." Reaching up, she tried to snag a pretty silver strand, but she was too short. She gave a valiant hop, putting all her effort into it, and her fingertips brushed it. "Shoot."

"Here, brat. Little tease." He bent, wrapped his arms beneath her buttocks and boosted her up his body to give her the extra head of height she needed. Marcie caught the beads, untangled them and drew down two, a silver and a shiny green. She was hyper-conscious of his arms around her, the way her mound pressed into his abdomen. When she looked down, bracing her hands on his shoulders, she could tell he wasn't unaffected either. He let her slide down his body but kept her close until she rested between his feet. His hands adjusted downward, way low on her waist, curling over the tops of her buttocks, pinching the folds of her skirt between his fingertips.

"I could have done it with a few more jumps," she defended herself. "It's just about building momentum. But your help was appreciated."

"Hmm." He stared down at her, and the unfathomable look quieted her. Dropping the silver strand over her head, she put the green on him. Her fingers slipped over his hair, touched his neck and ears, rested on his shoulders when she was done, her thumbs touching his throat because he'd loosened his tie, unbuttoned the collar. Because he didn't say not to do it, she stroked that small expanse of skin, scratched it with her nail.

His gaze heated, his hands dropping to take a firm hold of her ass, kneading, no matter the passing cars or sidewalk pedestrians. There weren't so many of those here, but the occasional matronly dog walker could make her more self-conscious than the anonymity and colorful nature of a big Canal Street crowd.

It was exactly why he did it. She knew it was a test. So she didn't look around, didn't squirm away. Fortunately, the passing hours and his and Rachel's combined tending had made her buttocks far less sore. "I'm going to do something now," he said. "As I'm doing it, you tell me what goes through that imaginative brain of yours."

Lowering his head, he nudged hers to the side with the touch of his mouth on her temple. Turning her face toward his broad shoulder, pressing her nose into the smooth line of his dress shirt over his pectoral, she shuddered as his mouth landed on the juncture of her throat and shoulder. He bit her there, a controlled motion, teeth slowly depressing as his tongue stroked her. Her breath shortened, and she almost forgot to do what he'd told her to do.

"You're winding a rope wrap from below my knees to my ankles." Her trembling increased as the pressure did, the clamp of the bite. "You do the same to my arms, from wrists to elbows, behind my back. My breasts...they're thrust way out because of that. So you do a binding there as well, one rope above, one below, a crossed knot in the middle, and then you attach that to the arm wrap. You put me over your shoulder, completely helpless. You take me to a sofa, bend me over the arm and…"

He relaxed his jaw, then started that depression again, interfering with her ability to think. His fingers were kneading her ass in rhythmic squeezes, and she was leaned into him, pressing her mound harder against him, sensation clenching in her pussy.

"Say it, Marcie. Say it the way you know I want to hear it."

"You'd fuck me in the ass until I was screaming to come, biting the cushions."

"Do I let you, or make you suffer? Make you beg?"

She smiled, though her fingers were digging into his biceps, holding on. God, how did he do this so well? "I'd come at your command, right now," she whispered.

"It takes awhile for a sub to learn how to do that. Come at her Master's command."

"Not if she's been practicing for seven years."

He stilled. She cursed herself for reminding him of that time when she was too young for him, since it underlined his belief that she was still too young for him. But it was true. In her fantasies, she'd work herself up with fingers or vibrator, but she wouldn't come, not until he was standing in her mind, real and strong and tall, commanding her to do so.

"I think we'll test that." He lifted his head then, brushing the abused area with his mouth before he adjusted her blouse back over it. He tweaked the green beads on his neck. "Why green?"

"They match your eyes. Sort of. They're sparkly and your eyes have fire, especially right now." She looked up into his face, her own flushed, and her eyes pretty much on fire as well, she was sure. "I want to do that for you. I want to come for you."

"You can tell me what you want, Marcie, but I run things, not you. You understand?"

"Yes, Ma—sir." She wouldn't mess it up, would play the game the way he wanted to play it, even if that made her dishonest.

His eyes narrowed, but he slid an arm around her, resuming their walk.

"So you've become a homeowner since I've been gone," she teased him. "An apartment in the Warehouse District *and* a house in the Garden District. When I was in high school, you were living in hotels."

He shrugged. "A hotel has concierge and maid service, dry cleaning. Choose one within walking distance to a good breakfast and dinner place, and you're all set. But property is a good investment."

"So why not rent them out and keep living in the hotels?"

"There are times I have the desire for privacy." He gave her an appraising look that sent heat washing over her.

"I figured you bought them so you could have a fully stocked kitchen."

He shrugged. "Not as important as it used to be."

He'd said he still brought a dish to the monthly dinners with the whole K&A family. But when she was in high school, he'd made her family meals all the time, taught any of the kids to cook who wanted to learn. Since Marcie had a driver's license, she was in charge of grocery shopping after school. He'd text her cell, instructing her on what he needed and expecting her to have it waiting for him at the house when he arrived after work.

Watching him cook was like everything else about him. A visual feast. He'd go through the groceries she bought, examine all of them carefully. He'd taught her how to pick out something at the right freshness, the brands that were better quality than others. He teased her, giving her a hard time if she brought him the wrong stuff. He'd affect a French accent, throwing up his hands and exclaiming, "I cannot work in theez coundiseeons..." In truth, the man could make an awesome meal out of a bag of flour and a tin can of sardines.

He'd taught her to cook the basics, but she'd been hopeless when it came to anything more complex. A truly great cook had an intimate relationship with the ingredients, understanding flavors and textures in a wandering, intuitive way she was far too literal and goal-oriented to ever comprehend. She preferred to provide the artist the supplies, watch him work and enjoy the fruits of his labor.

Now he said a kitchen "wasn't as important as it used to be". From that tightening around his mouth, she could tell they were getting into a tricky area. Not wanting to lose ground, she changed direction. "It's expensive, eating out all the time. Until Lucas married Cass, we only did it on really special occasions."

"Well, taking all of you out for a meal was like taking out an army of meerkats. You can hardly blame her."

"*We* were very good," she protested. "You were the one asked to leave the McDonald's play area for getting too aggressive."

"Not my fault those five-year-olds couldn't handle a little competition. That's what's wrong with America these days. Raising a bunch of pansies who don't want to win."

She pinched his side, but was gratified when he brought her closer. She threaded her arm around his waist, under his jacket, and he didn't discourage her. It was easier to walk that way, after all. His body was a sinuous ripple of motion under the shirt as he walked. She curled her fingers over his belt, held on.

"Speaking of dinner, let's get some before we head for the house." He gestured to a restaurant across the street. "Come on."

He kept pressure on her waist, holding her still until he was okay with their clearance, then they crossed the street.

She'd known how to cross the street on her own for some time, of course, but it didn't offend her. In truth, such gestures could be devastating to a woman's senses. All the more because Ben was oblivious to their potency. From watching Cass and the others, she'd learned it wasn't about denigrating a woman's independence. It had nothing to do with the men's opinion of female capability, but everything to do with their absolute conviction that a man's role was to protect and cherish.

The restaurant was one she hadn't tried before, an elegant place with full-length white table cloths, candlelight. The walls were pre-twentieth-century brick covered with artwork by local talent, and the place had the smell that the old, historic buildings did. A jazz band was jamming in the corner, filling the place with music. Ben had the maître d' show them to the upstairs level and a corner table on the balcony, though the round table could seat six. They could hear the music vibrating through their feet and drifting up the wide staircase, without their conversation being overpowered by it.

"If Noah's working tonight, I want him as our server," Ben told the maître d'.

"Of course, Mr. O'Callahan."

Ben held out the chair that was tucked in the corner, touching her shoulders briefly before he took his own seat next to her. "Any allergies?" he asked as the man disappeared down the stairs.

She shook her head. When she would have opened her menu, Ben took it away, sliding it under his own. "Take off your panties," he said.

Just like that, he took the reins, told her they were now Master and slave. Or Mentor and sub-in-training—to him. Either way, her body responded accordingly, with aching need and anxiety fluttering in her belly. Though it was difficult to do without rising, she worked the panties off under the snug skirt.

"Hand them to me. No balling them up."

No one was up here, but he'd anticipated her self-consciousness. There were people wandering the street below the balcony, looking up to study the diners. As attractive as Ben was, he'd probably get his share of looks. He wanted to see if she'd quake. Instead, steeling herself to be whatever he required, she hung them on one finger, let them dangle provocatively and extended them to him. His lips twisted, and he took them from her. Her face colored as he raised them to his lips, his nostrils flaring, taking in her heated scent. "These are wet. Who's been making you wet?"

"You. Only you."

"You sure that jogger's femoris didn't do it for you?" His tone was serious, despite the flash of humor. But either way, she'd give him no less than honesty. Not when he was completely in command like this.

"Yes sir. You made me wet."

"Hmm. I want your skirt up around your waist, your bare ass on the chair. Spread your knees out and hook your ankles around the chair legs to keep them that way. Tell me if the position becomes physically uncomfortable."

The reason he'd put her in the corner seat became obvious, since he was flanking her on one side, and the balcony rail and a profusion of potted plants were on the other. The table cloth was floor length, so it was pooled over her lap. But if the waiter moved around the table to grate pepper over her salad or refill her drink, he might see her skirt up, bare ass pressed to the chair's wooden surface.

Ben watched her follow his direction. "Might teach you to wear a looser skirt to work next time."

"Then whose ass would you stare at? Janet's? Even you're not that brave." She scraped the chair legs across the metal floor as she wiggled and managed it. The wooden seat reminded her of last night's punishment but, thanks to Rachel's balm, she could make full contact with it.

"Center yourself between two of the chair slats. I want your cunt right over an opening so you can feel the air flow." It was impossible to discern what he was thinking, his face impassive, voice even. Whereas she was getting more flustered with every word he spoke.

When she was in the proscribed position, her legs were spread, ankles hooked on the chair legs as he required, pussy exposed to the cool night air. Reaching out, he slipped the next button of her blouse so he had a better view of her breasts, cradled in lace. He stroked a finger over the top of the right one. *Oh God.* She had a feeling those two words were going to go through her mind quite a bit tonight, no matter how much trouble it gave her with the Higher Power. Hopefully, He understood. He'd made Ben, after all.

"Hold the chair sides by your thighs unless I tell you otherwise." He tucked the panties into his pocket, unhurried, even as their waiter topped the stairs. Another second and he would have seen what Ben held.

Noah was a Goth, complete with eyeliner and tongue stud. He wore the white shirt and slacks the restaurant required, but the tie was a pencil-thin black silk, the tack a tiny skull and crossbones. His hair was long and smooth, tied back from a slim, well-sculpted face. With all that and his thin, sensual lips, he made her think of a young vampire.

When he saw Ben, he smiled with genuine pleasure. "It's great to see you, Mr. O'Callahan." He gave Marcie a courteous nod, a quick appraisal that was flattering but not insulting, then cocked a brow at Ben. "You're not classy enough for this one. Is she slumming tonight?"

"There goes your tip," Ben said dryly. "I'll take the grilled porterhouse. She'll have the seared shrimp, and start us off with the goat-cheese salads." He added a few more instructions related to the cooking of the meat and the spices that would be used. He didn't ask Marcie her preferences, and of course she wasn't sure she could have made an intelligent response, regardless.

Her exposed sex was being teased by a rippling breeze moving over the balcony and coming up from the first level, filtering through the slim seams of the metal flooring, which allowed rainwater to flow out. Her breasts weren't graphically exposed, but as he bent to retrieve the menus, Noah's gaze slid briefly over the curves.

"We'll have those drinks and salads brought right back up, Mr. O'Callahan."

Ben nodded. As the waiter headed back down the stairs, he stretched his arm over the back of her chair, touched her nape. "Keep your back straight, Marcie."

She hadn't realized she'd hunched a little under Noah's perusal. She sent herself a mental slap for that one, tossing her hair back and giving Ben a smile as she made sure those breasts stood out high and proud for her Master. Then she almost swallowed her tongue as he put his other elbow on the table and traced a finger along the bra edge again, only this time he dipped into the cup, rubbed over her nipple. It was already puckered and eager. She pushed her ass harder into the chair, against the dull cut of those slats. It wanted to rise up, to communicate the throbbing desire from her pussy with a shameless undulation.

"Stay still. I expect you to behave, act like a good girl, even if you are a brazen slut."

"You make me into one." She locked everything down, trying to obey. "Like Lucas said, you're a corrupting influence."

His heavy-lidded green eyes were close, his firm mouth. "Bullshit. That pussy of yours is greedy for cock."

Your cock. But she didn't say it, knowing not to spar with him in this realm. When his hand dropped beneath the table's edge, she almost came off the chair as he calmly fingered her clit, slipping down to stroke the wetness of the labia. "Tilt your hips so I can reach your cunt."

She did, clenching the sides of the chair as he slid a finger in her, then two, then—holy God—three.

"So fucking wet," he rumbled in her ear, brushing his mouth beneath it, against her pounding pulse. "Tonight I'm going to put you on your knees. You're going to suck me off, and when I'm about to come, you're going to turn around, put your forehead to the floor, and I'll fuck your ass. I may not ever let you come. Keep you this fucking desperate to please me."

"Yes sir." She whispered it, closing her eyes as he withdrew his touch, then pushed in again, emulating what his cock could do there. Because she was tight and it was a narrow angle, it made it all the more excruciating.

Sliding his fingers free, he brought them to her mouth. She licked herself off them. Without prompting, she picked up her napkin, finished wiping them off using some of the water from her water glass. It wouldn't do for her Master to have sticky fingers while he tried to eat.

"An anticipatory sub. Sometimes that can get you into trouble."

She paused, remembering her thoughts about that last night. Her fingers lay on his. "Does taking care of you when you need it get me in trouble?"

"No. Not right now." As his eyes flickered with some unfathomable emotion, she returned her hands to the sides of her chair. Noah came back with their goat-cheese salads, arranged on attractive teal-blue square plates. When he poured their wine, she noted Ben stopped him when her glass was no more than a third full. She didn't hold alcohol well, was pretty much loose as a sun-warmed snake after two glasses. Given the night that was ahead of her, that might not be a bad idea, but with Ben and their battle of wills, she needed all her wits around her. And it was obvious Ben intended her to feel the full edge of anything he did to her.

"Thank you, Noah." Ben nodded. "I'd like an extra service, please."

"Anything, Mr. O'Callahan."

Ben turned his attention to Marcie. Instinct had her lowering her gaze instead of locking with his. When his next words came, she was glad for it.

"I want you to go down on my companion here, under the tablecloth. If she comes within three minutes, there's a hundred-dollar tip in it for you."

She was pretty certain she paled and flushed at once, a medical impossibility, but Ben leaned in, his hand sliding under her hair to tighten on her neck. "We'll see if you come on a Master's command, or if you're a mindless slut, just as I suspect. And when you come," he drew closer, his breath teasing her lips, her cheek, "I expect you to scream. Hold nothing back. The fact we're in public doesn't matter. Only what I desire does."

Okay, she'd never done anything like this. Sure, she'd fantasized about exhibitionism, but the reality was way different. As it moved into evening, the people on the sidewalks below were turning into larger groups. More patrons would eventually be brought out onto the balcony, given that it was a really nice night. If she wanted to stop, if it was too much, she was pretty sure Ben would stop, but that would mean she'd backed down. His usual subs would do a strip tease in the middle of Jackson Square if he commanded it.

Her throat was dry, so it came out as a whisper. "Yes sir."

When Ben gave him a nod, Noah put the tray on the adjacent table. With a graceful movement of lean male strength, he squatted and disappeared fully beneath their round table. When his hands touched her spread knees, Marcie tensed, she couldn't help it. She heard a muttered, reverent, "Jesus, she's got a gorgeous pussy," and clutched the chair, a tiny sound of protest coming from her throat.

"Ben…"

"Hold on, Noah." Ben was studying her face. His fingers on her nape were stroking. "Give her a moment."

"Not a problem." Noah's voice was muffled as his mouth brushed her inner thigh, a gentle reassurance. His fingers slid down her calf, more calming caresses.

Unless this was a hard limit for her, it was obvious Ben was going to proceed with it, but he was giving her time. Plus an unexpected reassurance. "I wouldn't allow anyone to touch you whom I didn't trust," he said, his fingers tightening on the back of her neck.

"I know." It was just so much, so fast. But she could handle it. She leaned her face into his hand, wished he would keep touching her. But Ben was a ruthless Master, she knew that. As soon as he could tell she was ready, he settled back in his chair, picking up his wine. Ready for the show he'd orchestrated.

"Proceed, Noah. Three minutes."

It took everything she had not to whip her legs out from behind the chair legs and close them, but Noah helped. He settled his grip on her quivering thighs, steadying and holding them open at once, and then he went right to the heart of the matter. She sucked in a breath, biting down on her lip. Holy God...the tongue stud vibrated. He played over her pussy lips with it, letting her get used to the feel of it, tickling her a little so she had to work hard not to squirm, and then he brought it right to her clit.

She sucked in a breath. He knew his business, working it against her in tiny movements that had her already aroused body rocketing up a ramp, set to take off and explode. She saw Ben's attention on her exposed breasts, the way they were vibrating with that compressed movement. She couldn't move, couldn't move, but oh God, she wanted to rise up, grind her pussy in Noah's face, throw her head back against the chair. But her Master didn't tell her she could come. Three minutes, three minutes.

Three minutes was an eternity when she couldn't count the seconds. Ben had a watch but it was under the cuff of his sleeve. She had no doubt he was counting it down in his head like a freaking NASA computer.

I serve my Master, I serve him, I serve you...

She didn't realize she was whispering it until she saw Ben's eyes darken, his mouth tighten. She was fighting with all she had against the orgasm. Noah was incredibly insistent. It was a battle of mind over matter. She imagined her clit encased in stone, all those sensations ricocheting against the inside, unable to be released, so she was imprisoned in this frenzy of need. Her fingernails cut into the chair, her thighs shaking under Noah's hands so that the chair made staccato noises on the metal balcony floor.

"I serve you...please, Master...let me come for you..."

Ben set down his wine, picked up his fork, took a bite of the salad, chewed. He necessarily took his eyes from her for the moment he had to do that, but then he studied her with a detachment that was anything but. His whole focus was on her, a heated intensity coming from him that vibrated against her body like that tongue stud. He continued to eat the salad, obviously considering the taste and texture as he monitored her reactions. The Knights were the only men in the world she knew who could multi-task, and they did it as if Lucifer himself had given them the ability.

She was whimpering, her whole body making tiny little jerks. Her nipples were so hard she could feel the way they stabbed the inside of her bra, constricting the barbell piercings so they added to the sensation.

Noah got creative, doing swirls and flicks, kneading the inside of her thighs, his thumbs tracing the crease of her buttocks beneath her pussy. It was too much...she couldn't hold on, yes she could. She would. She fiercely concentrated on all those masturbating fantasies, where she'd made herself wait longer and longer, until Ben's imagined command to release.

Ben slid the fork from his lips. His mouth was glistening from the oil of the salad, and she wanted to suck on that. Instead, he shifted forward. Plucking the blouse away from her body, he eased the fork into the bra cup, brought it over the nipple and pressed down, caging it behind those tines. She couldn't hold on any more. Fuck...

"Come for me, Marcie. Come now."

She would have screamed to raise the dead throughout New Orleans, she trusted him that much, wanted to surrender to him that much, but as she opened her mouth to do so, Ben covered it with his. He dropped the fork, cupped her head in one hand, his tight hold making her keep her position, bound by his will. She screamed into his mouth, shuddering, convulsing as Noah kept working her, holding her open with those surprisingly strong hands. Involuntary reaction took over and she struggled against their combined hold like a wild animal.

She came down in fits and starts, pleading nonsense in Ben's mouth, which he answered with unintelligible rumbles of response. Noah cleaned her up with strong licks of his now non-vibrating tongue, and then she felt the gentle pat of the wine towel he'd had. When he came back up, as graceful as he'd gone down, his hair was a tad rumpled and his face was flushed. He was also sporting a nice erection behind his slacks that didn't seem to discomfit him in the slightest. He nodded to her, turned his attention to Ben. "I failed, sir. My apologies."

Ben palmed some money from his coat, handed it over. "I wouldn't call it a failure. My compliments on your perseverance. Tell the maître d' others can be seated up here now."

Marcie was too dazed to do more than watch Noah go, but when she looked toward Ben, she somehow found her voice. "How...did I do?"

"Six minutes, twelve seconds. You're still a slut."

"But I proved I'm your slut, didn't I?" Her voice had a rasp from the strain to her vocal cords.

"Time to eat your salad," he said in quiet reproof, but he didn't deny it. Picking up his fork, he fed her. She needed that, because she was sure she wasn't steady enough to coordinate eating utensils. Her swollen folds were pressed against the wood, sending aftershocks rippling through her.

She wished she could stay mindless. As rationality returned, she was thinking of the seamless choreography of that scene. He'd done this before. Brought another woman here, maybe had her perform the same way for him.

She stopped chewing, pulled her face away, ostensibly to get a drink of wine. He reached to steady the glass for her, but she shook her head. "I can do it." She took it in about three swallows, but when she reached for the bottle to refill it, he moved it away.

"Enough," he said. "You'll make yourself sick."

"How did I do against the others?"

Why did she say that aloud? She couldn't be petulant and jealous. He wasn't a monk. For heaven's sake, she'd seen him fuck three women less than two weeks ago. It wasn't that. It was that he'd done to her something he'd done before, like she was some kind of mimeograph.

"Never mind. Sorry. Mentor-sub thing, no commitment. Forgot." She tried to keep the acid out of her tone, but of course she was unsuccessful. She was going to screw this up so badly if she couldn't sit on her mouth. Hell, she'd held out six minutes against Noah's tongue. It shouldn't be harder to sit on her emotional reactions than her physical ones, right?

"Noah is a regular at Progeny. He has a couple Mistresses who favor him, but he doesn't belong exclusively to any of them yet. Occasionally he's assisted me with a session there. This is the first time I've asked him to help me outside those walls, in this particular way, though I have come here for dinner before."

"Oh." She nodded. Picking up the napkin, she tried a quick dab at her eyes, to take care of the stress tears from the climax. She probably looked a sight.

"Marcie, did I tell you that you could remove your hands from the chair?"

Fuck, he hadn't. She'd been so dazed by the past few minutes, she'd just blanked on it. Setting aside the napkin, she returned her hands to the chair. "I'm sorry, sir."

"I'll let it pass, but only because you're still disoriented. I like it. Flushed and dazed, nipples still hard, and I can smell your cunt. Just the way I want you." He took his own napkin, dipped it in water as she'd done for his fingers. While she trembled from an entirely different reaction this time, he dabbed at her mascara. He stroked the cloth over her cheeks, the corners of her mouth. Even swiped at her nose, teasing her as she started to giggle and tried to squirm away from him. Then he lifted one of her hands from the chair, tucked the napkin into it so she could do that part for herself.

"Now that we've handled the appetizer course," he said, "eat the rest of your salad. You can lift both hands."

She had to get back on her game, but she remained unsettled, hyperaware that she was still exposed, open to him as he desired. In fact, as he was eating his salad, he settled his other hand on her thigh, stroking it up high. Her pussy was as attentive to him as if she hadn't just come. He was going to have her ready again in no time.

"Why anal sex?" she asked, just as the maître d' topped the stairs with another couple. Marcie bit her lip, but fortunately, it didn't seem they'd been paying attention. So she decided not to be deterred, particularly when the maître d' seated them at the other end of the balcony. "I've always wanted to ask. Will you tell me?"

Finishing his salad, Ben leaned back, picked up his wine. She continued to eat, giving him time, but his silence was encouraging. Usually he said no right off if he had no intention of answering a question.

"Most women have had sex by the time they reach legal age," he said at last, "at least in the usual ways. A lot still haven't had anal sex. Or, if they have, the guy had no clue what he was doing, so it left the woman feeling pretty neutral or, worse, it hurt like hell. She's nervous about that region for that or a variety of other reasons, unaware of what a pleasure zone it can be."

"There's also a lot of emotional reaction trapped in that area," Marcie observed. When Ben gave her a look, she shrugged. "Penetration would unlock it. I'm guessing that's a big draw for you."

"Really? How so?"

She ignored the trace of sarcasm as he invited her to tell her about himself. Wiping her lips delicately, she raised her gaze to his. "Getting a submissive to trust you, make herself vulnerable that way, challenges your ability as a Dom, and you like a challenge."

He flashed her that feral smile, a baring of teeth. "Actually, the main perk is not giving her a chance to claim I knocked her up."

"Yes. Having a little Ben running around is a scary thought." She considered him. "You want her to trust you, but you don't trust her. Doing it face-to-face makes it more emotionally naked for both participants. With the anal, you're stripping her down, taking her to a more vulnerable place, but you're staying removed. Untouched."

His expression flickered. "A fair point. But it's a conscious decision. I'm not looking to be touched."

She knew it was an attempt to tease, but the edge to his voice made his play on words a mockery, a warning to back off. She should leave it there, but she wasn't one of his club subs, or some trainee groupie so overwhelmed by him she'd be driven away by that formidable exterior. *Be who you are.* Jon's voice was in her ears, giving her enough courage to really fuck this up.

"When my brothers and sisters were little, you acted like a clown with them, wrestling, playing games. Matt and all of you took us to carnivals, ren faires, things like that. They loved it. But in your own life, you don't really go for relaxed fun, do you? I mean, you go out with the K&A guys, drink, do the male-bonding thing, but have you ever gone to a carnival and held your girlfriend's hand? You seem really focused on your career, the next goal, the next project. You play hard, but you don't play fun."

He raised a brow. "Is this based on your burgeoning career as my stalker?"

"You're not denying it."

"I've never had a girlfriend, Marcie."

Noah returned then to top off their wine, give them the status on their dinners. His hair was smoothed once again, his lips no longer glistening with her juices, but it was impossible not to remember what he'd been doing to her during the appetizer course. He gave her a slow smile when their eyes met, but he deferred to Ben on whether they required anything else at the moment, not asking her preferences. He knew how this game was played as well, and it was as distracting as all the rest of it.

But she wouldn't be distracted from this. No girlfriend. Thirty-two and he'd never sought a long-term relationship with anyone but the men with whom he worked. Even the women with whom the society column paired him for short durations were superficial, brief hook-ups with physical benefits for them both.

His mother had abandoned him in an alley outside a church when he was three, old enough to remember her. After that, he'd been in and out of foster-care situations, most of them bad, as if he'd been born with an unlucky star over his head. Before he hit puberty, he was on the street. It was then that star finally changed. He'd picked Jonas Kensington's pocket and gotten caught in the act by Matt's savvy father.

Even though things got better for him after that, his childhood hadn't been the kind where he kissed the pretty girl in his third grade class by the monkey bars, or hoped someone would ask him to the Sadie Hawkins dance in middle school.

She cocked her head, making sure her face didn't reflect the compassion she felt toward that boy. The man before her didn't need pity, not like that. He'd overcome, made something of himself, yet it had come at a cost. The cost was the wall she kept hitting, she knew that. She didn't have a psychology degree, only her intuition and her determination that she could love him like no one else — if he would just let her.

"I'll be your girlfriend then," she said lightly. "You can take me to a carnival. We can share a broken coin necklace, pass notes during work. I'll even take you to prom. If you promise to put out. Won't be worth my time otherwise."

Crossing his arms to lean on the table, he considered her at an intimate distance. The curve of those lips, the warmth that entered his gaze, eased some of her trepidation that she was treading dangerous waters. "What kind of notes would you pass me at work? Ones with Xs and Os, a lipstick mark pressed to the paper?"

She gave him an arch look. He hadn't let her bring her wallet, but she'd balked at not bringing some toiletries. Fishing her lipstick out of her small bag, she freshened her lips, cognizant of the way he watched the soft give of her mouth against the color. Then she pressed it to one of the extra napkins Noah had left by the bread basket. Pulling out a pen, she put a couple Xs and Os around it with a flourish and pushed it over to him. "There. We'll have to do the coin thing another time." She paused. "Do you still have the collar you took off me?"

"Do you want it back?"

"Yes, but only if you're putting it on me." She raised her chin.

"Not our agreement." His impassive expression returned and he sat back to sip his wine once more.

She pressed her moist lips together. She couldn't make this dinner about that. So she looked over the potted plants to gaze at the mural painted on the building across the street. It was of a trio of black musicians, blue and white dogs dancing around them. As whimsical as it was, her eye was caught by something much closer, on the rail, screened by the fern. "Ben, look."

He leaned forward. She started to rise to shift out of his view, but his firm touch on her elbow kept her sitting, reminding her of her exposed state from the waist down. Instead, he stood to look over her shoulder as she twisted around for a better view.

It was a pair of bright green salamanders. They'd been mating, or perhaps still were, because their lower bodies were connected. The much larger male was curled around the female in a tranquil, resting state, limbs and tails twined. Their tiny pulses rose and fell in their throats, and they seemed somnolent, relaxed.

"It's like they're spooning," Marcie said, keeping her tone quiet, not wanting to startle them. "Aren't they lovely?"

"Only you would notice that."

"No. You would have too. I was just blocking your view of them." She was aware of his chest pressed against her shoulder blade, his lips close to her ear. When she turned her head, they were close to her own mouth. She glanced up. "Kiss me, Ben. Please?"

Curling her hair around her ear, he studied her face. Then he bent, teasing her mouth with his own. When she sighed into his mouth, he turned it into a warm, lazy kiss that made everything settle, his tongue briefly caressing hers. When he sat back, though, she saw his face had that closed look once more.

"Adjust your skirt," he said. "We'll eat our dinner, then head for the house."

Marcie: What do you do when it becomes too much?

Ben: You take a breath, and make yourself a promise. The bastards aren't going to win.

Phone call between Ben and Marcie during final exam week

Chapter Eight

ഌ

A Master stayed in control, particularly with a new sub, one experiencing that wild vacillation of emotional and physical reactions for the first time. He was entirely responsible for her well-being while under his dominance. Yet Marcie had a way of taking him off guard. He shouldn't have given her that kiss. It was too intimate and personal, contradicting what he'd said only a few minutes earlier, that he was merely her mentor. Contradictions, inconsistencies. They would lead to real problems in an actual, intense session.

It wasn't the first time he'd told himself that, but it didn't seem to help much this time either. As they walked the few blocks to his place, she kept stopping to peer through the iron fences at the alley gardens, the hidden treasure trove of the Garden District. The gardens were as diverse as the people who lived there. One narrow space might look like a miniature English garden, right out of the pages of a home magazine; another was a chaotic design of homemade wire sculpture, English ivy and an old wooden chair painted to look like a cat's grinning face. Marcie was a sensual creature who noticed things like that, took pleasure in them. Like she had the salamanders.

Her attention to detail would make her an excellent corporate investigator. Hell, no "would" about it. She apparently knew his life up one side and down the other. It was outrageous. He'd noted her decision not to follow up on his statement that he hadn't ever had a girlfriend, which meant she knew why. She wasn't the type to hesitate over asking a question if she didn't know the answer, no matter how inappropriate the asking was. Yeah, he bet she was doing a bang-up job freelancing for Steve Pickard, impressing his veteran investigators.

When she turned to look at him, a small smile playing on her face, he reached out. She took his hand, that smile warming like a welcome touch of late afternoon sun on a winter day. As they kept walking down the street, her hand felt good in his, slim and restless, fingers tightening, little teasing strokes as she pointed out this or that, asked him questions about the neighborhood. The silver beads he'd helped her acquire still swung on her neck. He'd removed his, added them to hers, so the two colors sparkled together.

"Is Cass happy running Pickard's satellite office here?"

"Are you kidding? She loves it. She misses the Lakeshore house in Baton Rouge, but she and Lucas found such a nice place, she's feeling better about it. The Lakeshore house was one she bought with her own money, and after all she'd been through to reach that point, it meant a lot to her."

"After everything you'd all been through."

"It was hardest on her. She was in charge of everything."

"You were second oldest. When she was working, you were in charge of the kids. The nanny Pickard hired was only part-time."

"Well, I took over because I wanted extra spending money."

"Yes, that was your official story. Pickard paid you the money he was paying the nanny, and you turned around and used it to help out with expenses for the kids and the house."

She shrugged that off, but he wouldn't let it go. "All of you had to deal with what happened with your parents. Jeremy."

"It was okay. We were okay." She didn't like where this was going. Plus, she didn't want the uncertainty and stress that had marked most of her teenage years to mar this moment.

"Marcie." He stopped her. "You've been goal-oriented since you were in puberty. You were planning to be a business major before you were out of middle school. Your whole life was about taking care of those kids, dealing with your parents' instability and planning for a career. You didn't walk through a carnival holding hands with a boyfriend either."

"Well, I can now. Given the company, it was worth the wait." She lifted their clasped hands, put her other one over it. Daring, she dropped her head, pressed her lips to his knuckles, rubbed her cheek against him. His hand fit his large frame, the fingers deliciously thick when they pushed inside her, but in appearance they had a masculine elegance, like a master artist's. She thought of his cooking again, as well as the other things he could do with those talented digits.

Sighing, he brushed his other palm over her hair, tugged until she lifted her head. "You don't have to be goal-oriented in every aspect of your life anymore. You can still have your career, but enjoy dating, getting out and seeing the world. Having fun with friends."

She withdrew, went back to strolling. "It's funny how people say that. 'Put off getting married and having a family, because you need to live your life first'. To me, loving someone *is* living." She stopped then. "When you talk to someone who's done all that traveling, experiencing and 'living', you know what they say? That they wish they'd had someone special in their life, sharing it with them. Marriage isn't a prison sentence—it's an invitation for someone else to join you on your journey, experience all those things together."

She left it at that, only because she knew the dangers of getting too personal with him, too fast. Did he know he looked at the others with their wives like the lone wolf? Still part of the pack but somehow not. She'd seen it in his eyes at Jon and

Rachel's wedding. It had frustrated the hell out of her, knowing she was still too young to help ease that for him. In the deepening lines on his face, the more serious set to his mouth, it was more obvious to her now than it had been even then.

He took her hand once more. "It's impossible to argue with you if you're going to be unreasonable."

She slid her other hand around his elbow, so she could press her body against his. "That's your way of saying I'm right."

"I would never say anything so foolish. Telling a woman she's right is like giving a terrorist a nuclear weapon. Widespread destruction is inevitable."

Pinching his arm, she tried not to linger over the hard biceps that she was sure barely felt the impact. God, the man was built. Even in his suits it was obvious, that powerful cat way he had of moving, the breadth of his shoulders, the way his shirts fit across his chest. She remembered him in jeans, how he'd looked playing with the kids. If she was mayor of New Orleans, she'd pass a law that said he had to wear those all the time and nothing else.

He stopped in front of a row of townhouses that had obviously once been a large estate. It now continued its life of graceful historic beauty in three partitions, with the narrow dividing lines of more scenic alley nooks. "Since you know everything about me, I assume you know this is where I live."

"It was tough, because you've moved around a lot. In fact, you only bought this in the past year, and negotiated a price Satan would envy. Your place in the Warehouse District is close to the office, and you stay there most times." In fact, she thought it odd — and hopeful — he'd decided to bring her here instead, because of the two, the Garden District was more like a home.

He arched a brow at her. "Have pictures of me in the shower?"

"I tried to perch in an oak tree with my extended lens, but I'm not a great climber and didn't want to risk damaging the equipment."

She made an indignant noise when he swatted her ass, but she caught his quick grin as well. His hand came back to stroke, reminding them both she wore no panties beneath the skirt. Those butterflies swirled in Marcie's stomach again, excitement and apprehension.

"If I'm staying overnight," she ventured, "I should pick up a toothbrush or something."

"Cass is sending an overnight bag for you via one of the K&A drivers. It's probably already been dropped it off." He approached the security grate that blocked the alcove of his front door and peered in. She saw the duffel as well as a garment bag hung on the outdoor light fixture. "There we go."

"You guys are scary. Like Boy Scouts on steroids."

"Says my stalker." Opening the outer gate, he gestured her in underneath his arm. She let her fingers slide against his side as she did, under the pretense of the close quarters, but was surprised when he abruptly turned, lifted her up and pressed her against the shadowed wall of the alcove. Her eyes closed as his mouth took hers, his body pressing her hard against the oyster-shell stucco. Her legs wrapped around his hips instinctively, heels digging into the back of his thighs as he plundered her mouth. Digging his fingers into her hair, he tugged against her scalp mercilessly. She was gasping as he lifted his head.

"When we go through that door, you are a slave. You understand, Marcie?"

She nodded, then found her voice. "Yes sir."

"You don't look at me unless I tell you to do so. The second you step over that threshold, you strip. Everything. Jewelry, hairpins, rings, all of it. You leave the clothes folded neatly by the door. Then you sit down on the floor. Legs tucked underneath you, knees spread so I have access to your pussy. Fingers laced behind your head, tits thrust out. You hold that posture, and you stay silent, unless you get physically uncomfortable or I ask you a question. If you start to get uncomfortable, you ask for permission to speak."

He waited for her nod, then let her down. Turning away, he unlocked the interior door. Once again, he held it open, gestured her to precede him. When she stepped across the threshold, he moved past her without a glance, a dismissal, as he went down the hallway into what looked like the kitchen area.

She took off skirt, bra, shirt, heels. Earrings and bracelets, the ring Cass had given her that belonged to their mother. She put those things in a small dish on the hallway tree, then folded up her clothes beside them. Unclipping her barrette, she took out the couple of pins that held back the more unruly strands, put them with the rest. Then she followed his direction, folding herself down to the polished wood floor. She laced her fingers behind her head, spread her knees, thrust out her breasts.

It was a posture that made her instantly, shamelessly wet. Unlike the obeisance pose, which was a position of humble vulnerability, this one showed pride in her surrender, fully displaying what was her Master's. Her nipples were drawn up so that the barbells were a tingling burn in the piercings. Her clit piercing was the same.

She could see him through the opening to the kitchen, just a piece of him. He was flipping through his mail. He set something down, was reading it as he stripped off his tie, pulled open a couple buttons of his shirt. It made her mouth dry. She had no doubt he was completely aware of every move she made, yet he was also so…detached. It was heating her blood. Her pussy would be making her calves slippery in no time.

Stepping away from the table, he disappeared into another room of the house. She took the moment to look around. The floors were all hardwood, with that wonderful old wood smell. The narrow staircase probably led to a bedroom area, with a spacious window on the way up that let in afternoon sunlight. The kitchen looked modern and also full of sunlight. The house had obviously been remodeled inside, keeping the best of the old and integrating the new. It was tastefully decorated, but not female in the slightest. The walls were pale yellow with touches of bold earth-toned artwork here and there. No photos she could see.

Directly in front of her was the archway into a living area with a sectional sofa and wide-screen TV, as well as more artwork. A copper glaze vase was under a separate spotlight, obviously a gallery piece. A couple Japanese maples flanked it. Gifts from Jon, she was sure, since he said the delicate five-point leaf trees brought tranquility and blessings to a home. Cass had a few as well.

Though Ben had probably employed a decorator to reflect his tastes, the house had a good feel to it, like it was merely waiting for Ben to accept it as his home. She wondered what it would take for him to do that. He'd called the house a good investment, and the Warehouse District place was convenient to work. But this place felt like *him*. If he put down roots, staked his claim, this would be the place he'd do it.

And he'd brought her here.

She returned her gaze to the floor, everything within her coiling up in anticipation as his shoes tapped down the hall. She was completely naked. Naked in Ben's home, waiting for his demands. She had that shaking thing going on, just beneath the skin, little thrills of sensation running along the insides of her thighs.

"Close your eyes. Clasp your hands at the small of your back."

She did, and then he was touching her hair, gathering it up. He retrieved her barrette, used it to hold a flat twist on the back of her head.

"Since you have trouble obeying something as simple as not looking at me unless you have permission..."

She clutched her fingers hard as he fitted the head mask to her face. When her lashes fluttered, she found it had no eye holes, and then... She pushed down panic as he put ear plugs in those orifices before he brought the mask over them. The mask laced in the back, and he took his time, adjusting it and touching her face to ensure the opening for her nostrils was positioned properly. As he got the mask set, it constricted over her nose, cheekbones, forehead. The mouth opening was a mere slit, pressing against her lips.

When he was done with the lacing, she felt cool metal at her nape, a brief pressure, then a small weight. "I've inserted a small padlock in the last eyeholes of the lacing. Only I can remove this mask, Marcie."

He was speaking right against her ear, but any other sounds were muted. He'd just blinded her, taken away most of her hearing.

Now he was putting a collar on her. As he buckled it, he tested the constriction by sliding two fingers beneath it to caress her chin. It was a serviceable collar, wide and solid. Not a formal collaring, but still. Her quivering increased. She felt a tug. A tether.

"On your feet. Follow me."

He moved as soon as she rose, and he didn't set a slow pace, giving her time to feel her way or figure out where they were going. He was expecting her to trust him, to follow at a normal walk. She managed it, but she couldn't help some small flutters of panic. When he stopped, his hand touching her bare abdomen to bring her to a halt before she ran into him, she thought they were in the kitchen, but then he made a turn into a room she hadn't yet seen. It was warm, maybe a sunroom, which meant lots of windows. Was she on display to his neighbors?

"On your knees, forehead to the floor, arms out front, wrists crossed. Ass in the air. Thighs spread."

She obeyed. She wanted to talk, needed to speak, but it wasn't to ask a question. She needed to interact for reassurance. Imagining this and doing it were very different. She bit down on her tongue, stayed silent. He'd gag her with the least provocation, she was sure, and she definitely wasn't ready to lose the ability to speak.

Straps wrapped just beneath each of her knees, buckled snug so they wouldn't slip down her calves. Then something else, something that pushed her out a little wider, made her have to rest more of her weight on her elbows and forehead. A spreader bar, one that would hold her thighs open no matter what. She could hear her rasping breath in her head. He wasn't done yet, God help her. Cuffs around her ankles, and this time a light chain was run between them, a hobble. Moving around to her front, he cuffed her wrists together, and then she heard another chain run from them to something that anchored her there, perhaps the leg of a heavy piece of furniture, or a column in the sunroom.

He rose and was gone. No, not gone. She could barely hear him, but it sounded like...a chair scraping? A laptop turning on? Yes, the piercing chime of a boot-up filtered through the plugs. He was going to leave her in this position while he worked?

Not immediately, no. She drew in a breath as he touched her bare ass. Something rigid and small was inserted into her anus, followed by a feeling of warmth. Lube. He was lubing her up to fuck her, use her as he'd use a slave. More thick arousal trickled out onto her thighs. When she tied herself up, she always felt that peculiar stillness enter her, a dense type of arousal. This was ten times more intense, the volatility of an atom waiting to be split. She wanted to whimper, to moan, to cry a little. And she wanted him to keep wrapping her up in restraint after restraint until she couldn't move.

Shifting in front of her again, he curled his fingers into the strap on the top of the head mask, a replacement handhold with the hair trapped beneath it. Releasing the chain, he brought her up to her knees, wobbling precariously with that spreader between them, but he held her upright. Unhooking her wrist restraints to bring her arms behind her, he arched her back to attach them that to the spreader bar between her knees. Now she was dependent on her stomach muscles, her own unsteady balance and his hand to stay upright. But in another second that didn't matter.

Her lips parted as she smelled the heat and musk of his cock. She hadn't heard him remove any clothes, but she had a feeling he was still fully dressed, had just opened his slacks to have her service him.

He pushed against her mouth, and she had to adjust fast, because he didn't take his time as he had before. He was already hard and huge, sliding into the back of her throat. She reveled in it, knowing her submission, having her so helpless, was making him hot. So hot he stretched her lips cruelly, bumped against her throat. She flicked her tongue on him, sucked, teased, stroked, doing everything to convey how much she loved doing this for him. With her standing on her knees, that arousal was rolling down the insides of her legs.

She could come just from doing this. His other hand captured her breast, tugged on the nipple piercing, a sharp pain that made her cry out against him. He slapped the breast in reproof, making her gasp again. He did it to the other breast, a rough tweak and pull, followed by that sharp slap that made the breast wobble in reaction.

He was tearing her up inside, pulling her between cruel pain and pleasure, training her to respond to both the same way. She might know that rationally, but it was like nothing she'd ever experienced. It was frightening, feeling it all spin out of control, but at some visceral level, she understood. He wanted her to let go of everything. Identity, mind, everything but being his slave, because anything else was an attempt to control, and he wouldn't tolerate that. He held all the control. Whatever she'd imagined, it hadn't gone this far, but if she wanted him, she had to be willing to fall out of the boat and watch it float away, sink to the bottom of his ocean.

Now he'd let go of her head, leaving her to work him with her mouth while he grasped both breasts, pinched the nipples, rolled the barbells until she was trying so hard to focus, caught between ecstasy and flinching as he mixed pleasurable squeezes with sudden flicks that sent shards of pain through her nipples. Her back was starting to ache from her position, her jaw screaming, but she didn't care. He held her up with his cock impaling her mouth and his hands holding her breasts. As far as she was concerned, it was exactly where she wanted to be.

Taking hold of the headmask strap, he pulled her off him. Moving behind her, he freed her bound wrists from the spreader bar, and each other, but held onto them as he shifted his other hand to the back of her neck, pushed her face to the floor again. Her arms were brought back above her again so her elbows pressed into the wood. The way he took her to the floor was swift, a harrowing descent, blind and with nothing to control her speed but him, but again, she got the message. He was demanding her absolute trust. That was the kind of Dom he was, but she knew it was more than that as well.

She'd told him he sought his sub's vulnerability but withheld his own. He always played on the edge, but because he didn't like the truth she'd put in front of him, he'd take it even closer to that perilous drop because he wanted to scare the shit out of her, send her running back to her playground.

He was in for a surprise. She was scared, but she was also totally-out-of-control immersed in the world he was creating, and she'd never been so sexually stimulated in her life. They probably weren't even a fourth of the way through Ben's version of foreplay. A prayer for strength would probably not be out of line at this point, with an additional caveat for forgiveness for all the sins she was willing to commit for her Master.

He was being rough, but not violent. His touch was firm, strong, implacable. This wasn't romance. This was a hardcore Master out and out driving her to the upper level of madness, where her body was going to come completely to pieces before he was done. Cruel, but she craved his brand of cruelty.

She was moved forward, his arms briefly wrapped around her waist and chest. He pulled her arms out straighter, and directed her to wrap her fingers around what felt like the leg of that heavy piece of furniture before he chained her there, the links winding over her knuckles. Her forehead stayed pressed to the floor until he gripped her hips, bringing her to her feet, her head still down toward the ground, arms low and stretched before her, a modified Down Dog yoga position.

It strained her muscles in a new way. He wasn't keeping her in any pose long enough to become painful; just enough to stress the body, like a particularly stringent workout. Maybe he'd been going to Rachel's classes.

The desperate humor was gone in an instant as his hand made contact with her ass, a powerful slap. He followed it up with several more, warming her flesh. She was making soft cries in her throat, pleas of alarm, because if he so much as touched her pussy, she was going to come.

"None of that." She sensed the loss of his heat as he moved away from her, came back. Something cool and hard entered her pussy, sliding in like a knife into a peach, a scary thought when associated with her tender regions. Then she felt the discomfort of being stretched, and though she didn't hear the telltale clicks, a cold feeling ran through her belly as she realized he'd used a speculum, like the doctor used for pelvic exams. It held her wide open, reduced the ability of the pussy to spasm and create its own orgasm.

She cried out as something else closed over her clit, something ice cold. "Jon's version of the ice pack," he said. "It will feel like ice, at least for several moments. Until that hot pussy of yours warms it up."

It was impossible to stay still, but he'd anticipated that, with the way he'd bound her. She was twitching, convulsing, but he had her arms stretched out to that anchor point, her head toward the floor, her legs straight up and spread. Her range of movement was severely restricted. Then he went to work on her with two other tools.

The first was a flogger with thin straps that stung, eliciting tiny cries. He alternated that with the solid thunk of a weighted slapper, which had more impact. Back and forth, back and forth, and each time her pussy spasmed from the blow, she felt that speculum holding her open. He awoke the still-sensitive nerve endings from yesterday's caning and it became part of the spiraling agony.

Ben... Something was tearing open inside of her, something important and vital, and dark. Every fear, every childhood pain was swelling up inside of her, twining with this out-of-control lust in a macabre way, a parade of pleasure and agony that was going to drown her.

She didn't stop crying out even as he stopped using the weapons. She had no control over any of her reactions, verbal or physical. As his broad head pushed against her lubricated ass, she made a keening note. She was tight, but he worked against her, spurring her on with the words that filtered through the mask's cover.

"You can take me. You're soaking wet, you want my cock so much. Concentrate and take it. You were born to serve a Master who works you over until that smart mouth and far-too-clever mind of yours gives out and you just become mindless, serving him with everything you are."

"You... Born to serve...you." She didn't give a damn if he'd told her not to talk, she wouldn't let that one pass.

"I haven't used you hard enough, apparently." His cock withdrew, and she snarled in protest. Said some things she'd never thought would come from her mouth. Did she just call him a fucking bastard? In response, she got a diabolical chuckle and her mouth was forced open. She gagged as a thick rubber dildo was pushed in, so wide it held her tongue down and stretched the mask around her lips. When he buckled it tight around her head, he'd taken away her sight, most of her hearing, and now her ability to speak. She thought she'd been coming apart before. She realized then he wasn't going to stop until he'd shattered her into a million pieces.

* * * * *

"Fucking bastard, hmm? Baby, you don't know how much of a bastard I can be."

Her fingers dug into the floor but she screamed against the gag as something slapped against her ass. Rubber...flat...like a spatula. Fuck. The danger of a Master who cooked — he had a whole inventory of tools with more than one use.

Each time he hit her with it, the pain screamed through her nerve endings, made her shriek against the gag. But right after, he'd pause, his palm passing over her buttock. The throbbing would turn warm...and she'd want more. Until the next hit. It was crazy. She knew the type of person she was, that she craved pain as much as pleasure at his hand, but she'd had no ability to prove it other than her own experiments in the privacy of a dorm room or co-op apartment. Though the levels of pain she'd tried on her own might be similar, it was a hell of a lot different from the psychology of being helpless to whatever he wanted to do to her.

The cold on her clit was becoming an aching pain, it was all becoming agony and excruciating stimulation at once. He gave her four more hard strokes, alternating with stinging taps on the inside of her thighs.

"You ready to behave now? Don't bother to nod. I know you're a little liar."

He came back at her with his cock. She focused with all she had, and he worked himself against her sphincter muscles. She pushed against him, wanting him, wanting him now, and the muscles gave, letting him slide in deep, ruthless, irresistible. She wished she could flex the muscles inside her pussy. It was distressing to have him sunk deep in her while her pussy was held open, rendered as helpless to his will as any other part of her.

She was lost, just lost. All she had in this silent darkness was him. He began to thrust, shoving her forward so she had to brace her straining, trembling muscles against the onslaught. His fingers reached beneath, pinched that cold thing off her clit, slid the speculum free. There was a muffled clatter as he tossed it away, replaced it with his own fingers, sliding them into her cunt as his thumb and forefinger went to work on restoring the life to her frozen clit.

It swelled up in her like a finger-of-God cat-five tornado. "No, no, no." She was wailing against the gag. This orgasm was going to tear her apart, take her into places she hadn't known existed. He was beyond what she could handle, no matter how much she loved him. But he wasn't leaving her a choice. Hadn't even given her a safe word. He'd simply taken, because she'd told him that was what she wanted and because he was bound and damn determined to prove her wrong.

I love you, I love you... I want to serve you. You're my Master. She realized then there was a struggle happening inside her mind, and that struggle said she was still trying to hold onto control. She couldn't totally trust him because he was resisting the idea that she was the one meant for him. But she had to have faith for both of them, had to let go.

She couldn't. Oh God, she needed his tenderness, his heart, and this was a ruthless Master who was demanding she surrender everything while he gave her nothing.

But those were the terms. That was the risk she was taking. It didn't matter anyway. She was being dragged to the edge of the cliff by that punishing cock, those knowledgeable fingers, his heated breath on her spine. But what would happen if she stopped pushing back, if she just gave him a smile, her heart in her tear-filled eyes, and took the leap joyously?

"Come for me, Marcie. Come now. Obey me."

Heart, lungs, every major organ, were gripped in the squeezing moment of decision, then the orgasm crashed over her. He was pumping into her, the fingers at her clit working her like a maestro. Her nostrils flared, lips stretching to allow as much air past the dildo as possible. Her breasts wobbled beneath her with the motion of his thrusts, her fists in their cuffs and chains gripping that anchor point, her whole body chained and subjected to his will. His slave, in every way.

She screamed against the gag until her vocal cords gave out. Even then, she continued to convulse and buck as if gripped in a full epileptic seizure. Tears were on her lips. Her orgasm gushed forth so strong she spurted over his cock. Her legs buckled, but he had her by the waist, kept lifting her with his thrusts. He released then, taking her up once more with the heat of his seed. She shrieked as he kept massaging her clit, milking every last sensation from her. She strained to hear his release, a grunt, a moan, but the mask was too damn effective.

Still, he kept going even after she rode that tide to the end. He would fuck her as long as he wished, until her tissues were sore and begging for relief. Did he do it because he knew it was the key to his and her pleasure both, underscoring that she was his to do with as he desired?

With a mix of terror and other, less sensible, emotions, she realized he was still hard. She couldn't keep up. She couldn't be enough for him. No, she would be. She had to be.

At last, he was slowing down. She was panting. Easing her back to the ground, to her knees, he removed the spreader bar and the hobble chain, but he cuffed her ankles together. He adjusted her so she was lying on her back, her arms up above her head, for he left her attached to whatever furniture leg he'd chosen. When something silky touched her ankles, she realized he was binding her legs with nylon rope. He did a wrap from ankles to her thighs, tied off there. Then he took her arms down, unchained them.

For a moment her wrists were held in his hands, and she stretched out her fingers, seeking his face. *Please, please let me touch you.*

His mouth touched her palms, making her sob. She touched his jaw, his cheeks, stroking, desperate, needy. But then he was wrapping nylon rope between her forefinger and thumb, moving to the other fingers to lace them together so she was palm to palm before he did a similar snug rope wrap from her wrists to her elbows. *Oh God.* It was like her fantasy when he was biting her neck.

She couldn't follow what was going on anymore, floating in sensation. He slid his arms beneath her, lifted her. He smelled so good, heat and sweat, aroused male. Moving through a spiraling darkness, she focused on the way it felt to be held in his arms until he laid her face down over what felt like a sofa arm. He adjusted her arms before her, so her fingers gripped a cushion and there was space between her face and the couch surface, protecting air passage. Straddling her bound legs, he put his hands on her hips, thumbs on her buttocks, spreading them open. The opening was sore as hell, but then she made a dove's cry as he knelt and put his mouth there.

"Ahkh..." She was losing track of all the involuntary sounds he was wresting from her. God, that felt so good. His clever tongue was licking her rim, swirling inside, soothing and stimulating at once, setting off small contractions in her pussy, compressed by that rope wrap. His hands stroked her buttocks, reminding her of the punishing strokes he'd put there, but soothing them as well.

Then he rose. She couldn't help it; she made an apprehensive noise as he fitted his cock to that opening once more. She couldn't. She couldn't possibly.

"Easy, baby. Real, real, easy. Let me do all the work. You just feel."

He didn't thrust in hard this time. He worked his way slow. She whimpered throughout, because it was uncomfortable, but it was more than that as well. The desire to serve him, to give him whatever he wanted, superseded everything, made her pussy keep doing those little clenches. It was impossible that she could be getting aroused again so soon. But her nipples were brushing the stiff sofa material, hardening anew. He slid a hand between their bodies, petted her slick and compressed pussy with little strokes that had her mewling like a cat.

When he was all the way in, he leaned over her back, dropped a kiss on her nape, catching that padlock in his teeth and tugging, reminding her she was his prisoner. "Squeeze down on me."

She did, and earned a rasp of his breath against her neck, a reward that warmed her like the teacher giving her an A in front of the whole class. That squeezing motion made sensation ripple through her cunt and lower belly. She did it harder.

"Fuck. Keep doing that." He was close enough to her she could hear the rumble of his voice against her neck, through her back where his chest pressed against her. She'd been right. He still wore his dress shirt, though the tie was gone. She'd felt his open slacks against her ass and thighs when he was fucking her before, and now she felt them again. Somehow it just underscored her subjugation, him remaining in his work clothes. She imagined how it would feel to have him completely naked against her, hard muscle and curling male chest hair rough against her skin.

"Lift your tits off the couch."

His hands reached beneath her. No unkind pinches and tugs this time. Something far more devastating. He started brushing his palms over just the tips in a way that had her making little moans, increasing the rate of those constrictions in her ass. She could feel him swelling larger. They probably made Viagra out of whatever special hormone Ben carried in his DNA.

"That's it. Good girl. Keep working it." He laid another kiss on her nape, brought his other hand down beneath her to tease her clit with one finger, more light brushes. In a matter of minutes, she wanted to spread her legs with everything she had, open herself wide to him, but of course the rope wrap prevented her. What the hell was he doing to her?

"My sweet, sweet slut," he murmured. "You're so hot for it. I'm going to keep working you like this all night. We won't be stopping until my cock's had enough." His voice dropped to a whisper, right against her ear. "And baby, my cock never has enough of a sweet ass like yours."

Despite that thrilling threat, he surprised her. She expected him to take her to another completion, at least for him, but instead, after a few moments, he lifted her again. She was carried down a hallway, and then she was in another room, though she couldn't tell what function it served. Until he laid her down on what felt like a padded massage table.

"Lie still. No speaking unless I give you permission."

Unwrapping her legs and arms, he removed the phallic gag. Then he began to rub her limbs, back, shoulders and hips with firm, capable hands that knew exactly what they were doing. She had to bite back a moan as he worked over the sore muscles and strained joints.

"Your color's good. Wiggle your toes for me. Now your fingers. Any numbness anywhere? Yes or no."

"No."

She wasn't lying, not exactly, because she knew what kind of numbness he meant. He didn't mean the fact her lips could barely move because her body was trapped in a logy place where everything moved through molasses, even her thoughts. She felt like she was in a permanent world of hushed darkness.

When he was done with that, he turned her over, did the front. He cupped her breasts, passed his thumbs over her nipples, an idle caress as he checked her over. She knew he was looking for any discolorations or dangerous levels of tenderness. She'd learned that from watching Marcus do sessions with Thomas at their favorite New York club, and later she'd seen Ben do the same with the three women at Surreal. Only Ben was like a torturer who knew the limits of the human body exactly, straddling that border of pleasure and terror. A zone far wider for her than she'd realized, until she was under his command.

He slid his arms underneath her. "C'mon, brat." Was there tenderness in that murmur?

As he took a seat in what felt like a nearby recliner, he cradled her against his body. She turned her face into his neck. She wanted the mask off, wanted to feel him against her face. He must have known, because he removed the lock and unlaced it, pulled it off. She kept her eyes closed, fearing any brightness. He used what smelled like aloe wipes to clean her face, the mucus from her running nose, her tears, the sweat. He combed her hair with his fingers.

She'd bitten her lip, and he smeared something that smelled like coconut lip balm there. He leaned away from her and she heard the sound of a mini-fridge. Then he was plying her with sips of water. Fed her peanut butter crackers as he had at the office, gave her some juice. With a near giggle, she wondered if he kept supplies in every room of the house, like a Red Cross station after a bloodletting.

"Master…" She wanted to say it, wanted to call him that. He kept stroking her head, but said nothing. "Ben…"

"I'm here, baby. Just relax and get your strength back. We're not done. Not by a long shot."

"I haven't…made out a will. Tell Cass that Jess can have my clothes. But she gets…my birthday stilettos."

His lips pulled into a curve against her temple. "I'd like to see you in those stilettos, and nothing else. I'd cross your ankles, tie them together, run the rope under the soles of the shoes so it keeps them on, part of the binding."

"I'll wear them…in my casket."

He kissed her neck then, bit, earning a quiet sigh from her, a shudder as he clasped her breasts, gently massaged, pinched, toyed with the piercings. "Quiet now. Just feel. You're a slave. You don't speak unless your Master requires you to speak. You serve. Let everything else go."

She wanted to obey him, but her mind was in such an odd place. "I'm so, so sorry. About Jeremy. About the things… I was so lonely in college." She was sorry for everything she'd ever done wrong in her whole life. It was so strange, the desire to confess everything without choosing any one specific thing, just an overall purging.

He was silent a moment. "Jeremy wasn't your fault."

"It felt like it was. Why is that?"

"Because women are stupid about things like that." But he said it without rancor. Closing his arms around her, he held her tight. "I forgive you for everything, you understand?"

"Even the things I might do tomorrow? Or the next day?"

He snorted, not unkindly. "I should know you'd try to hedge your bets. Whatever you do tomorrow, I'll devise the appropriate punishment. But first, we get through today."

She opened her eyes at last, looked at him. The top three buttons of the shirt were open, so she could lay her hand on his chest. She didn't though. She kept her hands limp along her hipbones, out of his way so he could touch whatever he wished. There was simmering lust in his gaze, the banked embers of what they'd just done. He was hard beneath her ass, the size of him making a substantial impression in her buttock.

She wouldn't change a thing, but she wished there were two of her, one who could stand to the side and watch those green eyes go to pure emerald fire, watch him grip that large cock and push it inside her. See that strong jaw tighten, flex, his lips stretch back as he released, spent his seed inside her ass.

"If you want, we can stop now, Marcie." He drew her eyes back to his face. "You can clean up and go home."

She was home. He was home to her. It was so difficult not to say it, an ache in her heart. A submissive's honesty, her pure emotion, was what a Master demanded, a gift she could give him. But this Master wasn't ready for that kind of truth.

"I don't want to go. I want you to do everything you want to do to me. I'm yours." Laying her head back against his biceps, she lifted her gaze to the pressed tin ceiling. There was an elegant black and gold fixture, a slowly oscillating ceiling fan. "You remember when we all went to the state fair? You won me that giant bear, at the knife-throwing booth."

She'd expected Peter to have that skill, thanks to his military training, but Ben didn't miss. Ten balloons, ten knife throws, his movements smooth and certain. Thunk, thunk, thunk. She remembered the steady focus of Ben's eyes, the widening of the vendor's. He'd won her the largest bear in the kiosk, a black bear with green eyes. The furry taloned paws had bumped her knees as she carried him.

The other children already had prizes. She'd been the only one without, because of course she and Cass made sure the younger children got any winnings that day. But when Cherry and Nate were going to fight over that bear, Ben shook his head, spoke firmly.

"This one is Marcie's," he said. He'd handed it over to her with a smile, and a tug of her ponytail. *"He's the safest boyfriend you can have in college. Keep that in mind."*

"Yes, I remember." He spoke, bringing her back to the present.

"I did unspeakable things to that bear." With her legs and one arm wrapped around it, she'd held it on top of her while she slipped a hand between them, masturbating, imagining someone else's weight pressing her body into her mattress. Now she brought her gaze back to Ben. "I want you do unspeakable things to me. Please."

That jaw flexed, gaze heating. When she reached up to touch his mouth, he grasped her wrist before she made contact, held it between them. "You weren't supposed to speak without permission," he reminded her. "I think it's time for me to bind these hands again. Your ass was a pretty color from the spatula, but a red blush like that needs some caning marks."

She trembled under his intent scrutiny. "Yes sir," she said.

* * * * *

He was as good as his word. During the long hours of the night, she lost count of how many times she thought, *This is exactly as I imagined it, fantasized about it.*

Physically.

She'd had no idea what it would do to her emotionally. Her strange desire for confession was just the tip of the iceberg. She cried, she sobbed, she came, she pleaded, she said things against the replaced gag that were visceral, animal-like. Time and again, she thought she couldn't bear more, that the strain on mind and body had become too much, but then he'd wring another sensation out of her she couldn't resist. He'd murmur, "One more minute," and she could do another minute. The craving to be the most perfect slave he could ever want would rise to the top again.

She let go of things in those dark hours she couldn't give to anyone else. She wanted to tell him everything, things she couldn't even tell herself. He had her soul chained down with her body, helpless to him. As he tormented her, a sensual, ruthless inquisitor, she gave it all to him. He was so much more than she'd realized. She wasn't just in over her head, out in the middle of the ocean. Her life was literally in his hands, her right to breathe, to exist. All of it was at his mercy, and she would gladly stop breathing if that was what he wanted. She'd do anything to please him.

It was crazy, irrational. It scared her to death, because she couldn't stop feeling any of it. And he made it worse with every new thing he did to her. After her brief respite, he'd replaced the mask, put her over what felt like a spanking bench. Her nipple barbells were attached to a chain he threaded through a ratcheted buckle on the back of the collar. Each time he pushed that metal hasp left then right, it cinched in the chain another inch, increasing the pull on her nipples. He put her chin in a metal rest directly before her that he raised up until she felt the strain in her neck and more pull on the barbells.

Placing a slim dildo in her ass that was covered with a blissfully heated balm, he'd then slid a vibrator in her pussy with a clit attachment. Since that part of her had been achingly empty throughout their first session, it sucked on the vibrator greedily, earning a fervent expletive from him she treasured for the fascinated expression of male lust it was. As he changed the settings on that vibrator, he commanded her to clench her ass rhythmically over the dildo, working out those muscles, until she came again.

Next she was on her back. He strapped her to a table, buckled her calves in stirrups that kept her legs upright at a ninety-degree angle, increasing her sense of vulnerability. Her hands and waist were cuffed to the table, and then he positioned a thick dildo in her pussy. One that was connected to a fucking machine. She heard the muted whir of it as he started it. The dildo had a clit piece that hit her there with each slow thrust and retreat. That wasn't enough, however.

He fitted electrode pads on her areolas, holes to allow room for her nipples, and then those pads unpredictably sent low-voltage stimulus to them as the fucking machine did its thing. "I have some email to check," he'd said, as he teasingly brushed her lips stretched around the phallus gag. "I'm going to sit over there and answer it, rub my cock and enjoy watching my toy being fucked."

He had a remote control for both electric devices, a convenient addition provided by Jon, she was sure, since he was their mechanical genius. The electrodes were activated at unpredictable moments, and the fucking machine increased or decreased its rate without any rhyme or reason. It didn't matter. By the end, she was writhing and screaming at every level of stimulus. Then he let the machine pump into her like a jack hammer, and she came and came and came.

After that, he decided they both needed a late-night meal. He put her on all fours on his dining room table, with the mask still in place, but he removed the gag. He used a rope suspension system to bind her above and below her breasts, at the waist and curve of her hip.

"Not only for support," he told her. "I want you displayed the way I'd do it if I was entertaining business associates and wanted you as the centerpiece. I'd put the serving dishes around your knees and hands, let them decorate you if they'd like. Eat the food off your body."

As he told her that, he attached an additional hook to the crown of the hood mask. A tether attached to it tightened, forcing her head to be held up. She couldn't stop making noises at all now, so the guttural moan as he inserted the steel bulb of an anal hook into her rectum was just par for the course. He fastened a line to the eye hole of the anal hook and to the two lines that crossed her shoulder blades from the breast bondage. When he drew all of it taut from a ceiling hook, her head, shoulders and ass were held up at pert angles from the diabolical joining point.

He fed her then, a creamy soup with lots of protein, had her drink more fluids. Then he worked his fingers into her cunt, telling her to squeeze down on the steel bulb, and turned her into a screaming, mindless slut once more.

She lost track of how many hours, days, millennia passed as he was catapulting her into an alternative universe. He'd messed with her reality, her sense of time, spatial relationships. The only fixed point, the only anchor, was him.

Since time had no meaning, she measured it by climaxes, and of course eventually her mind even stumbled over that — was it fifth, seventh...tenth? They became increasingly more intense, rigid like an implosion, because her body had no energy to handle a more externally demonstrative response. It didn't matter. She was responding to his demands now, not her brain's limitations.

Now he had her kneeling on the floor, her body curled, her head pressed to the carpet between his feet, like the Child's Pose in yoga...or a position of utter subjugation before a Master. He'd kept her that way for a while. She smelled whiskey, knew he'd poured himself a glass and must be sitting in a comfortable chair before her, just watching her. She was shaking. She'd of course been shaking intermittently since the beginning, but somewhere during the past hour or so, it had become continuous. Her throat was hoarse, so screams were now weak gasps, making those hard climaxes even more potent, all the energy focused between her exhausted legs.

"All right then." He'd taken out the ear plugs after dinner, so she heard the glass being set on the side table. "Up on your heels, arms out to your sides."

She tried, and found her arms were noodles. She was losing motor control. Shouldn't that alarm her?

"Permission to speak, sir." She had to clear her voice, and it still came out a rough squeak.

"You have it."

"I can't lift them. I'm sorry. I'm trying."

"All right." Gripping her wrist, he drew her arm out to her side to cuff it to cool steel. The bar was laid over her shoulders, attached to her collar with a clip, and he lifted the other wrist, attached it to the other side of the spreader bar. He moved behind her then, and she heard a drawer opening and closing. She'd figured out that he kept a fairly well-stocked BDSM dungeon in this home, probably next to the room that held the massage cot.

She'd tried not to think why he had equipment here, because of course the truth of that was obvious. But she was pretty sure he'd been doing only club sessions for the past couple years. It might have been awhile since the dust had been knocked off this equipment, figuratively speaking. She'd take what she could get, hold onto the hope she was right about that.

"Easy now. Take this in." His arm wrapped around her waist, his fingers touching her well-used pussy, guiding in a dildo. She shuddered with the discomfort and yet the desire to please. He'd lubricated it well, and when it pressed against her perineum, she realized it was a double dildo he strapped in place. Then he turned on the vibration feature. She cried out. When he came back around her, keeping his hand on the spreader bar to steady her, he was close, such that her cheek was briefly pressed against his hip. As she turned her face into the soft stuff of his slacks, the strap of his belt, she couldn't hold back the quiet sob. She was so tired.

"We finish as we start, sweet slave. You suck me off until I come, then I let you rest."

He didn't move her back, such that she felt him pull off the belt, unfasten the pants, take down the zipper and the boxers beneath. She parted her lips, reaching for him. When the broad head pushed into her mouth, she sucked on it like a favorite treat, and remarkably it was like that, a pacifier. Yet that thing inside of her, depleted as it was, came to life again. Her Master was ordering her to service him, make him come, and that was what she was going to do.

212

He didn't make it easy, but that was part of it, wasn't it? He held out a long, long time, until she was crying in frustration, her tears bathing her cheeks and his cock, but it also made her even more determined, licking, swirling, sucking, biting. She made a triumphant noise in her throat when she felt the telltale convulsion of the shaft beneath her tongue, felt that first spurt against her throat. With a growl, he pulled out of her mouth, jacked his semen over her breasts. She welcomed the heat of it, the marking, keeping her lips parted to catch the stray drop splashed by the force of it.

She'd lost count of how many times he'd come, but what male could do that and not need IV fluids?

He was tucking himself back into the slacks. The rustle of clothing, a zipper, the clink of the belt being refastened. Dropping to a knee in front of her, he closed his hand over the spreader bar beside her right wrist. His other fingers touched her swollen clit, her cunt lips stretched over that dildo.

She couldn't. There was no way. But of course Ben didn't take no for an answer. She made a plea as his mouth closed over her left nipple, began to slowly suck. On their periodic breaks, he'd used different oils and balms to soothe the tissues of her ass and pussy, but she couldn't come. She just couldn't, she was so tired.

He was determined, though, teaching her that her mind could make impossible things possible when she surrendered her will to him. From somewhere low in her womb, that spiraling sensation was resurrected, leading to a quiet, shuddering detonation that had her bleating like a lost lamb as he continued to tease and suckle her nipples, squeezing her breasts throughout.

When she was done, he removed the spreader bar, eased her down to the floor, letting her lie on her hip. She was unable to do anything while he removed the double dildo, her mask and collar, the chains, all of it. When she opened her eyes, she couldn't do more than look up at him from the floor. Straightening, he had turned to pick up wipes and balm from a side table, the things he'd use to care for her, clean her. The shirt was all the way open, pulled free of the belted slacks so she could see the appealing ridges of muscle along his upper torso. External obliques...down to the iliac furrow, that lovely V-cut of muscles that arrowed down into the groin.

Emotions coiled up tight in her chest as she once again remembered her playful teasing with her pre-med roommate. Also known as the Adonis belt, a result of low body fat and tight internal obliques pulling on their origin, the inguinal ligaments highlighted the lower rectus abdominis and external obliques. Tempting the female tongue to trace them down, down... God, she never stopped wanting him.

She managed to roll to her elbow. If he moved back even a step, she wouldn't make it, but he didn't. She sensed him turning his attention to her, stilling. Waiting to see what she was about to do. Pulling herself over those few inches, she pressed her mouth to his foot, a hard, fervent gesture. She forced herself back up onto her wobbling knees, slid back into a slave's posture, hands behind her back, head bowed, breasts thrust out, knees spread. The way she'd begun.

"Thank you, Master," she said.

I saw your society date for the Spring charity ball on the NOLA online edition. The only thing made in nature on that woman was her cotton underwear.

Don't be too harsh, brat. We all start out made by nature, but we have to build other faces to survive in this world. Plus, I'm pretty sure she wasn't wearing underwear. At least, that's what I heard.

Letter exchange between Ben and Marcie, her sophomore year

Chapter Nine

౭౦

Having broken subs down to the deepest level, Ben had seen them do a lot of very emotional things, things which fed his need to make them that vulnerable, to prove, at least in that moment, that they trusted him utterly with their naked, shivering souls. He cherished those times, even as he didn't hold onto them. The point was getting them there, a catharsis for them and pure, undiluted satisfaction for him as a Dominant.

He'd given Marcie an incredibly intense workout, fueled as much by his own lust as her desire to learn what it was to serve a Master. Somewhere along the way, he'd gotten immersed in it, so he was no longer teaching as much as he was actually striving to take her deeper and deeper into her head, have her give more and more of herself to him. Fuck, what had he been thinking?

She'd told him he held himself away from his subs. He'd told her that was the way he wanted it, that it was intentional. Then he'd stepped across that line, gotten as deep into this as she had.

Watching her perform that remarkable act of obeisance, when she could barely sit up straight, when he knew every muscle in her body was shaking from stress, when her ass, pussy and nipples had to be sore as hell, it took the floor out from under him. For that one second, there was no rational thought. He wanted to fucking own her, make her follow him around naked, wearing nothing but those stilettos she'd mentioned and a diamond and emerald collar and leash he'd have made especially for her.

She'd do it, would strut proudly, sweet sassy thing that she was, letting that ass swing and breasts jiggle, and give him that challenging smile that told him she could handle anything he could dish out...even if it killed her.

Though he always asked club subs for their safe word, he took them far past where they'd have the sense to use it, so his intense scrutiny during a session had as much to do with their well-being as his own immersion in it. As he'd told Lucas and Matt, she was the type of sub who'd get so lost in her head she'd happily allow a Master to kill or permanently injure her, and smile all the way to the last breath.

A lot of Masters wouldn't touch that kind of sub, because it was too damn much responsibility. Twisted bastard that he was, she was exactly the kind of sub he considered a treasure. She'd trusted him more than any sub he'd ever had, no hesitation in obeying anything he demanded.

Fuck. He went to one knee, caught her as she toppled. "Easy," he murmured. She clutched his arms, opened her eyes to look at him. That hazy subspace disorientation was like crack to a Master. But her brown eyes were also full of devotion, care, a lot of things that made his chest tight.

"I need you," she said. Her voice was hoarse, words drunkenly slurred. "Stay with me? Sleep with me? Please."

In answer, he lifted her in his arms. She bowed up against him like a baby, letting out a little sigh. "First a bath," he said.

"Too tired."

"Tough. You need to soak before you sleep."

"Will drown."

"I won't let you drown. Unless you provoke me."

She let out a little snuffle at that, perhaps a chuckle. But she was in a half doze, completely dependent on him, no fight left...for the moment.

He set her on the padded wicker lounge in the master bath while he ran the Jacuzzi, added the salts. Then he turned to consider her. She was on her side, and her arm had fallen toward the floor, fingers half curled. She was boneless at this point. It would have made him smile, if it didn't make other things hurt, just looking at her. Taking off his clothes, he put a decanter of whiskey and a glass next to the tub. Then he lifted her once again, set them both down in it, putting the jets on a low boil. She didn't wake, merely shifting so her cheek was pillowed on his chest, her arms loosely around him. He slid his own arm around her back, resting his palm on her hip.

He'd doused the lights, only a street light outside casting a dim illumination up into the bathroom. Laying his head back on the tile, holding her, he took a swallow of the whiskey, swirling it in the glass with his elbow propped on the side of the tub. Fucking hell.

He passed his palm gently over her buttock under the water. Those marks would be there for a little while. He should be ashamed, but all the thought did was stir his cock back to life. Again.

No, he told it sternly. *Give her a break, you sadistic son of a bitch.* That one was directed at him, not his cock. His cock wasn't sadistic in the slightest. It just wanted pussy. Mindless beast. Actually, not quite so mindless, because right now he had no desire to turn his mind to any other woman available to him. Just the one in his arms.

He tried, thinking of some of the most beautiful, hardcore and willing subs he'd had the pleasure of enjoying. As he did, his cock started to deflate. *What the hell?* He pointed his mind back to the abused ass pressed against his inner thigh, the feminine breath stirring his chest hair, and his cock rose again. *Fuck.*

It didn't mean anything. She was real and in his arms, while the others were pale visions in his head. Guys were simple that way. When he pressed his lips to the crown of her head, she made a sweet noise of contentment, her fingers sliding along the small of his back, resting limply against the upper rise of his buttocks.

He liked that noise, liked the way she felt in his arms. She'd given his dungeon equipment a workout tonight, and it was about time. When he bought the townhouse, he'd liked the way it felt, except it never seemed right when he was there by himself. He'd cooked dinner for some of the guys and their wives a couple times, hosted a few business parties, but when he was alone, he preferred the Warehouse District apartment, which was really just an extension of his office with better kitchen facilities and a great flat-screen.

For a time, he'd kept most of his high-end dungeon equipment there, but he'd moved it here a couple years ago. There were two or three larger pieces at the other place, hidden behind a heavy plastic construction curtain he'd covered with decorative dark wood screens, since the Warehouse apartment was an open loft. At this house, he kept the high-end equipment behind a closed door. Both measures were to prevent the uninitiated from wandering into those areas.

That's what he told himself. It wasn't that he didn't like coming to either place and seeing the equipment waiting for something he didn't bring home to it anymore.

He had a discreet maintenance service that came in and kept everything cleaned and oiled, ready for use at any time. It was probably a waste of money, since he had access to Progeny's equipment and that was where he went now when his cock needed a workout. But questioning costs was Jon and Lucas' area, not his. He could wallpaper the house with Ben

Franklins if he wanted. So he spent the money. Tonight he was glad he had, because he'd put all of it through its paces, testing Marcie far beyond what he'd expected her limits to be.

When it was all over, she'd put her mouth on his foot, called him Master. And for one fucking insane moment, he'd thought, *You bet your sweet ass I am.*

Jesus. He finished the whiskey, set it aside. Didn't let himself pour another. *You're in charge of a beautiful girl tonight, buddy.* No getting shit-faced. He'd save that for sunrise, when she was going to hate his guts.

He got her out of the tub, summoning a tight smile at her sleepy grumbling. He made her stand while he dried her off one-handed, since the other arm had to stay around her waist to keep her from oozing back to the tile. Guiding her arm around his neck, he lifted her once more. It was ridiculous, how much he liked just carrying her.

He could put her in the guest bedroom, but he needed to watch over her until she was in control of her faculties again. It had been a long night. So he was going to put her in his bed, with him, no matter how bad an idea that was.

He'd been fooling himself about this mentoring shit. He was a one-way track to nowhere, and Marcie was a bright, beautiful star who deserved the whole universe.

He took her into his bedroom, to the king-sized canopy bed that filled most of the room. The ceiling fan rotated slowly. Lowering her to the bed, he paused, studying her. He'd laid her down facing away from him, so he was looking at his handiwork from that angle, every mark, bite, her ass still a brighter pink than the rest of her silky skin. The caning marks, those short lines and stippling, overlaid the faint square impression of the spatula strikes. She'd loved it. Fought it, cried through it, embraced it, come like a damn nymphomaniac from it.

He should put on sweats, a T-shirt. Fuck that. He wanted to feel her against his body, and she had passed out now, anyway. Sliding in behind her, he arranged the covers over her to keep her front warm while he pressed against her back. His cock had ignored him of course, and was hard and eager when it came in contact with the soft pillow of her buttocks. He wanted more, but he didn't want to cause her any pain.

Lifting her thigh, he slid just the head back into her ass. He'd lubricated her frequently, so there was plenty of oil there to allow him entry. He slid in a few more inches than intended but she made a soft sound, closed her muscles on him, just as he'd taught her, an automatic reflex. It made him growl, a satisfied predator. Cupping her breast, he murmured against her ear.

"Sleep, baby. You did well." What a fucking understatement.

* * * * *

Marcie woke to find herself comfortably nested in the covers. What she'd hoped might be Ben behind her was instead a brace of pillows. It was about three a.m., the hour when restless spirits were most plentiful, explaining why she'd woken to find herself alone.

Rising with caution, she found she was stiff and sore, but overall moving better than anticipated, since she hadn't expected to be able to move without undignified yowls of agony. She did yoga and MMA training, and those flexibility and strength workouts helped her, but she suspected the breaks Ben had taken between sessions had a great deal to do with it as well. He'd massaged her muscles and joints with those clean-smelling salves, washed her out with soothing tonics, changed her position at appropriate intervals, double- and triple-checked her bindings. Vaguely, she remembered him putting two pills on her tongue after that hazy bath, telling her to swallow, then making her finish up the glass of water.

Aspirin, brat. That, and the bath, should make things move easier tomorrow.

He knew just how extreme he was, and did the maintenance to ensure he left a lasting impression but not lasting damage. At least on a woman's body. Her heart was a whole different matter.

His dress shirt was hanging on the armoire doorknob, above a bag of laundry with a dry-cleaning ticket. A reminder to him to drop it off today, she was sure. Things a single lawyer had to do for himself. Fingering the cloth, remembering it close to her face when he carried her up here, she pulled it from its perch, brought the collar to her nose. A combination of aftershave, soap, dry cleaning and what she really wanted to detect—male sweat, earned from his sexual exertion with her.

Considering, she threaded her arms into the sleeves. *Oh my.* For all her teasing him about his expensive indulgences, the feel of tailored cotton was...luxurious. Particularly if it smelled like Ben. These fibers had the enviable job of stroking that superb upper body all day long.

When she moved out into the hallway, she saw the French doors on the second level open to a narrow balcony. There were several potted plants there, as well as a couple outdoor chairs to view the enclosed alley below. When they arrived, she'd stolen a quick glimpse of it. She remembered a statue of a laughing child placed under the rush of water from a fountain. Thick greenery had swayed around it, a cobblestone path and a single chair suggesting a perfect nook to read and dream the lazy New Orleans day away. She wondered if he ever used it, or if it was his neighbor's space.

Ben was leaning against the rail, but he wasn't looking down at that scene. He had his head turned as if studying the nearby street, but there was a lack of focus in the green eyes that suggested his focus was internal. All he wore was a pair of faded jeans that rode low on his hips. It was so carelessly sexy it made her mouth water, despite the fact her body felt as if it had been through the sensual equivalent of being drop-kicked by the entire New Orleans Saints team.

There was also a loneliness to him. The moonlight gleamed on his hair, reflected the brooding look in his eyes, the wooden quality of his expression. It tightened her heart, made her go to him.

She stepped over the threshold. Since the balcony was so narrow, it brought her right up behind him. He tilted his head, aware of her, and she dared, laying her hand between his shoulder blades. She hadn't buttoned the shirt, so when he reached back, took her hand beneath his arm to bring her closer, she pressed her bare breasts against him, her mound against the firm flesh beneath denim.

Laying her cheek on his back, she heard the strong thump of his heart. He held her hand against his abdomen, stroking her fingers and studying the night sky in silence. She touched those ridged muscles, traced them, and when she angled for more, he let her hand descend. Teasing the arrow of silky hair, she pressed her lips to his spine. He didn't move, but she didn't feel rebuffed. She thought he might be holding his breath.

Earlier, he'd clearly been Master to slave. It was what he'd wanted, what she'd wanted, and she'd reveled in the fact he loosed that desire upon her, given her the chance to prove she could match it. But this was different, indefinable. Something moved between them now, something that was part of it and yet even deeper. Holding *her* breath now, she reached the waistband of the jeans. She traced that, back and forth, aroused by the beauty of his fit body, the power of it he'd demonstrated so capably, again and again. Under her other palm, his heart was thumping a little faster. So was hers.

The jeans were loose, so she maneuvered beneath the waistband, found the trimmed pubic area, then lower, to the heated base of his cock. She was able to partly circle it with her thumb and forefinger. Her intent wasn't arousal, not exactly. She was gripping him, marveling at the heat and virility of the organ, at how much she could desire it inside her.

She explored the velvet skin stretched over the steel of it, because he was obviously hardening under her touch. His stomach muscles contracted as he shifted his hips, and she helped guide his shaft out of a folded position, letting it stretch up more comfortably beneath the zipper. It let her stroke her fingers more fully up and down its length, though the diminishing space was allowing less maneuvering room.

"You don't have any photos," she whispered. "Jon, Matt, any of them. Not even of my brothers and sisters. Or of you."

"No. I don't do photos." He sighed, looking up at the sky again as she let the other hand descend so she could use both. It required opening the jeans, but he didn't stop her as she did that, took a two-handed grip, started to explore more aggressively. Her nipples had tightened against his back, and she rubbed her mound against his ass. The jeans slipped a little lower. She wanted to go to her knees, kiss her way down his spine, tease that dip between his buttocks with the tip of her tongue, see if she could make him shiver as he'd made her shiver.

"You're messing me up, Marcie. You're just a baby."

She stilled, the rough quality of his voice bringing her heart into her throat. "I'm your baby," she said against his skin. "All yours. Love me, Ben. Love me in the dark, let me be whatever you want me to be. Stop worrying about me. Take what you need."

I am a baby. I'm scared to death, because I rely on your strength and your knowledge, but if I have to, I'll lead.

He turned in her arms, dislodging her hands. Gripping her wrists, he studied her. His expression was brittle stone, those eyes measuring. Old. Ancient, even.

"If my Master is lost," she said, her voice shaking a little, "I'll find him. I'll lead him back to himself, because to serve doesn't always mean to follow."

As he stared at her, she pushed against his hold. He didn't relent immediately, but she insisted, and then he let her put her hands on his face. Lifting on her toes, she brought her body up against him, laid her mouth softly on his. Teased his lips, touched them with her tongue, playing with him, coaxing him to respond. His head moved, his lips starting to answer her flirtation, and when he nipped at her, she smiled against his mouth.

He came to life then, summoning a pleased purr from her throat. His arms slid into the shirt and around her, one around her waist, the other dropping so his hand could grip her ass. He hiked her up in an effortless move that let her wrap her own arms around his shoulders. He didn't take her inside. Instead, he pushed her up against the balcony wall, his body pressed to the core of hers, and the kiss was suddenly much deeper, all consuming.

God, the man could kiss. Wet heat, just like what was gathering between her legs, rubbing against his cock. The cool teeth of the open zipper scratched against her inner thigh, where he'd slapped her with the spatula earlier. He had his other hand on her nape now, fingers tangled in her hair, tugging in that hard way he did, a Master's grip, reminding a slave of her place. She fought him, fought to deepen the kiss from her end, because she wasn't going to miss the chance to savor it even more fully.

She wondered if he'd take her here, under the night sky, where a neighbor might look out of the adjacent house and see their silhouettes mating among the flowers. Instead, he took a firmer grip on her, side-stepped over the threshold. He kissed her against that wall, and she moaned, telling him she wanted him.

"Insatiable," he murmured against her mouth. "You're insatiable."

"For you." She wasn't going to pretend otherwise, protected by the cloak of the night. He said nothing to that, just flexed his arm around her again, holding her to him to carry her down the dark hall, back into his bedroom.

She expected him to turn her over, bend her over the bed. Instead, he laid her down on her back in that nest he'd left her in before, only now he was over her, his knee pressed between her legs.

"Arms above your head," he said quietly, those emerald eyes gleaming in the dim light from the windows.

She complied, though she hated letting go of him. His gaze coursed over her as he adjusted the shirt so it was fully open, so he could see all of her. He trailed a knuckle down her sternum, under the curve of her left breast. The nipple jewelry gleamed, and when he caught one, tugging, she gasped, arching up to his touch.

"Stay still, *cher*."

Cajun. *Oh God.* She really had to ask how he did that, switched to different accents according to his moods, as if he was a split personality. Maybe he was, because she knew it had taken a lot of different Bens to become the man she was with tonight.

He bent, kissed her breast to the right of the piercing. He nuzzled her nipple but didn't suckle. Instead he moved to her sternum, rubbed his jaw between her breasts, teasing the tender skin with his beard shadow. Then he moved down, his lips on her navel, catching the dangling silver rose there in his teeth, tugging on it and eliciting another gasp. Then lower. Marcie's hands curled into balls as his heated breath skated over her clit. When he pressed his open mouth high on her thigh, so close that his hair brushed her labia, she moaned.

"You want me to eat your cunt, sweet darling?"

"I want…my Master to do…whatever he pleases." She let him see the absolute truth of it in her gaze. "I'm all yours." His pleasure was hers, one and the same.

"When you told me about your fantasy with Lucas and Cass…if he was eating your cunt tonight, while I fucked you from behind, how would that feel?"

"Like I'd died and gone to heaven, as long as it was what you command of me." She could barely breathe. "I want you, Master. It's all you."

He bent his head then, put his mouth on her. Oh holy…God. God. God. God. Lucas was known as the master of oral sex, but obviously he'd shared his talents, or Ben's were nothing to be sneezed at. His tongue flicked her clit at just the right pace, with erratic movements that kept her crying out, struggling not to move when she wanted to buck against his mouth. He thrust his tongue into her when she was so wildly excited that it made her scream aloud at the sensation.

Lapping at her cream, he suckled her so she could hear it. When he sealed his heated mouth over all of it, her cunt and clit both, started swirling, flicking and teasing, she came to pieces. She came, period, no time to ask permission, but it was obvious his intent was to drive her over that edge.

Right in the middle of that peak, he raised up, taking his mouth away, but before she could wrap her mind around the sudden, shocking loss, he was there instead, sliding his full, turgid length into her slick pussy, so slick that even with his size, he worked in with barely a pause, her tissues still spasming around him. He was stroking inside her almost immediately, so the aborted climax wasn't aborted at all. It was like a hurricane that did a somersault and came screaming back to the same center eye again.

"Be still, baby. Very, very still."

He slowed down, watched her frantic face as she fought not to move. She wanted to lift her hips, force him to continue the same pace or thrust. Instead, she made tiny pleas, caught in a string of spasms that drew out even further while he did those slow, dragging strokes. It became even more intense, so all her muscles locked, her lips stretched back from her teeth in a feral snarl.

Then he came to a full stop, lodged deep inside her. Marcie quaked, and when he framed her face with his hands, bringing his body down full on her, she bit his palm in ferocious need.

"Fierce kitten," he growled. "Touch me now. Move all you want."

She wanted to buck like a rodeo bronc spurred from confinement, but even through that roaring need, she wanted something else. She slid her arms around his shoulders, locked her legs over his hips like a drowning swimmer. "Can you take off the jeans without moving?" She pressed the gasp to his ear. "Will you let me feel you against me, nothing between us?"

It occurred to him then, to both of them. His muscles tensed, and he tried to pull out, but she held on tight. While he could overpower her, she made a noise of such vehement protest he paused.

"It doesn't matter," she said. "I'm protected from pregnancy. I have been for some time. I know you don't take risks. I know you're clean. You're my first...without wearing anything. Please don't leave me."

It startled him to the core that he'd forgotten to don protection, she could see it. If he withdrew from her now, unsettled by that realization, she wouldn't survive it. She wasn't near as confident as she seemed. She just loved him enough to bluff him into believing she could handle anything, no matter how rough or cruel he was.

But there was no cruelty now, only earth-shattering tenderness as he cupped her face anew, brushed her lips, gave her a nod. A slight smile touched his mouth, a trace of unexpected humor in his eyes. "If you can get your heel into the back of my jeans, you can push them to my knees. We can probably work them off from there."

His jeans were already mostly off his gorgeous ass, and she took full advantage of the sensory input through the soles of her feet as she curved one over his buttock, hooked her toes into the seat and worked the denim down to his thighs, maneuvering her other foot to get them to his knees. He did manage to get them off, but unfortunately it pulled him out of her as he did it, the tip of his cock leaving a delicious wet trail down her inner thigh. But her hands were between them in an instant, gripping him.

"Please, let me."

His jaw flexed as she guided him back to her empty pussy. She bit her lip, staring up at him so he saw every change in her expression as she pulled him deep inside her.

"I love how big you are," she whispered. "How it hurts and feels good at the same time."

Like love itself. From the shadows in his face, she could tell this was new ground for him. It was for her as well. So she buried her face in his neck then, taking a sharp nip of his neck, winding her arms and legs around him again.

"Please, Master. Fuck me. Use me for your pleasure." *All yours.* She repeated that in her mind, and then her mind was completely lost as he began to move.

He started with those slow thrusts forward and deep, dragging withdrawals that just devastated her, physically and emotionally. She loved having him on top of her, pinning her down, joined so closely. It made tears come to her eyes, the perfection of it all. As he started to pick up in speed and force, she held on, willing to go on the ride with him, now to eternity.

Her climax rekindled, the delay only concentrating it. His cock bruised, stretched and demanded more and more of her, and she met the challenge, clamping down on him, rippling her muscles along his length, holding his body tighter with the strength of her own. He would outlast her, because he was just that bloody strong, but as her strength flagged, he cinched his arm low on her waist, the other around her back, and he took over, driving into her so her body arched up like a doll's, helpless to his power as he took her to the edge he desired.

Everything caught fire, so fast it took her by surprise, but then the overwhelming storm of it drove away everything. She'd never had a climax like it, her heart, mind and soul fully pulled into the moment so she was almost sure the universe had stopped moving on this one fixed point. She was biting his shoulder, her fingers raking his back, finding blood. She exulted in his savage grunts as he released, spilling himself into her. The first time Ben O'Callahan had given his seed to a woman rather than to a condom.

She was sure of it.

It pushed her even higher, and he rode her to the finish, pulling every aftershock out of her until she was begging for mercy, a mercy she knew he would deny her, thank God.

Her Master was ruthless, demanding, all hers. At least for this one, perfect moment.

I went to a dance for the new freshmen tonight. Most of it was the usual loud techno-pop stuff, but then somebody played that Allison Krauss version of "When You Say Nothing At All". It made me think of you. I danced with a few guys, but mostly I just danced with part of a big group. It was nice, even though this one girl said I looked so serious, like I was studying for a test, instead of dancing. It occurred to me then that I'm used to you being the one who reminds me how to smile and laugh, and now I'll have to do that all on my own. I guess that's good. If I learn to do it on my own, I can remind you to smile and laugh when you get old and crotchety. Oh, forgot…you're already old and crotchety.

Letter from Marcie

Chapter Ten

ഇ

Dawn came. Even though it was beautiful, the sunlight on her face waking her in a bedroom that smelled like him and the musky scent of their sex, she knew from the first second something wasn't quite right. It wasn't just that he was absent. Her clothes had been laid out on a chair, and it looked like someone had ironed them. Ben probably had a bevy of domestic servants chained in his basement. She wouldn't put it past him.

She held her breath, listening, then relaxed as she heard movement on the lower level. If he'd bailed on her, gone on in to work, he would have at least left her a note and some coffee brewing. He might be an emotionally repressed bastard about certain things, but common courtesy wasn't one of them.

Pushing herself up, she saw he *had* left her a note, as well as a trio of Advil and a glass of water. A tiny wildflower lay on the note. *Take the Advil, drink the water, and do another soak in a hot shower. Get dressed for work. Breakfast will be waiting downstairs.*

He'd said they'd spend the day together, preparing to go to Progeny tonight. He'd changed his mind. Or maybe something had come up. It was a weekday, after all, and K&A sometimes needed their lawyer even on a planned day off. *Yeah right.* She picked up the wildflower, let it tickle her chin. It was a nice touch, but it still felt impersonal, removed. The type of thing a hotel might do. She'd figured out how he dealt with the women in his life, the easy charm that was devastating to their senses but didn't quite reach his eyes.

Cass said he'd worked up some awesome, elaborate dishes for Savannah during her pregnancy, when she didn't feel like eating anything else. For Nate's most recent birthday, he'd arranged a paintball party a general would have admired for troop mobilization and attack strategy. When he extended true affection, love, he went all out with it. In the right mood, Ben was more...rough, natural.

He'd have crushed flowers over her sleeping form, covered her in petals. Twined the stems around her wrists, a gentle bondage. But this...this was distance. Her stomach tightened into a cold ball. Surely after everything they'd shared last night, he wouldn't...

Yes, he would. Exactly because of what they'd shared last night.

She would take the shower, don the clothes because he'd told her to do it. It was her Master's order and she wanted to be compliant. But if he wasn't pulling back, work or no work, he would have wanted her to come down completely naked, still smelling of his scent. He would have had her kneel at his feet, fed her bits of breakfast from his fingertips as he read the morning stock reports, glancing at the flat-screen for live business news. She could live on *that* kind of detached connection like a drug.

Last night...there were no words for it. Until the reality, she hadn't known exactly what it was she craved, what she could take. Two walls of his shower were mirrored, and even with the steam, they showed her his marks.

She had bruises on the back of her legs from the slapper that had felt like a doubled-over fire extinguisher hose, weighted down inside to make the thud that much more significant. There was stippling on her ass cheeks from the rattan cane. When he went after her with his favorite tool, a flexible paddle, the burning and stinging sensations had come so close together she couldn't be still. At one point he'd laid his upper body over her back, pinning her down as she squealed from the pain.

She loved those marks, loved seeing them. She only hoped they weren't the only things that would be around for the next couple days. Suppressing a sigh, she got out, dried off and picked up the bag that Cass had left. She wasn't going to be fatalistic. She knew what she wanted, and she was going to get it. Ben wanted her to think she was imagining things she craved and he didn't, but she had to believe she knew what she knew, or her courage would falter.

The convoluted nature of the thought gave her lips a wry twist. Opening the overnight bag, she saw the folded note, recognized Cass' handwriting.

Jon said to remind you of this: To thine own self be true. This one's from me: Be careful and know that I love you. I'm here.

It made tears prick her eyelids, but she pushed them back. She was going to be less weepy today, no matter that Ben had torn open every shield she had last night. All but the one guarding her determination to have him as her permanent Master.

Fortified somewhat, she tucked that note inside her bra and went down the stairs. Sunshine was bathing the breakfast nook. Ben was wearing fresh work clothes, charcoal slacks and an open white shirt, green and black tie hanging off the back of the chair. He was barefoot, his shoes polished and waiting by the counter island with a folded pair of socks. He was going to work. He wasn't spending the day with her, at least not the way he'd said. Which meant he was likely backing out of taking her to Progeny.

She firmed her jaw, came into the kitchen. She'd stayed barefoot as well, but sat her heels down with a quiet click next to his shoes. He glanced up, though she expected he'd known the minute her feet crossed the upper landing. "Good morning. Have a seat and I'll bring you your breakfast."

"I don't mind getting it." She had to clear her throat, since the hoarseness from last night remained. He gave her a look.

"Sit." His tone was congenial, but firm, so she sat. She would have moved toward him, tried for a kiss, a caress, but he'd already moved away, gesturing to her chair with detached courtesy.

That cold ball in her stomach was getting worse. Removing a plate from the oven, he brought her an omelet so fluffy it was a couple inches thick. She could smell the mixture of appetizing cheeses, and it was scattered with half spheres of fresh garden cherry tomatoes. A long time ago, he'd told her the key to good cooking wasn't fancy combinations and syrup drizzled artfully on the plate, but fresh ingredients.

"This looks marvelous. Like the last meal for a death-row inmate." She shifted her gaze to his face, kept her voice even. "What is this, Ben?"

"Eat your breakfast, then we'll talk."

She pushed the plate away. "No. If you were standing on the other side of the Grand Canyon, you'd be closer to me than you are now."

"You're being melodramatic." He crossed his arms, leaned against the counter, his expression tight. There was a warning simmering in those green eyes, but she didn't really care.

"I don't think so. I'm talking in a calm, reasonable tone, just like you are." The edge in her voice earned her a narrow glance, but she continued. "I'm not capable of enjoying a breakfast this good if there's a ton of bricks already in my digestive tract."

"I'll pack it up for you then. Max will take you to work. Dana had a full schedule at the church and he was in the neighborhood. You can pick up the things you left in my office. I've had you reassigned to K&A's research department on the fifth floor. Given your career specialty, you'll learn more there. You're an exceptional investigator, Marcie. You shouldn't be wasting your time as my paralegal."

Things were replaying in her head. Everything that had happened last night. The times she'd cried and he'd wiped those tears away. The screaming orgasms. The way he'd completely taken her over, broken her open.

"Is this the way you do it? Give a woman the experience of her life, and then it's over?"

"You wanted to know more about serving a Master. Last night, I gave you what I intended to give you at Progeny, so that's no longer necessary. Lesson over. At least with me. There are some Doms I'll recommend who can mentor you at the club until you find someone willing to pair up with you according to your desires."

"You agreed to mentor me." She would keep her voice level, not accusatory. She would not stamp her feet or cry. She was going to do this as an adult, make him fucking admit he was the one acting immature.

He met her gaze with implacable eyes. His words remained cool, reasonable. Which was why she knew it was all bullshit. But he wasn't showing any cracks in the façade, anything she could use to break past that wall he'd built against her this morning. It was like he'd reinforced it with fucking concrete while she slept.

"You came to me for guidance, and I've given you that. If you've done your research, you know the protocol. When a Master or sub says it's over, it's over. You respect the boundaries and the consent."

He moved then, came to sit at the table with her. He didn't smile, didn't stab her in the chest with a gesture that patently dismissive of her feelings, but he did put his hand over hers. Now she saw his expression soften, become kind. "You were incredible last night. I couldn't have asked for a better submissive, so know that much. You just need to move on and look elsewhere. I have no problem helping you with that. You've told me you're not a child. I believe you, so I expect you to respect my decision like a reasonable adult. We've always been friends. I'm still your friend."

The Doms he had in mind were probably about her age, competent enough, but no one who would be a challenge, who could even touch what he'd been able to do to her. He might not acknowledge it consciously, but it would be deliberate. He wouldn't want anything that could compete with him. He refused to accept her, but he'd control the replacement candidate pool. If she could have bristled under his touch like a porcupine, she would have.

Rising, he picked up her plate. It made him lean over her, and the scent and strength of him, so close, was almost overwhelming. While he put her breakfast in a container as promised, she sat there numbly. When he disappeared briefly up the stairs, she stared out the window at a fence, a bird bath. An oak tree with a decorative lizard sculpture attached to it. He reappeared with her overnight bag. "I have a flight out this morning for an afternoon meeting in Houston. I'll touch base with you when I get back and we'll talk out the details. I told Research you're doing some freelance for Pickard, so they know you might need to be on a part-time schedule with them on some days."

How considerate of him. He had an appointment in Houston today; tonight, instead of going to Progeny with him, she'd have an appointment with a Dumpster, her latest strategy to uncover dirt about the company being sued by Pickard's client for insurance fraud. It was a fitting change of schedule, seeing as she was being kicked out like garbage.

Ben had his hand on her elbow to bring her to her feet. With smooth efficiency, he moved them toward the door. Probably a scenario he'd enacted with countless women before her. Except she wasn't them. He probably strolled to the door with them, rather than ushering them out like his ass was on fire. They'd been casual lays, after all, everyone reasonable adults about it. Unlike her.

"Tell Max if you need to stop anywhere before you get to the office. Take more Advil through the day if you need it, and another long soak in Cass and Lucas' hot tub tonight. I've put some more of that balm in your overnight bag for the sore areas." He brushed his lips over her cheek—*her cheek*—and opened the door, propelling her into the alcove. "Okay?"

"Mr. Calm and Reasonable?" She pivoted on her bare foot, looked up at him. "My shoes are still inside. If you throw them out onto the sidewalk, I might chase after them like a dog after a ball, giving you a chance to slam the door. But I'd rather not get them scratched."

He started, glancing down at her feet, her painted toes. As he stared at them a long moment, she could see him sorting through things. He didn't miss details. Not unless something had unsettled him. A casual, reasonable bed partner didn't unsettle him. She'd have let her lips curl in a satisfied smile if it wouldn't feel like a knife slash across her tight face.

He lifted his gaze to her. He at least had the decency to give her a wry quirk of his lips. "I'm sorry. You're right. I'm being an ass. This isn't personal, Marcie."

"This is so incredibly personal you can't get rid of me fast enough. If I was one of your easy ass fucks, you'd be ordering me to go down on you underneath the breakfast table while you ate your fluffy, pretty omelet." Ignoring the fact that as her voice rose, the squeaks and breaks of her abraded vocal cords got worse, she stepped back into him, locked her hands in his shirt front. "You made love to me last night. You let me inside you."

"It was a mistake. I care about you, Marcie." When he put his hands over her wrists, his face was locked down again, that expression she was beginning to hate. "We can't do this. There's no way any of it works, and you need to stop trying. I'll be cruel if you force me to it. That's a promise. Take what you've been given and leave it at that."

"What did I give *you*, Ben?" She stared up at him. He was looking at her, but not really at her. It was as if he'd blanked out her features and was staring at something faceless. She dug her nails into flesh. She'd marked him as well. He had claw marks in his back. "You figure if you give a woman Nirvana, she'll be okay with the fact you've taken nothing for yourself? It doesn't play with me. You thought I was out of it in the tub last night. I wasn't. You were intimate with me. Caring. And don't you dare deny what happened after, on the balcony."

His eyes went ice cold so abruptly it startled her. Putting his hands on her wrists, he detached her hands from his shirtfront. "Wait here."

He turned, shutting the door as if he didn't believe she'd obey, and she probably wouldn't have, except the frigid look in his eyes held her frozen, uncertain. When he came back, opened the door, he held her shoes. He locked her stiff fingers around them.

"I won't talk about this further. Not right now. You're not in the right frame of mind for it, and neither am I. Go to the limo." When she continued to stand there, staring at him, he physically moved her off the stoop onto the walkway, closed the grate to the alcove, shutting her out. He stared at her through the bars. She wondered if he realized it looked like he was shutting himself into a prison cell.

"I am your friend, Marcie, but from this moment on, only your friend. We are to each other what we were a few days ago."

She couldn't help it. She gave a bitter laugh. "Yeah, that much is true. The funny thing is, I'm the only one who accepts what that is."

"I'll talk to you when I get back from Houston." With that, he stepped back into the house and closed the door. Fucking closed the door in her face.

He wouldn't talk to her when he got back. He'd do everything he could to avoid talking to her. When they next saw one another, it would be at a Thanksgiving or Christmas gathering with the others, where he could treat her with smooth charm, like any other woman he held at arm's length.

What swept through her was so strong, it made her lightheaded. She swayed, closed her eyes. Which was a mistake, since images from last night once again went through her head. The power of them, the emotion, the all-consuming...everything. He'd say he'd given her what she wanted, and she only had herself to blame for putting her heart out there, when he'd told her what to expect. What total horseshit. What happened last night wasn't a one-sided experience.

She was young, but she wasn't stupid. She also wasn't some melodramatic teenager, imagining things. Even when she was in her teens, she'd looked at him and seen things others hadn't. She remembered it now, him standing in the shadows of Jon and Rachel's wedding, watching their first dance. For just a brief moment, there'd been a look in his eyes...

It recalled the many painful times she'd been reminded she had no parents to come to awards ceremonies, see her off to prom, ask her how her day had gone, things every other kid with functioning parents took for granted. He trusted very few, and those few were now married, somehow pulled away from him, even though it looked as if they were still standing right there, where they'd always been. Everybody dealt with change, but it broke her heart, seeing in that brief glimpse that this was a path he didn't know how to follow, shutting him out of their happiness.

Unable to see that desolation and not try to help, she'd gone to him. Yeah, she was a shy awkward teen, but she thought of him as her friend. Sidling up to him in those shadows, she'd elbowed him to catch his attention. His expression was back to being what was expected, congratulatory and amused, but that didn't matter. She pulled his head down to whisper in his ear, steeling herself to keep her cool, even though his whiskey-sweet breath was on her neck.

"Let's go put an 'I support offshore drilling' sticker on the back of Jon's hydroelectric getaway car."

"He'd retaliate. Put a Disney Gay Pride Day sticker on the back of the McLaren."

She smirked up at him, glad to see the sad look replaced by his smile. "Then let me have some of your drink."

"When you're twenty-one."

"Does everything fun happen then?"

"Only to boys. For girls, it's age thirty. Your lives totally suck until then."

She'd punched him in the side and he'd hugged her, pressing a brotherly kiss on the top of her head. Later she'd talked him into dancing with her, even doing the YMCA dance. She had incriminating photos to prove it.

She'd made it her private mission to keep an eye on him during that event. She knew what it was to hunger for what one might never have. It gnawed, it ached. At a key moment, that hunger could break loose and result in very, very bad behavior.

Coming back to the present, she studied her surroundings with narrowed eyes. Finding what she sought, she nodded to herself and pivoted toward the street, for the first time registering the limo and the man leaning against it, patiently waiting for her.

She wondered if Max had been standing there when she and Ben had her exchange at the door. Even if he'd still been sitting in the driver's seat, he would have known from their body language things weren't peachy. Max didn't miss much.

The K&A women joked about how much he looked like Peter, since he was Dana's regular driver. Blond, gray-eyed, with lots of muscles that had been used in his previous work as a Navy Seal. Why he'd spent the past few years working for the company motor pool was a mystery, but they'd speculated about it. As well as a lot more inappropriate things about the handsome, quiet male.

He wore a pair of belted tan khakis and white shirt open at the throat, a jacket over that. She had no doubt he had a weapon underneath it. Always prepared, after all. He nodded to her as she approached. "Miss Marcie. Good to see you."

"You too." It was a reflex answer as she handed him her bag and her shoes. The large fingers closing around the dainty straps would have amused her under normal circumstances, but right now, she had a different mission. Her hands now free, she turned around, headed back toward the front door.

She stepped off the path, smoothing her skirt modestly up under her thighs as she squatted. Selecting a handful of the smooth rocks that formed the mulch around the well-tended shrubs, she found they had a good weight and size in a woman's palm. Aware of Max's regard, she nevertheless ignored it.

Moving back onto the walkway, she backed up a sufficient number of steps, gauging her distance and studying her potential targets. Ben would have gone back upstairs. There was an office there, right off the bedroom. He preferred work when anything was aggravating him, and he'd made it clear she was an aggravation. His desk was close to that window. Perfect.

"*Ben.*" Her throat had resigned itself to being abused, so it was settling into a kind of sexy, intense Lauren Bacall sound. She'd been able to hear the muted rush of passing cars in the bedroom, so the window insulation wasn't soundproof. She was loud enough to be heard. "Here's how reasonable adults react when they have *feelings*."

The first rock hit the upper office window dead on, breaking through with a satisfying shattering noise. The lower panel went next. She hoped she'd winged him, bounced the damn thing off his stubborn head. It would probably break the rock. Then she adjusted her stance and aimed for the bedroom window, where that amazing moment of connection had happened. When he'd lain upon her, looking down at her, her legs coiled over his hips, his hands on her face. She'd leave an explosion of broken glass so he'd have to strip the bed, get the linens washed or get splinters in his ass.

She hesitated when she lowered her gaze to the first level. Yeah, she could send a rock zinging through the wrought iron bars and take out door panels, but they were beautiful old stained glass. Some things were sacred. She targeted the living area windows instead, and used the last couple rocks for the other side, his dining room. Though she was standing about twenty feet away, she didn't miss a single target. Before Jeremy had changed from her brother into an addict, he'd shown her how to throw a rock pretty damn well.

She was breathing a little erratically, but any desire to cry was gone. She was flat-out pissed, her blood on full boil. If he walked out that door, she wasn't entirely sure another rock wouldn't be aimed at his forehead as though a bull's-eye was drawn there. But of course he wasn't coming out. Stubborn bastard. No, worse than stubborn.

"If you're too chickenshit to take me to a club," she snarled up at the now fully aerated window treatments, "I will go by myself. *Fuck you*. How's that for reasonable?"

Yeah, she knew better than to bluff Ben O'Callahan, but this time, she wasn't sure it was a bluff. She was so mad, she was going to throw it out there. *To thine own self be true.*

It was time to fall back, regroup, or she was going to prove herself an obsessed stalker after all. She'd climb through one of those windows and beat him to death. Nothing said love like a two-by-four applied to soft tissue areas.

She marched toward the limo. Max was still leaning against the car, arms crossed over his broad chest. There was some sympathy in his gaze, some sardonic amusement. Apparently his scope of responsibility hadn't included stopping her. She would have liked to see him try. She was more than ready to kick someone's ass. Instead, she was going to have him take her home. She was doing exactly what she'd intended today. Mostly.

She'd call Research and tell them she'd report Monday, because she was in no mood to be at K&A today. She'd take care of that Pickard job in the early evening hours, but then she was going to a club, damn it. Not Progeny. She'd go back to Surreal, because she wouldn't run into someone she knew, and she was already familiar with their layout. She'd tell Cass she was driving up to Baton Rouge for an overnight to follow up on the Pickard work, which was plausible, because there were a couple things she could check out there after she handled the Dumpster job here.

Catching a movement in her peripheral vision, she noticed one of Ben's neighbors standing on the sidewalk, a trio of apricot toy poodles in her arms, too stunned to be yappy. The woman was staring at Marcie in a fascinated, horrified way. Marcie gave her a dignified nod. "He deserved it, I promise," she said.

The woman's lips twitched. Putting the poodles down, she continued on her morning walk with only a couple backward looks.

Max handed her his handkerchief. When Marcie glanced at him, puzzled, he touched a fingertip to her face, letting her feel the tears. "Oh shit," she muttered. She mopped her face with it, blew her nose with a ferocious snort that had his brows rising. "Please take me home, Max. I want to stop on the way for a brownie from Starbuck's. I'll treat you to a coffee and you can have this omelet. I think I'd choke on it at this point."

"Yes ma'am," he said, a glint in his eyes. Then he held the door for her.

Holy hell. He'd hit the floor like Peter under enemy fire when those first stones came through. "Fuck," Ben snarled, under a shower of glass. Only two things kept him from shoving up from the floor to wear her ass out. One, he got hard as steel from the thought of punishing her, which undermined the whole getting-rid-of-her scenario. Two — more importantly — he deserved her anger. It was his fault for letting it go this far, and so he would take the cost. Which was apparently eight perfectly preserved panes of pre-Civil War glass. Fuck, fuck and triple fuck.

Once she was done with her diatribe and he heard the limo pull away, he fished out his cell. Staying on the floor, he put in a call to his maid and maintenance services for glass cleanup and window replacement, respectively. But every word she'd shouted at him was echoing in his mind. He could imagine how she'd looked yelling at him, those gorgeous brown eyes flashing, her hair a swirl around her face, breasts heaving and fists clenched. Damn it, he was getting stiff against the floorboards, thinking about how he'd deal with her in such a temper.

I swear to God, I'm going to have to cut off my own dick.

Ben rolled to his back. He didn't feel like getting up yet. He'd heard her threat about the club, but he also heard the waver of uncertainty behind it. She was just working off a mad, even though he had no doubt she'd end up there by herself at some point if he didn't give her some direction. She was that stubborn. He'd make sure she had the numbers of those other Doms he'd talked about. Once she calmed down, she'd be smart enough to take them, even if her initial motive in doing so was to make him jealous. It wouldn't. That's what he told himself. They were nice, young, calm and sedate guys. Doms she'd find so boring they'd put her to sleep.

They were too lighthanded. Even when she was crying out from every blow, her ass kept rising up to the cane, the spatula, the flogger. Those strikes made her wet, made her beg for more. *Christ.*

He needed to get to Houston. If he was smart, he'd stay there for a couple months. Or he'd come back tonight, go to Progeny himself. No, too much risk of dealing with someone he knew. He might go to Surreal. Take a taxi from the airport, hang out there until closing, have one of the limos pick him up and bring him home. He'd find a sub who'd help him forget how he'd fucked this up. He'd call Lucas later, maybe, explain the situation, though he wasn't really sure how to do that. Maybe he'd wait and see what Marcie was going to do. She might not tell them. She was mad, and her pride was probably hurt.

He wanted to ignore the niggling thought that it went deeper than that, but he wouldn't duck that responsibility. He'd taken her too deep, let her get too close. It was better to wound her now, when it wasn't mortal.

He'd take her anger. Her tears would destroy him.

Ben: Congratulations on the five thousand you raised to help the off campus domestic violence shelter. Cass said you've been volunteering there. She also told me about that run-in with a husband ignoring a restraining order. She said you wouldn't let him come into the house, basically backed him down. You have a tendency to take things to extremes, brat. A guy won't stop to think about assault charges when he's got a red haze in front of his eyes. Btw, we're matching the funds you raised, and I've already authorized having a security system and panic button installed at the shelter.

Marcie: My knight in shining armor (lol). You guys are so overprotective, but I know the shelter will really appreciate it. As far as the asshole (aka husband) I just had to prove to him I had bigger balls. I did ☺☺. Seriously, don't worry about me. I'm no different from you guys. If I don't stick up for what's right, for what I know is truth, no matter what the world throws at me, then what kind of person am I?

Ben: Not a corpse. Just be careful, brat. Who will interrupt my day with her incessant letters, texts and emails if you're not around?

Marcie: That's true. I'm not sure if most of the women you date are literate.

Email exchange between Ben and Marcie

Chapter Eleven

හ

Marcie paused inside the foyer of Surreal, breathed deep. She'd chosen to spend some of her K&A intern salary on a car service to bring her here, because she'd made a deliberate decision to down a couple shots of tequila from Lucas' liquor cabinet before she left the house. The effect was still coursing through her veins, making her feel wild and loose, but she wasn't drunk. Underneath the storm waves, she was all deep ocean, focused and intent.

She'd gone through an extreme experience with a Dom less than twenty-four hours ago. She could handle any Master here. Tonight she'd get some nice marks to overlay Ben's, sashay into the office Monday, flip up her skirt and show him before she flounced down to her "place" in Research.

Of course, she'd have to use a Sharpie and circle the marks that were from her visit to Surreal. Otherwise he wouldn't be able to distinguish them from his, or those that had resulted from today's Dumpster adventure. She'd added a couple aspirin to the tequila to deal with that. She couldn't believe she'd let that security thug get the jump on her, but maybe she'd been spoiling for a fight. He'd gone the intimidation route, the usual tactic for big guys, and it had become ugly. Unfortunately, he also got the raw edge of her temper, so it was a fair trade. At least the mask covered her black eye. Nothing could cover swollen testicles, so he'd probably taken the night off.

Yeah, she was a badass. A badass whose palms were sweaty. She ignored that, handed her credit card to the hostess, a gorgeous ebony-haired pixie in corset, tight skirt and boots. When she'd come here masked to observe Ben, she'd had a definite plan, a focus. To watch him, gather information. He'd commanded her attention so decisively, nothing else had intruded on that path. No room for this open-ended anxiety, the what-if or what-trouble-am-I-going-to-get-into feeling.

The hostess nodded to the pirate chest full of rubber bracelets. The various colors denoted categories of play. She hesitated long enough that she had to move aside to let more decisive people pick up their choice. Then, feeling the hostess's curious glance, that sense that she was about to be asked if everything was all right, if she needed help, she firmed her chin and snatched up a silver one. It said she was a moderately experienced sub, that she was unattached and interested in invitations to play.

Of course, the fact she was here alone, and her outfit, made that patently clear. Her wet latex leggings looked poured on and rode low on her hips. They laced up the back, from crotch to just below the twin dimples of her pelvis, following the seam of her buttocks. She'd laced them snug enough that nothing was graphically revealed, but as her cheeks twitched along in a sauntering walk, interested parties might strain their eyes to see if they could discern any details through that shadowed sliver of exposure.

She'd left her tunic top in the Surreal locker room, so all she wore waist up was a shelf bra that pushed her up and almost out. The bra was the same bronze shimmering color as the leggings. The lace edges that barely covered her nipples were black, matching her five-inch stilettos.

Okay, she was tense, but it had nothing to do with the environment. The very first time she'd gone to a club, she'd expected to be nervous. Instead, watching the many different ways that Masters and subs fulfilled their mutual needs, soaking in the atmosphere through all senses, she'd felt like she'd come home. She'd known this world innately, even before she stepped across a club threshold.

She'd had a chance to let her guard down, immerse herself even more, when she'd visited clubs in New York City with Lucas' friend Marcus. She recalled how Thomas, Marcus' spouse and devoted submissive, had stood at her side. He'd slid an arm around her, letting her lean against his attractively half-naked form, since he wore only a pair of snug jeans and his wedding band, permanent proof of his bond with his Master. Looking down at her, he'd given her his slow, sweet smile that told her he understood exactly how she felt. Marcus had kept her close to the both of them on that initial trip, because she'd nearly floated off into a trance from voyeurism alone.

No, her tension was because of what lines she might cross tonight, and whether she could face herself in the mirror tomorrow. Everything about last night continued to haunt her, making her shiver at inappropriate moments.

She shoved that sentimental trash out of her head. This was her choice. If Ben refused what she offered, then she was going to see how she handled what else was out there. The copper-and-black eye mask bolstered her courage and hid the risk of tears. *Okay, Marcie. Go out and get what you want. Or, if you can't have that, let's prove he isn't going to change who you are just because he can't pull his head out of his ass.*

Taking one more deep breath, she stepped into the public play area. She was ready to be adventurous, to have a great orgasm and get her ass spanked. To hell with Ben O'Callahan.

Then she saw him at the bar.

He was cozying up to a blonde with tits so big they were practically in his drink. His hand was on her hip, giving her an idle stroke that ran his fingertips over the curve of her ass.

It hurt so badly, for a moment she hated him. From the beginning, she'd had to fight all the despicable voices of logic that said she was mistaken, that what she felt from him was imagined. That he truly wasn't interested in her, that she'd been throwing herself at him. But he hadn't been humoring her last night. She'd seen his eyes. Which made seeing this even worse.

She swayed on the five-inch heels. She couldn't do this. She really couldn't. She didn't want what she was about to do here. Ben had always been caring, compassionate, funny. He was being something he wasn't, she knew that, but his dysfunction didn't give him the right to be such an asshole. She loved him, truly loved him, and seeing him touch another woman like that, making it obvious he'd probably fuck her tonight, after all he'd done to her last night...

She was strong, but this required superhero strength. She didn't have it in her.

"You're trying to make someone notice you."

She stiffened at the warm comment. Glancing up and back, she found herself flanked by a man with red hair to his shoulders and direct blue eyes. The calm confidence, even more than the black bracelet, said he was an experienced Dom. He looked in his late twenties.

"Are you looking to play tonight?"

She turned her back on Ben. "Yes. Yes I am."

He took in the jut of her chin, the flash of her eyes. "I see. Have you played before?"

"Yes...but not like this. I was sort of...with a Dom, but now I'm not."

"Would you like to hang with me a little bit, see what might pique your interest?"

When she took a deep breath this time, there was a little shudder to it that translated into a twitch through her limbs, a quick jerk. *Damn it.* "I'm sorry."

"No apologies necessary." Giving her a reassuring smile, he took her fingers in a warm hand and rubbed them. "Relax. It's a playground, and we're all children here, looking to have fun. Is it all right if I touch you a little bit, help you relax? You can tell me to stop at any time, or if I'm doing too much."

She hesitated, then nodded. He slid his hand to her hip, his thumb coursing over the top of her buttock, a move remarkably like what Ben had just done to the blonde. His eyes darkened as her lips parted, moistened. "You wear the silver bracelet, but I'm thinking you're still fairly new to it. You just didn't want to be treated too gently. You're on that beginning edge, wanting even more."

She nodded. *But not with you, as nice as you seem to be.*

"I have another friend." When he gestured across the play area, she saw an older man watching them. Her mouth went dry as she registered he was leaning against an empty St. Andrew's Cross. "Would you like to be restrained on that? Let us give your beautiful ass a workout? We can do it over your clothes. Want to try it, see how it feels?"

She knew how it felt. She was glad the mask hid the stark pain she was feeling. "Sure," she managed. "Over the clothes will work." Hell, his touch on her hip had resulted in a reaction. Maybe it was all "touch button A to get reaction B". Maybe that floating sensation that happened last night was purely chemical, and if they had the expertise to get her to that level she'd get lost in her head, cut adrift. Then it wouldn't matter that the man she wanted the most wouldn't have anything to do with her.

"You can call me Master L. What should I call you?"

"Whatever you wish, Master L." She was just a faceless slave, here to be used. The thought tightened her stomach in a not entirely unpleasant coil.

She watched him kiss her knuckles. Was he the type Ben would put on his call list as the "perfect Dom" mentor? The thought curdled in her stomach like sour milk. But she followed him, comfortable in the span of his arm, one hand resting on her hip and the small of her back, the other holding her fingers as he escorted her. He smelled good, a nice aftershave. He was handsome but not overdone, wearing a simple pair of jeans and an untucked button-down. Cowboy boots with silver tips.

"Do you have a hat?"

Following her glance, he smiled, gave her a bit more of a Texas drawl. "Yes ma'am. But I don't wear it indoors, or in the presence of ladies." When he reached his companion, introduced as Frank, she found he was in his forties, with silver threaded through his dark hair. His eyes assessed her even more thoroughly, and he was more reserved, giving her only a courteous nod. It made her stomach flip inside that coil, gooseflesh rising on her arms as she recognized him as something closer to what her submissive nature craved. She had to steel herself not to drop her eyes in his presence. That wasn't required at this level, and he wasn't her Master.

Neither was Ben, was he?

They went over her safe word, what the boundaries would be. She explained the visible bruising on her upper body, saying she worked in a job that sometimes required full contact but that there was no injury. When they were satisfied they knew enough about her to keep her safe — she gave vague but accurate information about anything beneath the clothes — they lifted each of her hands, cuffed them to the cross, positioning her face forward against it.

The moment they started restraining her, that deep lower belly trembling started. But there was a wrong feeling to it. She put her forehead down on the wood crosspiece. She would do this. She could. She responded to Master L's questions. No, cuffs not too tight. Nowhere near as tight as what was around her heart.

"I'm going to start with just my hand, and work up to some other things, all right? Frank will take over as things escalate."

Frank stepped up behind her to test the bonds, pressing himself against her body. As he withdrew, he tangled his hands in her hair, gave her a sharp tug that elicited a gasp, a spiral of shameful pleasure at the rough treatment. When it turned into a desperate whimper, Master L stroked her back.

"It's all right. We can stop at any time. You obviously want this. Don't fight yourself. We'll get you where you want to be." He leaned in, touching her chin, and she stared into his knowing eyes. "We can take you to a place where you won't even know he's in the room. Is that what you want?"

"If you can make me believe he's not even on the planet, that would be better."

His lips firmed, and he nodded, glancing over at Frank. "She wants it rough."

"Just the way we like it."

She wished they'd bind her forehead to that crosspiece so she wasn't tempted to see what Ben was doing at the bar. It was still in her line of sight if she turned her head far enough.

Master L's hand landed on her buttock, a first slap, a test, an attention getter. It awoke the blows of last night, but not in an unpleasant way. It was a reminder of Ben's marks on her, which got her wet, no matter how much she despised him at the moment. Master L rubbed firm circles over her ass, took a healthy squeeze, tugged on the lacings of the leggings. His fingertips slipped into the spaces between the eye holes to do a brief caress of the seam of her buttocks before they moved on. Then another smack.

He was accomplished, alternating hard with soft, with those kneading caresses, so that she was shifting on the cross, that fluttery feeling in her belly settling into something pleasant. Frank ramped it up, doing a series of hard blows that made her arch into the sting. Then Master L returned. The unpredictability, the frequency and multiple sensations, were enough to get her aroused, get her body reacting without thought. So it was that, after one particularly stimulating series of blows, she turned her cheek to the crosspiece, seeking movement as an outlet for what was building inside her.

She was staring right at the bar. Realizing it, she started to turn her face away, no desire to torture herself, but Ben's glance slid her way. Passed over, then came back like a laser pointer.

She wasn't surprised he recognized her. That was part of what broke her heart about him, wasn't it? He knew her anywhere, the same way she knew him. But he was with that blonde, she'd come to this club for her own reasons, and she'd kicked the ass of a guy nearly twice her size today. Lifting her chin, she gave him a cool look, and then turned her face into Frank's hand as it cupped her face. She even let her lips drag across his palm. He smelled good too. Like powdery sawdust. He must like to do woodwork. It was nice, reassuring.

"She's warmed up. She's getting looser."

"Hmm." Master L had donned a vampire glove, and she flinched and shuddered, wriggling as he let the sharp edges scratch down her back, her upper arms. Frank lifted her hair and held it in a tight tail as Master L took the glove straight down her spine, over the bra strap and to the waist. They knew what they were doing, because the instinctive masochist was rising to the top, wanting more, even if it wasn't coming from the source she wanted.

You want me to prove I can be a shameless slut for anyone, Ben? You got it, baby.

A breath slid past her gritted teeth as Frank slapped her other buttock, making it wobble so hard she felt it in her pussy. She met Ben's gaze deliberately this time. His green eyes were ice, his jaw satisfyingly rigid. Good. Let him be mad. Wasn't a damn thing he could do to stop her. He'd relinquished any claim he might have, had tossed any leash she offered back at her feet.

"*Oh.*" It surprised her, the sudden ripple in her pussy as Master L reached around her, raked the glove across her belly, his breath on the back of her shoulder. She didn't know if it was a reaction to her defiance of Ben while two Masters had their way with her, or Master L's skill, but she was amping up her response. That was all that mattered. Another series of spankings from Master L, hitting her with consummate skill, a lighter stroke, harder, then one powerful clap that sent everything wobbling. Frank stepped back in with a cane. It slapped against the latex, awakening the blows of last night. The sting went right up through her core and to her nipples.

She was just a thing, a mindless slave who liked this, who liked the pleasure of serving Doms. So what if Ben didn't want her? She could do and be this, right? To hell with him, and with her hollow heart. It was like eating candy and knowing it was going to make you sick, knowing it didn't taste as good as you'd hoped. It was still eating candy, and who passed up the chance to do that? Tomorrow could be the *Titanic*, right?

She pressed her face against her upper arm, but Frank caught her hair, pulled her head back. "Eyes forward," he ordered. "Keep your head up, body still."

Holding poses increased the potency of psychological restraint. As her fingers curled in the cuffs, she was vaguely aware they were attracting an audience. A single drop of perspiration went from her throat down her sternum, and she thought of Ben's fingers trailing along that path the previous night.

"More," she whispered.

"What?" Master L's hand was on her shoulder. She turned her face into his knuckles, held her face there, hard.

"Please, more."

"You want it harder?"

She nodded. "And please...you can take off the clothes if you want. If it pleases you. Just leave the mask."

"Our pleasure." He unhooked the bra and the straps, his fingers sliding along that now bare track, and Frank removed the cups, caressing the soft underside of her breasts. Since her throat was aching, she closed her eyes. When they loosened the lacings enough, they pushed the leggings off her ass and down to her stilettos. Though they left the garment gathered at her ankles, she was now pretty much naked. Once again, just a thing. A slave.

She must have said it, for Master L spoke. "Yeah, you are. A beautiful slave. One any Master would want."

"With the proper discipline." That came from Frank, sending a thrill through her vitals. She was losing herself here, and that was okay. She could do that. It didn't matter that it all felt out of control, that she was afraid, that she had no idea where to go from here.

"She was worked over pretty good recently." That from Master L. His fingers trailed the bruises along her thighs, the welts underneath what they were doing. Ben's marks.

"Not good enough," she said. "*More.*"

"Quiet," Frank said. The cane struck her bare buttocks and she cried out, bucking against the cross. *More, more, more.*

But then there was a pause. No one touched her as they had between all the other blows. She didn't know why until she heard his voice.

"Frank, Master L, a word?"

Ben. Before she could turn her head, another male was gripping her hair, pushing her forehead against the crosspiece, telling her not to move. She knew that hand, knew firsthand how tight he could hold her. Even as something feral inside her wanted to struggle against it, bite and take a few of his fingers off, her arousal intensified threefold. Her pussy contracted, a short expulsion of cream. Damn traitorous body.

"Master L, this is my slave. She disobeyed me by seeking another Master tonight. My apologies for depriving you of the pleasure, but she needs discipline at my hand."

"Problem, gentlemen? Ben?"

Another voice, one she was sure belonged to the assigned dungeon master. Despite his obvious familiarity with Ben, an interruption to a session in progress was bound to catch his attention. In a moment, he'd ask her what she wanted, who she wanted. Whatever her decision, the DM would make a judgment as to what was best. If anything seemed hinky, he'd end the scene, period.

Ben explained the situation to him as he explained it to Master L and Frank, no more, no less, which of course left a lot unexplained. If he claimed she was bratting to get his attention, she swore she'd take his cock off with the nearest sharp object she could find. She hadn't come here looking for him, no matter that her body cried out for him the moment he'd released her hair, stepped back.

Even without his grip, she was all too aware she kept staring forward, just as he'd commanded with that physical cue. Now the DM was at her side. "Ma'am," he said quietly, "you're safe here. What do you want to do?"

She could tell Master L that Ben was lying. The DM would make Ben back off. Frank and Master L would continue to work their magic and she could get lost in the physical pleasure of the orgasm they'd undoubtedly give her. That would be that.

Her scalp was tingling from his touch, and the ache that they'd started from mere physical touch was now an agony of emotional need. She stared at the polished crosspiece. "Master L...Frank, sir, thank you both. But my Master is correct. I apologize for taking him away from Miss Big Tits at the bar to address my insubordination."

The DM had to work to disguise the half-snort, half-chuckle, but it puffed along her cheek. His tone remained serious, however. "All right, ma'am." He turned his attention to Ben. "Involving two other Doms without informing them that they're walking into an ongoing session with your sub is bad etiquette, and can be dangerous. I trust it won't happen again."

"No, it won't. My apologies to you gentlemen as well," Ben said, nothing given away in his voice. Marcie curled her fingers in the cuffs. He was taking the blame, the quickest way to get rid of them. What the hell did he want from her? She was torn between confusion and anger.

As the DM returned to his post, she heard Master L and Frank gathering their tools. "A good slave," Master L said dryly, probably from her double-edged apology. "Thanks for the pleasure of her, Ben. You're fortunate, despite her willfulness. If you need assistance with her punishment, I'd be happy to help."

"I'll keep that in mind. But for now..."

"Back off." There was a grin in Frank's tone. "No problem."

The two men moved away, leaving a blanket of silence around them. She wasn't sure what look Ben had cast around them, but she had the sense that the casual voyeurs had given them a little more distance. Sounds of whipping punctuated the air nearby, followed by cries of pleasure. An undercurrent of sultry music had been playing throughout, but now it all seemed muted against the roaring white noise in her head, the red haze over her vision. When Ben curled his hand in her hair once again, Marcie clenched her teeth. "If you untie me, try to make me go home, I'll go right back to them."

"I have no intention of untying you." His body pressed up against her as she drew in a breath at the size of the erection pressed against her sore bare buttocks. The deadly calm of his voice made a cold knot in her belly. "You're such a good little researcher, Marcella. Tell me what consensual non-consent is."

She swallowed. "It's when the slave or sub...when her safe word is only for a medical emergency. Within the boundaries they've set, the Dom can do anything he wishes."

"Are you willing to give me CNC?"

She was angry with him, frustrated beyond belief, confused. He'd had CNC with her from the very beginning. When he exercised his Mastery over her, the moment he touched her, she trusted him down to the level of her soul. It was one of the many reasons she knew what she knew. Could she set aside the hurt, the pain, to embrace that right now? Or would she tell him to fuck off and let her go?

She knew the answer to that. She closed her eyes. "Yes," she whispered.

"Boundaries?"

"You know them. What happened to the blonde you were going to fuck?"

In answer, he stepped away from her. A cane hit her upper thighs with the fast whipping air noise that made it even worse. She shrieked, not expecting the strike. Pressing her forehead back against the wood, she set her teeth, managing the pain that sang through her nerve endings.

"Your safe word is simple. Red. Like your ass is going to be. If you use it, I'll make the decision, based on your condition, whether you have a medical emergency."

He passed his hand over her buttocks, used it to slap her ass several times, warming it up anew. Whereas Master L and Frank had been cautious, he knew just how hard to hit to wake up everything he'd done to her last night. Then he picked up a switch. He wasn't playing or going for half measures. He was aiming for pain and punishment, pure and simple. If he thought he could beat her into submission, he was sadly mistaken. As he alternated its use with the spanking and the cane, she started to feel the burn, started to crave toward and writhe away from the blows at once. Honey from her pussy was running down her legs even as she shrieked at the pain.

Merciless, he bound her waist to keep her still, and as the volume of her cries rose, he strapped a rubber ball gag in her mouth to muffle the cries. She could still manage Red if needed, no matter how garbled, but if she went into full out screaming, as she had a feeling was going to happen, the gag would keep her from overwhelming the room.

The voyeurs were back. She could see them in the corners of her eyes. The K&A men mostly didn't do public performances, but in the past couple years, she knew Ben had done it more often. It was more impersonal, after all. Right?

The pain of that thought was replaced with another kind of pain. He brought down what felt like a thin, hardened strip of rawhide to crisscross the existing marks, rapid, light blows that raked across the nerve endings without real damage but which delivered intense pain. She was moving and wiggling her ass, trying to get away from the agony. She was screaming "no, no, no…stop, please" because it really hurt. After last night, then this morning, oh God, it was too much.

But she wouldn't use that safe word. She went in and out of pain, struggling for that zone, but it was too much. She was crying, even as her body was stoked for a release, nipples hard, pussy wet. When he put his hand in her hair, yanking her head back, she looked up into the face of the devil himself. He hadn't put a cloth with the ball gag, so she knew her saliva was running over her chin, her makeup smeared from tears, her nose running. Completely exposed to him, raw and vulnerable. "Five more minutes," he said.

"No..." she whimpered.

"You can do five more minutes." He dropped his hand to her cunt, rubbed through her slickness. "Wet and fuckable. Say it. You can do five more minutes."

She stared into his eyes. "Yes. I can." With the gag, the words were garbled, but clear enough for him.

It was the longest five minutes she'd ever experienced, and when it was over, she was gasping, hanging in her bindings. She let out a hoarse scream as he spanked her ass cheeks with both hands, hard, sending all the painful sensation reverberating through her. Then he pressed up behind her, clasping her buttocks in a bruising grip. Putting his mouth to her neck, he bit hard enough to draw blood. She wished there was a lower crosspiece to rub herself against, because her clit was throbbing.

He'd reacted the way he would if she belonged to him and had defied him, actively seeking punishment to reinforce the boundaries between them. There was something about that which was important, though she couldn't wrap her mind around it right this second, fighting the storm inside her.

Now he was pulling her pants back on. He left the laces loose, and she cried out as he found her secret, sliding into the lubricated channel. She worked herself against his hand shamelessly, wishing he'd touch her pussy. But of course he didn't.

"You came here to be fucked tonight."

She twisted her head around enough to give him a glassy half-glare, despite the tears. "Yeah," she rasped. "You got everything revved up, and if you weren't man enough to take care of the itch, I was going where it could be scratched. That's what a slut does, right?"

"You're better than that."

"When you fuck the blonde at the bar, are you hoping she'll help you forget last night?"

His lips tightened. He moved his hand around to rub her clit through the thin latex. She ground herself against his erection, trying to drive him as crazy as he was driving her. He was flexing against her ass, as if he was fucking her. Then he captured her breast, tugging on her nipple.

"God…" She was gasping as he worked her up higher. Her ass and thighs were throbbing, yet the wash of heat that came after that level of punishment made her want more, which was crazy because it had hurt like hell. Her mind was coming apart.

"Ben… Master…"

He stopped, pressing his forehead hard against her hair, his fingers spasming around her breast. "No," he said in a growl. "No."

"Yes." She set her teeth. "Master." *Don't pull away.*

He stepped back, hands leaving her. Retrieving her bra, he hooked it around her, positioned the cups and secured the straps. He tightened up the lacings on the pants with one jerk that drove the breath from her. Then he freed her wrists and ankles. Coiling his arm around her waist, he brought her back to the floor on the wobbling stilettos. He gripped her other hand, holding her fast as he led her out of the public play area.

When she saw they were headed toward the exit, she balked, but he simply hitched her up on his hip and kept going until she put her feet back down and let him walk her. "I'm not done tonight."

"Yeah, you are."

"I'm not going unless you are."

He suppressed a hard sigh. Yeah, he was probably like Mount Vesuvius about to blow, but she was already at the eruption point. She wasn't going to be shut down. Before she could say anything further, she was yanked through the door, and they were out on the sidewalk on the west side of the building. He was crossing the street, taking her toward a K&A limo.

"I'm...not...going." She planted her feet this time, yanked hard, and got away from him, though she almost tripped herself doing so. She kicked the shoes away, faced him on the balls of her feet.

When he turned toward her, she didn't give herself time to register his expression or anything else. She led with her emotions, did something she knew was wrong, on so many levels. She punched him dead in the mouth with all the strength she had.

Ben was pissed, torn up in twelve different ways. The guy he'd been a lifetime ago knew only one way to respond to a physical attack. Catching her arm and her hair, he twisted her around, slammed her against the side of the limo. He pulled his strength back at the last moment, he wasn't that crazed, but it wasn't that which could harm her. It was what was raging out of control in him, what had goaded him to get her out of there and into a limo, out of his sight. Now.

He hadn't restrained himself as much as he'd thought. She stumbled, hit her face on the metal corner of the rear window, letting out a surprised yelp of pain. When she managed to turn toward him, trying to regain her feet, he saw the bloom of blood. Worse, he saw her recognize the boiling, deadly rage pouring out of him. Every animal knew when they'd pushed a predator too far. The heart would leap into the throat, and the feet would automatically try to get into motion, to run, even as the mind's fear would slow them down, just as the predator got faster, calmer, colder.

Her eyes widened, but she didn't run. She wasn't that smart. She was trying to take another aggressive, fuck-you stance, and say something that would be entirely unwise.

He spun her back toward the limo before she could do it, startling another surprised cry out of her. "This is done," he said against her ear, pushing himself hard against her body, trapping her against the car. He could hear that pulse rabbiting beneath his grip. "We're not friends, we're not lovers. You don't know a fucking thing about me. You don't have what I need, you'll never have it. All your fucking useless dreams about me are just bullshit little-girl fantasies. That's it. We're done."

He was hot and hard, a rutting monster fueled by watching Frank study her, Master L's hands touching her skin, their eyes calculating how she would surrender to them.

"Let go of me," she said. Her voice was a shaky whisper that would have wrung mercy out of a stone. He felt nothing. He knew how to be mean, so mean that nothing in the world would fuck with him. When she tried to break free, he twisted her arm higher behind her back. Sliding his other hand around, he squeezed her breasts with no finesse, pure brutal possession, intending for it to be uncomfortable, to take only his pleasure and give her none. She struggled, but that just increased the pain to her arm, a deterrent. A sob caught in her throat.

"I'm not the prince in your Beauty and the Beast fairy tale." He wanted to die right now, because this was all wrong, but it had to be done. He had to do it. "You're going home, and this is over. You take that job in Milan, and you don't look back."

Suddenly, he knew he wasn't alone. Max stood to his left, just behind him. Tossing dark hair out of his eyes, Ben cocked his head. He gave Max a dangerous fuck-off look, but Max met it head on, his eyes cool. In control in a way Ben wasn't. "It's time to let her go, Mr. O'Callahan," he said. "Right now."

"Yeah. You're right about that." Ben released her, stepped back. He didn't watch her sag against the limo. He pivoted, was walking away when Max caught her. She would push away from Max immediately, would try to stand on her own. He knew that about her. It would have made him smile if a rusty knife wasn't cutting into his chest. He didn't see the tears or the broken look on her face, but he didn't need to do so. It was branded on his fucking black heart. He hadn't needed to remove her mask to see every terrible emotion go through those beautiful brown eyes.

You can take shit off the street, dress it up, but it's still shit. It stains everything eventually.

He didn't look back, his feet pointed toward the darkest hole of night.

* * * * *

Max didn't try to touch her again, but he did stay close. "Miss Marcie? Are you all right?"

Marcie stared at the shadowed edge of the parking lot where Ben had disappeared. "Isn't that a funny thing to say?" she said, her voice high and strange. "When everything is obviously not all right."

Max took a cautious step closer. Her legs were shaking hard. She had that lovely ass of hers pressed against the car door for support, but her wrist was red where Ben had gripped her, and she'd apparently hit her lip when he slammed her against the car. Jesus Christ, what was going on here? None of the guys had ever treated a woman like this. They'd kill any man who did. Yeah, Ben was into handing out the pain, but to women who craved it for the right reasons. Definitely not in this context.

"I guess people say that because the alternative is saying nothing," he ventured. "Being silent when it feels like something needs to be said."

Marcie's gaze shifted to him then, her eyes brimming. "Yeah," she said brokenly. "But sometimes there's nothing to say, Max." She took a deep breath that seemed to cost her dearly. "I need you to do me a really big favor."

"No."

Her expression flickered. "You don't know what I'm going to ask."

"Yeah, I do. I have to tell Mr. Kensington about this."

"I'm an adult. It's my decision to share or not share." Her voice quivered again. "I swear to God, if you say I'm not an adult, I'm going to find a blunt object and beat you to death with it."

Despite his best effort, his lips almost twitched. Jesus, she had spirit. Her eyes were actually flashing, even as she swiped at her tears with an impatient hand. "No ma'am. You're as adult as they get. Hey, no. You stay here."

She'd been about to push away from the car door, and from the direction of her look, he knew she was going to retrieve her shoes. Stilling her with a gentle hand and a firm look, he strode over to them. Picking them up, he marveled as he always did that women could walk in those things, but he bet Marcie had worked them to the nth degree.

She had a made-for-sex body, but one with a lot of strength to it. He'd seen that punch, was surprised Ben hadn't spurted blood. She'd had the balance, aim and force that said she knew what she was doing. Which meant she shouldn't have done it, but it was obvious there was a lot of emotional shit happening on both sides. Besides which, Max knew Ben was a way more lethal fighter than Marcie, even if she had ten black belts.

Since Ben had shown that side of himself in a way he shouldn't have either, it made Marcie's response now even more impressive. Max knew men who would have crapped themselves from that deadly backwash that Ben had dished out. They wouldn't be standing on their own bare feet, trying to hold it together and talk their driver into all sorts of foolishness.

He set his jaw, reminding himself of the dangerous influence of tears and a determined woman. As he came back toward the limo, he could see her gearing up for another try. But Max had his own code. "No," he repeated, before she could say anything. "I'm sorry, ma'am. Matt needs to know about this."

"Because I'm a woman."

"Yes. And you're one of theirs." He nodded into the night, after Ben. "There's nothing they take more serious than your well-being. He knows that." Which opened a whole other set of interesting questions.

"Can you at least give me twenty-four hours before you tell Matt?"

He suppressed a curse at that look, part plea, part demand. Jesus, what the hell was the matter with Ben? He was half tempted to go kick his ass himself. Except Max knew Ben. When she'd landed that punch, something had welled up in the guy, something Max had sensed before from him, but had never seen unleashed like that. He had comrades with PTSD, when the dark shit came up and took over, spilled out like pus running from an old wound. What he'd just seen had felt a lot like that.

Unless he was gravely mistaken about Ben's character, Max had a feeling that when the man's head got back on straight and he thought about what he'd just done to her... Hell, he was probably going to figure out a way to kick his own ass, even before Matt Kensington could do it. Which was coming, Max was pretty sure of that. Unfortunately, Ben had probably intended that with this stunt tonight. It was as if he was burning his bridges deliberately. Fucking bastard was all over the map. This wasn't good.

"I'll think about it. No promises. Let me get you home."

"Okay." She seemed to accept that was the best she was going to get. "Let me go in and clean up my face first. I'm not going back to my sister's looking like this." She unlaced the mask, scratching her snarled hair. "Damn, I'm a mess."

"Fucking hell. Did he do that?" When she raised a surprised face to him, showing the black eye even more clearly, Max was ready to discard any sympathy for Ben and lead the lynch mob himself.

Her brow furrowed, then cleared. "Oh no. That was work. An investigative case I was doing for Pickard. Security guy got the jump on me in an alley over at Pfeiffer. I was going through their Dumpster."

"Of course. Jesus, girl. You're a magnet for trouble."

"Magnet for everything but Ben, apparently." She stared off into the night again, and Max touched her arm.

"Come on," he said gently. "Let's get you home."

"Max, I have to go back in. Ben didn't let me get my clothes and purse out of the locker room. Asshole."

Max pressed his lips hard against a smile, though it was balanced with something far more grim, looking at her strained face. No way she was going back into Surreal. Not in this kind of mood. "I'll go get them. Tell me the number and the code you used."

When she gave him an obstinate look, he chose a different tack. "Do you really want to go back in there?" he asked quietly.

"No."

"Then let me go get your stuff. You can clean up in the limo. You'll find mirror, wet towels, all that girl stuff in the storage compartments."

"They're always prepared, aren't they?" She gave a bitter chuckle.

Not always, Max thought. When she slid into the limo, she gracefully accepted his steadying touch so she managed it without her knees buckling, but then she leveled a glare on him.

"If you engage the child locks while you're gone, I'll hotwire the limo and leave you here."

His lips pursed. "Deal. Just promise me you'll lock the doors until I get back."

"Yeah, because stealing a stretch limo is so inconspicuous."

It wasn't the limo that concerned him. The passenger was the real treasure. Shutting the door, he pointedly waited until she used the sharp painted nail of one forefinger and jabbed the door locks, engaging them. The exaggerated gesture, the fact she crossed her eyes at him, almost made him smile. The same way the streaked tracks of her tears squeezed his heart in a vise. She was a piece of work.

He was pretty sure Ben was out there watching, probably within hearing distance. He'd wait until he was sure Max was taking her safely home, Max knew it. None of this made sense. He didn't want to make Marcie unhappier, but he knew his responsibility. To her, to Matt Kensington…and to Ben.

* * * * *

Marcie held it together. She could deal with this. She'd get a good bath, a good night's sleep, then figure out what to do next. But when Max turned into the driveway, a variety of emotions rose up, nearly choking her. She'd forgotten what night it was. While Cass and the other K&A women had that monthly afternoon tea, they also had the occasional girls' night as well, which involved cocktails and lots of laughter. Unlike the tea parties, Marcie had never been home for one of those, because Cass made sure all the kids were at sleepovers or other activities on the night in question, probably so discussions could be far more adult.

There was another limo in the drive, and she saw Wade give Max a companionable wave. He was Savannah's regular driver, and Dana had probably carpooled with her, freeing Max up for the evening to chauffeur Ben.

She felt that surge of resentment again, pushed it away. Marcie had called her car service on the way back, letting them know she'd found another ride. It would save her some money, the only consolation so far for this terrible night.

"You going to be all right?"

She looked at Max, who'd come around to open the door for her. She'd washed her face, combed her hair, dabbed some makeup on the black eye, though Cass already knew about that. She was fine. As fine as porcelain. Giving him a nod, she took his hand to get out. "I'm sorry I changed your schedule this evening."

"Not by much. All I was doing was waiting on Ben, picking up some extra cash with the overtime. He was planning on watching tonight, not playing. He'd only been inside an hour when he came out with you, so I assume he never got past his first drink."

"Oh." Of course. She should have figured that one out herself. You couldn't actively play *and* drink at Surreal. It was a club rule and why she'd had the tequila before she came. It didn't matter. Ben could have taken the blonde outside the club to fuck her in the limo. Probably would have.

Max was a family friend, and normally she'd give him a hug, but at the moment he was too male, too virile, and her clothes were too scanty, even though she'd donned the thin tunic top. Before then, he'd made a superhuman effort not to be caught staring at her overflowing breasts. She didn't really mind that, but if those strong male arms surrounded her in a hug, she was either going to cry all over his shirt or take a swing at him.

She opted for a cordial nod. She was going to make it all the way to her bedroom with quiet dignity.

When she slipped in the door, she stood in the darkened foyer, staring down the hallway toward the light of the kitchen and sitting room areas. She listened to the women's laughter, women who were submissives of varying degrees to strong Masters. Masters who were bonded to Ben in an exceptional pack relationship that included these women. But not her.

She needed to go upstairs, go to her room, take a hot shower. At least get out of these clothes, which now felt cheap, tawdry, ridiculous. No, they weren't. She wouldn't let him make her feel like that. The outfit was damn sexy, intended to get the big-ass cock of one stubborn, asshole lawyer rock-hard. It had done that, or her behavior had done that, because what he'd pressed against her had definitely qualified as a raging hard-on.

She leaned against the wall, taking a breath. *Go upstairs. Go upstairs.*

Instead, she found herself moving past the staircase. They were in the sunroom, and she could hear their warm voices, drawing her to them.

It had been surprising to see Savannah here, but her bed rest was taking it easy around the house, not actual confinement to a mattress. She'd probably wanted to get out for a little while and insisted on the event not being relocated to her home.

All of the women were with strong Doms, but part of that was because they were such strong personalities themselves. She could just imagine the sparks flying between the two CEOs, but Savannah was here. With a limo driver to ensure her safety. Matt had likely already called him three times. Rachel having a medical background probably helped ease his mind some, and no doubt Savannah had used that fact for leverage.

"Look at this catalog. A twenty-four-carat diamond bracelet for a baby? Are they out of their minds?" Savannah's voice.

"The scary thing is I'm sure some idiot buys them," Dana responded.

"Yes, so your baby can be mugged in her stroller. For the love of God, let's stop looking at catalogs. I'm already addicted to the shopping networks."

"You sound cranky. I think you need to play a relaxing game of Twister. Rachel can post the video feed on Facebook."

"Give me her cane so I can beat her with it."

Cass' chuckle was dry. "You know that's just foreplay to Dana."

"Not if I beat her to death."

How many years had she dreamed of being part of that inner circle? Laughing, listening, knowing she was part of something incredibly special. Knowing she was *meant* to be part of it.

Maybe in the end, she was just a dumb fucking kid who had no clue. Maybe Ben O'Callahan didn't want her, and she'd made it all up in her head. The crush of a lonely teenager abandoned by her parents had evolved into the dysfunctional cliché of a delusional grown woman. That burning drive, the absolute certainty that she was meant to be with him, it had all been a dream. *A little girl's bullshit fantasy.* The reason she refused to face the truth was it knocked the bottom out of her world, destroyed everything she thought she was, because so much of it had to do with her feelings for him.

The seeds of doubt she refused to let grow, but which had lurked in her subconscious from the first moment she'd believed she was meant to belong to Ben, now grew into a monster beanstalk that covered everything else. If it was truth, if she had to face it once and for all, she needed her big sister, the only real mother she'd ever known.

She paused in the doorway. She needed to turn around, retreat, because there was no way she could do this and not completely embarrass herself. The women were curled up in a variety of positions on the wicker furniture. Dana had her head on Rachel's shoulder, grinning at something Cass was saying with expressive hands and a half-full glass of red wine.

Savannah was on her side on the lounger, a pillow propped between her knees to support her belly as she listened. She was always the perfect ice princess, even in that position, her blonde hair in a smooth tail over her silk-clad shoulder, but her expression was relaxed in a way usually only seen in this company.

Early on, Marcie had figured out what piece of jewelry served as a "collar" to each woman, primarily because they always wore it to the tea parties, and each woman wore it for any gathering where work demands or other fashion etiquette didn't make it inappropriate.

Savannah wore the delicate silver choker with rose quartz Matt had given her on their first anniversary. Cass had a pair of beaten silver cuff bracelets, etched with Japanese characters. She'd worn them at her marriage ceremony. Dana and Rachel's collars could be mistaken for nothing else. Dana's was a wide strap with a waterfall of decorative chains to soften it. The St. Christopher's medallion that belonged to Peter was on the D ring. Though it was her main collar, she sometimes alternated it with the more subtle jasper necklace with Peter's dog tags that served the same purpose. Rachel's reflected Jon's exceptional design skills, made of sterling silver wire, bound at intervals by vertical supports made of gold, and embellished with a wire-wrapped sapphire pendant.

That, as well as the whole scenario, told Marcie the harsh truth. She didn't belong here. Marcie took a step backward, but Rachel was the one facing the doorway. Her gaze lifted at the movement, and apparently she got a good look at her face.

"Cass," she said, her serious tone bringing the conversation to a halt.

Cass twisted around. In the very next moment, she was up and moving. Marcie stood frozen, watching her come forward. Suddenly she *was* a little girl again, she couldn't help it. Cass had always been there for her, the sister who'd become mother to them all, the one they all leaned upon when things became unbearable. Knowing that, seeing those keen blue eyes, the concerned set of her mouth, she couldn't hold it together.

"I'm sorry," she said brokenly. "I couldn't...I needed you. All of you."

I had an odd dream the other night. It was dark, I was running from something, but I ran smack into it. I screamed, but then it was gone and you were there, blocking the darkness. That wasn't the weird thing about it, though — you know it's not the first time I've dreamed about you when I get anxious about things. What was odd was that, this time, as I watched you stare out at that darkness, making sure it didn't come closer to me, I thought: When he dreams of darkness, who saves him?

Letter from Marcie, first few weeks of college

I always want to be there for you, brat, but in your dreams, don't you ever run. You stop and face that darkness, tell it to fuck off. Never let it drive you away from what you want. Once you show fear to something, it owns you. And yes, that's also the answer to your question. Someone can save you from darkness once or twice, but only you can kick its ass and send it running.

Ben's response

Chapter Twelve

ഹ

The sobs burst out of her, everything she'd been trying to manage since it all started, all the pretense and bravado swept away on a violent tide. Her knees buckled, but Rachel was already there, helping Cass catch her. They let her fold down to the floor, Rachel stroking her hair as Cass closed Marcie in her arms, practically holding her in her lap.

"I'm sorry. He doesn't want me…he hates me… I made him hate me."

Cass' hand whispered over her abraded wrist, then her gentle touch lifted her face, her thumb touching Marcie's mouth. Something fierce and dangerous went through her sister's expression. "Did he do this to your lip?"

"No." Marcie shook her head hastily. "I hit it on the car when he shoved me against it."

"Yeah, that's loads better." That tight comment came from Dana as she now crouched on the floor with Cass.

"We'll worry about that in a moment," Rachel said quietly. "Let's get her to the other lounger, take a look at her. She's not moving well."

"Here, let her take this one. It's longer, and I've warmed it up." Savannah had made it to her feet, and was gesturing them to the six-foot-long couch.

Marcie tried to protest, but they were moving her over there. She was hobbling a bit. The level of pain from the CNC session had worked her over pretty good, and then she'd tightened up further during her argument with Ben. On top of that her knuckles hurt from hitting him. She'd used that same fist earlier in the day, and the security thug had a rib cage like a steel vault.

When they had her sitting, Rachel's fingers moved over her, but Marcie shook her head, uncomfortable with the fussing. "'It's okay. He knew what he was doing, at least with the switch and the cane and…" She gave a hiccup, a near-hysterical snort. "That'd sound weird in the wrong crowd, wouldn't it? I…it felt good and bad at once, you know. I'm okay. Just…tough session."

Which she honestly might have loved if it wasn't driven by something so wrong between them. If Ben had been seeing how much she could take because he liked to push his slave to that level for their mutual pleasure, it would have been ecstasy for her. Another sob caught in her throat, made her clutch Cass harder, where she sat next to her on the couch. "I don't know what I'm saying. I'm sorry."

"Sssshh." Cass held her. "Just get it out, sweetie. It's all right. We're here. We've got you. Dana, can you find your way to my room and bring some warm clothes? I keep pajamas in the left top dresser drawer."

"Flannels and bunny slippers coming right up."

"She's okay," Rachel said, done with her cursory evaluation. "She's right. Just sore and stressed. Do you have heat and ice packs?"

"Master bathroom closet. This is one of her favorite rooms in the house. Can you work on her here?"

"Yes, this is a good space. I'll go get the packs and a warm throw for her to lie on while I work on her."

"I'm sorry," Marcie whispered. "I hate making you worry, making you have to do things for me."

"Oh love." Stroking her hair back, Cass kissed her forehead. "Do you know how long it's been since you've needed me to do anything for you? I'm so sorry this happened, but I've actually missed being there for you every once in a while. You ask so little for yourself, always handling everything so well." Marcie raised her head enough to see Cass smile through a sheen of tears. "I'm here for you, anytime."

"We all are," Dana said. She was back, and her fingers were loosening the laces of the pants. She'd been exploring them to determine their shape and workings. Now Marcie let out a combination sigh of relief and discomfort as they lifted her to her feet and removed them. She'd left the shoes where she'd crumpled and someone had put them neatly to the side of the couch.

When Rachel returned with a chenille throw, Savannah slid the tunic top over her head. Then her cool fingers caressed Marcie's back, releasing the catch of the shelf bra, letting it slide down her arms. She took the leggings that Dana handed her, folded them up with the bra and put the clothes with the shoes while the others eased Marcie down to her stomach on the couch. She was now fully naked, but the warm throw felt good against her skin.

"No shame, sweetheart," Cass said. "We're all girls here. All the kids are gone for the night. Jon has them making robots in his workshop or learning how to shape bonsai. One of his usual activities."

It made her smile a little, but she wasn't ashamed to be naked with them. If Ben wanted to strip her naked on St. Charles, tie her to a trolley stop sign and sit on a nearby bench to read his paper and enjoy the view, that wouldn't bother her. She was his. Because of the common elements that bound her to these women, particularly in this moment, she felt no more self-consciousness with them than she did with him. It might seem twisted to the rest of the world, but that was okay. It made sense to her.

Cass' fingers whispered over the cane marks. "Okay, some ice for these areas should be good enough. I give him credit. He never breaks the skin."

"Just every blood vessel beneath it," Dana chuckled. "I remember." She paused, as if realizing now might not be a good time to remind Marcie of that, but in answer, Marcie laced her fingers with the black woman's, laying her head on her knuckles. It was different with Dana. She couldn't really explain that either, but when you belonged to one of the Knights, in a peripheral way you belonged to all of them. Max's words came back to her.

You're one of theirs.

Dana stroked her hair, leaned down and kissed her temple, a soft nuzzle. "It wasn't all Ben," Marcie mumbled, wistfully passing her fingers over the St. Christopher's medal, briefly hooking in the D-ring when Dana made a soft noise of sympathy. "Master L and Frank did the first part."

Now there was a full stop. Cass squatted where Marcie could see her face. "What?"

"He wouldn't take me to the club, so I went on my own. To Surreal. I did go to Baton Rouge to get info for Pickard, that wasn't a lie. I just couldn't tell you the rest." It was important to let her sister know that, see Cass acknowledge it with a nod.

"Master L and Frank invited me to play with them. They were going to work me over on top of my clothes, which was fine at first, but they were really good at it. Ben was at the bar with this…woman. I didn't know he was going to be there, but when I saw he was, and he was with her…I just wanted it all to go away. Anyhow, Master L and Frank did a good job. None of them broke anything."

"I wouldn't go that far." Savannah was sitting on a broad and cushioned foot rest pulled over near them. She exchanged a glance with a tight-lipped Cass as Dana chuckled. She tugged Marcie's hair.

"Girl, you've got brass ones. Bigger than Ben's even. Damn, I bet he was pissed."

"Obviously." Cass' voice was frost. Dana quieted, but she reached out, found the older sister's knee.

"Not like that, hon. You know what I meant."

"I do." Cass sighed, rubbed her temple. It made Marcie flinch, seeing her worry. "Rachel, do you think we should put her in the hot tub?"

"Good idea. That'll help relax her, and then I can give her a full massage afterward."

They helped her to her feet, stayed close despite her protest that she could walk. The sun porch's annex held a hot tub that could seat a dozen people. There were a few wooden loungers around it, some of Jon's tranquil maples. He should start a nursery, call it Peaceful Plants. Ben could run a bakery right next to it. Steamed Buns.

She must have said the first part, because Rachel gave one of her musical chuckles. She and Cass were helping her into the hot tub, one on each side. "I'll suggest it as a retirement option for him. I think he has enough projects and ideas going right now to last him the next forty years."

"He took me by surprise," Marcie said. There was no filter on her mouth right now, no organization, just myriad thoughts drifting through her head. She remembered that breakfast, what he'd told her about touching Rachel. "One moment he's this peace-and-love super genius guru, the next, he's a Dom and he..."

"Turns the cartilage in your knees to jelly?" Rachel squeezed her waist carefully, brushed her cheek against Marcie's. "Yes, he does. It makes kneeling to him very convenient."

"For several reasons," Cass said wryly. "Here we go. We've got you. Just take the steps slow."

Marcie was vaguely aware of the front doorbell ringing and Savannah telling Cass she'd get it. When the heated water closed around her calves and Rachel pressed the control to start the jets, everything else was lost in the bliss and bubbling noise. She may have even moaned. She kept her wits about her enough to glance over her shoulder and watch Savannah move in a stately sway back across the sun porch, toward the front hallway.

"She doesn't even waddle. Wow."

"Yeah. But you should have seen her the night we got her to do Jell-O shots with us," Dana said. "Before she was pregnant, obviously. Even Matt had never seen her drunk. We have some blackmail photos. Or at least, I'm told they're blackmail material. She says if we ever share them she'll hire an assassin to take us all out. I'm not scared. We'll show them to you later."

Marcie smiled, she couldn't help it. Dana was just like that, the right combination of humor and calm assurance, with Rachel's earth mother support on the other side. No matter what, it was going to be all right.

* * * * *

She almost fell asleep in the hot tub, Dana and Rachel watching over her, but after twenty minutes, they brought her back out. Rachel moved one of the loungers to the sunroom, and Marcie was so loose they poured her back onto it. They'd moved the chenille throw with it, which felt wonderful on her naked skin. Dana sat in a chair near her head, to give Rachel room. Savannah had pulled her foot rest close as well. Matt's wife had a bowl of ice as well as prepared ice packs, which Rachel indicated would be used when she was done, to keep the swelling down where needed. Cass sat next to Dana, stroking Marcie's hair with her fingers, soothing.

Marcie listened to the murmur of voices, not really focused on any of it, just floating in her head. There was no pain there, all the things that hurt or disturbed pushed behind a gray mist. She closed her eyes as Dana's fingers twined with hers, the black woman's thumb sliding over her palm, her wrist pulse, caressing. She bit her lip as one of the ice cubes made a slow glide over the marks on her thighs, her ass. She felt the tips of Savannah's nails. It felt good, soothing...but a little more than that too.

The hot tub had loosened her up, but it had done something else. She hadn't come tonight. What had happened at Surreal had been a roller coaster, physically and emotionally, and since the latter had claimed center stage for the past couple hours, she'd assumed the former had settled down, but their touch was reawakening it. Were they doing it...intentionally?

"Um...Cass..." Her cheeks were warming. In a moment, she was going to be making it obvious how those slow, sensual glides of ice felt, the teasing touch on her wrist pulse, definitely an erogenous zone.

"It's all right. Let them take care of you in the way they know you need." The two sisters met eye to eye as Cass knelt before her, stroked her hair along her temple. "You're one of us, aren't you?"

Just like that, the key to the city, to the secret clubhouse, to the place she'd always known she belonged. It made tears spill forth anew. "Oh Cass."

"Sssh. It's okay. I've known for a long time what you are, haven't I? And I've never told you it's wrong. How could it be, when I'm cut from the same cloth? But I worry. Because you're young, reckless...and it goes so deep for you, deeper than me. Maybe more than any of us. There was a time I was afraid the life I gave you contributed to it, in the wrong way."

Marcie was already shaking her head, but Cass pressed a hand over hers, showing she'd made whatever peace she needed to make with that thought. "It doesn't matter. As long as this is what you truly want."

"It is. But with him. Only him. What if he doesn't..." She'd imagined being part of this circle for a long time, but she hadn't thought what it would be like to be the fifth wheel of it.

Torment. Just like it was for Ben.

"Marcie?" Savannah spoke in that quiet, steady way of hers that commanded instant attention. "No, you don't need to look toward me. Just feel. And listen, when it's time to do so."

She could do that. Cass pressed a kiss to her forehead, touched her nose then moved out of her view. Marcie's fingers curled into Dana's as Savannah sent that cube of ice gliding the length of what felt like one of the rawhide marks, down over the pitting caused by the rattan points. A drop of water rolled down her buttock, into the crease. It was pretty close to her pussy, and that was starting to throb. She had her legs closed, but she wanted them open, wanted to feel that ice glide over labia, touch her clit and make her writhe. *Get a grip, Marcie. This is* Savannah, *Matt's wife.* Who was probably the only woman in the history of the world who could walk with a regal sway, versus an adorable waddle, during advanced pregnancy.

But her mind couldn't help but turn to Ben, how he'd used ice in a far more invasive way to cool her down, to stop her orgasm when she couldn't do it herself. Dana made it worse, because now she bent her head, brushed her lips to Marcie's palm, her wrist. When she used the tip of her tongue, Marcie let out a breath, fingers gripping Dana's more tightly. "Guys...what..." Then she remembered what Savannah had said. *Feel. Listen.*

"That was Max at the door," Savannah said in that same conversational murmur. "He was making sure you were okay, that you'd come to us, rather than sneaking off to bed."

"They really are the most overprotective, interfering males *ever*," Marcie muttered. She'd tried to do that. Couldn't. What would happen when Max told Matt? Maybe she could get Savannah to intervene. This was between her and Ben, and if it was over, it was over. She didn't need anything else stirred up while her heart was already shattering and fragile. She didn't even have the energy to broach the topic now.

"Yes, God bless them. I've known Ben O'Callahan a long time. He is an extreme Master." Savannah's fingers followed the ice, the overlay of stripes and marks, two days' worth of his Dominance. "But anger never plays a role in that part of his life. He does have an Irish temper, but it's usually reserved for professional incompetence."

"And when the Saints lose," Dana added.

"He deserves to be horsewhipped, and we are not going to make excuses for him. But I am going to tell you this. In the time I've known him, he's never lost control with a woman like this. Matt agreed."

Marcie stilled. "You told him." Of course she had. She'd been in the hot tub twenty minutes, so that explained where Savannah had gone. Cass had joined her at some point, so did that mean Lucas knew too? Oh hell, if Matt knew, they probably all did.

"I don't want…this was between him and me."

"No, dearest." Savannah's voice was firm. Dana's hand had landed on her shoulder, anticipating Marcie trying to push up off the lounger. Rachel began a deep rub of her back designed to turn her into a limp noodle. As she struggled between alarm and the need to purr, Savannah continued.

"Women can fight their own battles, but thanks to Matt, I've learned true strength includes the ability to seek backup when needed. You took this on all by yourself. You brought the fight to Ben, did all sorts of dangerous things to draw him out. You knew enough about him to know what would work, but you had no idea how it would play out. That's the foolish courage of youth."

Marcie couldn't bristle over the simple truth. Not when Savannah's voice was kind, not patronizing. "You needed that type of courage, the belief that you could handle whatever kind of bull charged out onto that field. Because at a certain point, instead of the matador, you became the red cape."

That ache came to the surface again. "So I screwed up."

"Not necessarily." Savannah resumed her glide with the ice. Marcie bit her lip as she followed the curve of her buttock and touched down on her leg. Several more drops ran down her inner thigh, making her twitch. "I've no idea what the outcome will be, but set aside emotions. Focus on what you know of Ben, all that wonderful research I'm sure you did. Based on that, what is the most significant thing I've said to you?"

Marcie opened her eyes, glanced down the length of her body at the woman who met her gaze with piercing intelligence. Her mind was like a spaghetti soup, but when a successful Fortune-500 female CEO told her to review the details and come up with an answer, she dove into the tangle.

"In the time you've known him, he's never lost control with a woman like this."

"Good." Savannah nodded her approval. "By the way, when you start seeking permanent employment, I'll pay you twenty percent more than Pickard or K&A. Plus give you a corner office and your own assistant."

Marcie blinked. *Wow.* That certainly bolstered her, but her mind was turning over the statement. She wanted to believe, but... "He could have lost it because he sees me as a little kid. The big-brother protective thing."

Rachel snorted. She passed a hand over Marcie's buttock, offering a light scrape with her nails that made Marcie jump, not in an unpleasant way. The physical therapist's quiet chuckle had a sensual note to it. "No, Marcie. He most definitely doesn't see you as a child. No matter how much he's telling himself he does."

On the back of Rachel's collar, next to the locking mechanism, Marcie knew there was a Sanskrit word. *Owned.* To wear something like that of Ben's…it was all she wanted.

The gray mist parted, letting in some of those unsettling feelings, but their words were giving her wounded heart stray shots of hope. If they were wrong, she'd be opening herself to being stabbed again, and she wasn't sure if she was strong enough. Even now, remembering Ben's anger at the limo, his contempt, his…

She didn't want it to happen, but she'd pushed that part of tonight's events furthest behind the gray mist for a reason. She hadn't let it affect her in years, but in that moment, when he had her shoved against the limo, when she realized she couldn't fight him off, and he wasn't necessarily going to let her go, she'd remembered Allen, pushing her down on the floor, holding his forearm on her throat, not realizing she couldn't breathe as he tore at her clothes…

When a man attacked a woman, she never forgot it. It was in her head, the violence in his hands, the meanness in his face… Ben had betrayed what she knew of him, and she'd trusted him. The way she'd trusted Jeremy. Her brother hadn't pulled Allen off her. Cass had.

How could she trust Dr. Jekyll when she'd seen Mr. Hyde? She was shaking again. She'd told herself she wouldn't let her mind go in this direction. She was a clear-headed person, one who didn't let past baggage affect her present, but she was surrounded by women who knew what it was to be entirely vulnerable to the one they loved. It was a confessional she couldn't resist.

"He was…I've never seen him like that. I wasn't sure he wouldn't hurt me…like for real hurt, hit me in the face. It was someone else, some dark, terrible thing inside of him. It was like he hated me at that moment. I was…I was scared of him. I hate that. I don't want that."

She shouldn't be saying this. Cass was still in the room. But saying it out loud helped steady her, look at it with clearer eyes. Ben wasn't a chronic abuser of women. She knew that. Something else had happened tonight. It was as Savannah had implied. She needed to step back, look at all of it, not to make excuses for him, but to get all the information, figure it out, before she made the decision that was best for her. Even if it was a decision that broke her heart.

"I think it's time you and Matt talked," Savannah said after a quiet moment. "This is in your hands, Marcie. But you have a family. We'll help you."

And him. It was an odd thought, but being surrounded by their love and support made her wonder where Ben was, if he was still walking around in the cold darkness of the city streets, alone.

"Keep in mind, whatever you decide, I'm still going to kill him," Cass said. She put a small ice pack against Marcie's lip.

"Me too," Dana said. "As long as someone points me toward him. I'll break his kneecap, then he can't outrun me."

Marcie smiled beneath the ice pack. "I'd like to see that."

Peter's wife dropped another kiss on her knuckles. "You got to him, Marcie. This is a tricky, difficult situation, but I'll bet good money he doesn't know what the hell to do with how he feels about you."

That made two of them. Things had become more complicated and uncertain because of the evening's events, and she wasn't going to get it worked out in her head tonight. But that was what tomorrow was for, right?

"All right. Time to take care of some other things." As if discerning her thoughts, Cass rose. "I'm going to go make you some chocolate chip cookies."

"Nestle Tollhouse?"

"Is there any other kind? Hot out of the oven. I'll be back."

As Cass rose and moved to the kitchen, Savannah picked up another ice cube. Marcie had been listening for the tiny clicks of her manicured nails against the bowl, each time anticipating the first really cold touch of the frosted ice, then that combination warm-cold feeling as it melted against her skin, the beads of water working their way down, both agitating and soothing the welts. Savannah took this one on a different track. After she circled it over her buttocks, she pressed it between, a slow, slow glide into that crevice, over the rim, and then down, down, toward the aching center core.

Marcie's fingers tightened on Dana's, her thighs trembling, wanting to loosen. "What..."

"It's all right." This from Rachel, whose hands were still working their magic. "Just feel, Marcie. Enjoy. Do whatever your body wants you to do."

"But..." Her Master hadn't given her permission to enjoy this. To experience this. Given the night's events, though, it seemed a fair trade. She made a noise of sheer ecstasy as Rachel's strong hands worked a particularly good spot.

"There we go. That works, doesn't it? Roll with the feeling."

"Spread your legs out, if that's what you wish to do," Savannah said.

Tentative, Marcie shifted. Dana made a warm sound of approval. The black woman had shifted to her knees by the lounger, and her kiss on Marcie's palm this time became something more. She teased Marcie's pulse with her tongue, followed the vein.

"Ah..." A soft sound escaped as a result of that stimulation, as well as what Savannah was doing. The ice moved between her legs, Savannah tracing her labia, letting the tip of the ice slide between and letting it go, where it would melt, the drops following the path of gravity to drip over her clit. Another click in that metal bowl and Marcie's hips lifted to her, asking for more. She couldn't help it. Was she really doing this?

Yes, she was. Her sister had left the room, knowing they could provide this, knowing what she needed.

"I think it's time for you and me to change positions, Ice Princess." Dana directed that at Savannah. "If you think you can roll you and the mighty Matt mite in this direction."

"You are the only one who gets away with calling me that."

"Afraid to punch a blind girl?"

Savannah snorted, didn't answer that. "I don't need to roll," she said with dignity. "As long as I get a push from behind."

Marcie tilted her head to see Dana do just that, her hands incredibly gentle as she helped Savannah to her feet. She noticed Dana also caressed Savannah's swollen belly under the silk tunic, and Savannah's lips curved at the gesture. Matt's wife had always been the more austere aunt of the K&A family, even when Marcie eavesdropped on those tea parties. Cass told her it had taken Savannah far longer to trust their female circle than the other women, but that it had taken the K&A men a long time to win her faith as well.

"You understand him, don't you?" Maybe it was the moment, feeling like nothing was off limits, but that austerity that always kept her somewhat at arm's length with Matt's wife felt a little less restrictive right now.

Savannah paused long enough that Marcie was about to apologize, retreat, but then the elegant fingers wrapped around hers, tightened.

"I give Ben a great deal of credit for what he made of himself. When I met Matt, the official story about Ben was that he'd spent most of his formative years in New England, and he and Matt had met at Yale. Nothing about him suggested otherwise, as if he'd internalized that version of himself. They protected his past, not to make his life a lie, but so that he could stand away from it, not be defined by it, though of course emotionally, he still is.

"It is a mortal wound, when you realize that your parents don't love you. Don't want you. What dies is hard to resurrect, because we learn faith and trust on the foundation of our parents' love. Even if Ben carries such a wound, his behavior tonight seems extreme to me. However, my father's coldness was buffered by a house, servants, physical safety. A lack of material want. Ben didn't have any of those things."

"Okay." Marcie squeezed her hand. "I'm sorry. Both for asking and for the fact that happened to you. I've loved you since I met you, even though you've always been a little intimidating."

"She needs to come to the next Jell-O-shot night."

"Don't you have something you should be doing over there?" Savannah asked, narrowing her eyes at Dana. But when Marcie looked up at her again, Savannah's expression softened in a way she hadn't seen before. She touched Marcie's forehead. "They resurrected me," she said. "All of them. Don't worry, it will work out."

Marcie drew in her breath as Dana put another ice cube on her ass, only she was a little bit more forward about it than Savannah. She parted her buttocks, slid the ice right up against her anus, setting off a whole series of flashbacks. Ben's tongue there, his fingers, his cock stretching her. She whimpered, digging her nails into Savannah.

"Yeah, he has that effect on a woman." Dana's amusement had a sultry, serious purr to it, one that kept everything humming. Her slim fingers drew provocative circles on the marks. "He switched you good. Did you like it?"

"Yes." Marcie swallowed over her raw throat. She was going to have a permanent rasp from these past few days. "I like everything he does to me, and I just want more. The only thing I didn't like was how he was feeling, what he was feeling."

"Yeah. The boy has issues. Think we need to skip all this childhood therapy shit and just have Peter bash his head against a brick wall a few times."

"He has a very hard head."

"That ain't all."

The switch from grim amusement to mischief was welcome. An unexpected little giggle bubbled up in her. She must be feeling punchy. "The other night...I lost count of how many times he came. What guy can do that?"

"He's a cranky young god. Thor has his magic hammer, Ben has his hundred-horsepower cock."

Rachel chuckled while Savannah shook her head. "A long time ago, I told Dana that Ben wants a woman's soul, not her heart."

"Because the devil can take your soul," Dana added, brushing her mouth on the small of Marcie's back. "But he can't take a heart. It has to be given, and usually requires one given in exchange."

Marcie was pretty sure Ben already had her soul, but there was another caveat. In order to give a heart, someone had to accept it. Dana started kneading Marcie's buttocks, creating that low-level discomfort that made her shiver, made her want more. "Yeah, you like that," the blind woman observed. "You're a pain junkie. No wonder you've fucked with Ben's head so well. Let's get you up on your knees, little sister."

She didn't know what to say to any of that, but she didn't have to do so. Instead, she was clutching Savannah with both hands, because Dana slid one of those hands beneath her, enough to lift her a few inches off the lounger, and put her mouth between Marcie's legs. She'd never had a woman there, and the soft mouth, the feminine licks, were a different experience entirely from Ben's strong mouth and penetrating tongue. But Dana was focused, probably using her knowledge of what pleasured herself to bring Marcie to a different place, where thinking was no longer an option. She licked the cold labia, heating them up, stroked the clit with a broad then curling tongue. Two separate, dragging sensations. She tugged on the clit ring, making Marcie undulate against her with a moan.

Both strong brown hands now moved to Marcie's hips, thumbs nudging her inner thighs to spread her open. Marcie adjusted without thought, seeking more of that feeling, planting her knees out wide on the lounger.

She was propped on her elbows, and still holding Savannah's hands. When Savannah switched their grips, moving hers to Marcie's wrists, the suggestion of restraint was enough to send Marcie up another few notches. She could imagine Ben sitting in a corner, watching these women pleasure her, all at his command.

Rachel was no longer giving her a massage, at least not that kind. As she slid her hands under Marcie, Marcie dropped her forehead to the lounger. Jon's wife cupped her breasts, fingers closing over her nipples, tweaking the piercings.

"Oh...God..." It didn't take any time at all. She was pushing against Dana's face, her fingers now grabbing Savannah's wrists so they were holding each other. Then Rachel's touch slid back to her shoulder blades, up into her hair. At the key moment, as her lower belly was coiling up tight, tighter, Rachel dug into her scalp, pulled hard on her hair. The way Ben would if he was fucking her, to pull her head up and back.

She came hard, intense, fast. It shuddered through her, head to toe. It was a purely physical release, but there was an emotional purging involved, something the women obviously knew she needed. Taking out the trash, so tomorrow she could look around the psyche and see what was there.

She threw her head back farther, neck arching with the power of the climax. It was then Rachel caught her jaw, taking

that kiss Marcie had wanted at her house that day. It was so
startling and unexpected, Marcie stilled, quivering in the
aftershocks even as she explored the shape and pleasure a
woman's lips could offer, an easy girl kiss. It was like cotton
candy at the fair, a treat perfect when the environment was just
right, and in this moment, it was. When she murmured
something incoherent, Savannah's fingers joined Rachel's in
her hair. She stroked gently while Rachel kept giving her tugs
that made those aftershocks a steady bump of little waves
through her body.

Slowly, they eased her back to her stomach, Rachel
breaking the kiss to sweep her hands over her back and
shoulders, resuming the massage. Savannah kept stroking her
hair. She was falling into lassitude, until a sharp pinch made
her yelp. Her gaze snapped down to Dana, who gave her an
impish look. The woman picked up another piece of ice,
soothed the little bite of pain.

"Know you appreciate the sadistic side, girlfriend. Didn't
want to leave you unbalanced."

"Jesus," she breathed. "Some minister."

"Ministration comes in all forms, love."

She managed a snort, but she was well and truly limp
now. She mumbled something appropriate, no idea what. Eyes
closing, she gave herself back to their hands.

Cass came back a few minutes after the cries subsided.
The cookies were in the oven, but she knew her sister wouldn't
be eating them until later. Marcie was fast asleep, so deeply
her arm had fallen off the side of the lounger, the way it had
when she was ten. Tenderly, she knelt by Dana, tucked it into a
folded position under Marcie's chin. Glancing at Savannah,
she gestured, then helped the woman move over to a corner of
the sun porch, out of hearing distance, in case Marcie drifted
back to consciousness.

"Matt's spoken to Max since we talked. He confirmed what Max told us. He's never seen Ben like this. He thinks whatever he's been carrying inside him the past couple years may have ruptured, or at least cracked pretty hard. He told Matt the guys should go look for him, because he doesn't think he should be alone."

Savannah nodded, studied her tense face. "You're her sister, Cass. What do you think?"

"Matt asked me the same question." Cass sighed, shook her head. "I know she's loved him since she was sixteen years old. He's every woman's fantasy, but I don't know if he has what it takes to be a woman's reality. To be what Lucas and Matt are to us. We've always known he's the extreme one, Savannah. The one who carries the most demons. As her sister, it scares me to think of her exposed to that." She gave a tight smile. "At the moment, I want him dismembered and his body dumped in a swamp."

"I don't blame you."

Cass raised a brow. "There's something you want to say, but you're not sure it's appropriate."

"Using your negotiator skills on me?"

"Always. I'd miss good stuff if I didn't." Cass sobered though, glancing at the sleeping woman, the focus of their concern. "Tell me something that will make this all right, Savannah. Something that gives me hope of a happy ending."

"I believe Marcie is right. I think she is the one for Ben, the same way each of us has been for our husbands. Only they accepted the truth of that first, pursued us, convinced us of it. With some rather tempting and unorthodox methods."

Cass managed an amused eye roll. "A huge understatement."

Savannah nodded. "Ben had a very different history from the other men. He's never let a woman get close enough to hurt him. He has surrogates, the wives of his friends, safe targets for his affections, but it's different from having a woman of his own. He's armored against that level of intimacy, and behind that armor is a lot of darkness. Marcie had a way in no woman has ever had."

"Through our family connection."

"Correct." Savannah shifted on the footstool, adjusting swollen ankles onto the brace beneath Cass' chair. "We know these men have many traits in common. One of them is possessiveness, though they pretend to be civilized about it."

Cass snorted. "No disagreement here."

Savannah acknowledged that with a wry twist of her lips. "We love them, belong to them utterly, consider them ours as well. Ben is just as possessive and protective about what he considers his. However, he doesn't trust women, because the woman he was supposed to trust unconditionally, from his first breath in this world, abandoned and betrayed him. If his unconscious self recognized Marcie as his soul mate, seeing her with those two men tonight perhaps ripped something open that he's kept locked down for far too long."

"She's always had more bravery than sense," Cass said. "But he had no right—"

"No, he didn't," Savannah said evenly. "He had no right at all to do what he did. But figuring out why he did it, seeing what he will do next, that's the difference between whether there is a future for them or not."

Cass considered that. "Matt told Lucas. He'll be home later tonight. I'll have her in her pajamas by then, but he's going to know. Emotions are going to be running high."

"Matt will send Peter or Jon after Ben. He can face Lucas at the office Monday. In a reasonably public place, Lucas will hold off murdering him."

"I'm not so sure of that."

"Janet will cover their asses for many things, but not a capital crime."

"True." Cass sighed again. "I want to do something, Savannah."

"We did something tonight. Something important. She needed us." Savannah nodded toward Marcie. "Let the men deal with Ben right now. They'll know how to handle him. Marcie herself has a choice in all this, once she feels a little more herself. We don't want to step on that."

"You might feel less equable when you have your own child," Cass said, but without rancor. Rising, she moved back to Marcie, knelt by her. She couldn't bear looking at that strained and exhausted face any longer without touching, reassuring herself that her sister was okay. It made her think of Jeremy's pale, thin face. She'd seen him a couple weeks ago, and knew things were drawing to a close for him. The knowledge of that came forward now, making her feel even more fiercely protective, and more helpless.

"She's so sure, Savannah. Why is she so sure?"

"The letters," Marcie mumbled. "His letters." Her brown eyes opened, met Cass' blue ones. "I wrote to him in college, and he answered. I could tell…it's hard to explain. I just knew. The things he told me…to help me, they told me things about him as well." Pain suffused her expression. "Maybe I am too young, too stupid, too sure. But, Cass…I'm not sure I'll survive being wrong."

Tears spilled forth anew. Cass didn't know what to say to that, but she put her hand over the one Marcie had curled up under her chin. As she slid her arm over the younger woman's back, Dana and Rachel, who'd been stroking and keeping her comfortable, now drew closer once again. Marcie didn't seem to notice. She kept that lock on Cass' gaze, her chin tightening. "I'm sorry, I shouldn't have said that. If I am wrong, if he doesn't love me, if there's no chance…I'll go to Milan. I'll put it back together, Cass. It's okay. I'll be all right."

Did she know her words broke as she spoke them, her hand quivering in Cass'? When Marcie fixated on Ben as a teenager, Cass had been glad. Ben had been the big brother Jeremy failed to be. He'd also done what Cass couldn't—he'd taught her to relax enough to enjoy life, to have fun, to be young. But what Cass had called a fixation, a crush, had been something very different in Marcie's mind, evolving into this as she became a woman. If she had to go back, would she have discouraged Ben's friendship with her sister, seeing her like this now?

The answer to that question depended a great deal on what happened next, as Savannah said. They were a close-knit group for a lot of reasons, not the least of which was how much faith they had in this unique circle of men. She couldn't let this one night wipe away seven years of Ben being what he'd been to all of them. Just on principle, though, she might nurse a homicidal rage toward him for a day or two.

"You *will* be okay," Cass agreed, wiping away the tears. "You're very strong. You have family who loves you. Me, Lucas, all of us. We'll be here to take care of you, no matter what comes. I promise."

Her heart tightened at the thought of her husband, her Master, the man who meant so much to her. Lucas loved Marcie. Being the kind of Master he was, he would know what Ben had done to her with barely a glance. It wasn't the marks on her body. That was something Marcie craved. What would ignite Lucas was her shattered expression, her loss of faith, the evidence of betrayal. Ben broke down a sub with brutal methods, but only to bring her to a place where he gave her the maximum pleasure, the perfect experience. In this case, Ben had merely broken her, pushed her aside. Given his lethal talent at breaking a submissive, what he'd done was an unforgivable breach.

No way around it. Monday was going to be pretty ugly.

"Remember, we can still strap him down naked and go after him with a Taser. Combine that with a few chocolate truffles, and it'd be the perfect girls' night."

That helpful advice came from Rachel. "I think Dana's having a bad influence on you," Marcie said.

"Everyone always blames me," Dana complained. "No one realizes Rachel is really worse. I'm just her beard."

Marcie hiccupped, a half-chuckle. It also produced a few more tears, breaking Cass' heart a little.

Seeing it, Savannah glanced at Rachel and Dana. They picked up her cue without a word. The three of them slid their arms around both sisters, giving them an embrace that promised them all the love and support they needed.

Until tonight, the K&A men had never let any of them down, had rescued them from some unbearable situations. Savannah knew Ben would make this good. If he didn't, he wasn't the man she believed him to be. While she might call her own judgment into doubt on rare occasion, she knew one thing about Matt Kensington. He *never* misjudged people. It would all work out. If it didn't...she'd have a go with that Taser herself.

* * * * *

Ben knew he had no business being around anyone tonight. He wanted to pound on something. Fortunately, hanging around long enough to torture himself with that brief conversation between Marcie and Max had given him a target.

So Pfeiffer hired ham-handed security who liked to punch girls in the face. He'd stayed in the shadows long enough to hear that and be certain that Marcie didn't break Max, talk him into something stupid. Like Ben hadn't already won the hands-down prize for the stupidest act of the millennium.

She'd have been looking through that trash container when she had shadows and low foot traffic, which meant the security asshole who'd done it was a nightshift stiff. He wasn't oblivious to the irony of hunting down a guy who'd hurt her. But hypocrisy was the least of his crimes tonight. He knew he was out of focus, more than a little out of control. He should go home, bolt the door, get blind drunk and leave it at that. But he hated being closed in when he felt like this. He needed to move, to keep moving, until things evened out. He'd go beat this guy to a bloody pulp, buy a cheap bottle of whatever junk one of the convenience stores had, then go drink it on top of his cemetery perch. If he was lucky, he'd pass out, roll off the top and break his fucking neck.

Pfeiffer was within walking distance of the K&A offices. The building had a spiffy silver and glass façade revealing the lobby inside. He contemplated picking up one of the big stone planters up front and tossing it through, but then he noticed the security desk was visible. He could wave and get the attention of the two guys sitting there, entirely dissatisfying. He was going to throw the planter anyway.

Then he noticed Peter sitting on a sidewalk bench, ankle balanced on his knee, patiently waiting for him.

Max was too damn intuitive to be a fucking limo driver.

"If you're out trawling for paid pussy, that's up on Canal Street. Blind women can smell that kind of thing though, so you better sleep with one eye open. Dana will shoot you full of holes, even if she can't see you."

Peter gave him a level look. "You can't make me beat you into unconsciousness, no matter how much you deserve it."

"Stand back and watch me beat one of these guys into unconsciousness then. Other than doing the same to me, there's no way you're going to stop me." Ben tightened his jaw. "Go home, Peter. I don't want to be around anyone. Particularly anyone I know."

Peter rose, stretching his substantial bulk, cracking his thick neck. "The guy you want isn't working tonight. I happen to know where he lives."

"Why would you share that information?"

"Because I've seen him. I think you need to see him as well. It's not far." Sliding his hands into his jeans pockets, Peter began to walk up the street, literally whistling Dixie. Biting back a vile curse, Ben fell in with him in a few strides, since the asshole was ambling. Once there, Peter picked up the pace, but not by much. "Nice night."

"Not interested."

"Okay." He said nothing further, and in a few blocks, he made a left, taking Ben down a street where the buildings had upper-level apartments much like his own place nearby. Peter stopped in front of one with a side staircase that led to living quarters above the Ruby Slipper restaurant. Ben went there regularly for breakfast and sometimes to watch ball games on the several wide-screens. He and this guy were practically neighbors.

"What's his name?"

"Why? You thinking of exchanging Christmas cards?" Arching a brow, Peter rapped on a door that looked in need of painting.

"Hold on. Jesus. Like a fucking train station tonight." The rumbling voice within sounded like it came from a bear.

Ben gave Peter a look when they heard a thud, a curse, then a slow progression to the door. "How old is this guy? Ninety?"

The latch was thrown, and his target opened the door. Ben had to look up several inches. The guy freaking filled the door. Normally he'd throw Peter at him first, to soften him up, but Ben was riding on blood lust, wanting to work the guy over personally. Unfortunately, someone had beaten him to it.

The man held a frozen slab of meat against the side of his face, nursing the mother of a swollen eye and nose. The way he protected his side suggested bruised ribs, his reason for taking his time. As he shifted to lean on the door, Ben recognized the semi-hunched walk, the symptom of very sore balls.

"You did this," he accused Peter.

"No, asshole." The tenant gave him a grumpy look. "He came by, took a look at me, said he needed to bring someone else by to gawk. Paid me twenty bucks to open the door again.

Otherwise I'd have told him to fuck off. I've already lost a day's work this week, and I ain't no salaried suit. If I don't show up, I don't work."

Ben blinked, looked at Peter again. "You didn't do this."

The corner of Peter's lip curled. "Nope. Wanna guess who did?"

The bear looked between the two of them. "Oh fuck. You two know that crazy bitch?"

"Hey." Ben took a step forward, but Peter put a light hand on his shoulder. It didn't stop Ben from saying what was on his mind though. The guy's hands were the size of tennis rackets. "You popped a woman in the face who weighs less than a buck thirty. Have you lost your mind? You could have just picked her up over your shoulder and tossed her off the property."

Bear-guy looked at Peter incredulously, as if they were allies, then came back to Ben. "Sorry, is there something you missed about this steak on my face and the ice I'm having to put on my nuts? I could have picked up a porcupine easier than that bitch."

"You should stop calling her bitch," Peter said mildly, but with enough steel to warn the guy they weren't buddies. Even so, Ben knew he was still here to be his leash. It rankled, because he was feeling a little thwarted and conflicted. He remembered overhearing Marcie in the break room, telling Janet she didn't work out in the usual girl ways. She did MMA and strength training. At the time, he hadn't given any more thought to that choice, assuming that, like most women, she did it to maintain her toned and entirely hot body, not for functional purposes. He could almost hear her reaction to that.

Once again, sexist pig assumption triumphs over reason and logic.

"Okay, okay." The security employee held up his hand. "Hell, a little sympathy here. She cracked two of my ribs over a ream of papers."

"No, because you punched her," Peter said patiently. "She was defending herself."

"Fine. Listen, I don't want any crap for hitting her. Hell, if I brought assault charges, I'd not only lose my credibility, but a judge would look at the two of us and laugh me out of court. It doesn't change the fact I've taken easier beatings when I was a bouncer at a strip bar. Fuck, guys, she was caught red-handed, going through our garbage."

"If you throw something in a Dumpster in a public alley, there's no guarantee of privacy," Ben said automatically.

"Figures that you're a lawyer." The guy eyed Ben like he was a cockroach who'd crawled up on his mat. "Is that what this is about? You guys here to bring a suit against me or something?"

"No," Peter said, deadpan. "My colleague is thinking of hiring her for his own security needs."

The bear-guy relaxed considerably, grunted. "You'll have to stand in line. My boss says if she ever wants a job, he'll pay her twice what he's paying me."

* * * * *

Back out on the street, Ben stopped at a lightpost. Peter leaned on the other side of it, pulled out a candy bar and broke it in half, offering. Ben shook his head. He wanted a drink.

"Can't wait to tell Dana about this," Peter commented. "She's been looking for a sparring partner more her size. Maybe I'll ask that guy, since Marcie may be out of both our leagues."

"Yeah." She'd taken on a guy probably three times her size and come out on the winning end. Because she'd been level headed, prepared for what she faced. It was way different when an attack came from a blind spot, from someone she trusted. She'd let him tie her up, beat the living hell out of her, and came back asking for more, because she believed he'd never abuse the faith she put in him. The friendship she believed they'd shared. The fact they were family.

Yeah, she'd been kicking on a door he'd intended to keep shut, a place she had no business being, but for him to blame that on her made him more of a shit than he already knew he was. "I'm fucking going home."

"No you aren't." Peter chewed on nougat and chocolate. "You just think you'll ditch me if you tell me that."

"I don't need a babysitter."

"It's girls' night. Dana's out late. I'm lonely."

"Well, as much as I love being your substitute cuddle toy…" Ben drifted off. Fuck. Fuck. *Fuck.* "The girls were all at Cass'."

"Yeah. They took care of her, man. She's all right." Now Peter's expression changed from that neutral calm into something sharp and way more focused, though he kept his voice mild. "What the hell were you thinking?"

Nothing. He'd stopped thinking, which was why it had happened. If he closed his eyes, he saw her there again. Master L touching her, Frank undressing her. When he'd taken over, ironically he'd still been in control then. The practice of a lifetime had taken him through that session, every move choreographed, monitoring her stress level, her arousal, though something inside had been cold and numb. Then he'd hauled her outside and she'd hit him. That blow, the pain of it, and something had exploded. He'd just reacted, all that shit boiling up and over, all over Marcie.

Moving to the curb, he dropped down on it, to hell with whatever grime his custom tailored slacks were accumulating. "Fuck."

He was suddenly really tired. Nothing and nobody to be pissed at, other than himself. Nowhere to go. Just an empty place, and an empty hole inside himself.

When his head dropped into his hands, he felt Peter approach. "Don't fucking touch me."

That large hand settled on his shoulder, making him scoff. "You think I really deserve to be comforted? I hurt her, Peter. Just like I told that asshole. She weighs half of what I do, and I threw her up against the car like a doll. There's no coming back from this."

"Yeah, there is. It's just a hard road."

"You know what?" He shoved Peter's hand away, got back up. "I'm really sick of you all having that fucking tone with me. You don't know what a hard road is. Not with what you have in your corner. It's fucking Christmas every fucking day for you."

What the hell was happening? He was shouting, his voice was hoarse. What had happened to him tonight? He was Ben O'Callahan, a lawyer with K&A, a sexual Dominant who always held control. He always kept his shit together. He was the fucking foam on the latte that rose above all of it. He'd been there for them whenever they needed him, always. He hadn't let his friends down. But at this moment, he resented the hell out of every one of them.

"I'm going. Get the hell away from me."

Peter rose as he was walking away. "You know, Jon said something pretty interesting the other day."

"Doesn't he always? The guy never shuts up." Ben came to a halt though, bracing himself against another lightpost, fingers gripping it hard, the peeling paint over the metal.

"Yeah. He said that our women—Savannah, Cass, Rachel, Dana—when we met them, each was in a situation where she really needed someone's help. Someone strong to stand at her back. I'd say damsel in distress, but the lot of them would tie me down and pour acid on my manly parts."

Ben lifted his head. Peter met his gaze, those gray eyes as steady as the rock embedded in a cliff face. "Jon said maybe you were different. That maybe Marcie's supposed to rescue you."

"Yeah right." But he couldn't move, something keeping him rooted to this spot, listening to this bullshit.

Peter took another couple steps forward. "You've been alone a long time, Ben. You have us, but it's not the same. You don't think we all see it? You're struggling. You're going to go off somewhere, get drunk tonight. That's not the answer."

"When you don't know the answer, it works as good as anything else. What I do in my personal time is my business."

"Yeah. That works, if you were just a coworker. But the five of us are a hell of a lot more than that." Peter closed in another step. "We love you, man. We always have, we always will."

"Don't do this." Ben felt like a vise was closing over his rib cage. Something was going to crack. "I'm not worth loving and you know it."

A look of pained compassion passed over Peter's face, but then it was gone and he shrugged. "Well, tonight you're not. You're pretty much a piece of shit. But lucky I've seen you on better days."

"That moment at the limo...I *wanted* to hurt her, Peter. Not like when I have her tied up and want to make her ass red. Not the good kind of hurt."

"Why did you want to hurt her?"

"Because she makes me want things." Things he'd taught himself not to want, viciously hammering down any yearning for them, because those things couldn't be trusted. They didn't stay, didn't last, and if he made himself vulnerable to them, they'd become a black hole that would swallow him up.

"Look at her, Peter. She's young, and perfect..." Unspoiled. She was the face of what love was supposed to be. He knew everything about her, from every letter, from every word she'd spoken, every expression he'd seen cross her face. He didn't even deserve to be in the same room with her. "What if I had really hurt her?" Ben couldn't believe it, his voice broke. "I didn't mean to hurt her, Peter. I really didn't. Goddamn it, I wish Max had broken my fucking neck."

He wished he'd died on the streets before he'd ever picked Jonas Kensington's pockets, anything to avoid the shame of what he'd done tonight, becoming exactly what he'd spent his childhood facing. Ugly faces, screwed up with hatred and anger, hard fists, grasping hands. All of them wanting the same thing. To drag everything down into the muck with them, to confirm that life was a living hell, nothing perfect out there they couldn't trash and destroy.

There was no such thing as love and compassion, light and hope. Not on the streets. And once the dirt of the streets was ground into his soul by the heels of everyone he'd encountered, by supposed friends and unexpected foes, he was tainted.

Jesus, what the hell was he doing? He walked away, straight into an alley. When he realized he was facing a brick wall, he sat down on a pile of discarded packing pallets. Using the heels of his hands, he rubbed viciously at something that was dust in his eyes, damn it. His hands were shaking. No, he wasn't going to do this. He wasn't.

He pushed back the noise, the memories, and when he surfaced, gasping like a swimmer, Peter was sitting next to him. Just a few inches between their hips and shoulders, but not touching.

No. He wasn't a fucking victim, someone who deserved compassion. He had manhandled a twenty-three-year-old girl, stomped on her spirit with the intent of crushing it. He saw himself shout those unforgivable words at her, saw each one hit her like bullets. Then he'd left her bleeding, all for the crime of believing herself in love with him.

"I don't want to be around her anymore. She pushes my buttons too hard. What if I hurt her again?"

"Then we kill you, dump you in the swamp and be done with it." Peter laid a hand on Ben's shoulder again, though Ben refused to look up from the hole he was staring into the filthy concrete ground. "If you truly believe that's a risk, you get help. Lance the boil, let the past come out and deal with it. Dana's counselor is a woman who's worked with countless vets with PTSD."

"I'm not—"

"Yeah, you are. You think because it happened when you were a kid on these streets, instead of in a desert a few thousand miles away, that it's so different?"

Ben swallowed. He really didn't want to have this conversation. Everything in him was pulling away from it, but something kept him rooted. Marcie's wounded eyes, the fear he'd put in her eyes. The past two years, the nights when nothing filled the ache except things he knew weren't the answer, things that merely made the ache worse in the long run.

"Asking for help is the hardest thing for one of those guys to do. How can some fucking shrink sitting in her safe office, piping in Enya music, help you deal with the blood, the screams, the fucking noise in your head? The staring eyes of the dead, of the ones you feel like you let down? Of what you've lost? But she can, Ben. Dana used to have nightmares all the time. Now she doesn't. We all have battlefields we've survived, but until we make peace with them, we don't leave them behind. And your kind of battlefield? It can haunt you forever, keeping you from what you deserve."

Peter gripped his shoulder hard, drawing his eyes up to his face. "Your parents didn't abandon you because you weren't worth loving, Ben. They abandoned you because they were assholes."

He definitely heard a rib crack from the pressure inside. When Peter sensed it, moving his touch to his nape, rubbing there, Ben swallowed. "Get off me, you homo."

"Yeah, you know I've always wanted to suck your monster dick."

"Good of you to finally admit it."

Peter eased up on the touch but stared him down. "If you love her, if you want her, you do whatever you have to do to deserve her. Because she's gone to an awful lot of trouble to prove she wants your sorry ass. Got it?"

Rising, Ben rubbed a hand over his face. "Don't know where I am on that. I've got to go...to move. Don't follow me this time. I mean it. I need to work this shit out."

"If you make me a promise."

"What, we're girls now?"

When Peter shifted, blocking his way out of the alley, Ben sighed. Yeah, he could get into a major brawl with him, but he'd have to fight dirty to win, because fighting Peter was like facing a tank. Probably why Matt had sent him, knowing he was the only one Ben couldn't easily beat up. "What?"

The gray eyes were steady, implacable. "Tell me you're not going to do anything stupid."

"I'm not that kind of guy, Peter."

"Not usually, no. But I've seen the look you've got in your eyes. A guy so consumed with his demons he'd throw himself on a mine to escape it. Then they send the little polished medal home to the people who love him. You've got a lot of people who care about you, Ben. Don't do that to them. If you don't trust yourself tonight, then let me shadow you."

Ben sighed, looked back out in the darkness. "Fine, but keep a distance. I don't want anyone to think we're dating."

"No chance of that. I wouldn't be caught dead dating an ambulance chaser."

Yes, these will make your ass bigger. But they will be worth it. Remember, a good friend will always tell you the truth. A great friend will validate your decision when you decide to do something stupid anyway.

Ben's note on a box of homemade truffles for Marcie's birthday

Chapter Thirteen

ᔐ

Marcie woke at two a.m. She vaguely remembered being carried up to her bed by Lucas when he'd gotten home and the party had broken up. She'd almost immediately returned to a deep sleep, but it had been short-lived. A bad nightmare had sent her bolting out of the bed and practically into the wall. Cass was in the room with her in a flash, helping to calm her down. She hadn't had a nightmare in ages, but she guessed it made sense that it had happened tonight. She still hated it, because she didn't want anything about Ben tainted with that.

Her sister was still there, sleeping next to her, arm around Marcie's waist. Marcie studied her face, then leaned over, kissed her forehead. "I'm going downstairs to get a snack," she said.

"Mmph. Need help?"

"No. You go back to Lucas. He misses you. I'm all right now."

"S'okay." But Cass slept on. Marcie smiled. Lucas would undoubtedly come find her himself before long. Slipping out of the bed, she pulled on her robe and slippers and shuffled down the steps, wincing only a little at the shock to her joints.

What surprised her was seeing Savannah asleep on their comfortable wide sofa, a body pillow firmly clasped between arms and legs. An afghan had been laid over her. In sleep, her face was far more relaxed, approachable. Remembering that earlier job offer, Marcie felt a frisson of warmth. She had great friends.

Because she saw Savannah, she was less surprised but not sure how to feel about seeing Matt in the kitchen. His laptop was open at the kitchen table, along with a couple files, but he was heating a kettle of water at the stove, three mugs laid out on the kitchen island.

It was rare she saw him in more casual attire, but it wasn't an unpleasant experience. The jeans fit well, the dark blue T-shirt stretching over his broad shoulders.

"I thought I heard you up," he said. "Want some hot chocolate?"

"I didn't figure you for the hot-chocolate type."

"One's for you and one's for Savannah. The third will be for Talia. She'll arrive as soon as she smells chocolate, no matter how deep she's sleeping."

Marcie chuckled. "You know us pretty well."

Matt gestured to a stool at the kitchen island for Marcie to make herself comfortable. "How are you doing?"

Marcie shrugged. "I'm fine, Matt. Really. Is *Ben* okay?"

When he glanced up at her, his brow furrowing, she dropped her attention to one of the mugs, turning it in her hands. "I know you know what happened tonight. I also think... It would help if I understood more." She remembered again that glimpse of darkness in Ben's eyes, of a deep well that could swallow a soul whole. "Savannah said you might talk to me."

"I'm certain she didn't mean tonight."

"Well, I'm not doing anything, you're sort of not doing anything. At the moment." She knew she was treading on uncertain ground, but that rarely stopped her. She met his dark gaze. "I can research a lot of things, but it's not the same as getting information right from the mind and perspective of the person who probably knows him best. You."

Matt considered her. "You're very forthright."

"I've been told that's a bad thing."

"I hope you disregard that advice. However, I have another concern." He braced his hands on the counter. "I asked how *you* are doing. You turned the conversation immediately to Ben's well-being. I hope you realize that your well-being is as important as his, particularly if this relationship is going to succeed."

She had the grace to flush a little. His tone was mild, but his expression wasn't. She'd opened the door by being blunt, and he'd shifted into the role of patriarch.

"Does that mean you won't tell me?"

Matt studied her an instant longer. "Bring me the chocolate and marshmallows from the pantry."

She immediately moved to do that. Standing next to him at the island, she emptied the powder into the mugs at his direction, stirred as he poured her cup. "You know how Ben came into our family," he said at last. "Not the official story about growing up in New England, et cetera."

"I do."

Matt nodded, his lips quirking. "Because our ladies do tend to share secrets with one another."

"Well, fair's fair."

He gave her a full smile at that. Gesturing her onto the stool next to him, he steadied it until she was situated. Then he sobered. "Those first several years, he didn't like to be touched by anyone. Not men or women. It was obvious he trusted neither one, and I'm sure he experienced the expected list of atrocities a child on the street faces."

He'd straightened, turning to lean against the counter next to her. Her slippered feet brushed against his jeans leg, but he didn't discourage the casual contact. Marcie was glad, because in the aftermath of the night's events, and imagining the dark picture he was painting, the tactile connection was reassuring. "But the real wounds he carried were chronic betrayals, inflicted by everyone who mattered in his life. It was a long time before he learned to relax enough to enjoy the camaraderie you see between him and the other men now. But that's not the only difference.

"It's perhaps a sign of a divine plan that Lucas ended up as head of your household. He transitioned from losing his parents to an optimal adopted family early on, so optimal there's even a genetic resemblance between them. I'm not saying he doesn't remember the loss, but he had a strong familial structure to take its place fairly quickly. That's rare, but it gives him a stability that holds fast through everything. I saw it when we met at Yale. I was a few years late attending, because I had to take over my father's business, but that was a fortuitous delay, since it gained me Lucas as a roommate."

Matt brushed her hair from her face, a gentle touch. "The code of morality that we observe, toward women, business, service in our community...that was a code that already existed for Lucas and myself, Jon and Peter. It drew us together, and we deepened that bond in our daily actions." He met Marcie's gaze. "Ben needed that structure because he had lived entirely without it. Our code became a lifeline to what he was meant to be, instead of the scavenger he'd had to become. It defines him. When he lost control earlier tonight—"

"I pushed him. I was topping—"

"Stop."

Whoa. There was a reason the other men deferred to Matt. Her words froze in her throat at the look on his face. "What happened is entirely on Ben's shoulders," he said quietly. "He knows it, we all know it. If you want to be with him, Marcie, do not ever excuse a loss of control like that.

"Yes, topping from the bottom can be dangerous, because it mixes up who is holding the physical and emotional control, and it's important that the Dom keep a calm hand on those reins at all times, because of how intense a session can become. However, what I just said about our code…for Peter, Jon, Lucas and myself, it is an ideal, however vital we consider it. For Ben, it's an imperative. If you love him, you hold him to it, always. With the exception of Peter, within the confines of military action, none of us have lived lives governed completely by violence. Ben has."

She swallowed. He was waiting on her answer, and while he wasn't her Master, she knew exactly how to respond. "Yes sir."

Matt nodded. "Ben has another side of that same coin, which is why he will be harder on himself about what happened tonight than anyone. He has no tolerance for an attack on an innocent. If he had been part of your life the night Jeremy's friend attacked you, that friend would be dead. His body would be lost in the bayou, never to be found, and Ben wouldn't lose a night of sleep over cutting his throat."

Marcie blinked. "Are you trying to scare me away from him?"

"No. You asked me a question, and I'm giving you an answer. You're very young."

She scowled, automatic resentment rising in her breast. Here it went. The "you're so young" speech.

"Marcie." He had that authoritative gaze fixed on her again. "Drop the attitude. It's a simple fact. You don't have a lot of life experience to bring to a situation like this, the things I've described. Correct?"

She gave a grudging nod.

"Right. So you need to consider it carefully. Are you ready to handle that type of man, something entirely separate from your feelings for him? You may want to negotiate a million-dollar contract, but do you step into the room before you have the resources to handle it?"

She watched him pour more hot water, then patiently take up a spoon and stir a mug of chocolate for his wife. He had large hands, but they moved capably over the task. Savannah might be impatient with Matt's coddling, but the Tennyson CEO understood it. They all did. Savannah's mother had died as a result of her pregnancy. Though it was because of a virulent cancer that she'd refused to have treated to protect her unborn child, there was a lingering legacy there. Under Matt's collar, Savannah often wore the locket left to her by her mother. The past was important.

But it didn't dictate choices. Cass had taught her that.

"I don't know if I can handle him, but it's not that kind of decision." There was no going back now. Not for her. "From the moment we met, I knew I was his. That's who I want to be. So I have to figure it out, you know? Jon said it could only happen if I was myself, so that's got to be enough." She drew herself up. "I think it is."

Matt pursed his lips, nodded. "Considering how long you have pursued him, I think your argument is credible. It's also fueled by the passion of youth which, in this case, is not a bad thing."

When he pushed her mug closer to her, reminding her the chocolate was starting to cool, she saw the ceramic had a picture of a cat on it, one with a comically disagreeable face, a fly sitting on its whisker. It made her lips twitch.

She looked up at him then. He was still stirring, so she had the pleasure of studying the aristocratic bone structure of his face, the set of his mouth. Though none of the Knights shared their women outside their own circle, Savannah stayed pretty exclusive to Matt and him to her, except for indulging some soft pleasures within the group—like the women had done tonight. She wanted to ask about that, and about a million other questions, but she figured she'd wait until another time. Or seek other sources for the information. Best not to poke the lead wolf with a stick.

311

"I used to go crazy, reading the society pages," she admitted. "Whenever they hooked him up with someone for a charity event, or reported seeing him 'with' Miss So-n-So, I'd think—what will I do if someone gets him first? If one day I open up the paper and see his engagement notice?"

Matt arched a brow. "Did you have a plan to handle that eventuality?"

"Yes. It involved a shovel and a remote location."

Matt chuckled, heaping marshmallows in the top of Savannah's mug. "You and Ben may be a useful combination, if I ever need to be permanently rid of a competitor."

It made her grin at him. Lifting the hot chocolate, he gave her a wink, moved into the other room. When she followed him, she saw his timing was as uncanny as usual. Savannah was sitting up, restless from the discomfort of being on one side too long. She gave him a cranky look.

"I am exactly where I was when you checked on me thirty minutes ago. Oh except I had the baby. She slid right out, and now she's off somewhere playing with electrical sockets and curtain cords."

"That's a shame. I'll lose my deposit on that birthing suite at the hospital. Maybe we can just go there for a vacation stay and cancel that private island resort we've reserved for the fall."

"I'm surprised you haven't reserved the entire wing so I'll have the undivided attention of every obstetrician in New Orleans."

"Who said I didn't?" He gave her a lingering look, so full of warmth and gentle devotion that Savannah shook her head, a soft smile crossing her face. She glanced at Marcie.

"He's hopeless."

Hopelessly in love with his wife. It made Marcie ache and yearn...and hope.

* * * * *

312

Ben made sure he came into the office a bare few minutes before the nine o'clock staff meeting. He didn't want to chat over coffee or any other bullshit. He'd given Peter the slip about thirty minutes after their heart-to-heart in the alley. Yeah, it had been a crappy thing to do, but Peter needed to get home to Dana, and Ben didn't need a nursemaid. While the mushy moment hadn't been faked, it had made it easier to fool Peter into thinking Ben accepted being followed. One of the few times he'd been able to outwit the shrewd former captain.

His head was pounding from whatever toxic brew he'd poured down his throat in some of New Orleans' seedier dives throughout the weekend. He vaguely remembered getting into it in a pool hall with a trio of guys wearing a lot of biker leather. His ribs still hurt from being knocked down and kicked, but he didn't really remember much other than that. Except the guys being pretty affable about it, propping him up in the alley and watching over him until he regained consciousness. The biggest guy had even spotted him another beer, making the laconic comment, "She fucked you up, pal. Women'll do that. Go on home before you get yourself killed."

Since he didn't remember talking to anyone about Marcie, he supposed it was just an educated guess. Bikers could be pretty astute that way.

He barely nodded to Janet, went to his office, found the file he needed on his desk. Which either meant Janet had taken over Marcie's duties, or Marcie herself had come in and set it out. He'd had her reassigned, but she could be in the building. The very thought of it made his head hurt worse.

When he was sitting in the alley with the biker, deciding whether he'd sleep there and let someone steal his wallet, or struggle to his feet and find his way to the nearest hotel to hide out for the weekend, his thoughts had gone back to earlier in the night. Before the limo. She'd embraced the CNC treatment, but ultimately what she'd been seeking was that intense connection, the emotional input that promised a soul had a match in this world. It was the way she'd been from the very beginning, the first time he'd met her, when she was sixteen and not even on his sphere as a lover.

Friday night he'd felt that desire from her, overriding everything else, even the physical. The problem was, he'd felt it right back, and the more he'd felt it, the more he'd felt like a tiger trapped in a cage he didn't want opened. She just kept pushing and pushing. If he'd seen it through the way he should have, he would have sent her spinning through subspace, fucked her brains out.

He wouldn't have left her aftercare to the staff though. He'd have wrapped a blanket around her, held her as her teeth chattered and she shook, the effect of getting so deep in that zone, a place he could have gone with her, totally into topspace. Instead he'd been unable to leave his own fucking headspace, his anger, his frustration, his lack of balance. He'd had no business even touching her that night.

He wasn't a chickenshit, though. He'd do his penance today, get past it. Get back to what he knew how to be. Marcie would finish her internship and head to Milan, because that's where she belonged. It should be clear to her after last night. Everything fucking the way it fucking should be.

As he came into the conference room ten minutes later, he bit back an oath. He was hoping Janet would be set up to transcribe, a buffer to anything too personal, but it was just Peter all by his lonesome. He was in his usual relaxed sprawl, but with an expression that said he was going to give him shit about ditching his tail. Hell, Ben needed coffee before he did this.

He dropped the folder on the table, gave Peter an even, don't-fuck-with-me look, and turned right into Lucas' fist.

For all that he razzed Lucas about being a pussy-cyclist, the guy had a hammer of a right punch. It practically lifted him off his feet, knocked him back onto the conference table. He deserved it, but he wasn't going down defenseless. As he rolled and came back to his feet, ready to counter, Peter was already there, dragging him back while Jon and Matt did the honors with Lucas.

"What the hell is the matter with you?" Lucas snarled. "I swear to God, I'm going to put my foot so far up your ass you choke on it."

"She wasn't supposed to come to the club. She was supposed to be bluffing." Where the hell had that knee-jerk, dumbass response come from? Damn, he needed coffee.

When Lucas' blue eyes turned into ice frost from the Antarctic, Matt and Jon let him go. "For that, you get a free one," Matt decided.

Peter had let him go as well, but Ben was still seeing stars. Lucas got in another face punch and a gut shot before Matt and Jon pulled him back again. Ben was fervently glad he'd already puked up most of last night's intake in the hotel room. If he threw up on the boardroom carpet, Janet would make him clean every fiber with a toothbrush.

"You're pinning the blame on her for what you dished out? A twenty-three-year-old inexperienced sub who showed up where you didn't expect her to be? Let me go," Lucas told Matt and Jon. "I'm going to fucking rip his head off."

"He's our lawyer," Jon reminded him. "He can't get you off a murder rap if he's the victim."

"She may be inexperienced, but she's a sub, deep as they come," Ben said, surging against Peter's iron grip. "Friday, it was going to be me, or whoever she grabbed at the club. They were ten deep for that feeding trough. No one outside this fucking room is going to touch her, goddamn it. Not while I'm breathing."

He came to a full stop with that shouted declaration, feeling the shock of it reverberate off the walls and through his bones, settling into his gut. All heads turned toward him, four sets of eyes assessing, measuring. No. He wasn't that kind of Master. He wasn't possessive. He fucked women, let them go. Until last night. When he couldn't bear to see another Master's hands on what every blood cell in his body roared was his. Noah had been different, a sub under his command, a different tool, like the cane or rawhide.

He'd told Peter he needed to work it out, but he hadn't. He'd chosen alcohol and fists instead. Now he'd just blurted it out, bald as a naked newborn.

He struggled to be reasonable, calm. Sort of. "I told her I was mentoring her," he said. "Just her mentor."

The words sounded hollow, absurd. Weak. With a sudden weary sigh, he folded into a chair, nursing his aching temples and now his busted jaw. Lucas might have broken it. That'd be great, a lawyer with his mouth wired shut. The world would celebrate.

"What the hell is this?" Lucas demanded. "Spill it, Ben. Give me a reason to hit you again."

"Lucas." Matt put a quelling hand on the man's shoulder. "Ben. Tell us what's going on."

"I want her," Ben mumbled, so quietly that he didn't think they'd heard. Until he raised his gaze to Lucas' frozen features. "I want her," he repeated more strongly. "I didn't want to, but she wouldn't give up, and she got to me. It's all fucked up."

"Don't put this on her."

"I'm not." Ben leaped back to his feet, but Peter was there, steadying him. "Damn it, she's been nothing but what she should be. Beautiful, generous, full of life. It crept up on me. I thought if I scared her off...she'd be okay. I...It went too far. I just wanted her to find someone better for her."

"The problem is, she wants you just as much, Ben," Jon observed. "It was a damn fool thing to do."

"She woke up screaming Friday night," Lucas said. He was quieter now, but the harshness was still around his mouth, anger in his eyes. "A nightmare about when Jeremy's friend attacked her. She hasn't had one of those in years. Cass slept in her room."

Goddamn it. Yeah, they should let Lucas go. In fact, they should all beat him to a bloody pulp and then toss him out the window to hit the asphalt below. A hundred broken bones wouldn't hit him as hard as those few words.

"Fuck." Ben sat back down in the chair, wouldn't let himself look down, no matter how hard it was to meet Lucas' eyes. "I'm sorry, Lucas. You're right. It was unforgivable."

The CFO's face remained unreadable for several moments, then his jaw eased a fraction. "You're right. It is fucked up. But I'm not the one you owe an apology."

"If she's the one," Jon said quietly, "you can't push her away, Ben. You know that. Why are you trying so hard?"

Ben couldn't answer that. He just looked out the window. He didn't want to go there, didn't want to say it. But of course they knew. They'd always known. He just didn't want that shit dredged up. He wondered if he could make it to the door and escape, but Peter had casually shifted in front of it, anticipating him.

"Ben, look at me," Matt said. He had his firm, cool voice, the one that brooked no bullshit.

He didn't. Couldn't. "She's everything I'm not. She's clean."

"The one thing that can clean a man's soul is surrendering to a woman's love, Ben," Jon said. "You just have to give her the chance."

"Yeah, we saw how I dealt with that."

"Because you're fighting it. You're fighting yourself."

Matt took a step closer, and Ben felt that old terror, the one of being hemmed in. "Ben, look at me."

What the hell was the matter with him? He always met a man's eyes. But the part of him rising up, trying to choke him, reminded him of the uncomfortable moment with Peter last night. When he at last forced himself to meet those dark eyes, Matt was standing right in front of him. He put his hand on Ben's shoulder, fingers tightening. "You can choose to be a chickenshit bastard who runs away from a gift because you're scared it's going to abandon you one day, just like your parents. Or betray you, like pretty much everyone did when you were growing up. That decision will eat you like a cancer, but you can drink yourself into liver disease and beat that to the punch."

"Sounds swell. Option two?"

"It's time to come out of the cold, Ben. You were a child, fighting to stay alive on the streets, and you did what you had to do. You deserve love. Do the hardest thing a Master can do. Get your shit straight and accept the gift. Take the risk, the first step. Is she the one you want more than anything, now and forever?"

Matt really did have his father's eyes, so much it was sometimes like the son was channeling the sire. Not a bad thing, despite the fact the thought reeked of Jon's New-Age bullshit. Long ago, when Ben was a kid, he'd woken up in the Kensington guest bedroom screaming. Matt's dad had calmed him down, brought him cookies. Didn't make him talk, but Ben had talked anyway. When he'd settled down, Jonas had given him a brief hug, a squeeze of his shoulders. Ben had tensed, but that was all Jonas had done. The man had left the lamp on low setting so Ben didn't have to go back to sleep in the dark.

"Yeah, she is. I want her." He wanted to say more, but if he was going to do that, he wanted to say it to Marcie. She deserved that, and way more.

"God help her." Peter's lips twitched. He stepped up to Matt's side.

Ben rose, a self-defense measure. "Oh Jesus. Tell me this isn't a hugging moment."

"It's not a hugging moment." Then Peter gave him one of his bear hugs anyway, the kind where the monster squeezed his ribs and slapped his back to the point of pain, therefore making Ben still feel manly. When he released him, Peter put his hand on Ben's face in a brotherly gesture of affection, shoved it away so his neck popped. "You're such a dumbass."

Matt returned to the head of the table, gesturing to all of them to take their seats. After a moment, Lucas took his usual place at Matt's right, though he continued to regard Ben with an undecided expression. Ben had a futile wish for his coffee, but settled for taking a couple deep breaths and sitting down again. He wasn't sure how the hell he was going to concentrate on business after all that, but he needn't have worried. Matt had rewritten the agenda.

"You owe Marcie amends," Matt said. "That's the most critical consequence of your actions. But you also owe us. This circle is bound by a code, and you broke that code."

Oh hell. But Matt was right. Jesus, he wanted penance, wanted to do something to purge this shit from his soul, the look he'd put on Marcie's face. He had to fix it with her, but he also had to make it right with them. With Lucas.

"You're right." He nodded, straightened. "Whatever you think is fair."

"Making you cry like a little girl," Lucas said acidly, but there was a different set to his face now, one that said he might be forgiven. A few years from now. After a lot of groveling.

When they made their decision, Ben actually felt like bursting into tears. But he swallowed jagged glass, took it like a man. He deserved it, after all. Hard as accepting their ruling was, it was going to be worse, figuring out how to make it up to Marcie. But now that he'd accepted it…

He wanted her. He'd said it out loud, in front of all of them. It filled him with a strange sense of anticipation, reminding him of when each of them had come to this table, determined to make a chosen woman his. He'd spent so much time denying her, pushing her away, but he let it unfold now, looked at it from several different directions. *Come in out of the cold.* He felt like he was standing in the middle of a room where he'd cautiously opened a window, and then another…maybe one more. Letting the sunlight pour in.

I want her. I need her. If he hadn't fucked it up totally, she might consider being okay with that.

"I'm nearly a decade older than she is," he said suddenly. "When she's turning forty, I'll be hitting fifty."

Jon nodded. "You know Rachel is thirteen years older than me. We've dealt with those issues."

"How does *she* deal with it?"

"I think it's harder for a woman than a man. Some days she gets a little moody about it. But I point out that when I'm eighty and she's ninety-three, we'll both be on walkers and mixing up our teeth in the morning water glasses." A smile touched Jon's lips. "We never really grow beyond a certain age. We're all the same inside, our desires, our needs. We just get better impulse control.

Peter slanted Ben a grin. "Well, *most* of us get better impulse control."

"Blow me."

"You wish."

Jon waved the banter aside. "Ben, if you were fifty and Marcie was twenty-three, you'd be having the obvious epiphany about your mortality, trying to sate it in fancy cars and young girls, but that's not what this is. You're thirty-two and in love with an intelligent, vibrant woman nine years younger than you." His blue eyes twinkled then. "And Peter's right. You're emotionally immature for your age. Marcie is extraordinarily mature for hers, so you're a perfect fit."

"She said you told her I never grew beyond age thirteen."

"Which makes *you* emotional jailbait," Peter pointed out.

Ben shook his head, rose, went to the window. With his usual impeccable timing, Matt started hitting on today's business. Since the legal stuff wasn't relevant for the first couple agenda items, it gave him a strategic moment to take a breath. They'd give him that. They were his friends, after all. His family.

He thought about how Marcie had walked into his office on those killer legs, with that come-hither smile playing around her lips. More than that, he remembered her eyes. Determined, playful...nervous. He'd picked up on the active submissive in that first instance, and it ran bone deep in her. So to do what she'd done, shoving herself at him like that...it had to have been hard.

A submissive woman was often strong and driven in her career, but in the bedroom she yearned to submit, to surrender. Marcie had combined her mundane persona with her D/s one, and that was a stress. He'd seen it when she broke outside his front door and pelted his windows with rocks. She was pushed to the limits, and he'd pushed her there. While he did that regularly as a Dom, he didn't usually do it as a man, causing that kind of pain.

He'd deal with that. This time he really had to wrap his head around it, so he didn't screw up again. He'd spent so much time vacillating, sending out mixed signals, and he couldn't do that anymore. She deserved better from her Master. If he could just step away from his fucked-up head, he could work it through. Normally, he used the topspace he found as a Dom to help him with that, but he wanted his next session, every future session, to be with her, so it was a chicken and egg dilemma.

He was going in circles like a damn hamster. He wanted to go to her, talk to her. Right now. He didn't want to wait another minute. This wasn't a legal case he had to prepare. It had to be raw, from the heart, pure instinct. They could do without him in the meeting.

Lucas' cell rang with the ringtone he used for Cassandra. *Urgent* by Foreigner. Ben glanced over his shoulder as Lucas picked it up. Maybe Cass was letting him know how Marcie was doing. Maybe Lucas would hand him the phone and Cass would tell him how Marcie was doing. *Yeah right.* As pissed as

Lucas had been, Ben had a feeling it would take a truckload of diamonds to earn Cass' forgiveness. Even then, he'd probably have to hide behind the truck's steel reinforced cab. Cass kept a Beretta, after all.

"Hey, Marcie." Lucas' obvious surprise at finding Marcie on the line disappeared as his grip on the phone tightened, his eyes darkening with pain. "When? Okay. Are you with her? Okay. Just stay with her and the others. I'll be right there. Let me talk to her."

He shifted the phone to the other hand as the men rose, already anticipating the somber news. "Cassie? It's all right, baby. I know. I'm so sorry. I love you. I'm on my way. You keep Marcie and the kids with you, all right? I'll be there in a few minutes, promise."

As he clicked off, Lucas met Jon's eyes. "Jeremy died in Thailand early this morning."

I went to visit Jeremy at spring break. He was good, different. He's thin, looks like an old man, and he talks slow, moves slow. But when he looks at me, he sees me, he's no longer strung out. He took my hand, held it. Sat with me on a stone bench and we looked at the mist-covered mountains outside the temple together. He didn't say he was sorry, because it was as if he knew it wasn't needed anymore. That wasn't the same Jeremy. I cried all the way home on the plane. It felt bad to cry, but as much as I hated who he became on the drugs, he still isn't the brother I used to have. I guess I hoped I'd get him back at some point. I was grieving him on the trip home as if he was actually dead. Please don't ever tell Cass I said that.

Letter from Marcie to Ben, late sophomore year

All your secrets are safe with me, brat. Things change. You're a different person to him as well. You just need to figure out what you can be to one another now. When Jonas was killed, Matt and I didn't know each other well. I even resented him a little bit for being the real son of the only guy who was ever a decent father figure to me. But something inside said this was a relationship I didn't want to throw away. Look deeper, and you might find something in Jeremy of equal or even greater value than what you lost. Things happen for a reason.

Ben's response

Chapter Fourteen

ဆ

Jeremy was cremated in Thailand. While Lucas and Cass were there with Marcie, coordinating the arrangements, Jon and Rachel stayed with the children. Ben, Peter and Matt covered Lucas and Jon's workload at the office. Savannah handled phone calls and correspondence with family and friends.

Ben sent a wire transfer to their bank agent in Chiang Mai, a generous donation from all five of the K&A men, a sincere thanks to the clinic and the monks for the physical and spiritual care they'd given the troubled young man. Jeremy had come to them addicted to drugs and on death's door. The experimental clinic in Thailand recommended by Jon had given his body the additional years, but the monks' teachings and guidance had given his spirit renewed life Cassandra believed would be eternal. Ben hoped it was true. Lost souls needed all the help they could get, after all.

Even long distance, Marcie was working with Jessica to manage the memorial service details. He'd learned that through Peter, since Dana had been chosen to perform the service. It was to be held at Lucas and Cassandra's plantation home on the outskirts of New Orleans. The sprawling grounds had a manmade lake fed by the marsh tributaries, lots of garden paths to walk, and a back lawn flanked by ancient oaks, the perfect setting.

He'd been working long hours, taking the lion's share of Lucas' work, even when the others protested. "I owe him," he said briefly, and Matt let it go at that. Part of his self-imposed penance. The extra work helped the gnawing ache he had over other things as well. He was worried about Marcie, sure she was pushing herself too hard to support Cass and Lucas, trying to handle every detail in Thailand and at home. He checked in with Dana and Savannah regularly, confirming they and Jess were pulling everything off her shoulders that she'd let them take.

He hadn't been able to resolve things with his girl before she left. If things had been fixed between them, he could have sent daily emails to her phone with more personal words of encouragement, comfort, things to make her smile. Instead, he found a card service that created unique, artistic digital bouquets, and sent her one daily, with basic notes. *Thinking of you. Miss you. I'm here for you.* That one mocked him, because until they had a face-to-face, there was a lot of debris that told her the exact opposite. *Damn it.*

She didn't reply to them, but he saw the acknowledgments, knew she opened them all. He didn't need her to reply, didn't want to take up energy she needed for other things. The acknowledgment was enough. That's what he told himself, even as he told himself not to be an idiot and get caught up in a paranoid scenario where she wasn't replying because he'd lost her forever.

He sent two real bouquets the day they arrived back into town, one for Marcie, one for Cass. The card to Marcie said simply, *"I'm sorry. For everything. Will talk to you soon."* Cass' card had the appropriate condolences from a family friend. Now wasn't the time for him to seek her forgiveness. Forgiveness was a selfish thing to ask during something like this.

While he wished the reason had been different, the separation had given him time to think things through. He was steadier now. Stronger perhaps, or at least on the right path to it. Though he wanted Marcie with an urgency that bordered on painful, he wasn't going to screw it up again. Timing was everything.

* * * * *

Hell. He was late, despite breaking every traffic law to get there on time. He'd told Matt and Peter to go straight to the service while he went into the office to finish up a document for Lucas that needed to be filed today, and it had taken longer than expected. Crossing the back lawn quietly, he leaned against a tree a few feet back from the back row of chairs. It wasn't a large crowd, mostly family and close friends, like Steve Pickard and his wife, here to support Cassandra and her siblings. Jeremy hadn't had anyone in his life in the States not associated with his life as an addict. As Ben well knew, those kinds of acquaintances weren't attend-your-funeral types.

Though mindful of the reason they were all gathered, he couldn't help but seek out a glimpse of Marcie first. There. In the front row, her slim back even more fragile to him in the somber black, smooth hair in a barrette, the delicate line of her neck etched as she attended what Dana was saying. Her body leaned into Cass', giving comfort.

He turned his gaze to the podium, decorated with a beautiful spray of yellow lilies and purple iris. Dana stood on a step behind it so she was tall enough to be seen by the gathering. It was different, seeing Dana in her minister's robe, but her spiritual calling had always rested comfortably on her shoulders, despite the private side of her that some might say didn't mesh with a Christian message. Ben guessed it depended on how a person defined being a Christian.

Dana could be mischievous, playful, downright kinky and irrepressible. She also had a lake of calm inside her, a deep understanding of people's spiritual struggles in the face of physical and emotional adversity. She'd faced it firsthand herself with her injuries in Iraq. Her ministerial skills had already won her a loyal following at her New Orleans church, and they showed now, in her gentle but honest treatment of Jeremy's life.

"Over six years ago, Jeremy came to the monastery door a troubled soul. Addicted to drugs, terminally ill, lost in every way one of us can be lost. But God opens doors for us throughout our lives, and Jeremy finally stepped through one that was offered. The monks told his sisters that he'd learned to be a kind and humble soul, always willing to help with their daily tasks when he had the strength to do so.

"On his good days, he helped them in the garden. Cass and Marcie visited a patch of vegetables that he'd sown and watered. Each day, even if he was too weak to do anything else, he would make his way down to that small patch of ground to care for it."

Ben turned his gaze back to Marcie. Marcie had her arm around Nate, just entering his teen years, and Jess was between Talia and Cherry, holding them close to her sides. When Marcie's head turned enough for him to see her profile, she looked composed but tired. He could see the strain. She'd been doing what they were all doing. Attending to whatever details needed to be handled, trying to make things easier for Cass. They all knew what a blow this was for her, and now Dana hit that one straight on.

The blind woman tilted her head. She was wearing dark glasses, a way to keep her fixed gaze from being distracting, but they also gave the impression she was passing her glance over the assembled. "Marcie told me that, for all the love his family gave him, it was his older sister Cass who never failed Jeremy, no matter the pain and suffering his actions sometimes brought upon the family. She always loved him, as love is meant to be. Just, true and honest." She looked toward Cass then, unfailing in her direction. "Cass, as such, your siblings wanted me to conclude this service by reading 1 Corinthians 13. In your honor. They're certain Jeremy would agree."

Ben watched Cass' shoulders quiver and then buckle. Lucas' arm tightened around her, his head bending over hers. Marcie pressed her temple hard to her sister's as the words were read.

Ben kept his gaze fixed on Marcie, the tears that ran down that side of her face, the brittle expression, as Dana spoke the powerful words.

"If I have prophetic powers, and understand all mysteries and all knowledge, and if I have all faith, so as to remove mountains, but have not love, I am nothing... Love is patient and kind; love does not envy or boast; ...it bears all things, believes all things, hopes all things, endures all things..."

He should be sitting with her, as Matt was with Savannah, Jon with Rachel...Lucas with Cass. The front row of chairs had been for Jeremy's immediate family. There were a line of chairs right behind them for the K&A family and Steve Pickard, Cass' extended family. The single empty chair at the end was one he was sure Peter had kept open for him if he wanted to sit with them. He'd stayed back here, though, and not just because he was late and didn't want to be disruptive. He'd been listening, watching, looking...for something.

He drew a breath, a deep, slow one. When he was mastering a sub, everything went away but his body and her body. There was one singular focus, one intent, everything clear, nothing hidden or obscured. This moment felt like that. Everyone's focus on the minister, the quiet, tranquil surroundings, but there was a straight line between him and Marcie, connecting them. For the first time he put his hand on it, felt the tautness that confirmed it was tight and true, a true binding. Just waiting for him to have the courage to grasp it. To fight for it.

As the service concluded, people started filing back into the house for the hors d'oeuvres and to give the family their condolences. Matt saw him, nodded. Ben acknowledged him but stayed where he was. Matt understood, continuing to escort Savannah toward the house, Talia now under his other arm. Nate and the other siblings likewise had fallen in among the guys, or with Steve Pickard and his wife.

Marcie had turned Cass over to Lucas, but she stayed by her chair, watching them all leave. At first, he thought she knew he was there, but then he realized she didn't. She looked too alone, too lost in her head. Once everyone was well on their way, she turned and walked away.

He followed her. She went to the end of a finger dock at the manmade lake, stepping out of her black heels to sit down. Putting her feet in the water, she braced her hands on the rough planking. Taking off his own shoes and socks, he rolled up the legs of his trousers, and then came up behind her, putting a brief hand on her shoulder to warn her of his presence before he sat down next to her, trailing his feet in the water next to hers.

She kept looking down into the water, the mild wind keeping it rippling with movement. After seeing her in outfits that taunted and teased him beyond bearing, it was unexpected to realize she was even more beautiful to him like this. Her face pale but quiet, her hair drawn back from her face, the dark modest dress against soft skin. She looked both older than expected, and yet more vulnerable.

"If you could meet God and ask him one question, what would it be?" She had a wistful, sad look, and he knew he'd do anything to make her feel better.

"I'd ask him if there was anything in the world that hadn't been done, that hadn't happened. Not the significant obvious stuff, like world peace. The urban legend kind of thing, what people claim has happened before, but no one is certain about it. Like someone sitting down on the toilet and finding a snake in there."

She turned her head to look at him, her brows raised. "You ass," she said, and then she started laughing.

Extraordinary. That was the word Jon had used about her maturity, but it fit so much more about her. He couldn't help touching her face, but when he did, she stopped laughing. As she lifted a hand, hesitant, he waited on her. He knew it wasn't that she wasn't sure of his permission. She wasn't sure of herself, of what she wanted. What he'd done to her, the hurt, was still too close. He had to let her choose. Which meant he also had to swallow down the disappointment when she closed her hand into a fist, lowered it to her lap again. "What would you really ask?"

"Hell, I don't know." He shook his head. "If you're in the presence of God, all questions are supposed to be answered, right? At least that's what I'd hope."

She pursed her lips. "I wasn't sure you believed in God. Not specifically. I figured you were more of an agnostic, if not a complete atheist, because of how things went when you were little."

"When my mother left me in an alley, I was wearing a plastic rosary with a pressed shamrock pendant, suggesting she was Irish Catholic. Guess that's the only reason she didn't abort me. Or maybe she didn't want to waste the cash she could use on her drug habit." He shrugged before she could say anything to that. "When Jonas nabbed me for picking his pocket, he didn't turn me in to the cops. He found me a decent foster home. He checked in on me, made sure I went to school. A lot of things happened in my life, good and bad, but now I'm pretty well off. I worked my ass off for that, but certain things had to happen at the right moments to get me on the right track. It makes sense there's something out there that will help you, if you're willing to be helped."

"So if love is staring you right in the face, it'd be kind of stupid to turn your back on it, right?"

Touché, love. But before he could think of a proper answer to that, she spoke again. "I got your flowers. The bouquet. Forget-me-nots. But I don't want to talk about that right now, okay?"

"Okay."

She sat silently for a few minutes, gazing at the minnows clustering around her toes. "I don't know why I was thinking about this today. It was so long ago, and it seems somehow disrespectful, with how much further Jeremy came by the end, but I was remembering that night." Her shoulder jerked, a tic, and his brow furrowed when he saw it.

"Allen, that was his name. I was thirteen, didn't know anything. He was nineteen, and he came into my room, started flirting, but then he got mean and pushy. I was screaming for help, and he was tearing at my clothes, and all I could think was, 'why isn't Jeremy helping me?' I never thought…when I realized that he'd been sitting in the other room, too stoned to even pay attention…"

Ben put a hand over hers on the dock. He wanted to hold her, but recent and past history was pressing in too close, so he settled for that overlap of fingers. Hers were cold. She stared down at them. "Cassie got home just in time, pulled him off me. God, she was… I think about it now, and she was incredible. It was like watching a bear go after something attacking her cubs. A nineteen-year-old guy taller and heavier than she was and she pretty much kicked the crap out of him. All the shit I gave her growing up...and she was always there. But even after that, she loved Jeremy, just as much as she loved all of us." Her voice trembled. "I don't know if she's ever going to get over not being able to save him."

"She will. Because she's got you. And Lucas. All of us. We're here for all of you."

She looked at him then, and her eyes were sheened with tears. "Ben, please hold me. I promise I won't try to jump you. At least right now."

"Christ," he muttered, but he needed no further invitation to pull her into his arms. Or put his mouth over hers, despite the absolute stupidity of doing so. It was a soft, long kiss, with gentle heat and connection, and he could almost feel that line between them tightening, winding around them both, holding them together. But there was a tension to her, a caution. He'd caused that, and he needed to fix it. It would take time, and a hell of a lot more than a kiss.

She hadn't rebuffed him though. She'd asked him to hold her, even made a weak joke that made him hope she still wanted him. He needed her to want him with that same fierceness she'd had before, so he could honor it the way he should have from the beginning.

But today wasn't about that. When he finally lifted his head, her eyes were closed. He used his fingertips to carry away the few tears, and then those brown eyes opened, looking at him. "I should get back to the house. Cass will need me."

Looking at how pale she was close up, feeling the tremor in her hands, he shook his head. "She's surrounded by friends and family right now. Let's take a little bit of time for you."

"Ben—"

"No arguing," he said quietly. Her gaze flickered up to his face, uncertain. "If I thought she genuinely needed you right now, we'd go back. But she's all right. Give yourself a breath. You've gotten what, probably two hours' sleep this week?"

She shook her head. "I've been okay."

"You've been better than okay. You've been brilliant. But dim the wattage for a few moments, firefly. Let's walk somewhere. How about down to the gazebo?"

"Okay."

He helped her up, picked up her shoes. As Marcie watched him with those sad, tired eyes, he knelt, dried her feet with his handkerchief, guided each foot into the practical heels. She held onto his shoulder, and he felt the curve of her fingers in his coat. After he donned his own shoes and socks, straightened his trouser legs, he took that hand, pressed a kiss to her knuckles. Tucking it into the crook of his elbow, he guided her onto the path that followed the edge of the lake. For a little while she was quiet, just leaning against him, walking together, but then she pointed to the sky.

"Look at that. See how the sky is blue above the tree canopy, and directly beneath it, it's white, a perfect segue? I wonder what causes that?"

"We'll ask Jon. He knows all the science stuff."

"You're a lawyer. You know how to make up stuff that sounds right."

"Light refraction," he said solemnly. "Caused by the whosiwhatsit interacting with the thingamajig in a synaptic reaction."

"That's total nonsense. Good enough." They'd dropped to holding hands, and it felt pretty damn natural. Even more for him to pull her under his arm, guide her hand under his coat so she could settle her palm on his waist and he could put his around her shoulders. She laid her head on his chest.

They followed the boardwalk to the screened gazebo overlooking the marsh. It was a hushed place, a couple white herons fishing gracefully among the waters, the silence punctuated by the occasional sawing cricket or chirping note of a frog.

"Let's just sit here," she whispered. "We can listen and watch."

He shed his coat, put it over her shoulders, then took a seat in the Adirondack chair. Guiding her onto his knee, he let her lean back against his body, put her head next to his. The marsh grasses rippled back and forth, like conversations. Seed motes floated through the air. The heron stepped with stately slowness through the water, watching for fish.

"Do you have a quiet place like this, Ben? A place where everything makes sense?"

He'd been stroking her hair, carefully removing barrette and pins until it tumbled to her shoulders and he could comb through it, follow the line of her narrow shoulder blades. He could answer her question with more lawyer bullshit, things that sounded right, were somewhat true, but this was the first step. He wasn't going to be a chickenhearted bastard anymore.

"The St. Louis cemetery," he said, with effort. "I used to go there as a kid, at night. I still go there to think. If you sit on top of one of the bigger vaults, you can see most of the place. There's a sense of peace there, of problems set aside."

"Well, yeah. Everyone there is dead."

He tugged her hair, though he couldn't help a smile. He turned his head enough so they were eye to eye. Hers had a soft gleam of tired humor. "Brat," he said.

"Do you find it...when you do a scene?"

"You tell me. I think you already know the answer."

She pressed her lips together. "When I was watching you that night at Surreal—the first time—I saw it. You could have been in the middle of an empty desert, because it was just you and those three women. You were focused on finding the true root of their submission, and when you got them into subspace, you were right there with them, in a similar...Domspace, where everything made sense, their very lives, every movement, every breath, in your hand."

She nodded out to the marsh. "When I come here, for comfort, wisdom, or to be nothing for a little while, I imagine being held in God's hand. But the other night, when you took me over, Mastered me so completely, it was one and the same. I was held inside of you, because you had that same strength I sense here. I was nothing, in every good sense of the word, because it also felt like everything."

She gave a slight smile then, laced with tears. "How many times I imagined you holding me just like this, so I could lean against you, and you wouldn't give way." She looked at him then. "Tell me more about the cemetery. Will you take me there sometime?"

He had to clear his throat to answer. "Yeah. I'll take you anywhere you want to go." He thought about the cemetery, what would interest her. "There's one particular vault with a statue of a child on it. Just a small thing, nothing extravagant, but the face is soft, innocent, worn down from age. The vault says 'closed forever', because when the child died, the parents were too heartbroken to have it used again. Since the last family member died some time ago, I took over the maintenance fee for it."

"Why? Other than the fact you're a good guy."

He should have known she'd ask. *No cowards here, right?* He shrugged, looked out over the marsh. "Not so good. I did it because I envy that kid for being wanted that much, even though she was here for only three months."

He could feel her gaze on him, so he turned his face back to her, ran a knuckle along her cheek, kept talking. "When you're there at night, the statues remind you of silent angels, all white and gray. There's a guy who comes and plays a sax to his friend, and it's some of the best sax playing I've ever heard. But I don't go to him and ask him why he plays. Because in that place you whisper your secrets to those silent statues. To the angels of death."

"I wouldn't mind being one of those statues," she said. "All bathed in shadows, whites and grays, hearing you whisper your heart and secrets to me."

"My secrets might make your concrete feathers stand on end."

She wasn't smiling. Those brown eyes met his. "When you go to the cemetery, does it help? Help you deal with what you lost?"

Or what he never had. "Yeah, it does."

"Tell me how. Please?" She sighed, closed her eyes. "Jeremy died, but I lost him long ago. Just the same way we lost our parents. Not through death. Death is different, because it's over. No chance to hope, or to have hope crushed. Sometimes you can romanticize a dead person as time passes, or maybe remember some of the better things. When it came to you…I set myself up for loss there, I know it, so I don't blame you for what you can't give me. But I thought…maybe you could tell me how to deal with all of it."

It was hard to let that one stand. Yeah, he'd let her down. They hadn't hit the nail on the head yet, but he was gauging what she was seeking, figuring out how much she wanted right now. He was used to the guys or her knocking on that door, and him refusing to open it. This was a situation where opening it to her without being asked might be the key to whatever happened going forward.

He spoke to the sky. "You can't get it from the self-help shows, all that bullshit about coping with loss. There is no coping. It takes you over, and you're a drowning swimmer, trying to keep your head afloat, wondering sometimes why the hell you bother, except there's this compulsion to stay alive, this biological imperative you can't shake. It's part of why D/s called to me, the primal, straightforward, fuck-PC-and-all-its-bullshit-terminology.

"I could control things in that room, could get into the psyche of a woman and open her up, open her soul so I could find that part of her that's always raw and aching and open inside me. I could find what's real and not the façade. But each time I get there, I'm still empty. I touch that hand, find that spot, and it's not what I was seeking. So eventually you decide the point isn't finding something, but the search. You keep moving, avoid staying still."

"That's what Jon said," Marcie murmured. "You can't stay still. You're afraid of stillness."

"Not afraid." Ironically, Ben had to quell the urge to rise, move, but if he did that, he couldn't hold her. "Just nothing there I want to be with."

"What if I'm there? Can you sit in that stillness with me? For just a moment? See what we find there together?"

He turned his head to meet her gaze. "Yeah. I can."

The simple words kindled hope in her eyes. He wanted to fan it to a full-on blaze, but he let her keep the lead. She brushed his face with those gentle fingers, looking at him with eyes that were old and young at once. "If you died, I'd feel the way those parents did. It would break my heart. I would drown in a loss like that."

Jesus, she was ten times braver than he was. What he'd scoffed at as youthful drama and exaggeration was simple, pure faith in her own heart and what it wanted. He stayed silent for a moment, overcome by it, then caressed her cheek. "Why me, Marcie? Tell me why it's me."

When she worried her bottom lip with her teeth, he brushed her chin with his lips, a nip. "You can't say anything wrong," he said firmly. "Not in the past, not now, not ever. All right? Just say it as you're thinking it."

"Okay." She nodded. "Do you remember the weekend Cass and Lucas got married?"

"Like a minute after they met each other again at K&A?"

She smiled. "It might have been a little longer than that. They had to wait for Lucas' adopted family to fly in from Iowa to see the ceremony, after all. But I remember I'd wandered away from the wedding, sort of like I did today. You came to find me. Not Jon or Matt, the ones someone else might expect. You said 'I'm never going to let anything happen to you', as if you knew I was feeling uncertain about how fast things were changing. But what struck me was you didn't say, '*We're* going to take care of you'."

She glanced at him. "Maybe you think it was a slip, but I don't. Just like I don't think it was a coincidence that you came looking for me now, when it could have been anyone else. From the first moment I met you, you made me feel safe. I was cold then too, and you put your coat over my shoulders."

She took a breath. "I tried having other boyfriends. I pushed them, I yanked at their egos, not realizing at first why I was doing it. I needed them to be stronger than me, to put me in my place, prove to me they could hold the reins and they wouldn't let go. They couldn't. I believe in excelling in everything I do, Ben, and I won't take less than that. It's always been you. You've always been my safety, my laughter, my sense of salvation. I've always known you'd be the Dom who will give me what I need. Who I can trust with my secrets. And if you didn't mean it, about being honest, I'm probably going to drown you in this marsh, right here, right now."

It was crystal clear to him. She didn't know how to let go, a power submissive on turbo charge. The way she pursued him so relentlessly, the way she over-excelled at school, getting ahead of her grade levels. In essence, she'd been "topping from the bottom" all her life, with utter focus and determination. She craved a stronger hand to tell her it was okay to let go, to surrender. In return, she was the type of sub he'd always desired. A hundred percent devoted, loyal. Stubborn, independent, defiant. And overflowing with love to give, something he hadn't anticipated wanting so much.

"Keep going," he said softly, holding her gaze.

She nodded. "So often in my life, people told me I'm too young. When Cass had to take over from our mom, I *was* pretty young, but I was next oldest, so I helped Cass however I could. And then, when it was clear our father was never going to be around, and Jeremy got strung out on drugs, and his friend tried to attack me...all these different things, they give you a sense of fear, that the world isn't a stable place. You learn to be careful, and watchful, and you don't trust easily, though you keep hoping for something. You don't know exactly what it is, but you feel it... Maybe in the beginning all you know is it's a feeling you want to have and keep, to get more of it. But then, eventually, you realize what it is."

Ben stared at her. It echoed his own childhood experiences in a way he couldn't deny, resonating in the tightness of his chest. She was on a roll, the words tumbling out faster.

"It's a feeling of comfort and safety so strong, you know that's the place you're meant to be, your haven in the world. Whenever you were counseling me, or playing games with me, or carrying me piggyback to throw me in the pool in the backyard...I felt that. You didn't realize how much I liked the way your shoulders felt under my hands, how you felt against my body. You know I dreamed about that, the way it felt to have my legs wrapped around you?"

"I'm not surprised." He tried for a humorous note, but his voice was too thick. He had his fingers tangled in her hair, and he stroked his thumbs along her temples, holding her, just holding her and listening to her. Really listening, perhaps for the first time. Seeing the truth instead of pushing it away.

"I felt safe with you, but more than that, I felt I was where I needed to be. When we were together, everything was right and balanced. When things happened, and you wrote to help me, you were telling me about yourself at the same time. I wrote to you about losing my virginity and you told me how it was supposed to be. How, the first time you had sex that meant something, you'd wanted to hang onto that feeling of closeness, no matter how much of an illusion it was, because you'd sensed that was the important part, the seed of what it was really supposed to be like.

"You didn't use those words, but the meaning was there, between the lines. I've become a master of reading between the lines. I know I became the confidante that you were to me, no matter how you want to deny it. Then there was the most important thing. The way you —"

She bit her lip, coming to a full stop, cheeks flushing. "I'm sorry. I went into pushy mode, and I wasn't trying not to do that. I promised myself...after the other night, I was never going to do that again."

"Hmm." Cupping the side of her neck, he let his thumb play over her windpipe, watched her register the constriction, get short of breath not from the physical reaction but the psychological effect it had on her. "You know 1 Corinthians 13 also says 'It does not insist on its own way...'"

Marcie gave him her shy smile, strained at the edges. "That part was put in by the patriarchal guys who wrote the Bible and didn't want women telling them what was good for them."

"No doubt. They were wise to fear a determined woman. What was the most important thing?"

Marcie knew it might sound childish, such a small thing, but it was like the day he'd forgotten to give her those shoes, turning her out barefoot. He didn't miss details unless they were his blind spot. And Ben O'Callahan's heart was his blind spot.

"Did you look at the back of the forget-me-not pendant you took from me?"

His brow creased. Then, as her heart caught in her throat, he shifted to reach into his slacks' pocket. He was carrying it with him. Not the collar, just the small pendant, but he was carrying a part of her on his person.

He tilted his head, looking down at it, and she couldn't resist. She stroked his hair away from his forehead, a gesture of tenderness, of love. He had to understand when he saw it.

His eyes darkened, his mouth tightened, and his fingers clenched over the disk. Nodding, she wrapped both her hands around his and lifted his knuckles to her lips, closing her eyes. "Will you say it out loud? Please?"

"Always yours." His voice was husky.

"You started signing your letters that way on my twenty-first birthday, Ben. On the very day, in the card you sent me. Though we didn't correspond much during those two years, whenever I got any kind of card, email, letter or gift from you, that's how you signed it. Every time. Always yours. That kind of timing couldn't have been coincidental."

Ben stared down at their closed hands. She was right. It couldn't. He'd missed it entirely, yet there it had been, all the time. The way her submission had been there. Lucas and all of them had noticed it early, but he, the man who didn't miss details, had blocked it.

"Your card," she spoke softly now. "You said you were sorry. Is that your way of saying goodbye?"

How could she even ask? But it made sense. She knew her side of things — she was still trying to figure out where he was on all of it. As he paused, she bit her lip, looked back out toward the marsh.

Touching her chin, he brought her gaze back to him. Passing his thumb over that luscious lower lip, he curved his hand on her nape. Her brown eyes widened, then fluttered closed as he brought her to his mouth and kissed her. Deep and long. It wasn't an erotic, take-her-to-her-hands-and-knees-and-fuck-her kind of kiss. But in its own way, he thought it was the most all-absorbing, overwhelming kiss he'd ever experienced, because everything she'd just described happened in that kiss. He became everything and nothing at once.

Sliding his arm around her back, he turned her so she was cradled in his lap, her legs over the chair arm. Bracing his other hand on her hip and buttock, he took the kiss even deeper. She made a helpless little noise in her throat. Her hand slipped down, fingers tangling in his tie. His arms constricted around her, mashing her breasts pleasantly against his chest, and his grip on her hip shifted, so he was cupping her buttock to hold her even closer.

When at last he eased her back, her gaze was satisfyingly glazed, but he was knocked off his axis as well. Pretty amazing.

"No. It wasn't goodbye."

"I got that," she said breathlessly. There was a little curve to her lips, but uncertainty as well.

She sighed. "I'm out of courage, Ben. I know I went about it the wrong way, but I didn't know how else to do it. Now I'm thinking all I did was open myself up for the worst rejection of my life, something that will be hard to survive. But I can survive it."

Lifting her chin, she gave him a direct look. Though she was still in his lap, her body had tensed, ready to move away, to put distance between them. "Maybe you think you made the message clear enough at the club, but we were both pretty emotional that night. So here and now, when everything's quiet and clear, I need your final answer, no matter how scared I am of it. I don't want you as my mentor, unless it's part of you being my permanent Master. Am I wasting my time? Is there any chance you'll ever be in love with me, the way I am with you?"

She'd said she was out of courage, but he knew of no one, man or woman, who would risk an emotional blow as baldly as that. She kept her gaze locked on him, didn't flinch, even though he could tell how fragile she was, how vulnerable. A kitten and a lioness together. A shapeshifting sorceress.

"I'll answer you, but I want an answer from you first. I know you've thought a lot about what happened at Surreal. What was your conclusion?" He'd remind her to be honest, but at this point he realized she didn't know how to be anything else.

That chin lifted higher, tightened. "You wanted me. You didn't want anyone else touching me. And the way you acted at the car..." When a shadow passed through her eyes, he couldn't stop himself. He put his hands on her face.

"Was unforgivable. Unconscionable. I'd go through any level of hell if it could take me back to that moment. I never want you to be afraid of me, Marcie. I never want you to connect me in any way to what happened to you as a teenager."

"Damn it, Lucas," she muttered, but he increased his grip, bringing her eyes back up to him.

"He was right to tell me."

"I'm *not* afraid of you," she said, and she had no idea how it relieved him, down deep in his gut, to see the irritated truth of it in her eyes. "You were purposefully trying to hurt my feelings that night, and you succeeded. Yes, you're pretty scary when you're riled like that, but..." She shook her head, put her hands on his wrists, squeezing. "I know you, Ben. I was freaked out, I admit it, but after I thought it through, I knew the only reason you did it was because *you* were scared."

He blinked. Her fingers were cold and nervous on his, but she'd delivered the truth as steady as if she was the Head Mother in *The Sound of Music.*

Jesus Christ. Jon was right. She *was* more emotionally mature than him.

It made him smile, he couldn't help it. Her brow raised, her expression puzzled, but he just pushed her head back down next to his, stroked her hair as she lay in his arms, quiet, waiting on him. The water birds made their strange calls, the reeds rustling with the wind. He wasn't even really thinking.

He was feeling. She liked being a bad girl, would always push the limits. It was a symptom of the feelings she had inside her that she wanted to get out, that she trusted him to handle, to use to pleasure them both. She knew he liked challenges, and she was the challenge of a lifetime.

Closing his arms around her, he rose, bringing them both to their feet. She looked up at him, that uncertain, waiting look, but she still had that tightness to her chin. She was ready for whatever he decided. He stepped back, releasing her.

"On your knees," he ordered.

They were on a rough wooden dock, but it didn't matter. Everything inside him tied into a hundred different knots as she responded immediately, began to sink to her knees. He caught her elbow. Slipping his coat off her shoulders, he put it down to protect her knees. "Now."

"That's an expensive coat."

"Your legs rank up there with the Seven Wonders of the World."

She gave a tiny smile, though she was still too serious. Too sad. That wouldn't change today, because today was about far more than what was happening between them, but he could change this part, maybe make it better.

When she sank down to her knees, he touched her chin, making her look up at him. "A slave is braver than her Master, Marcie. That's the way it works. So you say it first, lay it all on the line for me. Take the risk."

By commanding her to her knees, he'd given her hope, and he loved seeing it spark in her brown gaze. She closed her hand over his wrist, a breach he allowed because her fingers felt too good to resist. He wanted the connection. "I've been in love with you since I was sixteen years old," she said. "Every guy I met, I compared him to you. I counted the days until break, when I might get a glimpse of you on the holidays. As soon as I realized what I was, I started calling you Master in my heart. I have a diary I wrote to you throughout college. I love you, Master. I love you with every part of me, and I love every part of you. I'm here, and I want you more than I've ever wanted anything."

He blinked, looked over the slow moving water, though her fingers squeezed his. "Please let me love you, Ben." Her whisper was a caress. "I won't let you down. I can survive your darkness."

To survive it himself, he'd rebuilt who he was from the ground up, locking away the person he'd once been. The other night had proven that wasn't the best strategy. In fact, Marcie's words felt like that cell was being unlocked, that she was standing there in its doorway, impossibly vulnerable yet completely unafraid of the monster within. Sunlight was streaming in behind her, inviting the beast out into the light.

It *was* Beauty and the Beast, when all was said and done. Because in the end, the Beast was willing to do anything to deserve her love.

"First off, you have never, will never, let me down. All you have to be is yourself." As her eyes filled with more tears, he squatted down, closed his arms around her, buried his face in her hair. "You asked if there's a chance I'll ever be in love with you. I already am." His throat closed up as a sob broke from hers, so strong it shook her narrow shoulders. "I'm crazy fucking in love with you, Marcella Moira. God help you. And I'm so, so sorry for every awful, cruel thing I've done to you."

Her arms wormed out from beneath his, locked around his shoulders, hands gripping his shirt as tight as they could. She made an incoherent sound of joy and sorrow at once, and he pressed his face harder into her hair. A chuckle strangled out of him as she spoke against his shoulder.

"You don't have to be sorry for *every* awful cruel thing."

"Sweet brat. Brave girl."

Her fingers convulsed on him with every word, and he held her, let her cry, murmuring to her as she got it all out. He wished he could have held her when she first learned about

Jeremy. He wished he could have been with her when she had that nightmare, soothed it away. But he'd make sure he was there to drive away any others she had. And he damn sure wouldn't cause any more of them. When she started to slow down a bit, he fished out another handkerchief, glad he'd brought a spare for today's emotional event. After she dried her eyes, he let her keep it.

"All right. Now I want you to stand."

He helped her, because she was a little shaky, and got even more so when he stayed on one knee, looking up at her. He put his hand against her face. "What happened in the parking lot at Surreal won't ever happen again."

She started to shake her head, but he wouldn't let himself off the hook for it. "It was inexcusable. If you want me as your Master, then you accept and understand that the guilt and blame for that night lies entirely with me."

She looked away, tears gathering once more, though she tried to wipe them away with the handkerchief she held in her free hand. She sniffed. "Dana said if you were really sorry, you'd let them tie you up naked, rub you down with kerosene and zap you with a Taser."

"Sorry doesn't mean I've taken leave of my fucking senses. Especially when it comes to Reverend Dana. She's about as bad as you are for taking advantage."

She cocked her head. That guarded look was still there, but it had lessened by a significant degree. He'd win her trust back. She was going to give him the chance to do so, thank God. He hadn't completely fucked it up.

"Cass said you'd owe *me* until the day you die, but that you'd made amends with Matt and the others. Something about restoring you to rights with the code of chivalry." Her silken brow rose, a small smile playing around her soft lips. "What did they make you do?"

He sighed, looked away. "Not going to tell you."

"Yes, you are." Her slim fingers crept under his jaw, teased his face back toward her. "You find me irresistible. You just told me so."

"I said I love you," he said sternly. "That's very different."

"No. It's not." She dimpled, and of course he couldn't resist her. Besides which, she'd worry it out of him like a terrier digging a rat out of a hole. Jesus, she was going to be so such a pain in his ass. He'd probably lose all his hair before he hit forty. "Tell me."

"Nope."

"Yes."

"No."

"Please? Pretty please?" She batted her eyes at him.

He chuckled. "Do that again and I'll smack your ass, right here in front of the fish."

Of course she batted her eyes again, then shrieked as he rose and tossed her over his shoulder, giving her a resounding slap on her soft buttock. He had to resist the urge to take hold of it, squeeze and enjoy the pleasure of touching what was his. She braced herself with hands curled in his shirt, docile in his hold, conveying that she would give him anything he wanted. It was an effort to put her back on her feet, even more so when her hands remained fastened to him, her body leaning against his. He could tell she was still waiting for an answer. Tenacious female. He relented.

"I'm not allowed to drink for a year."

Her eyes softened, her mouth getting serious, but he didn't want to take her there. So he gave her the other part of it. The *really* painful part. "And I gave away my car."

"What?" Those eyes widened to saucer shape. "The Mercedes? Your half-a-million-dollar sports car? The high-performance engineering piece of art?"

"Yeah. Thanks for reminding me. I donated it to the upcoming auction for the new domestic-violence shelter."

Marcie's gaze darkened then, and her hands cupped his face. "Ben, you didn't...even that night, when you were so angry...I knew you weren't going to hurt me."

"Marcie." He touched her lower lip. Though faint, the mark was still there where she'd hit the car. "I did hurt you. I laid hands on you in anger. That's the one thing a Master never does to his sub, and a man never does to a woman. Not *ever*," he repeated, underscoring it.

"You weren't angry. Not at me."

"Which made it even worse. I'm done discussing it," he said.

The voice Marcie heard was his Master's voice, which brought her nerve endings to full alert at once, even as his hand tightened on her wrist. To restrain, not to harm, an entirely different connotation. "It's done," he said. "Except for what I owe you."

There was no changing certain things about the K&A men, any more than a woman could change the shape of a knight's heart. She accepted that, loved him all the more for it. "How much will they get for it?" she asked.

He sighed. "Lewis, legal counsel for Sonoco, will bid on it. Matt sent him an email, telling him it's up for auction because I lost a bet. He knew Lewis won't be able to resist rubbing my nose in it, but he's a good guy—I'll deny that if you tell him. He'll bid a fair price. His revenge will probably take care of the shelter's operating expenses for the next two years."

"Or you could bid against him." She gave him a hopeful expression. "Since you insist that you owe me something, you could buy me your car. Even Cass would agree that's a sufficient level of remorse."

He snorted. "Not likely. I know Cassandra Moira. If I lie down under a convoy of semis, it wouldn't be sufficient. Plus, you behind the wheel of the McLaren would make me old before my time."

"Bet I could drive it faster than you ever have, you big pussy."

He slung her back over his shoulder despite her squeal, ignoring her thump on his broad back. Snagging his coat from the ground, he started back down the dock. "I can see all my spare time's going to be spent teaching you to be a proper slave. After we take care of what I should have given you from the very beginning."

"What?" She was trying to look up into his face, working her way around his side like a sinuous python. Once they were off the dock, he let her down, holding her by the waist. With her looking up into his face, wondering, it hit him square in the gut. She was so goddamn beautiful. So strong, so brave, so intelligent. It all underscored what he'd blocked when she was too young for it to be appropriate, the clues he'd ignored... Like how much he'd missed her letters the past two years. Or his punch-in-the-gut reaction when she walked back into his office.

It all boiled down to one thing — that overwhelming sense that she was his.

His slave, his submissive. He saw it even now, in the way her eyes searched his face, anticipating what it was he was about to say, what he wanted, how she could serve him. She didn't realize that the mere fact she was breathing and near was enough for him.

It was unexpected, and he wasn't sure he fully trusted it. He'd wanted something like it for so long, but he'd lied to himself over and over, run smoke screens over those yearnings. It was hard to clear all that out in a moment, particularly when he'd spent so much time rebuffing her. Now he was going to have the pleasure of fully embracing what she was offering, and though he was feeling a sharp urgency to get started, his Dom side impatient to fully claim her, he needed some time to adjust to it, to prepare. To make sure the experience was everything she desired and more.

Still, he'd opened a door, and she wasn't going to leave it alone. She was such a kid. It almost made him grin. "What should you have given me from the beginning?" she demanded.

He put the coat back over her shoulders against the incoming evening chill. Then he tucked her under his arm and started back toward the house. They'd set up a pavilion tent and soft music was drifting out from under it, a time for friends and family to relax and reminisce about Jeremy. About the importance of family, whether of blood or the kind that a person was lucky enough to find during his life. He tightened his arm around her.

"It's time to make you mine, the way I should have done it the moment you walked into my office. Not tonight, but soon." He stopped then, faced her. "Are you ready for that, Marcie? You know what belonging to me means."

She nodded, quivered under his hands. "Yes, Master. I do. I want that more than anything."

"All right then. In three weeks, I'll send you instructions and you'll follow them."

"Three—" She bit her lip. "All right, Master. Will the others—"

At his second quelling look, she broke off the question, settled. She wouldn't always be so malleable, God help him, but he expected that was part of what he loved about her.

He knew what she'd been about to ask. The other K&A men had always been involved in making a woman part of their circle. He saw no reason for Marcie to be any different, when she obviously wanted that. Yet she was unique to him, to his heart. His, in a way she wouldn't be to any of the others, even as they contributed to her pleasure. He felt the edge of it in his teeth, like blood to a predator, and had to curb that impatience once again. Not today. She was impatient with the idea of three weeks. She had no idea what that wait was going to do to him, but he was going to do it right.

Right now, she needed something else from him. She was starting to drag her feet, her eyes on that pavilion ahead. The past week or so had been about arranging all the details, the service. This was the epilogue, a pavilion of people saying goodbye and facing the truth that her older brother was gone. An older brother who'd once been her hero, until he'd become a nightmare.

They were crossing a footbridge over one of the creeks. When Marcie stopped, listening to the music coming from the pavilion, he stopped with her, giving her time.

"*I'll Stand By You*, by the Pretenders. Cass used to sing that when we were young." She started to hum it, closing her eyes.

She opened them when he turned her toward him. Sliding one arm around her waist, he took her other hand in his, against his chest, and began to sway with her. He picked up the hum, going along with it. Hell, people didn't dance at funerals, but he didn't really care. She let out a weary sigh, relaxed a little more in his arms.

He could be here for this, and for every need she had after this moment. She might think he was her Master, holding all the reins, but when push came to shove, he couldn't deny her anything.

* * * * *

Cass had gone into the house with Jessica and Nate to show Steve Pickard's wife some pictures of Jeremy. She'd told Lucas she'd be okay, and so he was sitting out in a corner of the pavilion, keeping an eye on Cherry and Talia. Steve had the two girls engaged in conversation about their school activities, so all the kids were handled, giving him a momentary break.

As he took a swallow of Scotch he'd poured from the self-serve wet bar, he glanced out over the marsh and saw Ben and Marcie coming back from the lake. He'd intended to go after her when he didn't see her come in from the service, but he'd gotten involved in other things. His moment of guilt was short-lived, though, seeing Marcie tucked under Ben's arm, a comfortable fit.

His lips twisted wryly. He hoped he'd done well by Cass' siblings, because he loved all of the kids. The rest of the guys felt the same way, but there'd been a special relationship between Ben and Marcie from the beginning, he couldn't deny it. He hadn't had to worry about Marcie all that much, because when she needed an adult friend, a shoulder, an ear, Ben had been there. Her playmate, her surrogate big brother, and now something else entirely.

As they stopped on the bridge and he saw her register the song, the sadness from it reflected in her face, he was ready to go to her. But Ben turned to her, going into that slow dance, his head bent protective and attentive over hers.

"She's the one for him, Lucas. You can tell." Jon was standing at his shoulder now, holding a beer and gazing at them. "He gave his heart to her a long time ago. She brought it back to him."

"Yeah, I know." Lucas sighed. "With all this other shit, I'd forgotten their history. There it is, right in front of us."

"Right where it was destined to be. That was why it took him so much longer. He had to wait for her to be ready. And figure out what he truly wanted."

"Hell, if his head's back on straight, there's no one in the world I'd trust with her more."

"You might want to tell Ben that at some point. I think he'd be surprised to hear it."

Lucas glanced at Matt as he took a seat next to him. The CEO nodded toward them. "She had to have enough faith for both of them. She's a remarkable young woman."

"In some ways, I get how Ben felt," Peter said. "I still don't know what I did to deserve a gift like Dana. I just try to do whatever's needed to earn it, every day, weighting the other side of that scale as much as I can." He gave a half smile. "She always gives me twice as much, so I'll never catch up. Some gifts take a lifetime to find the balance."

"For some of us, maybe not even then." Lucas nudged Matt. "Most of us still think Savannah married beneath her."

No argument there," Matt returned, unruffled. "Cass'll probably throw your midwest beancounting ass back into the pond any day now."

Lucas sobered, looking back at Ben and Marcie. Their lawyer had his hand curved around her jaw, thumb stroking her cheek as she pressed her face into his chest. "He'll protect her with everything he is. He's figured it out. He won't let her down."

"That's the job." Matt lifted his glass, tapped it to his. "And the blessing."

Marcie: I'm sitting in the student commons, and the sunset is spectacular. The reds are painted against the clouds, as if the sun is courting the moon.

Ben: Does the moon like being courted?

Marcie: What woman doesn't?

Marcie texting Ben, sophomore year

Chapter Fifteen

ഇ

Marcie stood on the footbridge, watching the sky and remembering the dance she and Ben had shared here, three weeks before. Tonight would be a full moon. She felt like its light was already filling her, lifting her up toward the heavens.

Ever since Jeremy's service, she'd received some type of whimsical gift or gesture from Ben every day. He'd made her dinner at his Garden District house. Her as well as Cass and Lucas, the other K&A men, her siblings. He'd had her come early, help him chop, mix, sauté. Driven her completely crazy when he laid kisses on her neck, holding her inside his armspan as he showed her exactly how he wanted things prepared. But her Master had been clear.

No sex right now. These next three weeks are for something different.

She tried really hard to change his mind. Alice had returned from her trip, but Peter needed some admin help on an offsite project. Therefore, Ben agreed to let Marcie split her internship between his office and the research department on the days Alice was gone. Of course, on those days, she always wore provocative clothes, doing a lot of bending over file cabinets in line with his office door. When he brought her close enough to touch, she made sure he knew what every inch of her felt like against him. She couldn't help herself, and it wasn't entirely her fault. While he'd said no sex, apparently that didn't mean he couldn't kiss her whenever he desired, long, drugging kisses that left her knees weak and her pussy soaked.

She'd lost count of how many times he'd had her come into his office, shut the door and then ordered her behind his desk to straddle his thigh while he kissed her, his hands dropping to knead her ass. Every time, no matter how she tried to control herself, she found herself rubbing herself on that hard muscle, straining against him like a complete out-of-control nymphomaniac. He'd stop her before she could come, make her stay completely still. Sometimes he'd open her blouse, stroke her breasts. Lay a kiss between them, then rearrange her clothes and send her back to her desk with a firm pat on the ass.

She was going to hack him up with his commercial grade, beautifully sharpened and polished meat cleaver. She'd be sorry, but no jury of her female peers would convict her.

He took her for long walks at lunch, holding her hand, buying her food from the sidewalk vendors. At night, he'd call her, give her bedtime stories that left her toes curling and her anything but sleepy. Especially with his parting good night.

"Remember, your hand and your vibrator stays away from what's mine. You come on my command alone."

"What about you?" She'd purred it into the phone, trying to cover the desperation. His sexy chuckle alone made her nipples harden.

"I'll be stroking my cock, baby. Thinking about you while I watch the evening news. And when I come, I'll say your name. Your punishment for trying to change your Master's mind with your tight skirts and those little stunts you pull at the office."

Hack, hack, hack. No, forget the meat cleaver. She'd use a power saw.

He'd told her he was her Master, which meant he held the reins. So she had to wait on him. He was testing her. She was trying, but God, she was going to go crazy.

On the flip side, Ben was making no secret of the fact he considered her his. There was no emotional uncertainty anymore. With every passing day, she became joyously more confident of his feelings. The night he'd prepared that dinner, Talia, as precocious a teenager as Marcie had ever been, had tracked every time Ben grazed his fingers over Marcie's hip, or brushed his lips against her temple when he handed her something to bring to the table. When her younger sister was helping her clear, she'd leaned in, whispered to Marcie, "Are you Ben's girlfriend now?"

Before Marcie could answer, Ben had come by with a stack of plates, pulled Talia's ponytail. "Yes, she is." And that was that.

She saw the exchanged looks between the other men and their wives that night, but she had a feeling it wasn't only because of the new dynamic between her and Ben. Something was easier about the K&A lawyer. The jokes he made, the fact he smiled a little more often…it was obvious that something was uncoiling inside of him, turning him in a better direction. Thinking she might have something to do with that was a good feeling, but just seeing him happier made her heart swell to bursting. It also touched something in her deeply, seeing him casually bypassing his normal whiskey, even abstaining from wine.

As remarkable as that was, other things were going on as well. They'd had other get-togethers, not just at Ben's house, but at Jon and Rachel's, and a concert at Audubon Park. During those events, she'd noted a distinct change in her relationship with the others. When Peter passed behind her chair at Jon and Rachel's, he'd playfully put his large hands on either side of the seat, his knuckles brushing her hips as he scooted her closer to the table so he could get his massive bulk in the narrow area between wall and chair. As he straightened, he'd laid his hands on her shoulders. The wide neckline of her cotton top had made it a simple, casual thing to hook his thumb under her bra strap, and he'd idly stroked her there as he exchanged a few remarks with Jon about a subject she couldn't possibly remember, not with that happening and Ben watching, leaned back in his chair, his green eyes intent on her reaction.

Later that same evening, when Matt was sitting on the couch with her and Savannah, he had his arm around his wife, but he also had his arm stretched behind Marcie. A couple times he stroked his strong fingers casually through Marcie's hair, tracing the shell of her ear. She'd stayed still, nerves tingling along her spine, everything coiling up tight at the touch, which couldn't be called anything but sexually proprietary. Once again, Ben had his eyes on her, his expression telling her that their subtle enjoyment of her had his full approval. When she leaned across him to accept Savannah's invitation to feel the baby kick, Matt's hand dropped to her waist, fingers wrapped over her hip bone. As the conversations continued, it was both more comfortable and titillating than expected, to stay leaning against him.

Of course, the big surprise was when Lucas demonstrated some of the same type of behavior. At the Audubon concert, Marcie had been sitting on her hip on the picnic blanket next to Cass. When Lucas asked them if they wanted more wine, he brushed a kiss along his wife's throat, taking a nip with teeth, but as he moved around Marcie to go get them both a glass, he let his fingertips trail up the inside of Marcie's thigh in what was undeniably a sexual caress. She felt a tingle all the way up her groin muscle.

She knew what this was. Dana had spoken of it once during those tea parties. Before Peter initiated her into the group, they'd done things like that to get her used to their touches, their scent. Ben was getting her ready, and it made her crazy with lust and anxiety, all the more because it was so subtle.

The same night, Ben left her with a kiss where he pressed her up against the car door, and she was ready to claw his clothes off him. When he called her at midnight, he was stretched out in front of his flat-screen, watching one of the latest offerings from an erotic filmmaker. Ben casually described the scene he was watching, of a woman on all fours being fucked from behind while she gave oral service to her Master. Ben asked her if she fantasized about such a scenario, made her tell him her reactions in detail, physical and emotional. Before long, she was sweating through her nightshirt.

"You're trying to make me into a lust-crazed lunatic," she accused.

"Lie down on your back," he said.

The switch from teasing seduction to command flipped a switch inside of her. She lay down immediately, aware her limbs were shaking.

"Legs spread. Arms to the headboard."

Everything stretched to snapping in another heartbeat. That dark, insidious edge to Ben, the edge he'd been holding back, was in his voice now. In an instant, she wanted to be punished, wanted more than that firm pat. She wanted to be gagged, roped down, beaten within an inch of her life and then fucked in the ass, into unconsciousness.

"Close your eyes."

She did, and bit her lip, hard, to keep herself still. She imagined his hands on her ankles, the sound of a cuff being wrapped around one, then the other, the tension as they were fastened to the end of the bed. He'd do the same to her wrists.

She hadn't worn any panties under the nightshirt, because she couldn't handle the friction. She wanted to be good for her Master, but she just couldn't be anymore. She imagined him bending over her in the dark, his green gaze intent, that mouth stern, uncompromising. As kind and romantic as he'd been these past few days, she knew that transition, when the sadist in him would rise to the top. He wanted to make her suffer, wanted to make her scream with pleasure, beg for mercy that he wouldn't give. He'd run his hand down her sternum, tug on her nipple piercing, and then his hand would go lower, lower.

Her hips jerked, imagining his hands there, his fingers sliding into her soaked pussy, pushing, stroking. He'd hook the clit ring, tug on it, sharp enough to send a pain through the tissues. Then he'd lift her up, lie beneath her, and put his cock in her ass. *Take all of me, baby. That's it, squeeze down on me. You keep coming down on me, lifting up...down. There you go. And every time you go up or down, you squeeze on me like your life depends on it.*

He was murmuring it to her, his voice a sexy rumble over the phone. She was gasping, telling him she was doing just that. Doing it to empty air, believing it was his cock, and the constricting of the muscles in her rectum were contracting her pussy, rippling along her clit.

"Ben...Master..." She whispered it, whimpered it. She needed him, needed him. She couldn't wait another moment for him. She loved him. She needed to serve him, which meant she needed to be good, she needed to wait. But she couldn't stop moving her hips up and down, up and down, imagining his cock deep inside her, his fingers working in her dripping cunt. "Please...oh God..."

Stretched out on the bed, nothing touching her but air, her imagination and his voice, she climaxed, a hard pull on her lower abdomen, thighs thrumming with the sensation, pussy spasming. "Oh God...Master..."

The words he spoke to her didn't matter. She clung to his voice, the rough edge of it that told her he was working his cock, listening to her come for him. When she came down, far too soon, needing more than just the empty imagining, she held the phone tight, quelling an odd desire to press it against her pussy, the closest she could get to him.

"You came without permission. I'll be taking care of that soon."

"How soon?" she demanded.

He gave a low, dangerous chuckle. "Careful what you wish for, brat."

* * * * *

Now it was day twenty-one. While he was merciless, the timeline had given her a blissful light at the end of the tunnel. The note had arrived yesterday, in a box containing a shimmering forest green short robe and matching slippers.

When you get up Friday morning, you won't be going into work. Do not shower. Wear only what's in this box and your nipple and clit jewelry. Unless you get dizzy from it, no food for twelve hours. Sips of water as needed. Whenever you sit or lie down today, your thighs will stay open. When your pussy gets wet (what I'd expect from a shameless slut like yourself), you will not clean your cream off your thighs.

A limo will pick you up at seven. Make no special preparations. Bring nothing but yourself and this robe. Leave your hair down, no clips or ties. Once you get into the limo, you will not speak unless asked a direct question. Until you see me, no male should touch you. No incidental brush against Lucas at the house, no taking the driver's hand to get into the limo. Every inch of your soft skin is mine to touch, mine alone. Your Master

A gardenia tied with a ribbon lay on the top of the robe. She'd brushed the petals over her cheek as she fingered the fabric. The silk was so thin it clung to her hips and breasts like skin. The kids had school, and were going to be picked up afterward by Rachel to go to the movies. With Cass and Lucas at work, Marcie had the house to herself all day.

She'd planned so hard for this day, had thought about it so long, that she found the reality dizzying. As the clock ticked so slowly toward seven, everything seemed dreamlike. She'd lain out by the pool, watching the clouds move overhead, and held the thought to her like a cherished doll. Ben O'Callahan was in love with her. He was going to claim her as his. Formally, as his submissive, his property. His lover. She knew what that meant to those five men who were an integral part of her blood family.

She'd refused to let the possibility of failure enter her mind until that dreadful night had forced her to confront the unthinkable. Until then, her certainty that she was meant to be his had driven her forward. With the goal achieved but not consummated, it left her oddly unbalanced, that part of her empty and waiting to be filled with something more substantial.

Returning to the present, she decided she felt like a harlequin, one half focused as a laser, steady as a rock, the other like nitro trapped in a bottle, ready to explode.

Putting her hand on her heart, she tapped out that song, *I'll Stand By You*, remembering their dance together. It made sense that it came to mind now, because she was standing on the same footbridge. She swayed, replaying the words in her head, so appropriate to everything she'd hoped and dreamed about when it came to Ben.

"You amaze me."

Opening her eyes, she saw her sister at the entrance to the bridge, watching her. She was glad to see Cass a little less tired today. She, Lucas and the others had tried their best to balance her natural need to grieve with distractions, things to keep the ache from being unbearable. It was going to take time, they all knew that, but it was hard to see her sister with that sadness in her eyes so often. Marcie had shed her own tears over Jeremy, but no matter how guilty she felt about it, the truth was Ben's behavior toward her these past several weeks had kept her preoccupied. She wouldn't put it past him to have taken into account that side effect. Ruthless Master, merciful lover. Good friend.

She went to Cass now, held her sister close. "I love you."

"I love you too. Don't you want to know why you amaze me?"

"Because I'm an incredible sister in all ways and you worship me?"

"Still not loaning you my Jimmy Choos."

"Bitch."

Cass grinned, as Marcie had hoped, and eased back. "This is beautiful." Cass fingered the hem of the robe. "The man does have good taste in clothes."

"I know. He's probably a repressed homosexual."

"Yeah, I'm sure." Cass snorted, then sobered. "You amaze me because you had such determination, such conviction. You didn't doubt yourself, or the way you felt for him, no matter how much it looked like an adolescent crush. You knew."

Marcie shrugged. "There were times I was afraid I was wrong, from his end of things. But the stories you've told me…each of them knowing which woman was the one? There was another side to that. Even though each of you had reasons to resist or doubt the inevitable, it was already inside you too, such that he was able to convince you of it pretty damn quickly. I remember how Dana put it. 'One look into Peter's gray eyes and I knew I was fucked. Literally and figuratively.'"

Cass' blue eyes twinkled. "Well, the soldier's as much a part of her as the minister." Then she grew somber again. "We should have supported you more. It wouldn't have been as difficult."

"No." Marcie shook her head. "That was part of it. You challenged the premise, tested it, Ben most of all. That's the way any deal is supposed to go, to make sure it's solid. And these past three weeks…he's been wonderful.

Her sister gave her that penetrating look. "There's a but in there."

"It sounds terrible." Marcie laughed at herself. "I'm just kind of going crazy, because he's keeping it to all romantic stuff. Most women complain about guys wanting to have sex and nothing else, but…"

"I've seen some of the romantic things he's doing." Cass lifted a brow. "Yes, it does fulfill emotional needs, but at the same time, it keeps a fire going under the physical. They're very good at that. He wants you worked up to the point you'd jump him on a public street corner if he told you to do so."

Marcie blinked at the bald assessment. "He's doing it intentionally?"

"Yes, and no. Yes, in that they can't help themselves. The romantic is integrated with the Dom, and no, in that I do believe he's truly trying to woo you, the way he knew he should have been doing from the very beginning. More than that, he's giving you time to trust him again. And maybe time for him to trust himself again as well."

Marcie nodded. "Much as I hate to admit it, I probably needed that. I'm not sure if…right after, I would have been ready. There needed to be some time for the air to clear. But honest to God, if he gives me another one of those neck kisses in front of you guys again I'm not going to be responsible for raping him on the kitchen island."

Cass put an arm around her, smiling, but then they contemplated the water together. "You had to grow up so fast," her sister said at last. "Are you sure you're ready for this?"

"Ben asked me the same thing. He called at lunch, and he was so gentle. Told me it wouldn't change anything for him. Said I could have more time if I needed it. But I don't need more time. I've wanted this for so long. I feel like a carnival's been set up within a stone's throw of my bedroom window for seven years, but I haven't been allowed on any of the rides."

At Cass' raised brow, Marcie chuckled. "Okay, maybe that didn't come out quite right."

"Probably came out pretty close." Cass gave her a teasing pinch. "Just have a care with some of those rides. There are some proprietary clauses involved."

Now it was Marcie's time to get serious. "Cass, we haven't really talked about it much... It's more than a little awkward. Lucas—"

"Don't." Cass put her hands on Marcie's shoulders, gave her a straightforward look. "There's no shame in it, love. You'll always be my little sister, which means I'll always see the child in you, but I also see the woman. This is who and what they are. Lucas and I have talked about it. I'm not confused about what will happen tonight, and his part in it. Of course, I've told him any fantasies he might have about some sister-sister action is confined to his late-night cable subscription," she paused as Marcie choked on a laugh, "but this...this is what we are. I'm mainly worried about you. Are you nervous?"

"More than I thought possible," Marcie said wryly. "But I'm really excited too."

"All right then. The limo arrived a few minutes ago. That's why I came out. It's time to go."

Marcie glanced toward the house, felt that trembling in her lower belly. "I don't know what to expect at all."

"You can expect everything, and things you never imagined. That's the way they work."

* * * * *

Max was her driver tonight, and she gave him a warm smile, remembering his kindness the night at the club. There was no awkwardness about that now. It was past, and she saw he was okay with things as well, no concern in his gaze tonight. He kept his attention courteously on her face as he held the door open for her, though she noted he sneaked a quick, sweeping glance over her nearly bare legs when she took her seat in the limo. It made her feel good. He was a guy, after all, and the robe was designed to highlight her full potential.

He didn't hand her into the vehicle as he normally would. That, and the fact they only exchanged nods, told her he had the no-talking and no-touching part of the instructions. She settled into the plush backseat, drawing deep breaths. There was a tray set up with a bowl of strawberries that had been dipped in chocolates of varying shades. Next to them was a thin black eye mask with lacings to hold it snug on the bridge of her nose and against the eyes. She read the notecard next to it.

Put on the mask, lace it tight, so you can see nothing. You may touch and smell the strawberries, but do not taste.

Picking up the mask in fingers that trembled, she followed the direction. The smell of the strawberries was too good to resist, so she lifted one, inhaled deeply. Oh wow. Ben had done these himself. She knew it, because Dana had talked about the night she was first shared with all of them. How they'd brought the juiciest, largest strawberries she'd ever tasted, coated in a chocolate that was as much an orgasm for the nose as the tongue. Peter's wife had learned later Ben had hand-dipped them himself in a special mixture of dark chocolates, vanilla and spices.

The richness of it brought saliva to Marcie's tongue. There was white chocolate, vanilla, butterscotch...praline coating. The evil man knew she lived for dessert. Her tongue longed to taste, her stomach rumbling, but she didn't.

His directions, so simple and straightforward, had nevertheless kept her in a state of wet longing through most of the day. With every hour that passed, she was more aware of her body. She wished he'd let her shower. She wasn't grungy, but it felt odd to come to him with hair that had been combed but not styled. She would have touched up her nails, done her makeup. Just as he'd anticipated, her arousal had formed damp tracks on her thighs more than once today, drying there.

To heightened male senses, she would smell like what she was. A female in raging heat.

She kept picking up the different strawberries, smelling each. The flavors seemed designed to stir her arousal further. She tried hard to hold them by the greenery at top, but she managed to get some of the melting chocolate on her fingertips. She couldn't find a towel or wipe, which left only the robe or the seat. Realizing it would qualify as tasting, she stopped with her hand halfway to her lips. Instead, she left her hands in a half curl on her parted thighs.

She couldn't ask Max where she might find a napkin, of course. For a devilish moment, she imagined extending her fingers over the seat back, a mute request that he oblige her with his mouth. She was sure that would break Ben's rules on several different levels, particularly the no-male-touching rule.

Another time, she might do it, because she had a sense of what kind of infractions Ben would enjoy punishing her for, but this was not that day. Playtime and challenges weren't part of this. All balls were now in Ben's court. In truth, she was more anxious than she'd let on to Cass. Because she'd had to fight so hard for her objective, she'd never completely surrendered herself the way she knew would happen tonight, the way a submissive was supposed to do. She hungered hard for it to come from Ben, but the reality was pretty unnerving.

She wanted to please him. Wanted to feel that sense of completion, of total belonging. She was as nervous about this night as a virgin on her wedding night. To her, it was the same, the level of commitment, the sense of no turning back.

While the physical was a big part of tonight, in the past three weeks, he hadn't neglected the emotional framework that would propel the physical to go to a far more intense level than she'd yet experienced, God help her. She remembered what Rachel and Dana had said about Ben taking a woman's soul, never her heart, because that meant he had to give her his.

If she read all the signals right, it would be a mutual exchange tonight. Ever since the day on the dock, he'd been cautiously handing her pieces of his heart, of who he was, and she cherished all of it. Holding the white-chocolate strawberry now, she remembered helping him prepare for that dinner with the others. As always, he'd gone through her grocery selections with meticulous care, but he'd taught her well. Everything was fresh. While he cut a cucumber, she'd asked him, "What made you want to learn to cook like this?"

Instead of a casual answer, like "I like food", he'd paused, knife in one hand, eyes on the vegetable he was slicing. "I know what it's like to be so hungry you'll eat garbage, Marcie. I know why Scarlett O'Hara felt the way she did."

Quiet, matter-of-fact. Honest. It was all he'd said, but she was fine with that. She didn't mind learning about his life in small pieces, if that was easier for him, and it gave her something new to discover every day. She'd slipped her arms around him, put her cheek to his back, just like she'd done on the balcony that night. Putting his hand over hers, he clasped them against his sternum, then he'd turned and fed her the cucumber piece, pleased when she said she liked the marinade he'd brushed over it.

The car stopped, bringing her back to the present. When the door opened, she sensed she was being studied. She lifted her chin, straightened her back.

"Take off the robe. Leave the slippers on for now. Come to me."

Ben's voice. It was like feeling rain on her face after the heat of a drought. She smiled at him, she couldn't help it. Slipping the tie carefully, so she didn't transfer the stickiness of her fingers to it, she shrugged the silk off her shoulders, let it pool on her hips. As she moved across the seat toward his voice, he touched her arm. Since she wasn't allowed to speak, she couldn't warn him about the chocolate. But he'd already seen it. He took her wrist, not her hand, and when he helped her out of the vehicle, he brought her fingers to his mouth.

It was incredibly intense, feeling that stimulation after a full day of waiting, imagining. The sight deprivation made it even more excruciating. She made a yearning noise as the wet heat of his mouth closed over each of the affected digits, his tongue swirling her clean.

"Did you taste any?"

"No, Master." She was standing naked before him, with no idea where she was, except she was outside, not in a parking deck. In the distance, she could hear cars, so they weren't in a secluded environment. The echo suggested they were surrounded by buildings…perhaps a side street. But it didn't matter. With the blindfold on, she was entirely at his mercy, and her mind settled into that mode, completely his. His.

"Lift your chin. This is temporary."

He buckled the slim collar on her, and she felt the tug of a tether snapped to it. "Follow my lead."

"Always, Master."

There was a pause at that, then the pressure increased. She stepped forward. It wasn't easy to walk normally when she couldn't see him, but she did her best, felt his hand brush her hip, guide and steady her to walk up two flights of steps. Then they were inside. The echo of the door closing suggested a large, open room. Maybe a loft? It had that old brick smell. Probably his place in the Warehouse District. She'd never been to that one.

"Take off the slippers. Kneel, submissive posture."

Folding her legs beneath her, she put her hands behind her back, kept her spine straight. Opened her knees. He let the leash drop so it dangled loosely between her breasts, down into that spread area.

"I'm putting your mind in the right place for becoming my property, now and forever. I'm going to immobilize you in a latex vacuum bed. It's like a cocoon, and has some nice modifications, thanks to Jon. I will decide when you've been in it long enough. I will not speak to you, but I will be here, watching you, checking your breathing. You will never be alone. You understand?"

She nodded. "Y-yes, Master."

"A stammer. Miracles can happen." His voice was amused, but it was also tender. She sensed him moving around her, wanted desperately for him to touch her, but she waited, holding the posture. "Are you scared, brat?"

"Yes, Master. A little."

"Good. That's the way I want you. Ass in the air, forehead to the ground."

She used her stomach muscles to control her descent. His hands brushed her stomach and shoulder, making sure she got there safely. Then he put his hands on her buttocks, probed between them. Lube trickled into her rectum, and she moaned as his finger pushed in, stretching her. Her pussy wept, but he didn't touch it. "You've been hot and wet a lot today, haven't you?"

"Yes, Master."

"Push out toward me. This is going to be thick, but you'll like the lubricant."

She complied, pressing her cheek into the floor as he worked the thick phallus into her ass. She moved her hips in eager response, wishing it was his cock, hoping she'd get that sometime tonight. When it was all the way in, and she felt split in two, he held onto it, rocked it as she shuddered and her pussy trickled a free flow of arousal down her thighs once more. He made a tsking noise.

"Sit up, slowly, reach in front of you. The vacuum bed is there. Lie down on it."

He helped, lifting her off her feet and positioning her on the frame, covered with thin fabric. He made sure the plug stayed in until she had her hips against the solid surface, which drove it deeper. Then he pulled a second layer of fabric over her. She heard the zipper being fitted, running up along the side, enclosing her. There were holes for her breasts. He was stretching them around those, and the restriction was tight, like rubber bands, so that the seal on the cocoon wouldn't be broken, but it made her breasts tingle.

"Legs spread as far as they can go, fingers flat on your thighs." While she made that adjustment, he coaxed her mouth open. A hollow gag was fitted there, her tongue depressed by it, her breath sounding fast and shallow. Okay, she was scared. This was...she was trusting all of herself to him. This was the real deal. Of course, she was also hot and revved up. It was worse than not licking the chocolate off her fingers, or resisting the overwhelming desire to touch her pussy these past few nights.

The zipper was now run behind her head, so she was enclosed fully in it, like a sleeping bag with the top closed. Way different from her childhood sleepovers though. "You're going to hear the vacuum engine now. It will take all the air out, and you'll be fully immobilized. You'll be left this way, until I feel you're in the proper state of mind. Nod if you understand."

She did.

The vacuum switched on, a much quieter motor than she expected, but then he had said Jon was involved in the modifications. She'd never seen one with cut-outs for the breasts like this. The tightening began, her body gradually being locked into the position. At first, she had a slight amount of movement, but the vacuum continued to remove even that slack area. Oh God...she was being completely held down. It was like having a laced mask on from head to toe, and being restrained at the same time. She couldn't see. She could hear though. He left the vacuum on to keep the restriction fully in force. Her fingers pressed hard on her thighs, so close to her pussy.

"You are just a body. My body, to do with as I wish. You have no identity except as my slave."

Yes, yes, yes. I love you, I want you, I serve you, Master. This was the full surrender she wanted, and God help her, she knew it was just beginning. He'd removed the collar and tether, so it was just her, and the piercings. The cocoon had to be etching her body out as if she were naked.

Silence settled in, and all that came with it. She wanted him talking again, to be sure he was here. The arousal was intense. Throughout her pursuit of him, so much had been about movement, thinking, doing. This was about stillness, waiting, submission. He not only required her obedience, he'd made it an irresistible demand, encasing her like this. She could let go and be whatever he wanted her to be in this moment, because that was all she'd ever wanted—to be what he needed and desired.

She'd heard how time could pass in such a situation, five minutes seeming like fifteen, but experiencing it firsthand was a lot more effort. She had to bite down on that tube so she didn't talk, call out to him. Her body shook in the cocoon. Her nipples stayed tight and hard, exposed to the air. The muscles in her ass and pussy kept contracting, a mute plea, and of course when she contracted over that dildo, it sent all sorts of reaction spiraling through her.

He wanted her broken down, reduced to pure sensation. Whether she wanted that or not, it was going to happen. It made her recall something she'd read on one of the fetish forums, a stream of consciousness offered by a submissive, right after she'd undergone a deeply intense session.

There's this threshold of panic, where you realize he has all the control. I'm not talking the safe word thing or being able to call a halt. He's plucked your free will right out of your hands, and you let him have it, and you don't want it back. That's what scares you shitless. You're just all his, and that's all you ever want to be. When you come out of the experience, you feel a bit like a kid coming out of a scary ride at Disneyland. Did that really happen? Will I have the courage to ride again? And you know you will.

That threshold of panic rose, heralded by the increased rasp of her breath. But that told him she was still breathing, so it wouldn't be cause for alarm. He wasn't going to respond to anything that wasn't physical distress. He wanted her to go through the emotional maelstrom. That was part of this.

Her fingers curled, best as they were able, beneath the latex. *Can't do this...too much...* She tried to focus on the breathing. *Need him to talk to me... Need his touch...*

He was asking her to have faith in him the way God did. Sightless, without touch or visible evidence of his presence.

But just like God, there *was* visible evidence of his presence. The cocoon was part of that presence. Him bringing her here, the instructions. He was present in her life and guiding her in a variety of ways.

She suppressed a hysterical giggle. Yeah, she was sure the Sunday preachers would admire her analogy. At least Dana would understand. "Ben, Ben..." She'd uttered his name before she could stop herself, before she could bite it back. Though it was a bare whisper of sound echoing in that hollow gag, she knew she'd screwed up. Spoken without being spoken to.

Then she did it again, louder, unable to help herself. "Ben. Ben. Please..." It came through like a disembodied humming, the syllables unintelligible except to the male who seemed to know so much about her.

He waited another five hours, or so it seemed to her. That panic built hard and fast in her, taking over. When his hand touched her forehead, she let out a sob of relief. She recognized the shape and strength of his fingers. The touch was far too brief though.

"Easy, brat. You have visitors. I want you on your best behavior."

"Look at those pretty tits, the nipples so hard."

Peter. Peter was in the room. She nearly choked.

"If you take out the gag, the opening's large enough she can get her tongue through the air hole. She can tease your cock with it." Jon, helpfully highlighting the features of the vacuum bed.

How long had they been here? She let out a strangled noise as a mouth touched her pussy, caressed her over the latex. Even with that thin barrier, the tongue and lips knew just how to work her up, get her wetter, make her whimper with the need to squirm against the erotic skill of that mouth.

"Nice. Slick and smooth, probably juicy as a peach on the inside. We need to open this up, let me smell her."

Lucas.

"Damn, I didn't realize the latex showed so much detail. It's molded right to her cunt. You can see how erect her clit is."

Unlike the others, he'd touched her intimately first, before speaking. His fingers trailed along her hip bone, over her pubic bone, a prominent mound. Her breath rasped through the tube. Pleasure, shock and thrilled amazement spiraled through her. He and Ben had chosen to address the elephant in the room head on. Lucas had just made it crystal clear he no longer saw her as a child. While Lucas would still be as protective as any of them, a guardian of her well-being, the shape of it had changed. She was Ben's, and therefore belonged to them all, in a far more adult way. She might be the youngest of the group, but she was now one of the Knights' *women*.

She'd never been so aroused in her life, so emotionally stirred up as she imagined them circling her, studying what they might do to her under Ben's direction.

"Jon, can we open it up?" His authoritative voice cut into her spinning mind, riveting her on his deep timbre.

"Not a problem. See the seam here?" She shivered as a finger, probably Jon's, traced her pussy. "Use a cutting tool to pop that seam, and it will stretch and seal around her cunt, just like her breasts. There's a second vacuum tube inserted in this area specifically to increase the seal there, compensate for it."

"Good. We'll handle that in a minute. Peter, take care of her nipples first."

"My pleasure." What she assumed were Peter's fingers took a gentle hold of one nipple, fondling it before he began unscrewing the ball of one of the barbells. Nipple piercings were sensitive, and she was literally helpless, completely immobilized, so she couldn't help some trepidation. Four men surrounding her, acting — as Ben said — as if she was just a body for their pleasure, no will or voice of her own.

But Peter removed both her barbells with amazingly competent fingers, given how large his hands were. "You'll feel a little discomfort here, nothing much."

She held her breath, that little quiver in her stomach a frantic butterfly in a jar. Someone's hands cupped her breasts beneath, squeezing them to push the nipples up even higher. She thought it might be Lucas, because she caught the pleasing scent of the cologne he wore.

A tiny whispering sigh caught in her throat as something was threaded through one nipple piercing, then the other. It was the same type of bar as her barbells, just a little thicker, and the slender steel bar went all the way across between them. Peter was adding fasteners to the sides to hold it in place, and then he pinched the bar between thumb and forefinger, tugging on both nipples at once. She let out a soft cry against the breathing tube.

"These teardrop weights can be added to the bar." She heard the click of metal objects, perhaps being rolled in Peter's palm. "It will make her feel the pinch and burn a bit more. You can also attach a cable to the bar, connect it to a hook and raise or lower it to stretch out the nipples as much as she can stand."

"Nice." Ben's hands replaced Lucas' on her breasts, squeezing, flicking that bar. "They've already gotten stiffer, bigger. She likes it. She'd take first prize in a wet T-shirt contest. Lucas, your turn. I want her dripping, close to coming, but not there."

A precise touch, some pressure between her legs, and the seam was released, probably by Jon. Myriad small noises vibrated in her throat as he stretched the latex around the outside of her labia, and that second vacuum tube engaged, giving her an increased sense of constriction around already swollen tissues. She imagined it looked like a peach cut open in truth, the juices squeezing forth from it, tempting the tongue…

She cried out through the open gag as Ben caressed her pussy, pushed a finger inside to test her wetness. She wondered about what Jon had said, if she could service Ben's cock through that breathing hole. She could suck on him while…

"She's more than ready. She's all yours."

She couldn't help it, she was so stimulated that she shrieked when Lucas' mouth touched her pussy. He flicked his tongue over her clit, traced the labia with lazy thoroughness, learning her. "Different scent from her sister, but similar. They're both screamers though. You've had bad, bad dreams about being in our bedroom, sucking my cock while I was going down on her, haven't you?"

"That's a direct question, Marcie."

A few moments ago she'd begged for someone to be talking to her. Now she wanted to be silent and just feel, but she managed to speak, garbled as it was. "Yes sir."

Not Master. She had only one of those in the room, but she'd give all of these men sir, because not to do so seemed unwise.

"A polite slave. I like that." That tongue slid up her clit, around, teased under the hood, hot breath bathing her labia. She squirmed the tiny amount possible, and the nipple bar tingled. Especially when Peter came back and tapped something against it, something that…

"*Argh.*" She arched up as much as possible, which wasn't much. It made the sensation all the more excruciatingly intense. Some type of electrical wand, sparking shock along that bar.

"Good response," Peter murmured. "Very nice. Give me the other one, Jon." Then he did it again, a different sensation.

Lucas tugged her clit ring in his teeth. She was going to come, she was going to... "Master...I need to come...going to come." She sounded like she had a mouth full of marbles, or in this case, tubing, but Ben understood.

"Not yet." His tone was sharp, stern. "You don't have my permission to do that. You're here to serve the Masters' pleasure, not your own."

She bit back a groan, but bore down, trying her best to hold out against the diabolical workings of that tongue. When she was younger, Marcie had wondered about the jagged rips in her sister's pillowcases, and why she'd had to replace them so often. Her sister had likely gnawed holes in them so the rest of the house wouldn't hear her screaming.

"You belong to me, Marcie." Ben's voice. "When it suits me, you belong to them. But to no one else. No other Master touches you, ever again."

She jolted from another mild shock through the nipple bar, the sensation arrowing down to where Lucas' mouth was working her. Then Peter's mouth got into the act, covering one of the nipples, licking above and under that bar.

Another shriek reverberated in her ears. She couldn't not come. She had to come. Had to...

"Sorry...can't...Master...*help*..."

It swept over her so hard, there was no stopping it. She wailed, cried out, pleaded for all sorts of unlikely things. Lucas kept working her with his mouth, Peter and Jon a mixture of mouth, fingers and tiny touches of electric stimulus. Ben hadn't touched her nearly enough.

It was indescribable, coming under that level of restriction and restraint, so hard, deep, dirty, so intense it was almost uncomfortable, because she had no ability to move herself against Lucas' mouth or Peter's touch. When they finally withdrew, she was making tiny jerks as if Peter was hitting her with far harder voltage.

She needed to see Ben. Needed Ben period, and then she heard his voice again.

"Put her on the web."

When the vacuum noise stopped, the touch of the latex began to ease. She still had that blindfold though. The hollow gag was pulled from her mouth. Her breasts and cunt tingled from the return of blood flow to those areas.

When she was freed from the cocoon, her legs had no ability to hold her, but she needn't have worried. She was swung up in Ben's arms. He was wearing his suit, his tailored shirt and silk tie pressing against her skin, his slacks and belt against her bare hip. Were they all dressed for the office, and her here, naked, stripped down to nothing but sticky arousal, mussed hair? It perversely turned her on even more.

He put her on her knees. "Jon's making a change to the web, so you have a minute. Get busy. And don't you let that dildo come out of your pretty ass. Keep those muscles tight, like it's my cock." She heard the sound of his slacks being opened and made a noise of eager hunger. She would have surged forward on her knees, but he clamped his hand down on her hair to hold her steady as he fed her his cock, thick and enormous, pre-cum oozing from the slit, telling her how her helplessness had affected him. He thrust in hard, ruthless, working her mouth the way he'd pound into her pussy when he wanted to sate his lust.

She loved it, sucked on him as hard as she could, working him in her mouth, taking him deep, loving how he stretched her lips, the tears of stress that came to her eyes as she tried her best to take all of him. Rough and hard was the way she wanted it. When she gripped him, he didn't stop her, so she made the most of the opportunity, working that thin layer of heated skin up and down his shaft, giving him that friction, tightening her fingers around his ridged head, using the lubrication from the slit to give him further pleasure.

Too soon, though, he pulled back. Peter's hands on her again, removing the nipple bar, then Ben lifted her beneath the arms effortlessly. She was placed face forward against a suspended rope net, like the rigging of a pirate ship. Her arms were threaded through two separate openings, wrists bound to the line above it. Her knees were guided into another pair of openings, so her weight wasn't pulling against her shoulders. More rope passed around her waist, then knotted at her sternum before the two ends were guided between her breasts and to her shoulders to form a Y-shape. Two sets of hands were working on her. Because of those three weeks of casual caresses, she realized she could tell who was who. Apparently both Peter and Jon knew the art of Japanese bondage. She was being trussed to that web, as well as having her upper body harnessed inside a complicated weaving of knots. Helpless, total restraint.

She made a quiet noise as her breasts were lifted in capable hands and worked through two openings in the web, reinforced by further weavings by Peter and Jon. In the end, her breasts were squeezed, constricted, the nipples becoming even more sensitive to the open air. They'd be jutting out, displayed and framed by the ropes, and with her bound this way, the men could do anything they liked to them. Peter replaced the nipple bar, which essentially locked her on the web with steel as well as rope. The lines that were taken over her shoulders had been reattached to the waist rope, leaving her pussy and ass unencumbered except for the wraps of rope that held her thighs firmly to the web. Since one of the horizontal lines was pressed against her clit, she squirmed against it, unable to help herself.

"None of that." She jumped as a switch touched her buttock, a sharp sting. Then Ben's hand was there, working that dildo in her ass. "Clench down, as if it was my cock. Like you were imagining, that night in your bed. Say what you were thinking, out loud for all of us to hear."

Her arousal shot up even higher, even as she blushed. "Fuck me...with your cock. Master...harder...please. Ohh..." She remembered how her climax had taken her over, without his permission to release. It made her pussy ripple with an aftershock even now.

She clenched over the dildo, groaning with the sensation. "Keep doing it," he ordered, and she obeyed as the others finished what they were doing. Even her head was secured to the web, a line that ran around her forehead. With her legs spread, knees tied down, her body completely restrained, she was able to be fucked, sucked, whatever they desired. The web gave them the flexibility to angle her as they desired.

"Beautifully done." He touched her flank with that switch again, a quick sting. "Thank the Masters properly, Marcie."

"T-thank you...Master Peter. Master Jon...Master Lucas. Thank you for using me for my Master's pleasure and your own."

"Gorgeous." That came from Jon. He caressed her shoulder as he tested the bindings once more. "Welcome to the family, love."

Then Peter cupped her breasts, a flick of his tongue over the sensitized nipples. "Your breasts are as beautiful as your sister's. Pure honey skin."

Finally, Lucas. His hand trailed over her face, a softer, more thoughtful caress, but then that hand dropped, found her dripping cunt, fingered her until she was growling like a needy cat.

"I think we'll be able to talk Cass into that fantasy I have, don't you? Particularly since it's your fantasy as well."

That sent a spasm through her, particularly when his fingers stroked her clit so knowledgeably. "Yes sir."

A touch of amusement entered his voice, tangled with a good degree of lust. When Lucas got home tonight, she was pretty sure Cass was going to get a good workout. "I'm sure I won't get that kind of deference when she's off this web, Ben."

"She still has a punishment coming," Peter offered, creating a spiral of anxiety in her lower belly. "Maybe that will help her remember to be more respectful. For a day or two."

"You know I have a certain code, Marcie," Ben said, staying frustratingly out of reach. She licked her lips, remembering the taste of his cock. "About letting my submissive top from the bottom. You need to remember your place is firmly on the bottom, always. Five switches from each of them to drive the lesson home."

Despite the threat, Marcie clung to his voice. She was in high gear, stimulated by all of this, but her emotional hunger was nowhere near sated. She needed him. Would eventually beg if she had to do so.

She remembered how much the switching had hurt from Ben, but how it had made her so hot, knowing she'd given him the right to do it. Now he was offering it to the others as a rite of passage, as part of her initiation. A ball gag was pushed into her mouth with cloth wadding to absorb the saliva. Then it was buckled tightly around her head, as her fingers clutched the ropes. She shook her head several times, trying to shake off the fear, the anticipation of the pain. She needed to do this. Punishment was necessary. Her Master said so.

She yelped as the first one hit. She didn't know who it was until he was done, alternating between the right and left buttock. "Nice striping," Peter commented. "Hand it over, Jon."

She was braced for five more strikes, but not for them being around her breasts. She let out a startled cry as the switch stung the top of her breast, brought down upon both of them from above, since Peter was a tall guy. His large hand curved around her nape, holding her there as he administered four more, at different angles, probably making a crisscross shape of red lines on her distended curves.

Lucas got her inner thighs, not quite hitting her pussy, but close enough she felt the reverberation through it. She was gasping, holding on to those ropes for dear life. Fire was spreading across her flesh, and then Ben gathered her hair, wrapping it into a tight tail, securing it high on her head, baring her neck for the press of his mouth.

She shuddered, moaned like a dove, needy. She wanted the gag gone. But she was at the mercy of her Master. Then he was removing it from her mouth, answering her prayers.

"No more topping. No more misbehaving."

"Yeah, I've had that conversation with Dana before." Peter's snort sent a ripple of humor through the men.

Dana misbehaved because she needed to feel her Master's yoke, its reassurance. That was a part of it for Marcie, but it was more than that also. Sometimes her Master needed her to misbehave, to give him the outlet of punishment, to feed his sadistic side. It gave her as much pleasure as it gave him. So in as demure a voice as she could muster, she managed two words. "Yes, Master."

Ben's snort was quite distinguishable from Peter's. "Just for that…"

She started out with "No, no, no…" because hell, it hurt so bad, having that switch strike her buttocks, her thighs. The pain was intense, excruciating, because it didn't take much with a switch. He knew her better than they did, knew how much she could take, what she craved. On ten, she gasped with relief, her legs quivering.

Things had gotten quiet again. She could hear Ben's breath, his shoes tapping as he moved, studying her stretched and tormented body from every angle, she was sure. She ached for him. Her pussy hadn't stopped dripping yet, and her ass, legs and breasts were on fire.

"What do you want, Marcie?"

"Whatever my Master desires."

"What do you think he desires?"

She couldn't help it, her lips curved, even as a few tears ran out from under the mask. "To fuck me. Please, Master."

She listened to the polished dress shoes move behind her. His fingers touched her ass, worked the dildo so that she spasmed in near climax once more, crying out. Then it was pulled free.

"Tell me what you want."

"Your cock, Master. In my ass. Please. If that's what you want."

"In a moment. We have a late arrival. Someone who takes the topping issue almost as seriously as I do."

A late arrival? There was only one... She hadn't expected him, not with Savannah pregnant, but then she felt his touch. Matt's firm hand was as unique as the four others. She recalled his fingers tracing the shell of her ear as they now slid along her spine, up to her nape. As he moved around her, he must have gripped the rope, because her body swayed on the web.

"I expect Ben will have to stay on his toes, keeping you in line." A statement of fact, not really a question, but the Master's tone was so clear, rippling through her every nerve ending, she knew a response was needed.

"Yes sir."

A masculine chuckle. "Lucky man. We're all lucky in that regard." She drew in a breath as Matt's hand caressed her throat, then cupped her cheek in a firm hold. "You won't push it to the lengths you've pushed it before this night though. Will you?"

She was incapable of lying, even to save her tender skin. "Unless my Master needs me to push it, sir."

Five more from Ben, and as she shrieked through the impact, she pressed her face hard into Matt's large hand, bit down to contain it all. The sound of her flesh being whipped just made it even more intense. Matt didn't move away, letting her lock her jaw on the calloused mound of his palm. With the other hand, he held her head rigidly still, reinforcing the rope bindings on it, his fingers tangled in her hair. When Ben finished, she was gasping for air. A handkerchief touched her face, Matt taking away her tears.

"Do you love him, Marcie?"

"More than anything," she sobbed. "Always. He's my Master."

Matt brushed his lips against her forehead, both cheeks. "Yes, he is. Make him deserve you, sweet girl. And love him like he deserves."

A reminder of their talk, and a blessing from the patriarch at once. She pressed her lips into his palm once more, soothing where she'd bitten with a shy touch of her tongue. Another chuckle, and he gave her hair a reproving tug. "She's a handful, Ben. She's all yours."

"Yes, she is." There was a silence, in which she imagined Ben and Matt exchanging a look that, like everything tonight, made things right. Balanced. Then she heard Matt moving away.

Now it was just her and Ben. Alone.

Chapter Sixteen

ഇ

At the blissful sound of his slacks being unbelted, opened, she was already pushing out toward him, her sphincter muscles contracting. He let out a soft oath, his fingers dipping in to caress that rim.

"You're flaring, love. A beautiful red rosebud, begging for my cock."

"Yes, Master."

He was wearing a condom, a surprise, but it made him nice and slick. He stretched her as she made those animal noises, which became a long cry when he slid in fully, pressing his thighs and pelvis firmly against her abused buttocks.

"Whose are you, Marcie?"

"Yours, Master. All yours."

"And if I want to fuck your ass all night?"

"That's your right. I belong to you."

"Make you suck my cock until your jaw cramps?"

"I belong…to you. Anything."

"Then clutch me with those muscles like I taught you."

She did, until she was struggling against exhaustion. But she reveled in every thrust, his grunts, the ropes rubbing against her flesh, the constriction around her breasts, her waist, her legs, everywhere she was bound. His pelvis pressing against her ass, making the welts from the switch burn, a reminder of his claim on her. The moist heat of his breath against her neck.

The others might still be watching, they might be gone, but for her there was only him right now. And then she was sure they were gone, because he loosened the blindfold, let it drop.

It was his loft apartment. Whereas the dungeon in the Garden District was full of luxurious pieces with satin polished wood and velvet, this one was a sparsely outfitted torture chamber, intended to be intimidating with its hard dark floors, blackened windows, single-bulb lights hanging from the ceiling. It was separated from the rest of the apartment by a thick curtain of overlapping thick plastic strips, like at a construction site.

"I'm glad I didn't move everything to the Garden District. I like the idea of having this equipment close to work. Particularly if I need to take a particular K&A employee home for lunch and discipline her."

"That employee might decide to work for Tennyson Industries. The pay's better."

He chuckled, a dangerous, thrilling sound, his breath on her neck. "Savannah can't match our benefits. I promise you that."

There was the sound of the condom being removed. When he came to stand before her, he'd left the slacks open, his erect cock pushing up and out of the fabric. He got up close and personal, so she was staring into those vivid eyes and his cock brushed against her belly through the opening of the ropes. He cupped her face, traced her cheekbone, caught strands of her hair. "My sweet slave," he murmured.

Stepping back, he unbuttoned his shirt, shrugged it off, dropped the slacks and shoved off his briefs, got rid of all of it. It was the first time he'd given her that pleasure when she was conscious enough to appreciate it. He was beautiful, every bare, perfect inch. She saw some unexpected scars, high on his thigh, at his abdomen, but they fit the tough, muscled body. The light mat of dark hair arrowed down to his groin and sprinkled his thighs and calves. A virile male animal. If this was Beauty and the Beast, she'd want him to stay the growling, dangerous Beast, never become the cultured, much-too-gentle prince.

"Eyes down, Marcie."

She obeyed, and had the pleasure and anticipation of watching him take that thick cock in his hand. She'd love to watch him masturbate, see how those strong fingers milked seed out of the thick organ. The night he'd told her he was doing that in front of the TV, she imagined him ordering her to stay on her knees next to him, eyes down while he jacked off. Then he'd torment her further by letting her clean him with her tongue, licking his seed off his balls and thighs, the base of his shaft, the broad head.

His other arm slid through the ropes, around her waist, palm settling on her buttock to use the ropes' flexibility to angle her properly for him. It tilted her away from him, so that with her head firmly anchored to the web, she had to strain her gaze to keep looking down as he'd ordered and see as much as she could within that range.

He pushed into her pussy, stretching her out with excruciating slowness, that harrowing, almost too-full feeling she'd never tire of experiencing. He kept going until his thighs pressed against the inside of hers. He kept his hand on her ass, but brought the other one back to the side of her neck, fingers twisting in her hair tight. He withdrew, then slid back in, keeping his eyes on hers.

No words; none needed. This was a taking, his mouth in that ruthless set, eyes unwavering, and she returned that in full measure, holding the lock, letting him see her helpless pleasure, hear the unintelligible pleas for her Master that broke from her lips, increasing the fire in his eyes. He was building her up to that incredible peak again, and bound as she was, she had no control. He had it all. But it wasn't a one-sided thing. She could see his total attention on her, how her surrender absorbed him...overwhelmed him, brought him into an untouchable space with her. It was just the two of them, giving, taking, until those two sides were fully twined together, the two of them fused.

He came closer, put his mouth on hers. It brought her to life like a detonator. She tried to devour him, would have if she hadn't been so completely restrained. As it was, she made little crazed sounds in her throat, conveying her madness without words. She needed him, needed him.

Oh God, his cock felt good. He was pressed to her now, his chest a broad wall against her bound breasts, pelvis rocking against her thighs. The angle was precarious, narrow, and it rubbed him against her clit in a tiny, teasing touch. In, out. With how thick he was, every thrust and withdrawal made her burn even hotter, the excruciating stretch of his size keeping the climax just out of reach for the moment. Scraping his teeth against hers, he nipped, tongue teasing her lips as he held her head still. He was a master at building an explosion inside a finite space, the pressure becoming so dense until she was sure she'd shatter from the inside out. But she squeezed down on him. She wanted him to come with her, get lost in this, stay in that bubble together.

"I love you," she whispered. "Please come for me, Master."

"You...first."

His voice was satisfyingly hoarse. It infused her with pleasure and power, and she had to hear him come, wanted to know she'd been able to give him that. "Please, Master."

"Always...trying to...argue." He pulled his lips back from his teeth, maybe a feral grin, maybe a rictus of control, trying to hold back his climax. "Right now, Marcie. Obey your Master. Your pussy is mine. You do what I tell you to do with it...or you won't be sitting for a week."

Putting his hand between them then, he found her clit. That mere brush of friction and she lost control. She protested, a brief plea, and then she was coming, milking him hard with the spasms, such that she got what she wanted as well. He came right in the middle of her own climax, grunting at the intensity of it, making tears spring to her eyes as his fingers bruised in their hold on her buttock. She liked the idea of those bruises, but it was all part of a whirling vortex of sensation as she screamed out her pleasure once again, her body unable to resist anything he desired of her.

He was her Master, after all.

When that climax left her, so did every scrap of energy she had. It wasn't just the physical. There was a haze over her mind, a numb aftermath of ecstasy, a postpartum experience that kept her drifting, malleable, limp. She was aware of him freeing her. He put the collar back on her, as well as the tether. Twining it around his wrist, he lifted her tenderly as a child cradled in his arms. He walked through those thick plastic curtains, and they were in a well-appointed loft apartment with masculine furniture, a big flat-screen, a kitchen full of silver appliances. There were intriguing pieces of art on the walls.

Moving across that space, he took her into a large bathroom. She smelled fragrant steam, sensed flickering candlelight.

She was shivering, but he stepped into a large Jacuzzi tub, sat down, putting her between his knees, wrapping an arm around her middle and pressing her head back on his shoulder. She didn't know how long the tub had been running or who had drawn the bath. Jon had likely invented something to keep the water nice and hot.

"No talking," Ben said quietly. "Not unless I give you permission."

She didn't think she could form words anyway, so that was good. But she drifted around in that haze as he wet her hair, cleaned it, fingers combing, massaging her nape. Then he shifted her around to all fours and attached the tether to a ring on the tub wall to keep her in that position. Using a moisturizing soap, he cleaned her skin, then followed that up with a warming oil he worked all over her body, paying particular attention to her joints and muscles. Her nipples still held that steel bar, replaced by him, and it was a provocative weight in her all-fours position. Then he turned his attention to her pussy and ass.

He cleaned her thoroughly, embarrassingly so, then worked in more soothing oils, spreading her legs out farther, making her whimper at the ripples of response he started. She was so sensitive, as if that climax had permanently awoken nerve endings that responded with jolts of pleasure to his every touch.

Unhooking the tether, he spoke in a quiet rumble against her ear. "Put your arms around me, baby."

She did, and he lifted her out of the tub, taking her to her knees on a stack of soft towels. He used a couple others to dry her while she leaned against the inside of his right leg. He massaged her head for a long time, almost putting her to sleep. She could barely keep her head up by the time he combed her hair, but he steadied her chin with one hand.

"Didn't think...you did this."

When his fingers stilled, she realized she'd spoken aloud. "Sorry," she mumbled. "Didn't mean to talk."

"I'll give you a pass on that one. Tell me what you meant."

She laid her head on his bare thigh, managed to lever her gaze open enough to see he'd donned a pair of short, clingy boxers. She could see the size of him beneath it, the generous curve of his balls, and she wanted to touch, nip. Squeeze. She took a steadying breath. "I guess...because of how you are, I thought you'd have somebody else handle aftercare."

"Hand you off like a serving girl who's met my needs?"

"Something like that. Which is kind of a turn-on, the psych...sic...psychology of it." She fumbled with her thick tongue. "But I like this even better."

"I like this too." He braided her hair into two tails, wrapped them together and used a band to hold them back off her face. Sensing he was gathering his thoughts, she didn't speak.

"In the not-too-distant future, I will take you to the K&A boardroom and allow the others to pleasure you there. It's another little tradition we have."

She knew that, thanks to Dana's provocative description. Savannah and Cass had both experienced the full sensual onslaught of the five K&A men in their boardroom, before either had committed their hearts to their respective Masters. Dana and Rachel had enjoyed it later. For Dana it had been a special birthday present; for Rachel, her first wedding anniversary.

In the short time Marcie had been working for Ben, she hadn't had the chance to sneak in and check it out, but from Dana she knew the K&A boardroom had some ingenious engineering, thanks to Jon's aptitude and the other men's imaginations. It was the ultimate adult Transformer, the table, screens and cameras able to serve an entirely different purpose when the men desired them to do so.

"I decided not to do that tonight," Ben continued. He stroked her hair, a more tender touch that drew her eyes up to his serious face. "For a long time," he said quietly, holding her gaze, "I rejected the possibility of someone belonging to me totally, of serving me the way I wanted. My demands can be extreme, so I learned to behave as if I didn't want that. But what I really wanted, always wanted, was someone to belong to me fully. Like this. I wanted to prepare her from head to toe, take care of everything, because you're mine, entirely. To care for, to punish, to pleasure. This first time, I wanted you to experience that in a more personal space. A space that was mine alone."

Her heart cracked open. "What can your slave do for you now?" she whispered.

"Whatever I demand." His hands remained gentle, despite the intriguing threat. "But she has a choice to make first."

Reaching toward a drawer, he opened it, removed a carved wooden box. When he flipped it open, her heart jumped in her throat and stayed there.

It was a collar. Simple, elegant stainless steel, with a key-pin-locking mechanism and matching cuffs. She'd seen a variety of more complex and decorative collars, but in a blink she understood that this meshed with the type of Master Ben was. Something that made it clear in no uncertain terms that this was a collar and cuffs for his property, his submissive. There was an etching on each. Three forget-me-nots. As she tilted the collar toward the light, her eyes stung. *Always yours* was etched on the inside.

He met her gaze. "Last chance, Marcie. I put these on, you're mine, irrevocably. You've been a student of who and what the K&A men are for a long time. You're my choice, and that's forever. You put these on, you take them off only when I give you permission to do so, and that's probably only going to be for their cleaning and care."

Remembering her earlier thoughts, she knew she'd been right. This moment meant as much to her as being presented an engagement ring, the commitment the same. Deeper in some ways, because she knew what it meant to him. While he finally understood and accepted what she was offering, it said he was now demanding it from her.

Tears were rolling down her face. Seeing them, his mouth softened. She lifted fingers to his lips, touched.

"Yes," she whispered. "I want to be yours, Ben. It's what I've always wanted. I've only been waiting on you."

His lips twisted in a wry smile. "Leave it to you to get that little dig in."

"Well, you didn't say I had to be docile and silent."

"And if I did?"

"I will do my very best, Master," she said prudently. "Unless you prefer me to fall short in that area, in which case I'm certain I can excel at that."

Though he chuckled, his response was somber, intent. "You embrace the hard stuff, love it, but I don't ever want to push you beyond what you can bear, Marcie. You're going to have to help me learn how to love you. I've done a lot of things with women, but that's one thing I haven't practiced much."

She shook her head. "You've been practicing a long time. Savannah, Cass, Dana, Rachel, my younger sisters...Ben, you love all of us. You love Peter, Matt, Lucas and Jon. You've looked out for them, been part of our family, no matter what." She met his gaze. "All those letters...you've been winning my heart, loving me, for seven years. I trust you. Please give me your collar, Master. I can't bear another moment without it."

A muscle worked in his jaw. Picking up the collar, he closed it around her throat. It lay lightly on her collarbone but had enough of a weight and a snug enough fit it stole her breath in all the right ways, sent her brain in a hundred different directions, while keeping one part of it very still, very focused.

His. His. His.

The cuffs just underscored it. He caressed her pulse beneath them, looked at her like that, all naked but for that mark of ownership. "All right," he said at last, then lifted her in his arms again.

He carried her back out into the loft. On this side, the thick plastic curtain was camouflaged by strategically placed screens. Tonight they'd been adjusted so she could still see the equipment, the latex vacuum bed where she'd lain. Turning her attention to the rest of the apartment, she found a king-sized bed on the lower level, piled up with pillows. She assumed that one was his. But he carried her up the stairs to the open room above it, where there was another king-sized bed and a window to look out at the New Orleans' lights.

Putting her arms around his shoulders, she pressed her face into his throat, her lips there.

"I feel so floaty."

"You were gone, baby. Off in subspace. You're still there. You don't worry about anything. I've got you."

He laid her down in the bed, arranged the covers over her. She suppressed a sigh. She didn't want him to leave, but she knew he didn't sleep with women, and there was another bed downstairs. Small steps. No. No, she didn't want that. He'd said to be herself, tell him what she wanted, needed.

As he moved back toward the stairs, she made a noise and he turned, eyebrow cocked. "What is it, Marcie?"

"I don't want you to go. Please…come sleep with me?"

He gave her a crooked smile, one that made those emerald green eyes an even deeper color. "Where else would I be sleeping, brat? I'm just turning off the light. The downstairs bed is a guest bed. Closer to the kitchen and bathroom."

"Oh." When darkness descended, the lights from the city cast a dim glow over the room. She waited with bated breath until he slid in behind her, lifting her thigh with a firm hand so he could slide his cock between her legs, rest it against her sore pussy, a reminder that she would serve him whenever he desired. But tonight, this was enough. She curved her fingers over his on her breast, glad when he didn't tell her not to do that. He put his lips against her neck, against that new collar. "Sleep. That's my last command of the night. Just sleep."

She was lost to dreams within minutes.

* * * * *

When she woke, it took her a moment to remember — joyously — where she was. But she was alone. Before she could panic over that, she realized two things. One, Ben was moving around the kitchen below. Two, she was still wearing his collar and cuffs. A wonderfully familiar aroma was drifting up from the kitchen, but she couldn't quite place it since it wasn't a normal breakfast smell.

Rising, she ran her hands through her hair. She didn't see clothes for her, not even his shirt, and before she could think about what that meant, he'd realized she was up.

"No clothes, unless you're cold. Just the collar and cuffs, Marcie. Come down here."

She did, her legs shaking a little from last night's exertions, and at the reality of what it all meant. Rising in his bed, coming to him as his, first thing in the morning, every day for the rest of her life. He was wearing only a pair of faded jeans, no shirt, and saliva gathered in her mouth just at the sight of him. As he straightened from doing something with the oven, she obeyed her first desire. Her eyes and mouth soft, she walked right into him, put her arms around his waist, pressed her cheek to his bare chest.

"Good morning, Master," she said against his skin.

He slid his arms around her tight, held her that way a long moment, lips in her hair. "Good morning, brat." Then she gave a little yelp as he hit her bare bottom with the heated spatula. "Go kneel on the pillow by my chair. Going to feed you some breakfast. We have to be in the office in a couple hours for the Chen meet. I assume you're ready for that?"

"I will be. Um, if I have clothes."

"Much as I'd love to see Chen's reaction to you sashaying in bare-assed naked, I had Cass pack you another overnight bag. Max brought it last night when he dropped you off. Do you have your Pickard job in the afternoon?"

She nodded.

"Tell him not to send you on any more investigative jobs that involve going toe to toe with security thugs or I'll have his ass."

"I handled that guy just fine."

"Yeah, you did." He gave her a bolstering grin, but a sharp look right along with it. "I mean it."

She pouted a little bit about that, started working on how she was going to get around it, just as he brought a sizeable piece of warm chocolate cake to the table, not yet iced. He'd brought a bowl of icing to take care of that. She stared at the plate, her mouth now watering for other reasons. "You made me cake."

Start every day with chocolate cake. That way, no matter what else happens, the day started with something perfect.

She lifted her gaze to him. "Are you worried about how the day will end?"

"Only if you're not going to be part of it." He tossed the spatula and the oven mitt onto the counter, then sat down on the chair, swinging his leg over her head so she was kneeling between his spread thighs. Her gaze couldn't help going downward and thinking about how good that chocolate icing would taste, spread on his cock.

He tweaked her breast, making her yelp. "Behave, brat. You get sick on icing, it'll spoil your appetite for the cake."

She didn't think anything could spoil her appetite for the man in front of her. Now all the way through forever. He liked the bad girl in her, would always like that. As much as she liked the bad boy in him. "Yes, Master."

"Save your strength. You have a busy day ahead. Tonight, after Pickard, I want you to come back to the office. Bring that mask you wore on the parking deck."

She looked up at him, but she had to open her mouth fast for the bite of cake or she would have been wearing it. She gave him a narrow glance as he patted at her lips with a tsking noise. Then the taste hit her. "Oh God. Oh my God. This is as good as sex."

When he laughed, it captivated her, the way it made him look younger, happier. She'd missed that side of him. But as he continued, her thoughts went to an entirely different but no less pleasurable place.

"I turn the car over to the auction tomorrow. So tonight I'm going to fuck you on the hood, exactly the way you were taunting me to do it on that security footage. *Then* Lewis can have it."

She vividly imagined it. Ben, tying her wrists to the rearview mirrors, bending her over the hood in those teetering heels, hand smacking her ass to get it good and red before he rammed into her... She was getting short of breath just thinking of it.

"Oh, Cass said that your package arrived, whatever that means. She put it in the bag and told me I wasn't allowed to look."

"Oh. Oh." Marcie brightened, momentarily distracted from lust. As she started to scramble off the pillow, over to the bag, she caught herself just in time. "Master, may I... I have something for you."

He gave her a quizzical look, but nodded with warm approval at her remembering to ask permission. It pleased her down to her toes. Then he got a devilish glint in his eyes. "If you do it on your hands and knees."

Which she was sure gave him quite a view of her ass and pussy as she moved the few necessary feet to the end of the kitchen counter. Opening the bag, seeing the wrapped package, a tiny smile bloomed in her heart. She loved the K&A women.

As she came back to him, she noticed he was just as fascinated by how her breasts swayed heavy and full in the all-fours position. During the night, he'd replaced the bar with the nipple rings strung with the emeralds, the ones she'd worn to match her clit piercing. Studying them and the movement of her breasts, he was getting hard and thick again against the jeans. It was obvious from that spread thigh position. They might just be late to that meeting after all. She could hardly wait. But first she wanted to give him this.

The package was wrapped in paper covered with a toy car pattern, a silver bow on top. He lifted his brow and she grinned. "The night at Surreal..."

The moment she said the words, his gaze shadowed. She couldn't stand that. Setting the package at his elbow, she rose on her knees, put one hand on his thigh, the other on his face. "If I have to accept you're at fault, you have to accept I've completely forgiven you. I can't regret that night, Ben. It resulted in you opening your heart to me. Because of that, I'd go through it again a hundred times."

"No, you wouldn't. I wouldn't let you. I'd cut off my arms first. Max would shoot me long before that."

When he pressed his lips to her eye, her nose, then her throat, his hands sliding up to cup her breasts, she lost her focus. "Stop," she said breathlessly, laughter in her voice. "I have to give you your gift."

"You're my gift."

Extricating herself from him, she snatched the package and thrust it between them. "I actually got this gift to remind you that I forgive you for that night." Sobering, she put a hand on his chest. "Always."

His look twisted her heart. She managed a smile. "Every time you see it, you can decide if I was worth it. Once you put it together, that is. You might need Jon's help. There's like a million pieces."

She liked his intrigued look, his obvious eagerness to open a gift from her. She couldn't wait to do Christmas with him. As he tore off the paper, Marcie couldn't suppress her grin when he recognized it as a model kit for a Mercedes-Benz McLaren Roadster. Cocking that handsome brow at her, he tapped the contents list. "It says 'glue gun required'. I can think of some interesting things to do with a glue gun."

"I'll bet." She sat back on her heels, her hands on his knees, but Ben noticed her attention was no longer on her gift. She was in the position she'd been in that first day, climbing over his legs to retrieve his pen, then sitting up between his knees just like this. Her gaze passed with a far more blatant appraisal over his erection before those mink lashes lifted. "Something I can do for you, Mr. O'Callahan?"

"I think so." Setting aside the model, he put his hand on her face, touching her mouth, imagining it about to be stretched by his cock, her lips swollen and glistening while her pussy worked itself into the same state, readying itself for him. "You make me come fast enough, you might just get a spanking before you go into work."

That was the only incentive she needed. Opening his jeans, she leaned forward, her lips already parted. Ben closed his hand on her shoulder as she teased his head with her tongue, tracing the broad head all the way around, and then doing a little nip-suck maneuver on the top like an ice cream cone, teasing the slit. Jesus...

She played with him like that for a good few moments until he'd had enough of it and moved his hand to her hair, tightening there. "Take me all the way in, brat. Deep throat."

Those sweet lips stretching, that slick, hot throat, so like her cunt, sucking him, tongue playing the throbbing veins on the underside like a damn violin. He thrust up into her mouth, and she made a noise at the stress, but it was a noise of pleasure. She liked it rough, his slave. She wanted icing on his cock, wanted to lick it off. He'd maybe give her that later, but right now he just wanted her sucking on him like this. Then he wanted to fuck her on the kitchen table, feel that wet pussy, that tight ass. Every morning for the rest of his life.

Her head was moving over him, her fingers digging into his thighs. Those pretty fingers, all that beautiful blonde hair, the delectable ass that he'd watched crawl away from him. God, it tempted him to command her to move around naked and on all fours in their home full time wearing his collar and those cuffs. In that position, he could see the pink lips of her cunt and rosebud of her ass, all of her so accessible and fuckable.

She brought both hands into it now, gripping him, sliding up, using his pre-cum to slick him up. She was devouring him, making animal noises in her throat. She knew how to give head like a pro, but it was all for him, her Master.

"Get up here." A lifetime of fucking women's asses, but now, he wanted her face-to-face. Wanted to be deep in her pussy, wanted to be staring into her eyes. It took her breath away, he could tell, the way he lifted her straight up off the floor, biceps flexing, to set her on his lap, make her straddle his cock. It took some angling, because of his size, but then he had her locked on, working her down that well-greased pole. Her mouth was slick from it, and he brought her to his lips, suckling and biting on it, tasting himself and her.

She moaned as he got her settled all the way on, and then he started moving. "Hang on, baby," he muttered. "I just want to fuck you this morning. Use you hard."

In answer to that, she coiled her arms around his shoulders. "Yeeeessss…" It drove him crazy, because she kept breathing little things like that, things that made him harder, needier, where Master and slave meant nothing, unless Master also meant slave. He was all hers. *Always yours.* He knew it for sure when he came, exploding inside of her like a heat missile. Not from the grip of her cunt, the press of her nipples, the slap of her ass against his legs, but from the words she whispered in his ear right before he released.

"I love you, Master. Love you…always…forever."

If Wishes Were Horses
Knights of the Board Room: Afterlife
Nature of Desire 1: Holding the Cards
Nature of Desire 2: Natural Law
Nature of Desire 3: Ice Queen
Nature of Desire 4: Mirror of My Soul
Nature of Desire 5: Mistress of Redemption
Nature of Desire 6: Rough Canvas
Nature of Desire 7: Branded Sanctuary
The Twelve Quickies of Christmas Volume 2 *(anthology)*
Virtual Reality

About the Author

∞

I've always had an aversion to reading, watching or hearing interviews of favorite actors, authors, musicians, etc. because so often the real person doesn't measure up to the beauty of the art they produce. Their politics or religion are distasteful, or they're shallow and self-absorbed, a vacuous mophead without a lick of sense. From then on, though I may appreciate their craft or art, it has somehow been tarnished. Therefore, whenever I'm asked to provide personal information about myself for readers, a ball of anxiety forms in my stomach as I think: "Okay, the next couple of paragraphs can change forever the way someone views my stories." Why on earth does a reader want to know about me? It's the story that's important.

So here it is. I've been given more blessings in my life than any one person has a right to have. Despite that, I'm a Type A, borderline obsessive-compulsive paranoiac who worries I will never live up to expectations. I've got more phobias than anyone (including myself) has patience to read about. I can't stand talking on the phone, I dread social commitments, and the idea of living in monastic solitude with my husband and animals, books and writing is as close an idea to paradise as I can imagine. I love chocolate, but with that deeply ingrained, irrational female belief that weight equals worth, I manage to keep it down to a minor addiction. I adore good movies. I'm told I work too much. Every day is spent trying to get through the never ending "to do" list to snatch a few minutes to write.

This is because, despite all these mediocre and typical qualities, for some miraculous reason, these wonderful characters well up out of my soul with stories to tell. When I manage to find enough time to write, sufficient enough that the precious "stillness" required rises up and calms all the competing voices in my head, I can step into their lives, hear what they are saying, what they're feeling, and put it down on paper. It's a magic beyond description, akin to truly believing my husband loves me, winning the trust of an animal who has known only fear or apathy, making a true connection with someone, or knowing for certain I've given a reader a moment of magic through those written words. It's a magic that reassures me there is Someone, far wiser than myself, who knows the permanent path to that garden of stillness, where there is only love, acceptance and a pen waiting for hours and hours of uninterrupted, blissful use.

If only I could finish that darned "to do" list.

I welcome feedback from readers - actually, I thrive on it like a vampire, whether it's good or bad. So feel free to visit me through my website www.storywitch.com anytime.

✂

The author welcomes comments from readers. You can find her website and email address on her author bio page at www.ellorascave.com.

Tell Us What You Think

We appreciate hearing reader opinions about our books. You can email us at Comments@EllorasCave.com.

Why an electronic book?

We live in the Information Age — an exciting time in the history of human civilization, in which technology rules supreme and continues to progress in leaps and bounds every minute of every day. For a multitude of reasons, more and more avid literary fans are opting to purchase e-books instead of paper books. The question from those not yet initiated into the world of electronic reading is simply: *Why?*

1. *Price.* An electronic title at Ellora's Cave Publishing runs anywhere from 40% to 75% less than the cover price of the exact same title in paperback format. Why? Basic mathematics and cost. It is less expensive to publish an e-book (no paper and printing, no warehousing and shipping) than it is to publish a paperback, so the savings are passed along to the consumer.

2. *Space.* Running out of room in your house for your books? That is one worry you will never have with electronic books. For a low one-time cost, you can purchase a handheld device specifically designed for e-reading. Many e-readers have large, convenient screens for viewing. Better yet, hundreds of titles can be stored within your new library — on a single microchip. There are a variety of e-readers from different manufacturers. You can also read e-books on your PC or laptop computer. (Please note that Ellora's Cave does not endorse any specific brands.

You can check our website at www.ellorascave.com for information we make available to new consumers.)

3. *Mobility.* Because your new e-library consists of only a microchip within a small, easily transportable e-reader, your entire cache of books can be taken with you wherever you go.

4. ***Personal Viewing Preferences.*** Are the words you are currently reading too small? Too large? Too... ANNOYING? Paperback books cannot be modified according to personal preferences, but e-books can.

5. ***Instant Gratification.*** Is it the middle of the night and all the bookstores near you are closed? Are you tired of waiting days, sometimes weeks, for bookstores to ship the novels you bought? Ellora's Cave Publishing sells instantaneous downloads twenty-four hours a day, seven days a week, every day of the year. Our webstore is never closed. Our e-book delivery system is 100% automated, meaning your order is filled as soon as you pay for it.

Those are a few of the top reasons why electronic books are replacing paperbacks for many avid readers.

As always, Ellora's Cave welcomes your questions and comments. We invite you to email us at Comments@ellorascave.com or write to us directly at Ellora's Cave Publishing Inc., 1056 Home Avenue, Akron, OH 44310-3502.

ELLORA'S CAVE

Romanticon

Annual convention
for women who
refuse to behave

*Discover for yourself why readers can't get enough
of the multiple award-winning publisher*
Ellora's Cave.
*Whether you prefer e-books or paperbacks,
be sure to visit EC on the web at
www.ellorascave.com
for an erotic reading experience that will leave you
breathless.*

Made in the USA
Lexington, KY
18 September 2012